Praise for Barbara Delinsky

"One of this generation's most gifted writers of contemporary women's fiction."
—*Affaire de Coeur*

"Women's fiction at its finest."
—*RT Book Reviews*

"Delinsky's splendid latest exploration of family dynamics combines her understanding of human nature with absorbing, unpredictable storytelling—a winning combination."
—*Publishers Weekly*

"Immensely readable...thought-provoking... highly recommended."
—*Library Journal*

"Readers looking for an engaging story will find it here."
—*Booklist*

"A polished drama...well-crafted and satisfying."
—*Kirkus Reviews*

BARBARA DELINSKY

Trust

Recycling programs
for this product may
not exist in your area.

ISBN-13: 978-0-373-60607-8

TRUST

Copyright © 2014 by Harlequin Books S.A.

The publisher acknowledges the copyright holder of the individual works as follows:

THE REAL THING
Copyright © 2002 by Barbara Delinsky

SECRET OF THE STONE
Copyright © 1999 by Barbara Delinsky

Printed in U.S.A.

CONTENTS

THE REAL THING   7

SECRET OF THE STONE   211

THE REAL THING

CHAPTER ONE

IT WASN'T EARTH-SHATTERING in the overall scheme of things. Nor was it unexpected. Yet coming as it did topping six weeks' worth of unpleasantness, it was the final straw.

Neil Hersey glared out the window of his office. He saw neither Constitution Plaza below him, nor anything else of downtown Hartford. The anger that blinded him would have spilled into his voice had not frustration already staked its claim there.

"Okay, Bob. Let me have it. We've been friends for too long to beat around the bush." He kept his fists anchored in the pockets of his tailored slacks. "It's not just a question of preferring someone else. We both know I'm as qualified for the job as any man. And we both know that Ryoden's been courting me for the past year. For some reason there's been an eleventh-hour reversal." Very slowly he turned. "I have my suspicions. Confirm them."

Robert Balkan, executive vice president of the Ryoden Manufacturing conglomerate, eyed the ramrod-straight figure across from him. He and Neil Hersey went back a long way. Their friendship was based on mutual admiration and genuine affection, and Bob respected Neil far too much to lie.

"Word came directly from Wittnauer-Douglass," he stated defeatedly. "Your release as corporate counsel there was a compassionate move. It was either let you go or bring you to trial."

Neil swore softly and bowed his head. "Go on."

"They alleged you were responsible for some transactions that were unethical, some that were downright illegal. For your own protection, the details remain private. The corporation is taking internal measures to counter the damage."

"I'll bet."

"What can I say, Neil? The charge was totally unsubstantiated, but it was enough to get the chairman of our board up in arms. One word in the old coot's ear and it became a crusade with him. Someone at Wittnauer-Douglass knew exactly what he was doing when he made that call. Then Ned Fallenworth got in on the act and that was that."

Fallenworth was the president of Ryoden. Bob had had reason to regret that fact in the past, but never as vehemently as he did now. "I've been spitting bullets since Ned gave me his decision. Ned's always been a coward, and what he's doing is a sad reflection on Ryoden. I gave it all I had, but his mind was closed. Narrow minds, Neil. That's what we're dealing with. Narrow minds."

Neil deliberately unclenched his jaw. "Narrow minds with a hell of a lot of power" was his own bleak assessment of the situation.

Leaving the window, he prowled the room, moving from parquet floor to Oriental rug and back, continuing the circle until he reached his gleaming mahogany desk. He leaned against the edge, his long legs extended and crossed at the ankles. His arms were folded over his chest. The pose might have been one of casual confidence under other circumstances. "Six weeks, Bob," he gritted. "This hell's been going on for six weeks. I'm being blackballed and it's touched every blessed aspect of my life. Something's got to give!"

"Do you need money? If it's a question of finances, I'd be glad to—"

"No, no." Neil waved aside the suggestion, then gentled his expression into a half smile of thanks. "Money's no problem. Not for now, at least." With the measured breath he took, the remnants of his half smile vanished. "The way things stand, though," he resumed, unable to stem his irritation, "my future as a lawyer in this town is just about nil, which is exactly what Wittnauer-Douglass intended."

"I think you should sue."

"Are you kidding?" Straightening his arms, he gripped the edge of the desk on either side of his lean hips. "Listen, I appreciate your vote of confidence, but you don't know that company as I do. A, they'd cover everything up. B, they'd drag the proceedings on so long that I would run out of money. C, *regardless* of the outcome, they'd make such a public issue of a suit that what little is left of my reputation would be shot to hell in the process. We're talking piranhas here, Bob."

"So why did you represent them?"

"Because I didn't *know*, damn it!" His shoulders slumped. "And that's the worst of it, I think. I just... didn't...know." His gaze skittered to the floor, dark brows lowered to hide his expression of deep self-dismay.

"You're human. Like the rest of us."

"Not much by way of encouragement."

Bob rose. "I wish I could do more."

"But you've done what you came to do and it's time to leave." Neil heard the bitterness in his voice, and while he detested it, he couldn't bring himself to apologize.

"I have an appointment at three." Bob's tone verged on apologetic, and Neil was quickly wary. He'd witnessed six weeks of defections, of so-called friends falling by the wayside.

Testing the waters, he extended his hand. "I haven't seen Julie in months. Let's meet for dinner sometime soon?"

"Sure thing," Bob said, smiling a little too broadly as the two shook hands.

Bob was relieved, Neil mused. The dirty work was done. And a "sure thing" for dinner was as noncommittal as Neil had feared it might be.

Moments later he was alone with an anger that approached explosive levels. Slumping into the mate of the chair Bob had just left, he pressed a finger to the crease in the center of his forehead and rubbed up and down. His head was splitting; he had to keep it together somehow. But how to remain sane when everything else was falling apart... Where was justice? Where in the hell was the justice in life?

Okay, he could understand why his working relationship with Wittnauer-Douglass would be severed after the abysmal scene six weeks ago. There had been, and was, a difference of opinion. A rather drastic difference of opinion. He wouldn't have wanted to continue serving as counsel for the corporation any more than they'd wanted him to. But should he be punished this way?

His entire life was twisted. Damn it, it wasn't right!

Okay, so he'd lost Ryoden. He could have lived with that if it hadn't been for the fact that he'd also lost three other major clients in as many weeks. He was being blackballed within the corporate community. How the hell could he counter it, when the enemy was so much larger, so much more powerful?

He took several slow, measured breaths, opened his eyes and looked around the office. Ceiling-high mahogany bookshelves filled with legal tomes; an impressive collection of diplomas and brass-framed citations; a state-of-the-art telephone system linking him to his secretary and the world beyond; a credenza filled with important forms and personal papers—all worthless. What counted was in his head. But if he couldn't practice law his mind was worthless, too; it was hammering at his skull now, hammering mercilessly.

Neil Hersey had never felt so furious, so bitter—so utterly helpless—in his entire life. He knew that something had to be done, and that he was the one who was going to have to do it. For the life of him, though, he didn't know what action to take. His thoughts were mired in that fury and bitterness. He couldn't think clearly.

Muttering a dark oath, he bolted from his seat. He needed a break, a change of scenery. More than anything at the moment, he needed out.

Rounding the desk, he snatched his personal phone book from the top right-hand drawer and flipped to the *L*s. Landry. Lazuk. Lee. Lesser. He set the book down, marking the place with his finger. Lesser. Victoria Lesser. Within seconds he'd punched out the number that would connect him with the stylish Park Avenue co-op high above the hustle of Manhattan.

A very proper maid answered. "Lesser residence."

"This is Neil Hersey. Is Mrs. Lesser in?"

"Please hold the phone."

Neil waited, tapping his foot impatiently. He massaged the throbbing spot on his forehead. He squeezed his eyes shut. Only when he pictured Victoria breezing toward the phone—wending her way through the most elegant of furnishings while, very likely, wearing jeans and an oversized work shirt—did he give a small smile.

Victoria Lesser was a character. Thanks to the husband she'd worshipped until his death six years earlier, she was extremely wealthy and influential. She was also a nonconformist, which was what Neil adored about her. Though never outrageous, she did what she wanted, thumbing her nose at the concept of a staid and proper fifty-two-year-old widow. She traveled. She entertained. She took up ballet dancing. She fantasized herself a painter. She was interesting and refreshing and generous to the core.

It was that generosity Neil was counting on.

"Neil Hersey...fine friend you are!" A good-natured tirade burst from the other end of the line. "Do you know how long it's been since I've heard from you? It's been months! *Months!*"

"I know, Victoria. And I'm sorry. How are you?"

"How I am is beside the point," Victoria said more softly. "The question is, how are *you?*"

Neil hadn't been sure how far word had spread, but he

should have realized Victoria would have heard. The mutual friend through which they'd originally met was an executive at Wittnauer-Douglass.

"You're speaking to me," he answered cautiously, "which makes me feel better already."

"Of course I'm speaking to you. I know what happened there, Neil. I know that board of directors. That is, I know how to recognize snakes. I also know what kind of lawyer you are—I haven't forgotten what you did for my niece—and I know the bind you're in right now."

"Then you know I need to get away." He broached the topic quickly. He was in no mood, even with Victoria, to pussyfoot around. "I can't think here. I'm too angry. I need peace and quiet. And seclusion."

"Something like a remote and uninhabited island off the coast of Maine?"

Neil's mouth lifted slightly at the corners. "Something like that."

"It's yours."

"No one's there?"

"In October?" She snorted. "People nowadays are sissies. Once Labor Day's passed, you'd think going north to an island was tantamount to exploring the Arctic. It's yours, Neil, for as long as you want it."

"Two weeks should do it. If I can't come up with some solutions by then…" There wasn't much more he could say.

"You haven't called me before, and knowing you, you'll want to work this out for yourself. But if there's anything I can do, will you let me know?"

Neil found solace in her words. She had the courage that others lacked. Not only was she unswayed by smear tactics, she would root for the underdog any day. "Use of the island is more than enough," he said gratefully.

"When were you thinking of going?"

"As soon as possible. Tomorrow, I guess. But you'll have to tell me how to get there."

Victoria did so. "Once you get to Spruce Head, ask for

Thomas Nye. Big fellow. Bushy red beard. He lobsters from there. I'll call ahead and alert him. He'll take you out to the island."

With brief but heartfelt thanks, plus a promise to call her when he returned, Neil hung up the phone. He spent the rest of the afternoon working with his secretary to clear his calendar for the next two weeks. It was a relatively easy feat, given the amount of work he'd recently lost. He met in turn with each of his two young associates, giving them enough direction to keep them marginally occupied during his absence.

For the first time in his memory, when he left the office his briefcase remained behind. He carried nothing more than a handful of Havana cigars.

If he was going to escape it all, he decided belligerently, he'd go all the way.

DEIRDRE JOYCE glowered at the thick white cast that sheathed her left leg from thigh to toe. It was a diversionary tactic. If she looked into the urgent faces that circled her hospital bed, she was sure she'd explode.

"It was an act of fate, Deirdre," her mother was saying. "A message. I've been trying to get it across for months now, but you've refused to listen, so someone higher up is spelling it out. Your place is in the business with your sister, not teaching aerobics."

"My teaching aerobics had nothing to do with this, Mother," Deirdre declared. "I tripped on the stairs in my own town house. I fell. I broke my leg. I don't see any message there, except that I was careless. I left a magazine where it shouldn't have been and slipped on it. It could as easily have been *Forbes* as *Runner's World*."

"The message," Maria Joyce went on, undaunted, "is that physical fitness will only get you so far. For heaven's sake, Deirdre, you'll be sidelined for weeks. You can't teach your precious dance even if you want to. What better time is there to help Sandra out?"

Deirdre looked at her sister then. Once upon a time she'd have felt compassion for her, but that was before six months of nonstop pressure had taken its toll. "I'm sorry, Sandra. I can't."

"Why not, Dee?" Tall and dark-haired, Sandra took after their mother, while Deirdre was more fair and petite. She had been different from the start. "You have the same education I do, the same qualifications," Sandra pressed.

"I don't have the temperament. I never did."

Maria was scowling. "Temperament has nothing to do with it. You decided early on that you preferred to take the easy way out. Well, you have, and look where it's gotten you."

"Mother…" Deirdre closed her eyes and sank deeper into the pillows. Four days of confinement in a bed had left her weak, and that annoyed her. It had also left her craving a hot shower, but that was out of the question. To say that she was testy was putting it mildly.

Her voice was quiet, but there was clear conviction in her words. "We've been through this a hundred times. You and Dad may have shared the dream of a family corporation, but it's your dream, not mine. I don't want it. I'm not suited for it. It's too structured, too demanding. I gave it a try once and it was a disaster."

"Eight months," Maria argued, "years ago."

"Your mother's right, Deirdre." The deep, slightly gravelly voice belonged to Deirdre's uncle. He had been standing, silent and innocuous up to that point, at the foot of the bed. "You'd only just graduated from college, but even then you showed potential. You're a doer, like your father, but you were young and you let things overwhelm you. You left too soon. You didn't give it a fair shot."

Deirdre shook her head. "I knew myself then," she insisted, scrunching folds of the coarse white sheet between tense fingers, "and I know myself now. I'm not cut out for the business world. Having a technical aptitude for business is one thing. Maybe I do have that. But emotionally—what with board meetings, conferences, three-martini lunches, client dinners, being constantly *on*—I'd go stark raving mad!"

"You're being melodramatic," her mother scoffed.

"Right. That's the way I am, and there's no place for melodrama in Joyce Enterprises. So please," she begged, "please leave me out of it."

Sandra took a step closer. "We need you, Dee. *I* need you. Do you think I'm any more suited to heading a corporation than you are?"

"At least you want to do it."

"Whether I do or not is irrelevant. Things have been a mess since Dad died."

Since Dad died. That was the crux of it. Six months before, Allan Joyce had died in his sleep, never knowing that what he'd done so peacefully had created utter havoc.

Deirdre closed her eyes. "I think this conversation's going nowhere," she stated quietly. "The only reason things have been a mess since Dad died is that not one of you—of us—has the overall vision necessary to head a corporation. What Joyce Enterprises needs is outside help. It's as simple as that."

"We're a family-run company—" her mother began, only to stop short when Deirdre's eyes flew open, flashing.

"And we've run out of family. You can't run a business, Mother. Apparently neither can Sandra. Uncle Peter is as helpless as Uncle Max, and I'm the only one who's willing to acknowledge that the time has come for a change." She gave an exasperated sigh. "What astounds me most is that the corporation is still functioning. It's been running itself, coasting along on Dad's momentum. But without direction it's only a matter of time before it grinds to a halt. *Sell it*, Mother. And if you won't do that, hire a president and several vice presidents and—"

"We have a president and several vice presidents," Maria informed her unnecessarily. "What we lack is someone to coordinate things. You're the organizer. You're what we need. You're the one who's put together all kinds of functions."

"Charity functions, Mother. One, maybe two, a year. Benefit road races and sports days," she replied wearily. "We're not talking heavy business here."

"You're your father's daughter."

"I'm not my father."

"But still—"

"Mother, I have a wicked headache and you're not helping. Uncle Peter, will you please take Mother home?"

Maria held her ground. "Now just a minute, Deirdre. I won't be dismissed. You're being selfish. You've always put your own needs first. Don't you have any sense of responsibility toward this family?"

The guilt trip. It had been inevitable. "I'm not up to this," Deirdre moaned.

"Fine." Maria straightened. "Then we'll discuss it tomorrow. You're being discharged in the morning. We'll be here to pick you up and drive you to the house—"

"I'm not going to the house. I'm going to my place."

"With a broken leg? Don't be absurd, Deirdre. You can't climb those stairs."

"If I can't handle a flight of stairs, how can I possibly run a multimillion-dollar corporation from a seventeenth-floor office?"

"There are elevators."

"That's not the point, Mother!" Deirdre threw an arm over her eyes. She felt tired and unbelievably frustrated. It was nothing new. Just worse. "All I know," she managed stiffly, "is that I'm checking out of here tomorrow morning and going to my own town house. Where I go from there is anyone's guess, but it won't be to Joyce Enterprises."

"We'll discuss it tomorrow."

"There's nothing to discuss. It's settled."

Maria's chin gave a little twitch. It was a nervous gesture, one that appeared when she wasn't getting her way. Deirdre had caused it more times than either of them could count. "You're upset. It's understandable, given what you've been through." She patted her daughter's cheek. "Tomorrow. We'll talk tomorrow."

Deirdre said nothing. Lips set in a grim line, she watched her visitors pass one by one through the door. Alone at last, she pressed her finger hard on the call button.

Her head throbbed. Her leg throbbed. She needed aspirin.

She also needed a magic carpet to sweep her up, up and away.

This time when she glowered at her cast, there was no diversion intended. How could she have been so careless as to slip on that magazine? Why hadn't she caught herself, grabbed the banister? Why hadn't she just sat down and bumped her way to the bottom of the stairs?

But that would have been too simple. Deirdre the athlete had had to tumble head over heels. She'd had to catch her ankle in the banister, breaking her leg in three places.

Given the picture of coordination she'd projected day in, day out for the past five years, it was downright embarrassing. Given the physical exertion her body was used to, her body craved, her present state was downright stifling.

It was also depressing. Her future was a huge question mark. Rather than a simple break, what she'd done to her leg had required intricate surgery to repair. She'd been trussed up in the hospital for four days. She'd be in the cast for six weeks more. She'd have to work her way through several weeks of physical therapy after that, and only *then* would she learn whether she'd be able to teach again.

As if her own problems weren't enough to bear, there was the matter of her family…and Joyce Enterprises. That provoked anger. Ever since her initial eight-month fiasco of a professional introduction to the company, she'd insisted that she wanted no part of it.

While he'd been alive, her father had put in repeated plugs. *Try it again, Deirdre. You'll grow to like it, Deirdre. If the business isn't for my children, who* is *it for, Deirdre?*

After his death, her mother had picked up the gauntlet. Her sister and her uncles in turn had joined in later. And as the company had begun to fray at the edges, the pressure had increased.

Deirdre loved her own career. It was an outlet—demanding, creative and rewarding. She took pride in the fact that she was a good teacher, that she'd developed a loyal following, that her classes were packed to overflowing and that she'd become known as the queen of aerobics at the health club.

Her career had also been a convenient excuse, and now she was without.

A pair of aspirin eased the pain in her leg and, to some extent, her headache. Unfortunately, it did nothing to ease her dilemma. The prospect of leaving the hospital in the morning, and by doing so putting herself at the mercy of her family, was dismal. She could see it now—the phone calls, the drop-in visits, the ongoing and relentless campaign to draft her. Dismal. Unfair. *Unbearable.* If only there were someplace quiet, distant, secluded...

Sparked by a sudden determination, she grabbed the phone, dealing first with the hospital operator, then New York City information, then the hospital operator once more. At last her call went through.

A very proper maid answered. "Lesser residence."

"This is Deirdre Joyce. Is Mrs. Lesser in?"

"Please hold the phone."

Deirdre waited, tapping her finger impatiently against the plastic receiver. She shifted her weight from one bed-weary hip to the other. She squeezed her eyes shut, relieving herself of the sight of the sickroom. And she pictured Victoria, dressed no doubt in an oversized shirt and jeans, wending her way through the most elegant of surroundings to pick up the phone. Would she be coming from the music room, having just set down her cello? Or from tending African violets in her rooftop greenhouse?

Victoria was neither a musician nor a gardener, if skill

was the measure. But whatever she did she loved, which was more than enough measure for Deirdre. Of all the family friends Deirdre had come to know in her twenty-nine years, Victoria Lesser was the one she most admired. Victoria was a freethinker, an individual. Rather than withering when the husband she'd loved had died, she'd blossomed and grown. She shunned parochialism and put protocol in its place. She did what she wanted, yet was always within the boundaries of good taste.

Deirdre enjoyed and respected her. It had been far too long since they'd seen each other.

"Hey, stranger," came the ebullient voice from the other end of the line, "where *have* you been?"

Deirdre gave a wan half smile. "Providence, as always, Victoria. How are you?"

"Not bad, if I do say so myself."

"What were you doing just now? I've been trying to imagine. Was it music? Gardening? Tell me. Make me smile."

"Oh-oh. Something's wrong."

For an instant Deirdre's throat grew tight. She hadn't spoken with Victoria in months, yet they could pick up a conversation as though it had been left off the day before. Despite the more than twenty years separating them, their relationship was honest.

Deirdre swallowed the knot. "What were you doing?"

"Stenciling the bathroom ceiling… Are you smiling?"

"A little."

"What's wrong, Dee?"

"I've always hated that nickname. Did you know? The only people who use it are members of my family…and you. When they do it, I feel like a child. When you do it, I feel like…a friend."

"You are," Victoria said softly, "which is why I want you to tell me what's wrong. Are they at it again?"

Deirdre sighed and threw an arm across the mop of sandy hair on her forehead. "With a vengeance. Only this time I'm operating from a position of weakness. I broke my leg. Can you believe it? Super athlete hits the dust."

Silence.

Deirdre's voice dropped an octave. "If you're laughing at me, Victoria, so help me…"

"I'm not laughing, sweetheart. I'm not laughing."

"You're smiling. I can hear it."

"It's either that or cry. The irony of it is too much. Of all the people to break a leg, you can stand it the least…no pun intended. Are you going stir-crazy?"

"I can see it coming fast. It's bad enough that I can't work out. Lord only knows when—or if—I'll be able to teach again. But they're closing in on me, and they're not about to let up until I either give in and go to the office or flip out completely." She took an uneven breath. "I need to get away, Victoria. There'll be no peace here and I have to think about what I'm going to do if…if I can't…" She didn't need to finish; Victoria felt her fear.

There was a pause. "You're thinking of Maine."

"If it'd be all right with you. You've mentioned it so often, but the timing's never been right. It might be just what I need now—distant enough, quiet, undemanding."

"And there's no phone."

"You do understand."

"Uh-huh." There was another pause, then a pensive, "Mmmm. Maine might be just what you need. When were you thinking of going?"

For the first time since her fall down the stairs, Deirdre felt a glimmer of spirit. "As soon as I can." Definitely. "Tomorrow, I guess." Why not! "But you'll have to tell me how to get there."

Victoria did so, giving her route and exit numbers. "Can you get someone to drive you?"

"I'll drive myself."

"What about your broken leg?"

"It's my left one."

"Ahhh. Be grateful for small favors."

"Believe me, I am. Okay, once I get to Spruce Head, what do I do?"

"Look for Thomas Nye. Big fellow. Bushy red beard. He lobsters from there. I'll call ahead and alert him. He'll take you out to the island."

Deirdre managed a smile then. "You are a true friend, Victoria. A lifesaver."

"I hope so," Victoria replied cautiously. "Will you give me a call when you get back to let me know how things went?"

Deirdre agreed, adding heartfelt thanks before she finally hung up the phone and lay back on the bed.

Victoria, on the other hand, merely pressed the disconnect button. When the line was clear, she put through her second call in as many hours to Thomas Nye. She wore a distinct look of satisfaction when she finally returned the receiver to its cradle.

IT WAS STILL RAINING. Strike that, Neil amended sourly. It was pouring.

He scowled past his streaming windshield to the rain-spattered road ahead. The storm had followed him north, he decided. Just his luck. From Connecticut, through Massachusetts, to New Hampshire, then Maine—four-plus hours of nonstop rain. Leaden skies promised more of the same.

His windshield wipers flicked from left to right and back in double time, yet the passing landscape blurred. He hadn't minded the lack of visibility when he'd been on the superhighway—there hadn't been much to see. But he was well off the turnpike now, following Route 1 through towns such as Bath, Wiscasset and Damariscotta. He would have welcomed the diversion of an occasional "down east" sight.

But all he saw was the dappling and redappling sweep of grays and browns, in the middle of which—demanding his constant attention—was the road. The only sounds he heard were the steady beat of rain on the roof of the car and the more rhythmic, if frantic, pulse of the wipers. The world smelled wet. He was tired of sitting. And his mind... His mind persisted in rummaging through the baggage it had brought along on the trip.

Shortly before three in the afternoon, his mood as dark as the clouds overhead, Neil pulled his black LeBaron to a stop alongside the weathered wharf at Spruce Head. He should have been relieved that the arduous drive was over. He should have felt uplifted, filled with anticipation, eager to be nearing his destination.

What he felt was dismay. The docks were mucky. Visibility beyond the moored but wildly bobbing boats was practically nil. And the stench in the air, seeping steadily into the car, was nearly overpowering.

Distastefully he studied the large lobster tanks lined up on the wharf, then the nearby vats filled with dead fish, rotting for use as lobster bait. His own fondness for lobster meat in no way made the smell easier to take.

A gust of wind buffeted the car, driving the rain against it with renewed fury. Neil sat back in the seat and swore softly. What he needed, he decided, were a fisherman's oilskins. As far as he could see, though, not even the fishermen were venturing outside.

Unfortunately he had to venture. He had to find Thomas Nye.

Retrieving his Windbreaker from the back seat, he struggled into it. Then, on a single sucked-in breath, he opened the car door, bolted out, slammed the door behind him and raced to the nearest building.

The first door he came to opened with a groan. Three men sat inside what appeared to be a crude office, though Neil doubted he'd interrupted serious work. Each man held a mug filled with something steaming. Two of the chairs were tipped back on their hind legs; the third was being straddled backside-to.

All three men looked up at his entrance, and Neil was

almost grateful for his disheveled appearance. His hair was damp and mussed; a day's worth of stubble darkened his cheeks. His Windbreaker and worn jeans were rain spattered, his running shoes mud spattered, as well. He felt right at home.

"I'm looking for Thomas Nye," he announced straight-away. Fishermen were laconic; that suited him fine. He was in no mood for polite chitchat. "Big fellow with a bushy red beard?"

One chair and one chair only hit the floor. Its occupant propped his elbows on his knees and gestured with a single hand. "Down a block…feust left…second house on y'or right."

Nodding, Neil left. Head ducked low against the torrent, he dashed back to the car and threw himself inside. Rain dripped from his Windbreaker onto the leather seats, but he paid no heed. In the short minutes since he'd arrived at Spruce Head, his focus had narrowed. Reaching Victoria's island and shutting himself inside her house to avail himself of that highly acclaimed master bedroom with its walls of glass, its huge stone fireplace and its quilt-covered king-size bed seemed all-important.

Taking a minute to decide which way was "down" the block, he started the car and set off. One left later he turned, then pulled up at the second house on the right. It was one of several in a row on the street, and he might have said it had charm had he been in a better mood. It was small, white with gray shutters and, with its paint peeling sadly, looked as aged as he felt.

Loath to waste time, he ran from the car and up the short front walk. Seeing no doorbell, he knocked loudly enough to make himself heard above the storm. Shortly the door was opened by a big fellow with a bushy red beard.

Neil sighed. "Thomas Nye."

The man nodded, held the door wide and cocked his head toward the inside of the house. Neil accepted his invitation instantly.

LESS THAN AN HOUR LATER, Deirdre pulled up at the same house. She looked in turn at the humble structure, then at the sporty black car parked in front of her. Even had she not seen the Connecticut license plate she would have bet it wasn't the car of a lobsterman.

Thomas Nye apparently had guests and the thought didn't thrill her. She wasn't exactly at her best—an assessment, she realized, that was decidedly kind.

She'd been lucky. A passerby at the wharf had given her directions, sparing her a dash from the car. Not that she could dash. Or even walk. Hobble was more like it.

But her luck had run out. She was at Thomas Nye's house and there was no way she could speak to the man without leaving the haven of her car. That meant hauling out her crutches, extricating her casted leg from the hollow to the left of the brake and maneuvering herself to a standing position. It also meant getting wet.

Well, why not! she snapped to herself. The day had been a nightmare from the start. What was a little more grief?

Tugging her hip-length Goretex parka from the back seat, she struggled into it. Then, taking a minute to work out the logistics of dealing with cast, crutches and rain, she opened the car door and set to it.

By the time she reached Thomas Nye's front door, she was gritting her teeth in frustration. What might have taken ten seconds, had she been operating on two strong legs, had taken nearly two minutes—long enough for the storm to drench her. Her hair was plastered to her head and dripping in her eyes. Her sweatpants were noticeably heavier. Her wet grip on the crutches was precarious. And her armpits ached.

Tamping down her irritation as best she could, she shifted her weight to one crutch and knocked. As the small porch overhang offered some protection from the gusting rain, she wedged herself closer to the door.

She twitched her nose. The rank odor that had hit her

full force at the wharf was less pungent here, diluted by the fresh salty air and the rain.

She tugged at her collar. She was cold. Impatient, she knocked again, louder this time. Within seconds, the door was opened by a big fellow with a bushy red beard.

Deirdre sighed. "Thomas Nye."

Eyes skittering away, he nodded, held the door wide and cocked his head toward the inside of the house. She hitched her way into the narrow front hall, and at another silent gesture from the large man, into the small living room.

The first thing she saw was a low table spread with papers, charts and what looked to be bills. The second was the television set, broadcasting *Wheel of Fortune* in living color. The third was the dark, brooding figure of a man slouched in a chair in the far corner of the room.

The fourth thing she noticed, unfortunately, was that Thomas Nye had calmly settled into a seat by the table, returning to the work her knock had apparently interrupted.

She cleared her throat. "You were expecting me."

"That's right," he said. He had already lifted several papers, and didn't look up. "Want to sit?"

"Uh...are we...going?"

"Not now."

She ingested that information with as much aplomb as she could, given that the last thing she wanted was a delay. "It's the weather, I take it?" The possibility had been niggling at the back of her mind for the past hour. She'd done her best to ignore it.

The man in the corner grunted.

Thomas Nye nodded.

"Do you have any idea when we *will* be able to go?" she asked, discouraged; it seemed like forever since she'd awoken that morning. She now had to admit that making the trip on the same day as her discharge from the hospital may have been taking too much upon herself. But it was done. The best she could hope for was that the delay would be minimal.

In answer to her question, the bearded man shrugged. "As soon as it lets up."

"But it could rain for days," she returned. When a second grunt came from the man in the corner, she darted him a scowl. At the moment all she wanted was to be dry and warm beneath a heavy quilt on that king-size bed in the house on Victoria's island. Alone. With no one to stare at the sorry sight she made and no one to make her feel guilty about anything.

She willed her concentration on Nye. "I thought you went lobstering rain or no rain."

"The wind's the problem." At precisely that moment a gust howled around the house.

Deirdre shuddered. "I see." She paused. "Is there a forecast? Do you have any idea when it will let up?"

Nye shrugged. "An hour, maybe two, maybe twelve."

She leaned heavily on the crutches. An hour or two she could live with. But twelve? She doubted she could last twelve hours without that warm, dry bed and heavy quilt. And where would she be waiting out the time?

She glanced again at the man in the corner. He sat low in his chair, one leg stretched out, the other ankle crossed over his knee. His elbows were propped on the arms of the chair, his mouth pressed flush against knuckle-to-knuckle fists. His eyebrows were dark, the eyes beneath them even darker. He, too, was waiting. She could sense his frustration as clearly as she felt her own.

"Uh, Mr. Nye," she began, "I really have to get out there soon. If I don't get off this leg, I'm apt to be in trouble."

Nye was jotting something on the top of one of the papers that lay before him. He lifted his gaze to the game show and gestured with his pencil toward a faded sofa. "Please. Sit."

Deirdre watched as he resumed his work. She contemplated arguing further but sensed the futility of it. He looked calm, satisfied…and utterly immovable. With a grimace she plodded to the sofa. Jerking off her wet parka, she thrust it over the back of the worn cushion, coupled her crutches to one side of her and eased her way down.

When she lifted her eyes once more, she found the man in the corner staring at her. Irritated, she glared back. "Is something wrong?"

He arched a brow, lowered his fists and pursed his lips. "That's quite an outfit." It wasn't a compliment.

"Thank you," she said sweetly. "I rather like it myself." Actually, when they were dry, the roomy pink sweatpants were the most comfortable ones she owned, and comfort was a high priority, what with a cast the size of hers. Unfortunately, while dressing, she'd also been fighting with her mother, and consequently she'd pulled on the first sweatshirt that came to hand. It was teal colored, oversized and as comfortable as the pants, though it did clash slightly. And if the man had an argument with her orange leg warmers, that was his problem. The left one, stretched out and tucked into itself beyond her foot, had kept her toes warm and her cast dry. Her lone sneaker on the other foot was pitifully wet.

So she didn't look like Jaclyn Smith advertising makeup. Deirdre didn't care. In the immediate future, she was going to be all alone on an island. No one would see her. No one would care what she wore. Practicality and comfort were the two considerations she'd made when deciding what to bring with her. The man with the dark, brooding eyes could thank his lucky stars he wouldn't have to see her beyond this day.

Muted pandemonium broke loose on the television screen as a player won a shiny red Mercedes. Looking up, Thomas grinned at the victory, but Deirdre merely lowered her head and pressed chilled fingers to the bridge of her nose. She hated game shows almost as much as she hated soap operas. On occasion when she passed through the lounge of the health club, the set would be tuned to one or the other. Invariably she'd speed on by.

Now she was speeding nowhere. That fact was even more grating than the sound of the show. Disgruntled, she shoved aside the wet strands of hair on her brow and focused on Thomas Nye.

Head tucked low once again, he was engrossed in his paperwork. He looked almost preppy, she reflected, appraising his corduroy pants, the shirt and sweater. A man of few words, and those spoken with a New York accent, he was apparently a transplant. Deirdre wondered about that. Was he antiestablishment? Antisocial? Or simply... shy? He seemed unable to meet her gaze for more than a minute, and though he was pleasant enough, he made no attempt at conversation. Nor had he introduced her to the man in the corner.

Just as well, she decided as she shifted her gaze. The man in the corner didn't appear to be anyone she'd care to meet. He was frowning toward the window now, his fist propped back against his cheek. The furrow between his brows was marked. His lips held a sullen slant. And if those signs of discontent weren't off-putting enough, the heavy shadow of a beard on his lower face gave him an even less inviting appearance.

Just then he looked her way. Their eyes met and held, until at last she turned her head. No, he wasn't anyone she'd care to meet, because he looked just as troubled as she was, and there was precious little room in her life for compassion at the moment.

At the moment, Neil Hersey was thinking similar thoughts. It had been a long time since he'd seen anyone as pathetic-looking as the woman across the room. Oh, yes, the weather had taken its toll, soaking her clothes and matting her short, brown hair in damp strands that grazed her eyelids. But it was more than that. The weather had nothing to do with the fact that she had one fat leg and an overall shapeless figure. Or that she was pale. Or that her crossness seemed to border on orneriness. He assumed Nye was shuttling her to one of the many islands in the

Gulf of Maine. But he had woes enough to keep him occupied without bothering about someone else's.

His immediate woe was being landlocked. Time was passing. He wanted to be moving out. But Thomas Nye was calling the shots, a situation that only exacerbated Neil's dour mood.

He shifted restlessly and absently rubbed his hand over the rough rag wool of his sweater. Was that heartburn he felt? Maybe an incipient ulcer? He took a disgusted breath, shifted again and was about to glance at his watch, when he saw the woman do it.

"Mr. Nye?" she asked.

"Thomas," Nye answered without looking up.

"Thomas. How long will the crossing take?"

"Two hours, give or take some."

She studied her watch again, making the same disheartening calculations Neil did. "But if we're held up much longer, we won't make it before dark." It would be bad enough negotiating rugged terrain in daylight with her crutches, but at night? "That...could be difficult."

"Better difficult than deadly," Thomas replied gently. "As soon as the wind dies down, we'll go. We may have to wait till morning."

"Morning! But I don't have anywhere to stay," she protested.

Thomas tossed his head toward the ceiling. "I've got room."

She gave an exaggerated nod, which said *that* solved everything, when in fact it didn't. It wasn't what she wanted at all! She wanted to be on Victoria's island, comfortably settled in that spectacular master bedroom she'd heard so much about. She pictured it now—huge windows, an elegant brass bed, dust ruffles, quilt and pillows of a country-sophisticate motif. Silence. Solitude. Privacy. Oh, how she wanted that.

The awful fatigue she was fighting now she did not want. Or the ache in her leg that no amount of shifting could relieve. Or the fact that she was in a room with two strangers and she couldn't throw back her head and scream...

Neil had returned his attention to the window. What he saw there wasn't pleasing; the thought of spending the night in the fisherman's tiny house was even less so. *I've got room.* It was a generous enough offer, but hell, he didn't want to be here! He wanted to be on the island!

He was exhausted. The day's drive through the rain had been a tedious cap to six tedious weeks. He wanted to be alone. He wanted privacy. He wanted to stretch out on that king-size bed and know that his feet wouldn't hang over the edge. Lord only knew most everything else had gone wrong with his life lately.

"Does the boat have radar?" he asked on impulse.

"Yes."

"So we're not limited to daylight."

"No."

"Then there's still a chance of getting out today?"

"Of course there's a chance," Deirdre snapped, testy in her weariness. "There's always a chance."

Neil shot her a quelling look. "Then let's put it in terms of probability," he stated stubbornly, returning his attention to Thomas. "On a scale of one to ten, where would you put the chances of our making it out today?"

Deirdre scowled. "How can he possibly answer that?"

"He's a fisherman," Neil muttered tersely. "I'm asking for his professional estimate based on however many number of years he's worked on the sea."

"Three," Thomas said.

Deirdre's eyes were round with dismay. "On a scale of one to ten, we only get a *three*?"

Neil eyed her as though she were daft. "He's only been lobstering for three years."

"Oh." She then focused on Thomas. "What *are* the chances?

Thomas straightened a pile of papers and stood. "Right now I'd give it a two."

"A two," she wailed. "That's even worse!"

Neil glowered toward the window. Thomas stood. The Wheel of Fortune spun, gradually slowing, finally stopping on "bankrupt." The groans from the set reflected Deirdre's feelings exactly.

But she wouldn't give up. "How do you decide if we can leave?"

"The marine report."

"How often does that change?"

"Whenever the weather does."

The man in the corner snickered. Deirdre ignored him. "I mean, are there periodic updates you tune in to? How can you possibly tell, sitting here in the house, whether the wind is dying down on the water?"

Thomas was heading from the room. "I'll be back."

She looked at the man. "Where's he going?" He stared back mutely. "You're waiting to get out of here, too. Aren't you curious?"

Neil sighed. "He's getting the forecast."

"How can you tell?"

"Can't you hear the crackle of the radio?"

"I can't hear a thing over this inane show!" Awkwardly she pushed herself up, hopped to the television and turned the volume down, then hopped back. She was too tired to care if she looked like a waterlogged rabbit. Sinking into a corner of the sofa, she lifted her casted leg onto the cushions, laid her head back and closed her eyes.

Moments later Thomas returned. "Raise that to a seven. The wind's dying."

Neil and Deirdre both grew alert, but it was Neil who spoke. "Then we may make it?"

"I'll check the report in another half-hour." The lobsterman said no more, immersing himself back in his work.

The next half-hour seemed endless to Deirdre. Her mind replayed the events of the day, from her hospital discharge through the cab ride to her town house, then on to the unpleasant scene with her mother, who had been positively incensed that Deirdre would even think of leaving Providence. Deirdre would have liked to believe it was maternal concern for her health, but she knew otherwise. Her refusal to tell Maria where she was headed had resulted in even stronger reprisals, but Deirdre couldn't bear the thought that somehow her mother would get through to her on the island.

She needed this escape. She needed it badly. The way she felt, she doubted she'd get out of bed for days…when she finally reached the island.

Neil didn't weather the half-hour any better. Accustomed to being constantly on the move, he felt physically confined and mentally constrained. At times he thought he'd scream if something didn't happen. Everything grated—the lobsterman's nonchalance, the flicker of the television, the sight of the woman across the room, the sound of the rain. Too much of his life seemed dependent on external forces; he craved full control. Misery was private. He wanted to be alone.

At long last Thomas left the room again. Deirdre raised her head and held her breath. Neil waited tensely.

From the look on the fisherman's face when he returned, it seemed nothing had changed. Yet the first thing he did was flip off the television, then he gathered up his papers.

Aware that the man in the corner was holding himself straighter, Deirdre did the same. "Thomas?"

He said nothing, simply gestured broadly with his arms. Deirdre and Neil needed no more invitation. Within seconds, they were up and reaching for their jackets.

CHAPTER TWO

THE STORM MIGHT HAVE ABATED over the water, but Deirdre saw no letup on shore. The rain soaked her as she limped on her crutches to her car, which, at Thomas's direction, she moved to the deepest point in the driveway. Transferring her large duffel bag to the pickup was a minor ordeal, eased at the last minute by Thomas, who tossed her bag in, then returned to stowing boxes of fresh produce in the back of the truck. The other man was preoccupied, parking his own car, then loading his bag.

Gritting her teeth, she struggled into the cab of the truck. No sooner was she seated than the two men—the dark one, to her chagrin, had turned out to be every bit as large as the lobsterman—boxed her in, making the ensuing ride to the wharf damp and uncomfortable. By the time she was aboard Thomas's boat, propped on a wood bench in the enclosed pilothouse, she felt stiff and achy. Her sneaker was soggy. Her jacket and sweatpants were wet. She was chilled all over.

The nightmare continued, she mused, but at least its end was in sight. She'd be at Victoria's island, alone and in peace, by nightfall. It was this knowledge that kept her going.

The engine chugged to life and maintained an even growl as the boat left the wharf and headed seaward. Deirdre peered out the open back of the pilothouse for a time, watching Spruce Head recede and finally disappear in the mist. Burrowing deeper into her jacket, she faced forward then and determinedly focused on her destination. She pictured the island forested with pines, carpeted with moss, smelling of earth, sea and sky, kissed by the sun. She envisioned her own recovery there, the regaining of her strength, the rebirth of her spirit. And serenity. She conjured images of serenity.

Just as Neil did. Serenity…solitude… Soon, he told himself, soon. He'd wedged himself into a corner of the pilothouse, not so much to keep a distance from Nye's other passenger as to keep his body upright. It had been a long day, a long night before that. He'd grown accustomed to sleeplessness over the past weeks, but never had its effects hit him as they did now.

Though his fatigue was in large part physical, there was an emotional element as well. He was away from the office, relieved of his duties, distanced from his profession. This wasn't a vacation; it was a suspension. Brief, perhaps, but a letdown. And more than a little depressing.

A tiny voice inside accused him of running away; his abrupt departure from Hartford was sure to be seen by some as just that. Maybe he had run away. Maybe he was conceding defeat. Maybe…maybe… It was very depressing.

His pulse was steadily accelerating, as it always did when he pursued that particular line of thought. He wondered if he had high blood pressure yet. It wouldn't have surprised him, given the kind of nervous tension he'd been living with for days on end. He needed an outlet. Any outlet.

His gaze settled on the woman just down the bench. "Don't you think it's a little stupid going out in all this like that?" He jerked his chin toward the fat leg she'd painstakingly hauled up beside her on the hard bench.

Deirdre had been wondering apprehensively if the rhythmic plunge of the boat, noticeable now that they'd left the harbor behind, was going to get worse. She looked at him in disbelief. "Excuse me?"

"I said, don't you think it's a little stupid going out in all this like that?" He found perverse satisfaction in the verbatim repetition.

"That's what I thought you said, but I couldn't believe you'd be so rude." She had no patience. Not now. Not here. "Didn't your mother ever teach you manners?"

"Oh, yes. But she's not here right now, so I can say exactly what I want." Ah, the pleasure in blurting words out at will. He couldn't remember the last time he'd done it as freely. "You haven't answered my question."

"It's not worth answering." She turned her head away and looked at Thomas, who stood at the controls, holding the wheel steady. His body swayed easily with the movement of the boat. Deirdre wished she could go with the flow that way, but her own body seemed to buck the movement. She was glad she hadn't eaten recently.

In an attempt to divert her thoughts from various unpleasant possibilities, she homed in on the baseball hat Thomas had been wearing since they'd left the house. It had fared unbelievably well in the rain. "Are you a Yankees fan, Thomas?" she called above the rumble of the motor.

Thomas didn't turn. "When they win."

"That's honest enough," she murmured under her breath, then raised her voice again. "You're originally from New York?"

"That's right."

"What part?"

"Queens."

"Do you still have family there?"

"Some."

"What were you doing before you became a lobsterman?"

A grumble came from the corner. "Leave the man alone. He's hardly encouraging conversation. Don't you think there's a message in that?"

Deirdre stared back at him. "He's a Maine fisherman. They're all tight-lipped."

"But he's not originally from Maine, which means that he *chooses* not to speak."

"I wish *you* would," she snapped. "I've never met anyone as disagreeable in my life." She swung back to the lobsterman. "How'd you get saddled with this one, Thomas? He's a peach."

Thomas didn't answer, but continued his study of the white-capped waves ahead.

Neil propped his elbow on the back of the bench, rested his cheek in his palm and closed his eyes.

Deirdre focused on a peeling panel of wood opposite her and prayed that her stomach would settle.

Time passed. The boat had the ocean to itself as it plowed steadily through the waves amid an eerie air of isolation. The smell of fish mingled with a decidedly musty odor, whether from wet clothing, wet skin or aged wood Deirdre didn't know, but it did nothing for the condition of her insides. She took to doing yoga breathing, clearing her mind, concentrating on relaxation. She wasn't terribly successful.

At length she spoke again, clearly addressing herself to Thomas. "Two hours, more or less, you said. Will it be more, in weather like this?" The rain hadn't let up and the sea was choppy, but, to her untrained eye, they were making progress.

"We're in luck. The wind's at our back."

She nodded, grateful for the small word of encouragement. Then she shifted, bending her good knee up and wrapping her arms around it.

"You look green," came an unbidden assessment from the corner.

She sighed. "Thank you."

"Are you seasick?"

"I'm fine."

"I think you're seasick."

Lips thinned, she swiveled around. "You'd like that, wouldn't you? You'd like to see me sick. What's the matter? Are *you* feeling queasy?"

"I'm a seasoned sailor."

"So am I," she lied, and turned away. Straightening her leg, she sat forward on the bench. Then, fingers clenched on its edge, she pushed herself up and hopped toward Thomas.

"How much longer?" she asked as softly as she could. She didn't want the man in the corner to hear the anxiety in her words. Unfortunately Thomas didn't hear the words at all. When he tipped his head toward her, she had to repeat herself.

"We're about halfway there," he replied eventually. On the one hand it was reassuring; halfway there was better than nothing. On the other hand, it was depressing; another full hour to endure.

"His island's near Matinicus, too?" The slight emphasis on the "his" told Thomas who she meant.

"There are several small islands in the area."

She moved closer and spoke more softly again. "Will you drop me first? I'm not sure I can take much more of this."

"I'm heading straight for Victoria's island."

She managed a wan smile and a grateful "Thank you" before maneuvering back to her seat. She avoided looking at the man in the corner. He raised her hackles. She didn't need the added aggravation, when so much of the past week had been filled with it.

Neil was brooding, thinking of the last time he'd been on a boat. A seasoned sailor? He guessed it was true. Nancy had had a boat. She loved boats. Supposedly she'd loved him, too, but that had been when he'd had the world on a string. At the first sign of trouble she'd recoiled. Granted, her brother was on the board at Wittnauer-Douglass, so she'd been in an awkward position when Neil had been summarily dismissed. Still…love was love… Or was it?

He hadn't loved Nancy. He'd known it for months, and had felt guilty every time she'd said the words. Now he had a particularly sour taste in his mouth. Her words had been empty. She hadn't loved him—she'd loved what he was. She'd been enthralled by the image of a successful corporate attorney, the affluence and prestige. With all that now in doubt, she was playing it safe. And it was just as well, he knew, a blessing in disguise, perhaps. A fair-weather lover was the last thing he needed.

He looked over at the woman on the bench. She was another can of worms entirely. Small and shapeless, unpolished, unsociable, unfeminine—quite a switch from Nancy. "What did you do to your leg?" he heard himself ask.

Deirdre raised her head. "Are you talking to me?"

He glanced around the pilothouse. "I don't see anyone else with crutches around here. Did you break it?"

"Obviously."

"Not 'obviously.' You could have had corrective surgery for a congenital defect, or for a sports injury."

A sports injury. If only. There might have been dignity in that. But falling down a flight of stairs? "I broke it," she stated curtly.

"How?"

"It doesn't matter."

"When?"

Deirdre scowled. "It doesn't *matter*."

"My Lord, and you called *me* disagreeable!"

She sighed wearily. "I'm not in the mood for talking. That's all."

"You still look green." He gave a snide grin. "Stomach churning?"

"My stomach is fine!" she snapped. "And I'm not green...just pale. It's the kind of color you catch when you've been surrounded by hospital whites for days."

"You mean you were just released?" he asked with genuine surprise.

"This morning."

"And you're off racing through the rain to get to a remote island?" Surprise gave way to sarcasm once more.

"It's only a broken leg! The rest of me is working fine."
Not quite true, but an understandable fib. "And, in case
you're wondering, I didn't personally request the rain. It
just came!"

"You were crazy to come out. Didn't your mother try
to stop you?"

She heard the ridicule in his tone and was reminded of
her earlier shot at him. Hers had been offered facetiously,
as had his, yet he'd unwittingly hit a raw nerve. "She certainly did, but I'm an adult, so I don't have to listen to her!"
She turned her head away, but it did no good.

"You don't look like an adult. You look like a pouting
child."

Her eyes shot back to him reproachfully. "Better a
pouting child than a scruffy pest! Look, why don't you
mind your own business? You don't know me, and I don't
know you, and before long, thank goodness, this ride will
be over. You don't need to take out your bad mood on me.
Just stay in your corner and brood to yourself, okay?"

"But I enjoy picking on you. You rise to the occasion."

That was the problem. She was letting him get to her.
The way to deal with a man of his ilk was to ignore him,
which she proceeded to do. Whether it worked or not she
wasn't sure, because she suspected he had freely chosen
not to speak further.

But he continued to look at her. She could feel his eyes
boring into her back, and she steadfastly refused to turn.
The man had gall; she had to hand it to him. He wasn't
spineless, as Seth had been....

Seth. Sweet Seth. Parasitic Seth. He'd slipped into her
world, taken advantage of her home, her job, her affec-
tions, and then turned tail and run when the family pressure
had begun. Seth hadn't wanted ties. He hadn't wanted responsibility. And the last thing he'd wanted was a woman
whose career demands and family responsibilities took
precedence over his own needs.

The irony of it, Deirdre reflected, was that he'd had such

little understanding of her. She'd never wanted Joyce Enterprises, and she'd told him so repeatedly. But he'd still felt threatened, so he'd left. In hindsight, she was better off without him.

She was drawn from her reverie when the man in the corner rose from the bench, crossed the pilothouse and positioned himself close by Thomas. He spoke in a low murmur, which, try as she might, Deirdre couldn't hear over the guttural drone of the engine.

"How much longer?" Neil asked.

Thomas glanced at one of his dials. "Half an hour."

"Where's she going?" He put a slight emphasis on the "she."

"Near Matinicus."

"Lots of islands, are there?"

"Some."

"Who gets dropped off first?"

"I'm heading straight for Victoria's island."

Neil considered that. "Look, it's okay with me if you drop her off first. She's really pretty pathetic."

Thomas's eyes remained on the sea. "I thought you didn't like her."

"I don't. She bugs the hell out of me. Then again—" he ran a hand across his aching neck "—just about anyone would bug the hell out of me right about now. She just happens to be here." He was feeling guilty, but was torn even about that. On the one hand, arguing with the woman was thoroughly satisfying. He needed to let off steam, and she was a perfect patsy. On the other hand, she was right. He'd been rude. It wasn't his normal way.

Head down, he started back toward his corner.

Deirdre, who'd been thinking just then about how badly she wanted, *needed* a bath, and what an unbelievable hassle it was going to be trying to keep her cast out of the water, stopped him midway. She was feeling particularly peevish. "If you think you can con Thomas into dropping you off first, don't hold your breath. He's already set a course and it happens that *my* island's up there at the top of the list."

"Shows how much *you* know," Neil mumbled under his breath. He passed her by, slid down into his corner of the bench, crossed his arms over his chest and stared straight ahead.

Deirdre passed his comment off as a simple case of sour grapes. He was an ill-humored man. Soon enough she'd be free of his company. Soon enough she'd be at the island.

"There it is," Thomas called over his shoulder a little while later. "Victoria's island."

Deirdre pushed herself to her good knee and peered through the front windshield. "I can't see a thing."

Neil, too, had risen. "No harm," he muttered.

"Do you see anything?"

"Sure. There's a dark bump out there."

"There's a world of dark bumps out there. How do you tell which one's a wave and which one's an island?"

"The island has trees."

The logic was irrefutable. "Swell," she said, sinking back into her seat. When they reached the island they'd reach the island. She'd have plenty of time to see it, time when she wouldn't be tired and uncomfortable and thoroughly out of sorts.

Neil stood by Thomas, watching the dark bump swell and rise and materialize into an honest-to-goodness land mass. It wasn't large, perhaps half a mile square, but it was surprisingly lush. Neither the rain, nor the clouds, nor the approach of dusk could disguise the deep green splendor of the pines. And the house was there, a rambling cape-style structure of weathered gray clapboard, nestling in a clearing overlooking the dock.

Deirdre was on her knee again. "That…is…beautiful," she breathed.

Neil, who was feeling rather smug at the perfection of his destination, darted her an indulgent glance. "I agree."

"For once. I was beginning to wonder if you had any taste at all."

His indulgence ended. "Oh, I've got taste, all right. Problem is that I haven't seen a thing today that even remotely appealed to it." His eyes didn't stray from her face, making his meaning clear.

It was an insult Deirdre simply couldn't let pass. "The feeling is mutual. In fact—"

"Excuse me," Thomas interrupted loudly, "I'll need everyone's help here. And it's still pouring, so we'd better work quickly." He was already cutting the engine and guiding the boat alongside the short wooden dock. "Neil, you go outside and throw the lines onto the dock, one at the bow, one at the stern. Then hop ashore and tie us up on those pilings. I'll pass supplies to you and Deirdre. Watch yourself on the dock, Deirdre. It'll be slippery."

Deirdre nodded and worked at the wet zipper of her parka, thinking what a waste it was to give a nice name like Neil to such an obnoxious man. But at least he was helping. She'd half expected him to insist on staying dry while Thomas got her set up on shore.

Neil zipped up his jacket and headed for the open pit of the boat's stern, thinking how ironic it was that a woman with as flowing a name as Deirdre should prove to be so thorny. But at least she'd agreed to help. That surprised him. Of course, Thomas hadn't exactly given her a choice.

"The line, Neil. We're here." Thomas's call ended all silent musings.

Head ducked against the rain, Neil raced to tie up the boat, bow and stern.

Biting her lip against a clumsiness foreign to her, Deirdre managed to lumber onto the dock with only a helping hand from Thomas. When she would have thanked him, he'd already turned away to begin off-loading. He handed things, first to her, then to Neil when he reached her side.

"I'll be back in a week with fresh supplies," instructed

the lobsterman hurriedly. "These should be more than enough until then. Keys to the front door are in an envelope tucked in with the eggs. If you run into a problem, any kind of emergency, you can reach me on the ship-to-shore radio in the den. The directions are right beside it."

Deirdre nodded, but she was too busy concentrating on keeping her balance to answer. When her large duffel bag came over the side of the boat, she rearranged her crutches and somehow managed to hook the wide strap of the bag over her shoulder, then return the crutches to their pre-scribed position without falling.

Neil, busy piling boxes of supplies atop one another to keep them as dry as possible, looked up briefly when Thomas handed over his canvas cargo bag. He set it down on the dock, finished up with the supplies, put a box in one arm and the cargo bag's broad strap over his other shoulder, then turned back to thank Thomas.

The boat was already drifting away from the dock, which didn't surprise Neil. Thomas had said they'd work quickly. But there was something that did surprise him....

Deirdre, whose eyes had gone wide in alarm, cleared her throat. "Uh, Thomas?" When the boat slipped farther away, she tried again, louder this time. "Thomas?"

The engine coughed, then started.

This time it was Neil who yelled. "Nye! You've forgotten someone! Get back here!"

The boat backed around the tip of the dock, then turned seaward.

"Thomas!"

"Nye!"

"There's been a mistake!" Deirdre shrieked, shoving her dripping hair from her eyes, then pointing to Neil. "*He's* still here!"

Neil rounded on her. His face was soaked, but his eyes were hard as steel. "Of course I'm still here! This is my friend's island!"

"It's *Victoria's* island, and Victoria is *my* friend."

"*My* friend, and she didn't mention you. She said I'd have the place all to myself!"

"Which was exactly what she told me!"

They glared at each other amid the pouring rain. "Victoria who?" Neil demanded.

"Victoria Lesser. Who's your Victoria?"

"The same."

"I don't believe you. Tell me where she lives."

"Manhattan. Park Avenue."

"She is Mrs. Arthur Lesser. Tell me about Arthur."

"He's dead. She's a widow, a wonderful...wacky..."

"Conniving..."

Scowling at each other amid encroaching darkness on that windswept dock in the rain, Deirdre and Neil reached the same conclusion at once.

"We've been had," he stated, then repeated in anger, "we've been had!"

"I don't believe it," Deirdre murmured, heart pounding as she looked out to sea. "Oh, damn," she breathed. "He's going!"

Simultaneously they began to yell.

"Thomas! Come back here!"

"Nye! Turn around!"

"Thomas! Don't do this to me, Thomas! Thomas!" But Thomas was well beyond earshot and moving steadily toward the mainland.

"That creep!" Neil bellowed. "He was in on it! Victoria must have known precisely what she was doing, and he went along with it!"

Deirdre didn't remember ever being as miserable in her life. All that she'd faced at home, all that she'd escaped was nothing compared to this having been manipulated. Her frustration was almost paralyzing. She took a ragged breath and tried to think clearly. "I've come all this way, gone through hell..." She brushed the rain from her cheek and looked at Neil. "You can't stay! That's all there is to it!"

Neil, who felt rain trickling down his neck, was livid. "What do you mean, I can't stay? I don't know what brought you here, but whatever it was, I need this island more, and I have no intention of sharing it with a sharp-tongued, physically disabled...urchin!"

She shook her head, sure she was imagining it all. "I don't have to take this," she spat. Turning, she set her crutches before her and started along the murky dock toward the even murkier path.

Neil was beside her. "You're right. You *don't* have to take it. I'll put through a call to Thomas and get him to come back tomorrow to pick you up."

Deirdre kept her eyes on the wet boarding, then the muddy dirt path. "I have no intention of being picked up, not until I'm good and ready to leave! You can put through that call to Thomas and have him pick *you* up!"

"No way! I came here for peace and quiet, and that's exactly what I'm going to get."

"You can get peace and quiet somewhere else. You sure can't get it with me around, and I sure can't get it with you around, and I don't know how you know Victoria, but she's been a friend of my family's for years and I'm sure she'll give me the right to this place—"

"*Right* to this place? Look at you! You can barely make it to the door!"

He wasn't far off the mark. The path was wet and slippery, slowing her progress considerably. It was sheer grit that kept her going. "I'll make it," she fumed, struggling to keep her footing on the slick incline. "And once I'm inside I'm not budging."

They reached the front steps. Deirdre hobbled up, then crossed the porch to the door. Neil, who'd taken the steps by twos, was standing there, swearing. "Tucked in beside the eggs..." He dropped his bag under the eaves, out of the rain, set down the box he'd carried and began to rummage through it. He swore again, then turned and retraced his steps at a run.

Weakly Deirdre leaned against the damp clapboard by the door. Pressing her forehead to the wood, she welcomed its chill against her surprisingly hot temple. The rest of her felt cold and clammy. She was shaking and perilously close to tears. How could the perfect solution have gone so wrong?

And there was nothing to be done about it, at least not until tomorrow. That was the worst of it.

Then again, perhaps it wasn't so bad. Once inside the house, she intended to go straight to bed. She didn't care if it was barely seven o'clock. She was beat and cold, perhaps feverish. Neil whoever-he-was could do whatever he wanted; she was going to sleep through the night. By the time she got up tomorrow, she'd be able to think clearly.

Neil dashed up the steps, his arms laden with boxes.

"I can't believe you did that," she cried. "You've got every last one of them piled up. It's a miracle you didn't drop them on the path, and then where would I be?"

He tossed his head back, getting his hair out of his eyes and the rain out of his hair. "Be grateful I did it myself. I could have asked you to help."

She wasn't in the mood to be grateful. "The key. Can you find the key?"

He'd set the bundles down and was pushing their contents around. "I'm looking. I'm looking." Moments later he fished out an envelope, opened it, removed the key and unlocked the door.

Deirdre, who feared that if she waited much longer she'd collapse on the spot, limped immediately inside. It was dark. She fumbled for a light switch and quickly flipped it on. In one sweeping glance she took in a large living room and an open kitchen off that. To the left was a short hall, to the right a longer one. Calculating that the hall to the right would lead to bedrooms, she single-mindedly headed that way.

There were three open doors. She passed the first, then the second, correctly surmising that they were the smaller guest bedrooms. The third… She flipped another light switch. Ah, she'd been right. It was much as she'd imagined it—a sight for sore eyes.

Swinging inside, she slammed the door shut with her crutch and made straight for the bed. She'd no sooner reached it than her knees buckled and she sank down, letting her crutches slip unheeded to the floor. Hanging her head, she took several deep, shaky breaths. Her limbs were quivering from weakness, exhaustion or chill, or all three. She was wet, and remedying that situation had to take first priority. Though the room was cold, she simply didn't have the wherewithal to confront that problem yet.

With unsteady fingers, she worked down the zipper of her jacket, struggled out of the soggy mass and dropped it on the rag rug by the side of the bed. She began to apologize silently to Victoria for making a mess, then caught herself. After what Victoria had done, she didn't owe her a thing!

She kicked off her sodden sneaker and tugged the wet leg warmer off her cast. The plaster was intact. Gingerly she touched the part that covered her foot. Damp? Or simply cold? Certainly hard enough. So far, so good.

Bending sharply from the waist, she unzipped her duffel bag and began pushing things around in search of her pajamas. Normally the neatest of packers, she'd been in the midst of the argument with her mother that morning when she'd thrown things into the bag. She'd been angry and tired. Fortunately everything she'd brought was squishable.

She'd finally located the pajamas, when the door to the bedroom flew open and Neil burst in. He'd already taken off his jacket, shoes and socks, but his jeans were soaked up to the thigh. Tossing his cargo bag onto the foot of the bed, he planted his hands on his hips.

"What are you doing in here? This is my room."

Deirdre clutched the pajamas to her chest, more startled than anything by his sudden appearance. "I didn't see your name on the door," she argued quietly.

"This is the largest bedroom." He pointed at the bed. "That is the largest bed." He jabbed his chest with his thumb. "And I happen to be the largest person in this house."

Deirdre let her hands, pajamas and all, fall to her lap. She adopted a blank expression, which wasn't hard, given her state of emotional overload. "So?"

"So...I want this room."

"But it's already taken."

"Then you can untake it. The two other rooms are perfectly lovely."

"I'm glad you feel that way. Choose whichever you want."

"I want this one."

For the first time since she'd entered the room, Deirdre really looked around. Nearly two complete walls were of thick, multi-paned glass, affording a view that would no doubt be spectacular in daylight. The large, brass-framed bed stood against a third wall; out of the fourth was cut the door, flanked by low, Colonial-style matching dressers, and, at one end, the pièce de résistance; a large raised hearth. Over it all was a warm glow cast by the bedside lamp.

Deirdre looked Neil straight in the eye. "So do I."

Neil, who'd never been in quite this situation before, was thrown off balance by her quiet determination. It had been different when she'd been yelling. This was, strangely, more threatening. Deirdre whoever-she-was was a woman who knew what she wanted. Unfortunately he wanted the same thng.

"Look," he began, carefully guarding his temper, "it doesn't make sense. I need this bed for its length alone. I'm six-three to your, what, five-one, five-two? I'll be physically uncomfortable in any of the other rooms. They all have twin beds."

"I'm five-three, but that's beside the point. I have a broken leg. I need extra space, too...not to mention a bathtub. From what I've been told, the master bath is the only one with a tub. I can't take a shower. It'll be enough of a challenge taking a bath."

"Try," Neil snapped.

"Excuse me?"

"I said, try."

"Try what?"

"To take a bath."

"And what is that supposed to mean?"

"What do you think it means?" he asked rhetorically. "You're filthy." He hadn't been able to resist. When he'd tried logic on her, she'd turned it around to suit herself. He didn't like that, particularly when he had no intention of giving in when it came to the master bedroom.

She looked down at her mud-spattered orange leg warmer and plucked at the odious wet wool. "Of course I'm filthy. It's muddy outside, and that boat was none too clean." She raised her head, eyes flashing. "But I don't have to apologize. Look at you. You're no prize, yourself!"

Neil didn't have to look at himself to know she was right. He'd worn his oldest, most comfortable jeans and heavy sweater, and if she could see the T-shirt under the sweater... The stormy trip had taken its toll on him, too. "I don't give a damn how I look," he growled. "That was the whole purpose in coming here. For once in my life I'm going to do what I want, when I want, where I want. And that starts with this bed."

Jaw set, Deirdre reached for her crutches. "Over my dead body," she muttered, but much of the fight had gone out of her. Whatever energy she'd summoned to trade barbs with Neil had been drained. Draping the pajamas over her shoulder, she stood. "I have to use the bathroom. It's been a long day."

Neil watched her hobble into the bathroom and close the door. Again he found himself wishing she'd yell. When she spoke quietly, wearily, he actually felt sorry for her. She looked positively exhausted.

But damn it, so was he!

Taking his cargo bag from the foot of the bed, he put it where Deirdre had been sitting. He then lifted her soaked jacket by its collar, grabbed her duffel bag by its strap and carried them down the hall to the more feminine of the two guest bedrooms.

She'd get the hint. With luck, she'd be too tired to argue. Either that, or she'd come after him once she left the bathroom, and they could fight it out some more.

He sighed, closed his eyes and rubbed that throbbing spot on his forehead. Aspirin. He needed aspirin. No. He needed a drink. No. What he really needed was food. Breakfast had been a long time ago, and lunch had been a Whopper, eaten in sixty seconds flat at a Burger King on the turnpike.

Stopping briefly in the front hall to adjust the thermostat, he returned to the kitchen, where he'd left the boxes of food piled up. Plenty for two, he mused dryly. He should have been suspicious when Thomas had continued to hand out supplies. But it had been rainy and dim, and he hadn't thought. They'd been rushing. He'd simply assumed the girl would get back on the boat when the work was done.

He'd assumed wrong. Thrusting splayed fingers through his hair, he stared at the boxes, then set about unloading them. Soon he had a can of soup on to heat and was busy making a huge ham-and-cheese sandwich.

The kitchen was comfortable. Though small, it was modern, with all the amenities he enjoyed at home. He hadn't expected any less of Victoria. At least, not when it came to facilities. What he hadn't expected was that she'd foist company on him, not when he'd specifically said that he needed to be alone.

What in the devil had possessed her to pull a prank like this? But he knew. He knew. She'd been trying to fix him up for years.

Why now, Victoria? Why now, when my life is such a goddamned mess?

The house was quiet. He wondered about that as he finished eating and cleaned up. Surely Deirdre would be finished using the bathroom. He hadn't heard a bath running. Nor had he heard the dull thud of crutches in the hall.

Not liking the possible implications of the silence, he headed for the smaller bedroom where he'd left her things.

It was empty.

Nostrils flaring, he strode down the hall to the master bedroom. *"Damn it,"* he cursed, coming to a sudden halt on the threshold. She was in bed, albeit on the opposite side from his bag. She was in his bed!

His feet slapped the wood floor as he crossed the room and came to stand on the rug by that other side of the bed. "Hey, you! What do you think you're doing?"

She was little more than a series of small lumps under the quilt. None of the lumps moved. The bedding was pulled to her forehead. Only her hair showed, mousy brown against the pillow.

"You can't sleep here! I told you that!"

He waited. She gave a tiny moan and moved what he assumed to be her good leg.

"You'll have to get up, Deirdre," he growled. "I've moved your things to the other bedroom."

"I can't," came the weak and muffled reply. "I'm...too tired and...too...cold."

Neil glanced helplessly at the ceiling. *Why me? Why here and now?* He lowered his gaze to the huddle of lumps. "I can't sleep in any of the other beds. We've been through this before."

"Mmm."

"Then you'll move?"

There was a long pause. He wondered if she'd fallen asleep. At last, a barely audible sound came from beneath the covers.

"No."

He swore again and shoved another agitated hand

through his hair as he stared at the bundle in the bed. He could move her. He could bodily pick her up and cart her to the next bedroom.

"Don't try to move me," the bundle warned. "I'll cry rape."

"There'll be no one to hear."

"I'll call Thomas. I'll make more noise than you've ever heard."

Rape. Of all the stupid threats. Or was it? There were just the two of them in the house. It would be her word against his, and "date rape" had become the in thing. If she was cruel enough to go through with it, she could really make a scene. And a scene of that type was the last thing he needed at this point in his life.

Furious and frustrated, he wheeled around and stormed from the room. When he reached the living room, he threw himself into the nearest chair and brooded. He threw every name in the book at Victoria, threw many of the same names at Thomas, then at the woman lying in *his* bed. Unfortunately, all the name-calling in the world didn't change his immediate circumstances.

He was bone tired, yet there was enough adrenaline flowing through him to keep him awake for hours. Needing to do something, he bolted from the chair and put a match to the kindling that had so carefully been placed beneath logs in the fireplace. Within minutes, the fire was roaring. It was some comfort. Even greater comfort came from the bottle of Chivas Regal he fished from the bar. Several healthy swallows, and he was feeling better; several more, and his anger abated enough to permit him to think.

After two hours he was feeling far more mellow than he would have imagined. He wandered into the den off the shorter of the two halls and studied the directions taped beside the ship-to-shore radio. *Piece of cake.*

Unfortunately no one responded from Thomas's house. *Bastard.*

Okay, Hersey. Maybe he's not back yet. After all, it

was still raining, and the man was working in total darkness. No sweat. He'll be there tomorrow. And in the meantime...

Neil banked the fire, nonchalantly walked back to the master bedroom and began to strip. *Let her cry rape,* declared his muzzy brain.

Wearing nothing but his briefs—a concession that later he'd marvel he'd been sober enough to make—he turned off the light, climbed into his side of the bed and stretched out.

"Ah..." The bed was firm, the sheets fresh. He might have imagined himself in his own bed at home had it not been for the faint aroma of wood smoke that lent an out-doorsy flavor to the air. Rain beat steadily against the roof, but it, too, was pleasant, and beyond was a sweet, sweet silence.

He was on a remote island, away from the city and its hassles. Taking a deep breath, he smiled, then let his head fall sideways on the pillow and was soon sound asleep.

CHAPTER THREE

SEVERAL HOURS LATER Neil's sleep was disturbed. Brow puckering, he turned his head. The mattress shifted, but he hadn't been the one to move. He struggled to open an eye. The room was pitch-black.

When the mattress shifted again, he opened the other eye. Was it Nancy? No, Nancy never stayed the night, and he wasn't seeing Nancy anymore. Then...

It took him a minute to get his bearings, and by the time he did, a dull pounding had started at the back of his head. He rolled to his side, tucked his chin down and pulled his knees up. He'd fall back to sleep, he told himself. He'd keep his eyes closed, breathe deeply and steadily, and fall back to sleep.

A soft moan came from the far side of the bed, followed by another shift in the mattress.

Eyes flying open, Neil swore silently. Then, gritting his teeth, he moved nearer his edge of the bed and closed his eyes again.

For a time there was silence. He was nearly asleep, when another moan came. It was a closed-mouth moan, more of a grunt, and, as before, was followed by the rustle of bedding and the shimmy of the mattress.

His head throbbed. Cursing, he threw back the covers and stalked into the bathroom. The sudden light was glaring; he squinted against it as he shoved the medicine chest open. Insect repellent...Caladryl lotion...antihistamine...aspirin. Aspirin. He fought with the child-proof cap for a minute and was on the verge of breaking the bottle, when it finally opened. Shaking three tablets into his palm, he tossed them into his mouth, threw his head back and swallowed, then bent over and drank directly from the tap. Hitting the light switch with a blind palm, he returned to bed.

The aspirin had barely had time to take effect, when Deirdre moaned and turned again. Neil bolted upright in bed and scowled in her direction, then groped for the lamp. Its soft glow was revealing. She was still buried beneath the covers, but her side of the quilt was pulled up and around every which way. Even as he watched, she twisted, lay still for several seconds, then twisted again.

"Deirdre!" He grasped what he calculated to be a handful of her shoulder and shook her. "Wake up, damn it! I can't sleep with that tossing and turning."

There was movement, independent of his shaking, from the lumps beneath the quilt. One hand emerged, slim fingers clutching the quilt, lowering it until a pair of heavily shadowed and distinctly disoriented brown eyes met his.

"Hmm?"

"You'll have to settle down," he informed her gruffly. "It's bad enough that I have to share this bed, but I refuse to do it with a woman who can't lie still."

Her eyes had suddenly widened at the "share this bed" part; they fell briefly to the shadowed expanse of his naked chest, then flew back up. Slowly, slowly they fluttered shut.

"I'm sorry," she whispered with a sincerity that momentarily took the wind from his sails.

"Were you having a nightmare?"

"No. My leg kills."

He studied the thick wedge that had to be her cast. "Is there something you're supposed to do for it? Didn't the doctor give you any instructions? Shouldn't you elevate it or something?"

Deirdre felt groggy and exceedingly uncomfortable. "They kept it hitched up in the hospital—to minimize swelling—but I thought that was over."

"Great." Neil threw off the covers and headed for the door. "I'm stuck here with a dimwit whose leg may swell to twice its normal size." His voice was loud enough to carry clearly back to her from the hall. "And if that happens your circulation may be cut off by the cast, and if *that* happens, gangrene may set in. Terrific." He stomped back into the master bedroom, carrying two pillows under each arm, went straight to her side of the bed and unceremoniously hauled back the quilt.

"What are you doing?" she cried, blinking in confusion.

"Elevating your leg." He had two of the pillows on the bed and was trying to sort out the legs of her pajamas. "There's so much damned material here... Can you move your good leg? There, I've got it." With surprising gentleness, he raised her casted leg just enough to slip the pillows underneath.

"Gangrene won't set in," she argued meekly. "You don't know what you're talking about."

"At least I know enough to prop up your leg." With a flick of his wrist, he tossed the quilt back over her as he rounded the bed to reach his side. "That feels better, doesn't it?"

"It feels the same."

"Give it a minute or two. It'll feel better." He turned off the light and climbed back into bed, dropped his head to the pillow and massaged his temple. Seconds later he was up again, this time heading back to the bathroom. When he returned, he carried a glass of water and two pills. "Can you sit up?"

"Why?"

"Because I think you should take these."

The only light in the room was the sliver that spilled from the bathroom. The dimness made Deirdre feel at a marked disadvantage to the man who loomed above her. "What are they?"

"Aspirin."

He was so large…shadowed…ominous. He wasn't wearing much. What did he intend? "I don't take pills."

"These are harmless."

"If they're harmless, why should I bother to take them?"

"Because they may just help the ache in your leg, and if that happens you'll lie quietly, and then maybe I'll be able to sleep."

"You can always try another bedroom."

"No way, but that's beside the point. Right now we're discussing your taking two innocent aspirin."

"How do I know they're innocent? How do I know they're aspirin at all? I don't know you. Why should I trust anything you give me?"

Amazed that Deirdre whoever-she-was could be as perverse in the middle of the night as she was during the day, he gave an exasperated sigh. "Because, A, I took these pills from a bottle marked Aspirin, which I found in Victoria's medicine chest. B, I took three of them myself a little while ago, and I'm not up, down or dead yet. And C, I'm Victoria's friend, and that's about as good a character reference as you're going to get." He sucked in a breath. "Besides, it works both ways, you know."

"What does?"

"Character references. I have to trust that you're clean—"

"What do you mean, clean?"

"That you don't have any perversions, or addictions, or contagious diseases…"

"Of course I don't!"

"How can I be sure?"

"Because I'm Victoria's friend—"

"And Victoria knowingly stuck us together, so we have to trust that neither of us is an unsavory character, because we both do trust Victoria. At least I do. Or did." He threw his clenched fist in the air. "I don't believe I'm standing here arguing. Do you, or do you not, want the damn aspirin?" His fist dropped and opened, cradling the tablets.

"I want them."

Neil let out an exaggerated breath. "Then we're back where we started. Can you sit up?" He spoke the last very slowly, as though she might not understand him otherwise.

Deirdre was beyond taking offense. "If I can't, I have no business doing what I do," she muttered to herself, and began to elbow her way up. With her leg elevated, the maneuvering was difficult. Still, she was supposedly agile, an athlete, an expert at bending and twisting…

Neil didn't wait to watch her fall. He came down on a knee on the bed, curved his arm beneath her back and propped her up. "The pills are in my right hand. Can you reach them?"

His right hand was by her waist; his left held the glass. She took the tablets, pressed them into her mouth and washed them down with the water he offered.

Neither of them spoke.

Neil lowered her to the sheets, removed his knee from the bed and walked back to the bathroom. Quietly he set the glass by the sink, switched off the light and returned to bed.

Deirdre lay silent, unmoving, strangely peaceful. Her leg felt better; her entire body felt better. She closed her eyes, took a long, slow breath and drifted into a deep, healing sleep.

When she awoke it was daylight—overcast still, raining still, but daylight nonetheless. She lay quietly, gradually assimilating where she was and what she was doing there. As the facts crystallized, she realized that she wasn't alone in the bed. From its far side came a quiet breathing; she turned her head slowly, saw the large quilt-covered shape of Victoria's other friend, turned her head back. Then the crux of her dilemma hit her.

She'd fled Rhode Island, driven for hours in the pouring

rain, been drenched, mud spattered, nearly seasick—all to be alone. But she wasn't. She was marooned on an island, some twenty miles from shore, with a grump of a man. Now what was she going to do?

Neil was asking himself the same question. He lay on his side with his eyes wide open, listening to the sounds of Deirdre's breathing, growing more annoyed by the minute. He did believe what he'd said the night before. If she was Victoria's friend—and she knew a convincing amount about Victoria—she couldn't be all bad. Still, she was disagreeable, and he wanted to be alone.

Pushing back the quilt, he swung his legs to the floor, then paused to give his head a chance to adjust to the shift in position. His head ached, though he was as ready to blame it on Deirdre as on the amount of Scotch he'd drunk the evening before.

"Don't you have something decent to wear?" came a perturbed voice from beneath the quilt.

His head shot around. Mistake. He put the heels of his hands on his temples and inch by inch faced forward. "There's nothing indecent about my skin," he gritted.

"Don't you have pajamas?"

"Like yours?"

"What's wrong with mine? They're perfectly good pajamas."

"They're men's pajamas." Even as he said it his arm tingled. It was his right arm, the one he'd used to prop her up. Sure, she'd been wearing men's pajamas, but beneath all the fabric was a slender back, a slim waist and the faintest curve of a hip.

"They're comfortable, and warm."

"I don't need warmth," he growled roughly.

"It's freezing in here. Isn't there any heat?"

"I like my bedroom cold."

"Great." It was an argument to be continued later. For the moment, there was something more pressing. Vividly she recalled the sight of his chest, the corded muscles, the dark swirls of hair. "It might have been considerate of you to put *something* on when you decided to crawl into bed with me."

"Be grateful for the consideration I did make. I usually sleep in the buff."

She clenched a fistful of quilt by her cheek. "So macho."

"What's the matter?" he shot back. "Can't handle it?"

"There's nothing to handle. Macho has never turned me on."

"Not enough woman for it?"

The low blow hit hard, causing her to lash out in self-defense. "Too much of a woman. I hate to disillusion you, but machismo is pretty shallow."

"Ah, the expert."

"No. Simply a modern woman."

Muttering a pithy curse, Neil pushed himself from bed. "Save it for Thomas when he comes back for you later. Right now, I need a shower."

She started to look up, but caught herself. "I need a bath."

"You had your chance last night and you blew it. Now it's my turn."

"Use one of the other bathrooms. They've got showers."

"I like this one."

"But it's the only one with a tub!"

"You can have it as soon as I'm done."

"What happened to chivalry?"

"Talk of chivalry from a modern woman?" he chided, and soundly closed the bathroom door behind him.

Deirdre did look up then. He'd had the last word...so he thought. Rolling to her side, she grabbed her crutches from the floor and hobbled from the bedroom. Off the short hall on the other side of the living room was a den, and in the den was the ship-to-shore radio.

She checked her watch. Ten-forty-five. *Ten-forty-five?* She couldn't believe she'd slept round the clock and then some! But she'd needed it. She'd been exhausted. And she'd slept soundly once she'd been settled with her leg propped up and aspirin dispersing through her system.

Ten-forty-five. Had she missed Thomas? Would he be home or out on the boat? It was rainy, true, but windy?

She studied the directions beside the radio and, after several unsuccessful attempts, managed to put through the call. A young man responded, clearly not the lobsterman.

"It's urgent that I reach Thomas," she said.

"Is there an emergency?" the young man asked.

"Not exactly an emergency in the critical sense of the word, but—"

"Are you well?"

"Yes, I'm well—"

"And Mr. Hersey?"

Hersey. "Neil? He's well, too, but it really is important that I speak with Thomas."

"I'll have him call you as soon as he can."

She tightened her fingers on the coiled cord of the speaker. "When do you think that will be?"

"I don't know."

"Is he on the boat?"

"He's in Augusta on business."

"Oh. Is he due back today?"

"I believe so."

Frustration. She sighed. "Well, please give him the message."

After the young man assured her he would, Deirdre replaced the speaker and turned off the set. In Augusta on business. She wondered. Thomas would know precisely why she was calling; he'd known precisely what he was doing yesterday when he left both of his unsuspecting passengers on Victoria's island together.

She thought back to the things he'd said. He'd been smooth. She had to hand it to him. He'd been general enough, vague enough. He'd never lied, simply given clever, well-worded answers to her questions.

She wasn't at all sure she could trust him to call back.

Scowling, she turned at the sound of footsteps in the hall. So Neil had finished his shower, had he? And what was he planning to do now? She listened. The footsteps receded, replaced by the sound of the refrigerator door opening, then closing. He was in the kitchen. Good. Now she'd take her bath, and she'd take her sweet time about it.

In truth, she couldn't have rushed if she'd wanted to. Maneuvering herself into the tub was every bit the hassle she'd expected. Particularly awkward—and annoying— was the fact that the tub was flush against one wall, and in order to drape her casted leg over its lip she had to put her back to the faucets. Her decision to climb in before she ran the water resulted in a considerable amount of contortion, not to mention the fact that when she tried to lie back, the spigot pressed into her head. She finally managed to wedge herself into a corner, which meant that she was lying almost diagonally in the tub.

It was better than nothing, or so she told herself when she gave up the idea of relaxing to concentrate on getting clean. That, too, was a trial. With both hands occupied soaping and scrubbing, she slid perilously low in the water. Just as well, she reasoned. Her hair needed washing as badly, if not more than the rest of her. How long had it been since she'd had a proper shampoo? A week?

"Yuk."

Tipping her head back, she immersed her hair, doused it with shampoo and scrubbed. Unfortunately she'd used too much shampoo. No amount of dipping her head in the water removed it completely, and by then the water was dirty. She was thoroughly disgusted. In the end she drained the tub, turned on fresh warm water, sharply arched her back to put her head in the stream and hoped for the best.

By the time she'd awkwardly made her way out of the tub, she was tense all over. So much for a refreshing bath, she mused. But at least she was clean. There was some satisfaction in that. There was also satisfaction in rubbing moisturizing lotion over her body, a daily ritual that had been temporarily abandoned during her stay in the hospital. The scent of it was faint but familiar. When she closed her eyes she could imagine that she was back home, in one piece, looking forward to the day.

She couldn't keep her eyes closed forever, though, and when she opened them, the truth hit. She was neither home, nor in one piece, nor looking forward to the day. Rather, she was in self-imposed exile on Victoria's island. Her left leg was in a heavy cast, her face was decidedly pale and she was pathetically weak. And she was not looking forward to the day, because *he* was here.

Angrily she tugged on her underwear, then the mint-green warm-up suit she'd brought. It was loose, oversized and stylish, and the top matched the bottom. He couldn't complain about her clothes today.

Propping herself on the toilet seat, she worked a pair of white wool leg warmers over her cast, then her good leg, put a single white crew sock on the good foot, then a single white sneaker. She towel-dried her hair with as much energy as she could muster, then, leaning against the sink, brushed it until it shone.

She studied her face. A lost cause. Squeaky clean, but a lost cause nonetheless. It was pale, bland, childlike. She'd always looked younger than her years. When she'd been in her late teens and early twenties, she'd hated it. Now, with women her age doing their best to look younger, she had her moments of self-appreciation. This wasn't one of them. She looked awful.

A pouting child? Perhaps, but only because of *him*. With a deep breath, she turned from the mirror and began to neaten the bathroom. *Him*. What an unpleasant man, an unpleasant situation. And a remedy? There was none, until she reached Thomas, until she convinced him that, for her sanity alone, Neil Hersey should be removed from the island.

A few minutes later, she entered the kitchen to find the

remnants of bacon smoke in the air, two dirty pans on the stove, the counter littered with open cartons of juice and milk, a bowl of eggs, a tub of margarine, an open package of English muffins and miscellaneous crumbs. Neil Hersey was nonchalantly finishing his breakfast.

"You're quite a cook," she remarked wryly. "Does your skill extend to cleaning up after yourself, or were you expecting the maid to come in and do it?"

Neil set down his fork, rocked back in his chair and studied her. "So that's why Victoria sent you along. I knew there had to be a reason."

Deirdre snickered. "If you think I'm going to touch this disaster area, you're crazy. You made the mess, you clean it up."

"And if I don't?"

"Then you'll have spoiled juice and milk, stale muffins and dirty dishes to use next time." She stared at the greasy pans. "What did you make, anyway?"

"Bacon and eggs. Sound tempting?"

Her mouth was watering. "It might if you didn't use so much fat. I'd think that at your age you'd be concerned about that, not to mention the cholesterol in however many eggs you ate."

"Four. I was hungry. Aren't you? You didn't have supper."

"I had other things on my mind last night." She sent him a look of mock apology and spoke in her sweetest tone. "I'm sorry. Were you waiting for me to join you for dinner?"

His lips twisted. "Not quite. I had better company than you could ever be."

"A bottle of Scotch?" At his raised brows, she elaborated. "It's sitting right there in the living room with a half-empty glass beside it. Now that was brilliant. Do you always drown your sorrows in booze?"

The front legs of his chair hit the floor with a thud. "I don't drink," he stated baldly.

"Then we must have a little gremlin here who just happened to get into the liquor cabinet."

Faint color rose on Neil's neck. "I had a couple of drinks last night, but I'm not a drinker." He scowled. "And what's it to you? I came here to do what I want, and if that means getting drunk every night, amen."

He was being defensive, and Deirdre found she liked that. Not just because she was momentarily on top. There was something else, something related to that hint of a blush on his neck. "You know, you're really not all that bad-looking." Her gaze fell to take in his large, maroon-and-white rugby shirt and slimmer fitting jeans. "Aside from a receding hairline and all that crap you've got on your face—"

Neil reacted instantly. His eyes narrowed and his jaw grew tight. "My hairline is not receding. It's the same one I've had for years, only I don't choose to hide it like some men do. And as for 'all that crap' on my face, they're whiskers, in case you didn't know."

"You could have shaved."

"Why should I?"

"Because I'm here, for one thing."

"Through no choice of mine. This is my vacation you're intruding on, and the way I see it, you don't have any say as to what I do or how I look. Got that?"

Deirdre stared mutely back at him.

"Got that?" he repeated.

"I'm not hard of hearing," she said quietly.

He rolled his eyes. "Thank goodness for that, at least."

"But you've got it wrong. You're the one who's intruding on my time here, and I'll thank you to make yourself as invisible as possible until Thomas comes to pick you up."

Neil stood, then drew himself up and slowly approached her. "Make myself invisible, huh? Just how do you suggest I do that?"

He came closer and closer. Even barefoot he towered

over her. Deirdre tipped back her head, stubbornly maintaining eye contact, refusing to be cowed. "You can clean up the kitchen when you're done, for one thing."

"I would have done that, anyway…when I was done."

"For another, you can busy yourself exploring the island."

"In the rain?"

"For a third, you can take yourself and your things to one of the other bedrooms."

His voice suddenly softened. "You didn't like my taking care of you last night?"

His question hung in the air. It wasn't that the words were shocking, or even particularly suggestive, but something about his nearness made Deirdre's breath catch in her throat. Yes, he was large, but that wasn't it. Yes, he looked roguish, but that wasn't it, either. He looked…he looked…warm…gentle…deep?

Neil, too, was momentarily stunned. When he'd come up so close, he hadn't quite expected—what? That she should smell so fresh, so feminine? That the faint, nearly transparent smattering of freckles on the bridge of her nose should intrigue him? That she should have dusty brown eyes, the eyes of a woman?

Swallowing once, he stepped back and tore his gaze from hers. It landed on the littered counter. With but a moment's pause, he began to close containers and return them to the refrigerator. "How does your leg feel?"

"Okay," Deirdre answered cautiously.

"Any worse than yesterday?"

"No."

He nodded and continued with his work.

Deirdre took a breath, surprised to find herself slightly shaky. "I, uh, I tried to call Thomas. He wasn't in."

"I know."

So he'd tried, too. She should have figured as much. Hobbling on her crutches to the stool by the counter peninsula, she propped herself on its edge. "We have to find a solution."

"Right."

"Any thoughts on it?"

His head was in the refrigerator, but his words carried clearly. "You know them."

She certainly did. "Then we're stalemated."

"Looks that way."

"I guess the only thing to do is to dump the problem in Victoria's lap. She caused it. Let her find a solution."

The refrigerator door swung shut. Neil straightened and thrust a hand on his hip. "That's great. But if we can't reach Thomas, how in the hell are we going to reach Victoria?"

"We'll just have to keep trying."

"And in the meantime?"

She grinned. "We'll just have to keep fighting."

Neil stared at her. It was the first time he'd seen her crack a smile. Her teeth were small, white and even; her lips were soft, generous. "You like fighting."

"I never have before, but, yeah, I kinda like it." She tilted her head to the side, tipped her chin up in defiance. "It feels good."

"You are strange, lady," he muttered as he transferred the dirty pans to the sink with more force than necessary. "Strange."

"Any more so than you?"

"There's nothing strange about me."

"Are you kidding? I haven't been arguing in a vacuum, you know. You even admitted that you enjoy picking on me. I dare you to tell me how that's any different from my saying I like fighting."

He sent a leisurely stream of liquid soap onto a sponge. "Give me a break, will you?"

"Give *me* a break, and hurry up, will you? I'm waiting to use the kitchen, or have you forgotten? It's been twenty-four hours since I've eaten—"

"And whose fault is that? If you'd stayed home where you belonged, you wouldn't have missed any meals."

"Maybe not, but if I'd stayed home, I'd have gone crazy!"

Neil stared at her over his shoulder; Deirdre stared back. The question was there; he was on the verge of asking it. She dared him to, knowing she'd take pleasure in refusing him.

In the end he didn't ask. He wasn't sure he wanted to know what she'd left that was so awful. He wasn't sure he wanted to think of someone else's problems. He wasn't sure he wanted to feel sympathy for this strange woman-child.

Perversely disappointed, Deirdre levered herself from the stool, fit her crutches under her arms and swung into the living room. Though it was the largest room in the house, it had a feel of coziness. Pine, dark stained and rich, dominated the decor—wall paneling; rafters and pillars; a large, low hub of a coffee table, and the surrounding, sturdy frames of a cushioned sofa and chairs. The center of one entire wall was bricked into a huge fireplace. Deirdre thought she'd very much like to see the fire lit.

Propping her hip against the side of one of the chairs, she gave the room a sweeping overview. No doubt about it, she mused sadly. The room, the house, the island—all had high potential for romance. Miles from nowhere…an isolated, insulated retreat…fire crackling mingled with the steady patter of rain. At the right time, with the right man, it would be wonderful. She could understand why so many of Victoria's friends had raved about the place.

"It's all yours," Neil said. Momentarily confused, Deirdre frowned at him. "The kitchen. I thought you were dying of hunger."

The kitchen. "I am."

"Then it's yours."

"Thank you."

He stepped back, allowing more than ample room for her to pass. "There's hot coffee in the pot. Help yourself."

"Thank you."

Just as she was moving by, he leaned forward. "I make it thick. Any objections?"

She paused, head down. "What do you think?"

"I think yes."

"You're right. I like mine thin."

"Add water."

"It tastes vile that way."

"Then make a fresh pot."

"I will." She looked up at him. His face was inches away. Dangerous. "If you don't mind…"

Taking the hint, he straightened. She swung past him and entered the kitchen, where she set about preparing a meal for the first time in a week.

It was a challenge. She began to remove things from the refrigerator, only to find that she couldn't possibly handle her crutches and much else at the same time. So she stood at the open refrigerator, balancing herself against the door, taking out one item, then another, lining each up on the counter. When she'd removed what she needed, she balanced herself against the counter and, one by one, moved each item in line toward the stove. A crutch fell. Painstakingly she worked her way down to pick it up, only to have it fall again when she raised her arm a second time.

For a woman who'd always prided herself on economy of movement, such a production was frustrating. She finally gave up on the crutches entirely, resorting alternately to leaning against counters and hopping. Each step of the preparation was an ordeal, made all the worse when she thought of how quickly and effortlessly she'd normally do it. By the time she'd finally poured the makings of a cheese omelet into the pan, she was close to tears.

Lounging comfortably on the sofa in the living room, Neil listened to her struggles. It served her right, he mused smugly. She should have stayed at home—wherever that was. Where was it? He wondered what would have driven her crazy had she not left, then he chided himself for wondering when he had worries aplenty of his own.

He thought of those worries and his mood darkened.

Nothing had changed with his coming here; the situation would remain the same in Hartford regardless of how long he stayed away. He had to think. He had to analyze his career, his accomplishments and aspirations. He had to decide on a positive course of action.

So far he was without a clue.

The sound of shattering glass brought his head up. "What the hell…" He was on his feet and into the kitchen within seconds.

Deirdre was gripping the stove with one hand, her forehead with another. She was staring at the glass that lay broken in a puddle of orange juice on the floor. "What in the devil's the matter with you?" he yelled. "Can't you manage the simplest little thing?"

Tear-filled eyes flew to his. "No, I can't! And I'm not terribly thrilled about it!" Angrily she grabbed the sponge from the sink and knelt on her good knee.

"Let me do that," Neil growled, but she had a hand up, warding him off.

"No! I'll do it myself!" Piece by piece, she began gathering up the shards of broken glass.

He straightened slowly. She was stubborn. And independent. And slightly dumb. With her cast hooked precariously to the side, her balance was iffy at best. He imagined her losing it, falling forward, catching herself on a palm, which in turn would catch its share of glass slivers.

Grabbing several pieces of paper towel, he knelt, pushed her hands aside and set to work cleaning the mess. "There's no need to cry over spilled milk," he said gently.

"It's spilled orange juice, and I'm not crying." Using that same good leg, she raised herself. Her thigh muscles labored, and she cringed to think how out of shape she'd become in a mere week. "You don't have to do that."

"If I don't, you're apt to do even worse damage."

"I can take care of myself!" she vowed, then turned to the stove. The omelet was burning. "Damn!" Snatching up a spatula, she quickly folded the egg mixture in half and turned off the heat. "A crusty omelet. Just what I need!" Balling her hands against the edge of the stove, she threw her head back. "Damn it to hell. Why me?"

Neil dumped the sodden paper towels in the wastebasket and reached for fresh ones. "Swearing won't help."

"Wanna bet!" Her eyes flashed as she glared at him. "It makes me feel better, and since that's the case, I'll do it as much as I damn well please!"

He looked up from his mopping. "My, my, aren't we in a mood."

"Yes, we are, and you're not doing anything to help it."

"I'm cleaning up."

"You're making me feel like a helpless cripple. I told you I'd do it. I'm not totally incapacitated, damn it!"

He sighed. "Didn't anyone ever tell you that a lady shouldn't swear?"

Her lips twisted. "Oh-ho, yes. My mother, my father, my sister, my uncles—for years I've had to listen to complaints." She launched into a whiny mimic and tipped her head from one side to the other. "'Don't say that, Deirdre,' or 'Don't do that, Deirdre,' or 'Deirdre, smile and be pleasant,' or 'Behave like a lady, Deirdre.'" Her voice returned to its normal pitch, but it held anger. "Well, if what I do isn't ladylike, that's tough!" She took a quick breath and added as an afterthought, "And if I want to swear, I'll do it!"

With that, she hopped to the counter stool and plopped down on it with her back to Neil.

Silently he finished cleaning the floor. He poured a fresh glass of juice, toasted the bread she'd taken out, lightly spread it with jam and set the glass and plate before her. "Do you want the eggs?" he asked softly.

She shook her head and sat for several minutes before slowly lifting one of the slices of toast and munching on it.

Neil, who was leaning against the counter with his ankles crossed and his arms folded over his chest, studied her defeated form. "Do you live with your family?"

She carefully chewed what was in her mouth, then swallowed. "Thank God, no."

"But you live nearby."

"A giant mistake. I should have moved away years ago. Even California sounds too close. Alaska might be better—northern Alaska."

"That bad, huh?"

"That bad." She took a long, slow drink of juice, concentrating on the cooling effect it had on her raspy throat. Maybe she was coming down with a cold. It wouldn't surprise her, given the soaking she'd taken the day before. Then again, maybe she'd picked up something at the hospital. That was more likely. Hospitals were chock-full of germs, and it would be just her luck to pick one up. Just her luck. "Why are you being so nice?"

"Maybe I'm a nice guy at heart."

She couldn't bear the thought of that, not when she was in such a foul mood herself. "You're an ill-tempered, scruffy-faced man."

Pushing himself from the counter, he muttered, "If you say so," and returned to the living room, where he sat staring sullenly at the cold hearth while Deirdre finished the small breakfast he'd made for her. He heard her cleaning up, noted the absence of both audible mishaps and swearing and found himself speculating on the kind of person she was at heart. He knew about himself. He wasn't really ill-tempered, only a victim of circumstance. Was she the same?

He wondered how old she was.

By the time Deirdre finished in the kitchen, she was feeling a little better. Her body had responded to nourishment; despite her sulky refusal, she'd even eaten part of the omelet. It was more overcooked than burned and was barely lukewarm by the time she got to it, but it was protein. Her voice of reason said she needed that.

Turning toward the living room, she saw Neil sprawled in the chair. She didn't like him. More accurately, she didn't want him here. He was a witness to her clumsiness. That, on top of everything else, embarrassed her.

In the back of her mind was the niggling suspicion that at heart he might well be a nice guy. He'd helped her the night before. He'd helped her this morning. Still, he had his own problems; when they filled his mind, he was as moody, as curt, as churlish as she was. Was he as much of a misfit as she sometimes felt?

She wondered what he did for a living.

With a firm grip on her crutches, she made her way into the living room, going first to the picture window, then retreating until she was propped against the sofa back. From this vantage point she could look at the world beyond the house. The island was gray and wet; its verdancy made a valiant attempt at livening the scene, but failed.

"Lousy day," Neil remarked.

"Mmm."

"Any plans?"

"Actually," she said with a grand intake of breath, "I was thinking of getting dressed and going to the theater."

He shook his head. "The show's sold out, standing room only. You'd never make it, one-legged."

"Thanks."

"Don't feel bad. The show isn't worth seeing."

"Not much is nowadays," she answered. If she was going to be sour, she mused, she might as well do it right. By nature she was an optimist, choosing to gloss over the negatives in life. But all along she'd known the negatives were there. For a change, she wanted to look at them and complain. It seemed to her she'd earned the right.

"I can't remember the last time I saw a good show, or, for that matter, a movie," she began with spirited venom. "Most of them stink. The stories are either so pat and contrived that you're bored to tears, or so bizarre that you can't figure out what's happening. The settings are phony, the music is blah and the acting is pathetic. Or maybe it's the casting that's pathetic. I mean, Travolta was wonderful in

Saturday Night Fever. He took Barbarino one step further—just suave enough, just sweet enough, just sensitive enough and born to dance. But a newspaper reporter in *Perfect*? Oh, please. The one scene that might have been good was shot in the exercise class, but the camera lingered so long on Travolta's pelvis it was disgusting!"

Neil was staring at her, one finger resting against his lips. "Uh, I'm not really an expert on Travolta's pelvis, disgusting or otherwise."

"Have *you* seen anything good lately?"

"In the way of a pelvis?"

"In the way of a movie."

"I don't have time to go to the movies."

"Neither do I, but if there's something I want to see— a movie, an art exhibit, a concert—I make time. You never do that?"

"For basketball I do."

She wondered if he himself had ever played. He had both the height and the build. "What team?"

"The Celtics."

"You're from Boston?"

"No. But I got hooked when I went to school there. Now I just drive up whenever I can get my hands on tickets. I also make time for lectures."

"What kind of lectures?"

"Current affairs-type talks. You know, by politicians or business superstars—Kissinger, Iacocca."

Her eyes narrowed. "I'll bet you'd go to hear John Dean speak."

Neil shrugged. "I haven't. But I might. He was intimately involved in a fascinating period of our history."

"He was a criminal! He spent time in prison!"

"He paid the price."

"He named his price—books, a TV miniseries, the lecture circuit—doesn't it gall you to think that crime can be so profitable?"

Moments before, the conversation had been purely incidental; suddenly it hit home. "Yes," he said stiffly, "it galls me."

"Yet you'd pay money to go hear someone talk about his experiences on the wrong side of the law?"

Yes, he would have, and he'd have rationalized it by saying that the speaker was providing a greater service by telling all. Now, though, he thought of his experience at Wittnauer-Douglass and felt a rising anger. "You talk too much," he snapped.

Deirdre was momentarily taken aback. She'd expected him to argue, either for her or against her. But he was cutting the debate short. "What did I say?"

"Nothing," he mumbled, sitting farther back in his seat. "Nothing important."

"Mmm. As soon as the little lady hits a raw nerve, you put her down as 'nothing important.'"

"Not 'nothing important,' as in you. As in what you said."

"I don't see much difference. That's really macho of you. Macho, as in coward."

Neil surged from his chair and glared at her. "Ah, hell, give me a little peace, will ya? All I wanted to do was to sit here quietly, minding my own business."

"You were the one who talked first."

"That's right. I was trying to be civil."

"Obviously it didn't work."

"It would have if you hadn't been spoiling for a fight."

"Me spoiling for a fight? We were having a simple discussion about the ethics involved in giving financial support to convicted political criminals, when you went off the handle. I asked you a simple question. All you had to do was to give me a simple answer."

"But I don't have the answer!" he bellowed. A vein throbbed at his temple. "I don't have answers for lots of things lately, and it's driving me out of my mind!"

Lips pressed tightly together, he stared at her, then whirled around and stormed off toward the den.

CHAPTER FOUR

WITH NEIL'S EXIT, the room became suddenly quiet. Deirdre listened, knowing that he'd be trying to reach Thomas again. She prayed he'd get through, for his sake as well as hers. She and Neil were like oil and water; they didn't mix well.

Taking advantage of the fact that she had the living room to herself, she stretched out on the sofa, closed her eyes and pretended she was alone in the house. It was quiet, so quiet. Neither the gentle patter of rain nor the soft hum of heat blowing through the vents disturbed the peaceful aura. She imagined she'd made breakfast without a problem in the world, and that the day before she'd transferred everything from Thomas's boat without a hitch. In her dream world she hadn't needed help, because her broken leg was good as new.

But that was her dream world. In reality, she had needed help, and Neil Hersey had been there. She wondered what it would be like if he were a more even-tempered sort. He was good-looking; she gave that to him, albeit begrudgingly. He was strong; she recalled the arm that had supported her when he'd brought her aspirin, remembered the broad chest she'd leaned against. He was independent and capable, cooking for himself, cleaning up both his mess and hers without a fuss.

He had potential, all right. He also had his dark moments. At those times, given her own mood swings, she wanted to be as far from him as possible.

As she lay thinking, wondering, imagining, her eyelids slowly lowered, and without intending to, she dozed off. A full hour later she awoke with a start. She'd been dreaming. Of Neil. A lovely dream. An annoying dream. The fact that she'd slept at all annoyed her, because it pointed to a physical weakness she detested. She'd slept for fourteen hours the night before. Surely that had been enough. And to dream of *Neil*?

She'd been right in her early assessment of him; he was as troubled as she was. She found herself pondering the specifics of his problem, then pushed those ponderings from her mind. She had her own problems. She didn't need his.

What she needed, she decided, was a cup of coffee. After the breakfast fiasco, she hadn't had either the courage or the desire to tackle coffee grounds, baskets and filters. Now, though, the thought of drinking something hot and aromatic appealed to her.

Levering herself awkwardly to her feet, she went into the kitchen and shook the coffeepot. He'd said there was some left but that it was thick. She didn't like thick coffee. Still, it was a shame to throw it out.

Determinedly she lit the gas and set the coffee on to heat.

Meanwhile, Neil was in the den, staring out the window at the rain, trying to understand himself. Deirdre Joyce— the young man who'd answered at Thomas's house had supplied her last name—was a thorn in his side. He wanted to be alone, yet she was here. It was midafternoon. He still hadn't spoken with Thomas, which meant that Deirdre was going to be around for another night at least.

What annoyed him most were the fleeting images that played tauntingly in the corners of his mind. A smooth, lithe back…a slim waist…the suggestion of a curve at the hip…a fresh, sweet scent…hair the color of wheat, not mousy brown as he'd originally thought, but thick, shining wheat. Her face, too, haunted him. She had the prettiest light-brown eyes, a small, almost delicate nose, lips that held promise when she smiled.

Of course, she rarely smiled. She had problems. And the fact of the matter was that he really did want to be alone. So why was he thinking of her in a way that would suggest that he found her attractive?

From the door came the clearing of a throat. "Uh, excuse me?"

He turned his head. Damn, but the mint-green of her warm-up suit was cheerful. Of course, she still looked lumpy as hell. "Yes?"

"I heated up the last of the coffee, but it really is too strong for me. I thought you might like it." Securing her right crutch with the muscles of her upper arm, she held out the cup.

Neil grew instantly wary. It was the first attempt she'd made at being friendly. Coming after nonstop termagancy, there had to be a reason. She had to want something. "Why?" he asked bluntly.

"Why what?"

"Why did you heat it up?"

She frowned. "I told you. I thought you might like it."

"You haven't been terribly concerned with my likes before."

"And I'm not now," she replied defensively. "It just seemed a shame to throw it out."

"Ah. You're making a fresh pot, so you heated the dregs for me."

"I don't believe you," she breathed. She hadn't expected such instant enmity, and coming in the face of her attempted pleasantness, it set her off. "You would have had me drink the dregs, but suddenly they're not good enough for you?"

"I didn't say they weren't good enough." His voice was smooth, with an undercurrent of steel. "I reheat coffee all the time because it saves time, and yes, it is a shame to throw it out. What I'm wondering is why the gesture of goodwill from you. You must have something up your sleeve."

"Boy," she remarked with a wry twist of her lips, "have *you* been burned."

His eyes darkened. "And just what do you mean by that?"

"For a man to be as suspicious of a woman, he'd have to have been used by one, and used badly."

Neil thought about that for a minute. Funny, it had never occurred to him before, but he had been used. Nancy had been crafty—subtle enough so the fact had registered only subliminally in his brain—but crafty nonetheless. Only now did he realize that often she'd done small things for him when she'd wanted something for herself. It fit in with the nature of her love, yet he hadn't seen it then. Just as he hadn't seen the potential for treachery at Wittnauer-Douglass.

"My history is none of your damned business," he ground out angrily.

"Fine," she spat. "I just want you to know that it's taken a monumental effort on my part to get the dumb coffee in here without spilling it. And if you want to know the truth, my major motivation was to find out where you were so I'd know what room to avoid." She set the mug on a nearby bookshelf with a thud. "You can have this or not. I don't care." She turned to leave, but not fast enough to hide the hint of hurt in her expression.

"Wait."

She stopped, but didn't turn back. "What for?" she asked. "So you can hurl more insults at me?"

He moved from the window. "I didn't mean to do that. You're right. I've been burned. And it was unfair of me to take it out on you."

"Seems to me you've been taking an awful lot out on me."

"And vice versa," he said quietly, satisfied when she looked over her shoulder at him. "You have to admit that you haven't been the most congenial of housemates yourself."

"I've had…other things on my mind."

He took a leisurely step closer. "So have I. I've needed to let off steam. Yelling at you feels good. It may not be right, but it feels good."

"Tell me about it," she muttered rhetorically, but he took her at face value.

"It seems that my entire life has been ruled by reason and restraint. I've never spouted off quite this way about things that are really pretty petty."

She eyed him askance. "Like my using the master bedroom?"

"Now that's not petty. That's a practical issue."

"Then what about heat? The bedroom is freezing, while the rest of the house is toasty warm. You purposely kept the thermostat low in that room, didn't you?"

"I told you. I like a cool bedroom."

"Well, I like a warm one, and don't tell me to use one of the other bedrooms, because I won't. You'll be leaving—"

"You'll be leaving." His voice had risen to match the vehemence of hers, but it suddenly dropped again. "Only problem is that Thomas still isn't in, so it looks like it won't be today."

"He's avoiding us."

"That occurred to you, too, hmm?"

"Which means that we're stranded here." Glumly she looked around. "I mean, the house is wonderful. Look." She gestured toward one wall, then another. "Hundreds of books to choose from, a stereo, a VCR, a television—"

"The TV reception stinks. I tried it."

"No loss. I hate television."

"Like you hate movies?"

"I didn't say I hated movies, just that lately they've been awful. The same is true of television. If it isn't a corny sit-com, it's a blood-and-guts adventure show, or worse, a prime-time soap opera."

"Opinionated urchin, aren't you?"

Her eyes flashed and she gripped her crutches tighter. "Yes, I'm opinionated, and I'm in the mood to express every one of those opinions." Silently she dared him to stop her.

Neil had no intention of doing that. He was almost curious as to what she'd say next. Reaching for the mug she'd set down, he leaned against the bookshelf, close enough to catch the fresh scent that emanated from her. "Go on. I'm listening."

Deirdre, too, was aware of the closeness, aware of the breadth of his shoulders and the length of his legs, aware of the fact that he was more man than she'd been near for a very long time. Her cheeks began to feel warm, and there was a strange tickle in the pit of her stomach.

Confused, she glanced around, saw the long leather couch nearby, and inched back until she could sink into it. She raked her lip with her teeth, then looked up at him. "What was I saying?"

"You were giving me your opinion of the state of modern television."

"Oh." She took a breath and thought, finally saying, "I hate miniseries."

"Why?"

"They do awful things to the books they're adapted from."

"Not always."

"Often enough. And they're twice as long as they need to be. Take the opening part of each installment. They kill nearly fifteen minutes listing the cast, then reviewing what went before. I mean, the bulk of the viewers know what went before, and it's a waste of their time to rehash it. And as for the cast listings, the last thing those actors and actresses need is more adulation. Most of them are swell-headed as it is!" She was warming to the subject, enjoying her own perversity. "But the worst part of television has to be the news."

"I like the news," Neil protested.

"I do, too, when it is news, but when stations have two hours to fill each night, a good half of what they deliver simply isn't news. At least, not what I'd consider to be news. And as for the weather report, by the time they've finished with their elaborate electronic maps and radar screens, I've tuned out, so I miss the very forecast I wanted to hear."

"Maybe you ought to stick to newspapers."

"I usually do."

"What paper do you read?"

"The *Times*."

"New York?" He was wondering about her connection to Victoria. "Then you live there?"

"No. I live in Providence."

"Ah, Providence. Thriving little metropolis."

"What's wrong with Providence?"

"Nothing that a massive earthquake wouldn't fix." It was an exaggeration that gave him pleasure.

She stared hard at him. "You probably know nothing about Providence, much less Rhode Island, yet you'd stand there and condemn the entire area."

"Oh, I know something about Providence. I represented a client there two years ago, in the middle of summer, and the air conditioning in his office didn't work. Since it was a skyscraper, we couldn't even open a window, so we went to what was supposed to be the in restaurant. The service was lousy, the food worse, and to top it all off, some bastard sideswiped my car in the parking lot, so I ended up paying for that, too, and *then* my client waited a full six months before settling my bill."

Deirdre was curious. "What kind of client?"

"I'm a lawyer."

"A lawyer!" She pushed herself to the edge of the seat. "No wonder you're not averse to criminals on the lecture circuit. The proceeds could well be paying your fee!"

"I am not a criminal attorney," Neil stated. The crease

between his brows grew pronounced. "I work with corporations."

"That's even worse! I hate corporations!"

"You hate most everything."

Deirdre's gaze remained locked with his for a moment. He seemed to be issuing a challenge, asking a question about her basic personality and daring her to tell the truth. "No," she said in a quieter tone. "I'm just airing certain pet peeves. I don't—I can't do it very often."

He, too, had quieted. "What do you do?"

"Hold it in."

"No. Work-wise. You do work, don't you? All modern women work."

Deirdre dipped one brow. "There's no need for sarcasm."

He made no apology. "You pride yourself on being a modern woman. So tell me. What do you do for a living?"

Slowly she gathered her crutches together. She couldn't tell him what she did; he'd have a field day with it. "That—" she rose "—is none of your business."

"Whoa. I told you what I do."

"And I told you where I live. So we're even." Leaning into the crutches, she headed for the door.

"But I want to know what kind of work you do."

"Tough."

"I'll bet you don't work," he taunted, staying close by her side. "I'll bet you're a very spoiled relative of one of Victoria's very well-to-do friends."

"Believe what you want."

"I'll bet you're here because you really wanted to be in Monte Carlo, but Daddy cut off your expense account. You're freeloading off Victoria for a while."

"Expense account?" She paused midway through the living room and gave a brittle laugh. "Do fathers actually put their twenty-nine-year-old daughters on expense accounts?"

Neil's jaw dropped. "Twenty-nine. You're pulling my leg."

"I wouldn't pull your leg if it were attached to Mel Gibson!" she vowed, and continued on into the kitchen.

"Twenty-nine? I would have given you twenty-three, maybe twenty-four. But twenty-nine?" He stroked the stubble on his face and spoke pensively. "Old enough to have been married at least once." He started after her. "Tell me you're running away from a husband who beats you. Did he cause the broken leg?"

"No."

"But there is a husband?"

She sent him an impatient look. "You obviously don't know Victoria very well. She'd never have thrown us together if one of us were already married."

He did know Victoria, and Deirdre was right. "Okay. Have you ever been married?"

"No."

"Are you living with someone?" When she sent him a second, even more impatient look, he defended himself. "It's possible. I wouldn't put it past Victoria to try to get you to forget him if he were a creep…. Okay, okay. So you're not living with someone. You've just broken up with him, and you've come here to lick your wounds."

"Wrong again." Seth had left four months before, and there had been no wounds to lick. Propping her crutches in a corner, she hopped to the cupboard. She was determined to make herself a cup of coffee. "This is sounding like *Twenty Questions*, which reminds me of what I *really* hate, and it's game shows like the one Thomas was watching yesterday. I mean, I know why people watch them. They play along, getting a rush when they correctly guess an answer before the contestant does. But the contestants—jumping all over the place, clapping their hands with glee when they win, kissing an emcee they don't know from Adam…" She shook her head. "Sad. Very sad."

Neil was standing close, watching her spoon coffee into the basket. Her hands were slender, well formed, graceful. There was something about the way she tipped the spoon that was almost lyrical. His gaze crept up her arm, over one rather nondescript shoulder to a neck that was anything but nondescript. It, too, was graceful. Strange, he hadn't noticed before....

Momentarily suspending her work, Deirdre stared at him. Her eyes were wider than normal; her pulse had quickened. It occurred to her that she'd never seen so many textures on a man—from the thick gloss of his hair and the smooth slope of his nose to the furrowing of his brow and the bristle of his beard. She almost wanted to touch him...almost wanted to touch...

She tightened her fingers around the spoon. "Neil?"

He met her gaze, vaguely startled.

"I need room. I'm, uh, I'm not used to having someone around at home."

His frown deepened. "Uh, sure." He took a step back. "I think I'll...go take a walk or something."

Deirdre waited until he'd left, then slowly set back to work. *Take a walk. In the rain?* She listened, but there was no sound of the door opening and closing. So he was walking around the house. As good an activity as any to do on such a dismal day. She wondered when the rain would end. The island would be beautiful in sunshine. She'd love to go outside, find a high rock to sit on, and relax.

Surprisingly, when she thought of it, she wasn't all that tense, at least not in the way she'd been when she'd left Providence. In spite of the hassles of getting here, even in spite of the rain, the change of scenery was good for her. Of course, nothing had changed; Providence would be there when she returned. Her mother would be there, as would Sandra and the uncles. They'd be on her back again, unless she thought of some way to get them off.

She hadn't thought that far yet.

Carefully taking the coffee and a single crutch, she made her way into the den. She could put some weight on the cast without discomfort, which was a reassuring discovery. Carrying things such as coffee became a lot easier. Of course, it was a slow trip, and that still annoyed her, but it was better than being stuck in bed.

Leisurely sipping the coffee, she sat back on the leather sofa. Her duffel bag held several books, yarn and knitting needles, plus her cassette player and numerous tapes. None of these diversions appealed to her at the moment. She felt in limbo, as though she wouldn't completely settle down until Neil left.

But would he leave? Realistically? No. Not willingly. Not unless Victoria specifically instructed him to. Which she wouldn't.

Victoria had been clever. She'd known she was dealing with two stubborn people. She'd also known that once on the island, Neil and Deirdre would be virtually marooned. Thomas Nye was their only link with the mainland, and Thomas, while alert to any legitimate physical emergency, appeared to be turning a deaf ear to their strictly emotional pleas.

It was Neil and Deirdre versus the bad guys. An interesting prospect.

On impulse, she set down her cup and limped from the den. The house was quiet. She wondered what Neil was doing and decided that it was in her own best interest to find out. He hadn't returned to the living room while she'd been in the den, and he wasn't in the kitchen.

He was in the bedroom. The master bedroom. Deirdre stopped on the threshold and studied him. He lay on his back on the bed, one knee bent. His arm was thrown over his eyes.

Grateful she hadn't yet been detected, she was about to leave, when the whisper of a sound reached her ears. It was a little louder than normal breathing, a little softer than snoring. Neil was very definitely asleep.

Unable to help herself, she moved quietly forward until she stood by his side of the bed. His chest rose and fell in slow rhythm; his lips were faintly parted. As she watched, his fingers twitched, then stilled, and correspondingly something tugged at her heart.

He was human. When they'd been in the heat of battle, she might have tried to deny that fact, but seeing him now, defenseless in sleep, it struck her deeply. He was tired, perhaps emotionally as well as physically.

She found herself once again wondering what awful things he'd left behind. He was a lawyer; it was a good profession. Had something gone wrong with his career? Or perhaps his troubles related to his having been burned by a woman. Maybe he was suffering the effects of a bad divorce, perhaps worrying about children the marriage may have produced.

She actually knew very little about him. They'd been thrown together the moment she'd arrived at Spruce Head, and he'd simply provided a convenient punching bag on which to vent her frustrations. When she was arguing with him, she wasn't thinking of her leg, or aerobics, or Joyce Enterprises. Perhaps there was merit to his presence, after all.

He really wasn't so bad; at times she almost liked him. Moreover, at times she was physically drawn to him. She'd never before had her breath taken away by a man's nearness, but it had happened several times with Neil. For someone who'd always been relatively in control of her emotions, the experience was frightening. It was also exciting in a way….

Not trusting that Neil wouldn't awaken and lash out at her for disturbing him, she silently left the room and returned to the den. Her gaze fell on the ship-to-shore radio. She approached it, eyed the speaker, scanned the instructions for its use, then turned her back on both and sank down to the sofa. Adjusting one of the woven pillows beneath her head, she yawned and closed her eyes.

It was a lazy day. The sound of the rain was hypnotic, lulling, inducing the sweetest of lethargies. She wondered at her fatigue and knew that it was due only in part to her physical debilitation. The tension she'd been under in Providence was also to blame.

She needed the rest, she told herself. It was good for her. Wasn't that what a remote island was for? Soon enough she'd feel stronger, and then she'd read, knit, listen to music, even exercise. Soon enough the sun would come out, and she'd be able to avail herself of the island's fresh air.

But for now, doing nothing suited her just fine.

She was sleeping soundly when, some time later, Neil came to an abrupt halt at the door to the den. He was feeling groggy, having awoken only moments before. He wasn't used to sleeping during the day. He wasn't used to doing nothing. Oh, he'd brought along some books, and there were tapes here and a vast collection of old movies to watch, but he wasn't up to any of that just yet. If the weather were nice, he could spend time outdoors, but it wasn't, so he slept, instead.

Rationally he'd known that it was going to take him several days to unwind and that he badly needed the relaxation. He'd known that solutions to his problems weren't going to suddenly hit him in the face the moment he reached the island. Nevertheless, the problems were never far from consciousness.

Ironically Deirdre was his greatest diversion.

Deirdre. Looking down at her, he sucked in his upper lip, then slowly released it. Twenty-nine years old. He thought back to when he was that age. Four years out of law school, he'd been paying his dues as an associate in a large Hartford law firm. The hours had been long, the work boring. Frustrated by the hierarchy that relegated him to doing busywork for the partners, he'd set out on his own the following year. Though the hours had been equally long, the work had been far more rewarding.

Now, ten years later, he was approaching forty, sadly disillusioned. He knew where he'd been, saw his mistakes with vivid clarity…but he couldn't picture the future.

If Deirdre was disillusioned about something at the age of twenty-nine, where would she be when she reached his age? What did she want from life? For that matter, what had she had?

Lying there on her side, with her hands tucked between her thighs and her cheek fallen against the pillow, she was the image of innocence. She was also strangely sexy-looking.

He wondered how that could be, when there was nothing alluring about her in the traditional sense. She wore no make-up. Her hair was long in front, short at the sides and back, unsophisticated as hell. Her warm-up suit was a far cry from the clinging things he'd seen women wearing at the racquet club. The bulky fabric was bunched up in front, camouflaging whatever she had by the way of breasts, and yet…and yet…the material rested on a nicely rounded bottom—he could see that now—and she looked warm and vaguely cuddly. He almost envied her hands.

With a quick headshake, he walked over to the ship-to-shore radio, picked up the speaker, shifted it in his hand, frowned, then set it back down. Ah, hell, he told himself, Thomas wouldn't be there; he was conspiring with Victoria. Short of a legitimate physical emergency, he wouldn't be back soon. And that being the case, it behooved Neil to find a way to coexist in relative peace with Deirdre.

But what fun would that be?

Deirdre was, for him, a kind of punching bag. He felt better when he argued with her. She provided an outlet and a diversion. Perhaps he should just keep swinging.

Smiling, he sauntered into the living room. His gaze fell on the fireplace; the ashes from last night's fire lay cold. Taking several large logs from the nearby basket, he set them atop kindling on the grate and stuck a match. Within minutes the kindling caught, then the logs. Only when the fire was crackling heatedly did he settle back in a chair to watch it.

Strange, he mused, but he'd never come to the wilderness to relax before. He'd been to the beach—southern Connecticut, Cape Cod, Nantucket—and to the snow-covered mountains of Vermount. He'd been to the Caribbean and to Europe. But he'd never been this isolated from the rest of the world. He'd never been in the only house on an island, dependent solely on himself to see to his needs.

Nancy would die here. She'd want the option of eating out or calling room service. She'd want there to be people to meet for drinks. She'd want laundry service.

And Deirdre? Broken leg and all, she'd come looking for solitude. Perhaps stupidly, with that leg, but she'd come. Was she indeed a spoiled brat who had run away from all that had gone wrong in her life? Or was she truly self-sufficient? It remained to be seen whether she could make a bed....

"Nice fire."

He looked up. Deirdre was leaning against the wall by the hall, looking warm and still sleepy and mellow. He felt a lightening inside, then scowled perversely. "Where's the other crutch?"

Her eyes grew clearer. "In the kitchen."

"What's it doing there?"

She tipped her chin higher. "Holding up the counter."

"It's supposed to be under your arm. You're the one who needs holding up."

"I've found I can do just fine with one."

"If you put too much strain on the leg," he argued, "you'll slow the healing process."

"You sound like an expert."

"I broke my own leg once."

"How?"

"Skiing."

She rolled her eyes. "I should have guessed. I'll bet you sat around the ski lodge with your leg on a pedestal—the wounded hero basking in homage."

"Not quite. But what I did is beside the point. What you're doing is nuts. The doctor didn't okay it, did he?"

"*She* told me to use common sense. And what's it to you, anyway? You're not my keeper."

"No, but it'll be my job to do something if you fall and crack the cast, or worse, break the other leg."

She smiled smugly. "If anything happens to me, your problems will be solved. You'll get through to Thomas, zip, zip, and he'll be out to fetch me before you can blink an eye."

Neil knew she was right. He also knew that she had momentarily one-upped him. That called for a change of tactics. He took a deep breath, sat back in his chair and propped his bare feet on the coffee table. "But I don't want him to come out and fetch you. I've decided to keep you."

Her smile faded. "You've what?"

"I've decided to keep you."

"Given the fact that you don't *have* me, that's quite a decision."

He waved a hand. "Don't argue semantics. You know what I mean."

She nodded slowly. "You've decided to let me stay."

"That's right."

"And if I decide I want to leave?"

"Thomas won't give us the time of day, so it's a moot point."

"Precisely, which means that you're full of hot air, Neil Hersey. You can't decide to keep me, any more than I can decide to keep you, or either of us can decide to leave. We're stuck here together, which means—" Her mind was working along pleasurable lines. The grin she sent him had a cunning edge. "That you're stuck with me, bad temper and all." The way she saw it, he'd given her license to fire at will, not to mention without guilt. Battling with him could prove to be a most satisfying pastime.

"I think I can handle it," he said smugly.

"Good." Limping directly between Neil and the fire, she

took the chair opposite his. "So," she said, sitting back, "did you have a good sleep?"

"You spied on me?"

"No. I walked into my bedroom and there you were. Snoring."

He refused to let her get to him. "Is that why you took your nap in the den?"

"You spied on me."

"No. I walked in there intending to call Thomas. Then I decided not to bother. So I came in here and built a fire. It is nice, isn't it?"

"Not bad." She levered herself from the chair and hopped into the kitchen. A bowl of fresh fruit sat on the counter; she reached for an orange, then hopped back to her seat.

"You're a wonderful hopper," Neil said. "Is it your specialty?"

She ignored him. "What this fire needs is a little zip." Tearing off a large wad of orange peel, she tossed it into the flame.

"Don't do that! It'll mess up my fire!"

"It adds a special scent. Just wait." She threw in another piece.

Neil stared into the flames. "I hate the smell of oranges. It reminds me of the packages of fruit my grandparents used to send up from Florida every winter. There was so much of it that my mother worried about it spoiling, so we were all but force-fed the stuff for a week." His voice had gentled, and his lips curved at the reminiscence. "Every year I got hives from eating so many oranges."

She pried off a section and held it ready at her mouth. "You said 'we.' Do you have brothers and sisters?" The orange section disappeared.

"One of each."

"Older or younger?"

"Both older."

"Are you close?"

"Now? Pretty close." He shifted lower in his seat, so that his head rested against its back, and crossed his ankles. "We went our separate ways for a while. John is a teacher in Minneapolis, and Sara works for the government in Washington. They're both married and have kids, and all our lives seemed so hectic that we really didn't push reunions."

"What changed that?" Deirdre asked.

"My mother's death. Something about mortality hit us in the face—you know, life-is-so-short type of thing. That was almost seven years ago. We've been much closer since then."

"Is your father still living?"

"Yes. He's retired."

"Does he live near you?"

"He still lives in the house where we grew up in West-chester. We keep telling him to move because it's large and empty but for him most of the time. He won't sell." Neil was grinning. "He travels. So help me, nine months out of twelve he's galavanting off somewhere. But he says he needs the house. He needs to know it's there for him to come home to. Personally—" he lowered his voice "—I think he just doesn't want to displace the couple who live above the garage. They've been overseeing the grounds for nearly twenty years. They oversee *him* when he's around, and he loves it."

Absently Deirdre pressed another piece of fruit into her mouth. She chewed it, all the while looking at Neil. It was obvious that he felt affection for his family. "That's a lovely story. Your father sounds like a nice man."

"He is."

She took a sudden breath. "So how did he get a son like you? By the way, aren't your feet freezing? I haven't seen you with socks on since we got here, but it's cold."

He wiggled his toes. "I'm warm-blooded."

"You're foolhardy. You'll get splinters."

"Are you kidding? The floor's been sanded and waxed.

Only the walls have splinters, and, thank you, I don't walk on walls." He swung his legs down and stood. "So you'll have to find something else to pick on me for."

"I will," she promised. "I will." She watched him escape into the kitchen. "What are you doing?"

"Contemplating dinner."

"We haven't had lunch!"

"Breakfast was lunch." He flipped on a light in the darkening room. "Now it's dinnertime."

She glanced at her watch. It was well after six o'clock. She supposed she was hungry, though the thought of preparing another meal was enough to mute whatever hunger pangs she felt. So she remained where she was, looking at the fire, telling herself that she'd see to her own needs when Neil was done. She didn't want an audience for her clumsiness. Besides, between her hopping and Neil's size, they'd never be able to work in the kitchen at the same time.

She listened to the sounds of his preparations, wondering how he'd come to be so handy. Various possible explanations passed through her mind, but in the end the question remained. Then she heard the sizzle of meat and began to smell tantalizing aromas, and her admiration turned to annoyance. Why *was* he so good in the kitchen? Why wasn't he as clumsy as she? The men she'd known would have been hollering for something long before now—help in finding the butter or sharpening a knife or preparing vegetables for cooking. Why didn't he need her for something?

Pushing herself from the chair, she limped peevishly to the kitchen. What she saw stopped her cold on the threshold. Neil had set two places at the table and was in the process of lowering one brimming plate to each spot.

He looked up. "I was just about to call you." Her expression of shock was ample reward for his efforts, though his motives went deeper. If he helped Deirdre with things he knew she found difficult, he wouldn't feel so badly when he picked on her. Good deeds for not-so-good ones; it seemed a fair exchange. Not to mention the fact that keeping her off balance seemed of prime importance. "Steak, steamed broccoli, dinner rolls." He beamed at the plates. "Not bad, if I do say so myself."

"Not bad," she echoed distractedly. "You'd make someone a wonderful wife."

He ignored the barb and held out her chair. "Ms Joyce?"

At a loss for anything better to do, particularly when her mouth was watering, she came forward and let him seat her. She stared at the attractive plate for a minute, then looked up as he poured two glasses of wine. "Why?" she asked bluntly.

"Why wine? It's here for us to drink, and I thought it'd be a nice touch."

"Why me? I didn't ask you to make my dinner."

"Are you refusing it?"

She glanced longingly at her plate. Hospital food was nearly inedible; it had been days since she'd confronted anything tempting. "No. I'm hungry."

"So I figured."

"But you must have something up your sleeve."

He sat at his place, nonchalantly shook out his napkin and spread it on his lap. "Maybe I'm thinking of Victoria's kitchen. You broke a glass this morning. Another few, and we'll run low."

"It's not the glass, and you know it. What is it, Neil? I don't like it when you're nice."

He arched a brow as he cut into his steak. "Prefer the rough stuff, do you? A little pushing and shoving turns you on?" He put a piece of steak into his mouth, chewed it and closed his eyes. "Mmmm. Perfect." His eyes flew open in mock innocence. "I hope you like it rare."

"I like it medium."

"Then you can eat the edges and leave the middle." He gestured with his fork. "Go ahead. Eat. On second thought—" he set down the fork and reached for his wine

"—a toast." When Deirdre continued to stare at him, he dipped his head, coaxing. "Come on. Raise your glass."

Slowly, warily, she lifted it.

He grinned. "To us." The clink of his glass against hers rang through the room.

CHAPTER FIVE

To US. Deirdre thought about that through the evening as she sat pensively before the fire. She thought about it that night when she lay in bed, trying her best to ignore the presence of a large male body little more than an arm's length away. She thought about it when she awoke in the morning. By that time she was annoyed.

Victoria had fixed them up. Deirdre had always resented fix-ups, had always fervently avoided them. She'd never been so hard up for a man that she'd risk taking pot luck, and she wasn't now. Who was Neil Hersey, anyway? She asked herself that for the umpteenth time. After spending thirty-six hours with the man, she still didn't know. She did know that she'd been aware of him in some form or another for the majority of those thirty-six hours, and that her body was distinctly tense from that awareness.

She turned her head to study him. Sleeping, he was sprawled on his back with his head facing her. His hair was mussed; his beard sported an additional day's growth. Sooty eyelashes fanned above his cheekbones. Dark swirls of hair blanketed his chest to the point where the quilt took over.

One arm was entirely free of the covers. Her gaze traced its length, from a tightly muscled shoulder, over a leanly corded swell to his elbow, down a forearm that was spattered with hair, to a well-formed and thoroughly masculine hand. As though touched by that hand, she felt a quiver shoot through her.

Wrenching her head to the other side, she took a shallow breath, pushed herself up and dropped her legs over the side of the bed. For a minute she simply sat there with her head bowed, begrudging the fact that she found Neil attractive. She wanted to hate the sight of him after what he'd done to her dreams of solitude. But the sight of him turned her on.

She didn't want to be turned on.

Slowly she began to roll her head in a half circle, concentrating on relaxing the taut muscles of her neck. She extended the exercise to her shoulders, alternately rolling one, then the other. Clasping her hands at the back of her head, she stretched her torso, first to the left, then to the right. The music played in her mind, and she let herself move to its sound, only then realizing what she'd missed during the past week, finding true relaxation in imagining herself back at the health club, leading a class.

"What in the hell are you doing?" came a hoarse growl from behind her.

Startled from her reverie, she whirled around, then caught herself and tempered the movement. "Exercising."

"Is that necessary?"

"Yes. My body is tense."

"So is mine, and what you're doing isn't helping it." He'd awoken with the first of her exercises and watched her twist and stretch, watched the gentle shift in her absurdly large pajamas. And he'd begun to imagine things, which had quickly affected his own body. In other circumstances he'd have stormed from bed right then. As things stood—literally—he didn't have the guts.

"Then don't look," she said, turning her back on him and resuming her exercises. It was spite that drove her on, but all petty thoughts vanished when a strong arm seized her waist and whipped her back on the bed. Before she knew what had happened, Neil had her pinned and was looming over her.

"I think we'd better get something straight," he warned

in a throaty voice. "I'm a man, and I'm human. If you want to tempt me beyond my limits, you'd better be prepared to take the consequences."

Deirdre's trouble with breathing had nothing to do with exercising. Neil's lunge had dislodged the quilt, leaving his entire upper body bare. The warmth of his chest reached out to her, sending rivulets of heat through her body, while the intensity of his gaze seared her further.

"I didn't know you were tempted," she said in a small voice. "I'm a bundle of lumps to you. That's all." She'd been a bundle of lumps to most men, lumps that were conditioned by steady exercise, lumps that were anything but feminine. She'd always known she couldn't compete with the buxom beauties of the world, and she fully assumed Neil was used to buxom beauties. The way he'd looked at her that first day had left no doubt as to his opinion of her body. Then again, there had been other times when he'd looked at her...

"You are a bundle of lumps," he agreed, dropping his gaze to her pajama front. "That's what's so maddening. I keep wondering what's beneath all this cover." His eyes made a thorough survey of the fabric—she felt every touch point—before lazily meeting hers. "Maybe if I see, I won't be tempted. Maybe what we need here is full disclosure."

Deirdre made a reflexive attempt at drawing in her arms to cover herself, but he had them anchored beneath his and gave no quarter.

"Maybe," he went on, his voice a velvety rasp, "what I ought to do is to unbutton this thing and take a good look at all you're hiding."

"There's not much," she said quickly. Her eyes were round in a pleading that she miraculously managed to keep from her voice. "You'd be disappointed."

"But at least then I wouldn't have to wonder anymore, would I?"

Her heart was hammering, almost visibly so. She was frightened. Strangely and suddenly frightened. "Please. Don't."

"Don't wonder? Or don't look?"

"Either."

"But I can't help the first."

"It's not worth it. Take my word for it. I'm an athletic person. Not at all feminine."

Neil was staring at her in growing puzzlement. He heard the way her breath was coming in short bursts, saw the way her eyes held something akin to fear. He felt the urgency in his body recede, and slowly, gently he released her. Instantly, she turned away from him and sat up.

"I'd never force you," he murmured to her rigid back.

"I didn't say you would."

"You were talking, rationalizing as though you thought I would. I scared you."

She said nothing to that. How could she explain what she didn't understand herself: that her fear had been he'd find fault with her body? She didn't know why it should matter what he thought of her body....

"You didn't scare me."

"You're lying."

"Then that's another fault to add to the list." She fumbled for her crutches and managed to get herself to her feet. "I'm hungry," she grumbled, and started for the door.

"So am I," was his taunting retort.

"Tough!"

DEIRDRE MADE her own breakfast, grateful to find such easy fixings as yogurt and cottage cheese in the refrigerator. She waited in the den until she heard Neil in the kitchen, then retreated to the other end of the house for a bath.

At length she emerged, wearing the same bulky green top she'd worn during the drive up. This time she had gray sweatpants on, and though the outfit didn't clash, it was less shapely than yesterday's warm-up suit had been.

Reluctant to face Neil, she busied herself cleaning up the bedroom. Making a king-size bed by hobbling from one side to the other and back took time, but for once she welcomed the handicap. She went on to unpack her duffel bag. It wasn't that she hadn't planned on staying, simply that she hadn't had the strength to settle in until now. Yes, she did feel stronger, she realized, and found some satisfaction in that. She also found satisfaction in placing her books, cassette player and tapes atop the dresser. Neil had put his things on the other dresser; she was staking her own claim now.

Under the guise of housekeeping, she crossed to that other dresser and cursorily neatened Neil's things. He'd brought several books, a mix of fiction and nonfiction, all tied in some fashion to history. A glass case lay nearby, with the corner of a pair of horn-rimmed spectacles protruding. Horn-rimmed spectacles. She grinned.

Completing the gathering on the dresser was a scattered assembly of small change, a worn leather wallet and a key ring that held numerous keys in addition to those to his car. She wondered what the others unlocked, wondered where his office was and what it was like, wondered where he lived.

Moving quickly into the bathroom, she wiped down the sink and shower, then the mirror above the sink. She'd put her own few things in one side of the medicine chest. Curious, she slid open the other side. Its top shelf held a number of supplies she assumed were Victoria's. Far below, after several empty shelves, were more personal items—a comb, a brush, a tube of toothpaste and a toothbrush.

Neil's things. He traveled light. There was no sign of a razor. He'd very obviously planned to be alone.

Strangely, she felt better. Knowing that Neil was as unprepared for the presence of a woman as she was for the presence of a man was reassuring. On the other hand, what would she have brought if she'd known she'd have company? Makeup? Aside from mascara, blusher and lip gloss, she rarely used it. A blow dryer? She rarely used one. Cologne? Hah!

And what would Neil have brought? She wondered.

Sliding the chest shut with a thud, she returned to the bedroom, where a sweeping glance told her there was little else to clean. She could always stretch out on the bed and read, or sit in the chaise by the window and knit. But that would be tantamount to hiding, and she refused to hide.

Discouraged, she looked toward the window. It was still raining. Gray, gloomy and forbidding. If things were different, she wouldn't have been stopped by the rain; she'd have bundled up and taken a walk. All too clearly, though, she recalled how treacherous it was maneuvering with crutches across the mud and rocks. She wasn't game to try it again soon.

Selecting a book from those she'd brought, she tucked it under her arm alongside the crutch, took a deep breath and headed for the living room. Neil was there, slouched on the sofa, lost in thought. He didn't look up until she'd settled herself in the chair, and then he sent her only the briefest of glances.

Determinedly she ignored him. She opened the book, a piece of contemporary women's fiction and began to read, patiently rereading the first page three times before she felt justified in moving on to the second. She was finally beginning to get involved in the story, when Neil materialized at her shoulder.

Setting the book down, she turned her head, not far enough to see him, just enough to let him know he had her attention. "Something wrong?" she asked in an even tone.

"Just wondering what you were reading," he said just as evenly.

Leaving a finger to mark her place, she closed the cover so he could see it.

"Any good?" he asked.

"I can't tell yet. I've just started."

"If it doesn't grab you within the first few pages, it won't."

"That's not necessarily true," she argued. "Some books take longer to get into."

He grunted and moved off. She heard a clatter, then another grunt, louder this time, and, following it, a curse that brought her head around fast. "Goddamn it. Can't you keep your crutches out of the way?" He had one hand on the corner of her chair, the other wrapped around his big toe.

"If you were wearing shoes, that wouldn't have happened!"

"I shouldn't have to wear shoes in my own home."

"This isn't your own home."

"Home away from home, then."

"Oh, please, Neil, what exactly would you have me do? Leave the crutches in the other room? You were the one who was after me to use them."

He didn't bother to answer. Setting his foot on the floor, he gingerly tested it. Then he straightened and limped across the room to stand at the window. He tucked his hands in the back pockets of his jeans, displacing the long jersey that would have otherwise covered his buttocks. The jersey itself was black and slim cut, fairly broadcasting the strength and breadth of his shoulders, the leanness of his hips. She wondered if he'd chosen to wear it on purpose.

Returning her eyes to her book, she read another two pages before being interrupted again.

"Crummy day" was the information relayed to her from the window.

She set the book down. "I know."

"That's two in a row."

"Three."

"Two full days that we've been here."

She conceded the point. "Fine. Two in a row." She picked up the book again. Several pages later, she raised her head to find Neil staring at her. "Is something wrong?"

"No."

"You look bored."

"I'm not used to inactivity."

"Don't you have anything to do?"

With a shrug he turned back to the window.

"What would you do at home on a rainy day?" she asked.

"Work."

"Even on a weekend?"

"Especially on a weekend. That's when I catch up on everything I've been too busy to do during the week." At least, it had been that way for years, he mused. Of course, when one was losing clients right and left, there was a definite slackening.

"You must have a successful practice," she remarked, then was taken aback when he sent her a glower. "I meant that as a compliment."

He bowed his head and rubbed the back of his neck. "I know. I'm sorry."

Deirdre glanced at her book, and realized she wasn't going to get much reading done with Neil standing there that way. She was grateful he hadn't made reference to what had happened earlier, and wondered if he was sorry for that, too. If so, she reflected, he might be in a conciliatory mood. It was as good a time as any to strike up a conversation.

"How do you know Victoria?" she asked in as casual a tone as she could muster.

"A mutual friend introduced us several years ago."

"Are you from the city?"

"Depends what city you mean."

For the sake of civility, she stifled her impatience. "New York."

"No." He was facing the window again, and for a minute she thought she'd have to prod, when he volunteered the information she'd been seeking. "Hartford."

A corner of her mouth curved up. She couldn't resist. "Ah, Hartford. Thriving little metropolis. I went to a concert there last year with friends. The seats were awful, the lead singer had a cold and I got a flat tire driving home."

Slowly Neil turned. "Okay. I deserved that."

"Yes, you did. Be grateful I didn't condemn the entire city."

He wasn't sure he'd have minded if she had. At the moment he felt the whole of Hartford was against him. "My allegiance to the city isn't blind. I can see her faults."

"Such as…?"

"Parochialism. Provinciality."

"Hartford?"

"Yes, Hartford. Certain circles are pretty closed."

"Isn't that true of any city?"

"I suppose." Casually he left the window and returned to the sofa. Deirdre took it as a sign of his willingness to talk.

"Have you lived there long?"

"Since I began practicing."

"You mentioned going to school in Boston. Was that law school, or undergraduate?"

"Both."

"So you went from Westchester to Boston to Hartford?"

He had taken on an expression of amused indulgence. "I did a stint in San Diego between Boston and Hartford. In the Navy. JAG division."

"Ah. Then you missed Vietnam."

"Right." He had one brow arched, as though waiting for her to criticize the fact that he hadn't seen combat.

"I think that's fine," she said easily. "You did something, which is more than a lot of men did."

"My motive wasn't all that pure. I would have been drafted if I hadn't signed up."

"You could have run to Canada."

"No."

The finality with which he said it spoke volumes. He felt he'd had a responsibility to his country. Deirdre respected that.

"How did you break your leg?" he asked suddenly.

The look on her face turned sour. "Don't ask."

"I am."

She met his gaze and debated silently for a minute. He'd opened up. Perhaps she should, too. Somehow it seemed childish to continue the evasion. She gave him a challenging stare. "I fell down a flight of stairs."

He held up a hand, warding off both her stare and its unspoken challenge. "That's okay. I'm not laughing."

Averting her gaze, she scowled at the floor. "You would if you knew the whole story."

"Try me. What happened?"

She'd set herself up for it, but strangely she wasn't sorry. It occurred to her that she wanted to tell the story. If he laughed, she'd have reason to yell at him. In some ways, arguing with him was safer than...than what had happened earlier.

Taking a breath, she faced him again. "I slipped on a magazine, caught my foot in the banister and broke my leg in three places."

He waited expectantly. "And...? There has to be a punch line. I'm not laughing yet."

"You asked what I did for a living." She took a breath. "I teach aerobic dance."

His eyes widened fractionally. "Ah. And now you can't work."

"That's the least of it! I've always been into exercise of one sort or another. I'm supposed to be ultracoordinated. Do you have any idea how humiliating it is to have done this slipping on a magazine?"

"Was the magazine worth it?" he asked, deadpan.

"That's not the point! The point is that I'm not supposed to fall down the stairs! And if I do, I'm supposed to do it gracefully, with only a black-and-blue mark or two to show for it." She glared at her leg. "Not a grotesque cast!"

"How does the leg feel, by the way?"

"Okay."

"The dampness doesn't bother it?"

"My thigh is more sore from lugging the cast around, and my armpits hurt from the crutches."

"That'll get better with time. How long will the cast be on?"

"Another five weeks."

"And after that you'll be good as new?"

Her anger was replaced by discouragement. "I wish I knew. The doctor made no promises. Oh, I'll be able to walk. But teach?" Her shrug was as eloquent as the worry in her eyes.

Neil surprised himself by feeling her pain. Wasn't it somewhat akin to his own? After all, his own future was in limbo, too.

Leaning forward, he propped his elbows on his thighs. "You'll be able to teach, Deirdre. One way or another you will, if you want to badly enough."

"I do! I have to work. I mean, it's not a question of money. It's a question of emotional survival!"

That, too, he understood. "Your work means that much to you."

It was a statement, not a question, and Deirdre chose to let it rest. She wasn't ready to go into the issue of Joyce Enterprises, which was so much more complex and personal. Besides, Neil was a corporate attorney. He'd probably take *their* side.

"Well," she said at last, "I guess there's nothing I can do but wait."

"What will you do in the meantime?"

"Stay here for as long as I can."

"There's nothing else to keep you busy in Providence while your leg mends?"

"Nothing I care to do."

Neil wondered at her mutinous tone, but didn't comment. "What had you planned to do here? Besides read."

Still scowling, she shrugged. "Relax. Knit. Listen to music. Work up some routines. It may be a waste of time if it turns out I can't teach, but I suppose I have to hope."

"You could have done all that in Providence. I'd have thought that with a broken leg and all, you'd be more comfortable there. The drive up couldn't have been easy, and if Thomas had dumped you on that dock alone, you'd have had a hell of a time getting everything to the house."

Her scowl deepened. "Thomas knew what he was doing. *You* were here. Otherwise he'd probably have helped me himself."

"Still, to rush up here the day you left the hospital... What was the rush?"

"The telephone! My family! It was bad enough when I was in the hospital. I had to get away!"

"All that, just because you were embarrassed?"

Deirdre knew that she'd be spilling the entire story in another minute. Who in the devil was Neil Hersey that he should be prying? She hadn't asked *him* why he'd been in such a foul mood from day one. "Let's just say that I have a difficult family," she concluded, and closed her mouth tightly. Between that and the look she gave him, there was no doubt that she was done talking.

Neil took the hint. Oh, he was still curious, but there was time. Time for...lots of things.

She opened her book again and picked up where she'd left off, but if her concentration had been tentative before, it was nonexistent now. She was thinking of that difficult family, wondering what was going to change during the time she was in Maine that would make things any better when she returned.

From the corner of her eye she saw Neil get up, walk aimlessly around the room, then sit down. When a minute later he bobbed up again, she sighed.

"Decide what you want to do, please. I can't read with an active yo-yo in the room."

He said nothing, but took off for the bedroom. Moments later he returned, threw himself full length on the sofa and opened a book of his own. He read the first page, turned noisily to the last, then began to flip through those in between.

"Are you going to read or look at the pictures?" Deirdre snapped.

His face was the picture of innocence when he looked up. "I'm trying to decide if it's worth reading."

She was trying to decide if he was purposely distracting her. "You brought it along, didn't you?"

"I was in a rush. I took whatever books I had around the house and threw them in the bag."

"Then you must have decided it was worth reading when you bought it. What's it about?" She wondered which he'd chosen.

"World War I. History fascinates me."

"I know."

His eyes narrowed. "How would you know?"

"Because I saw the books lying on your dresser, and every one of them dealt with history in some form. You know, you really should wear your glasses when you read. Otherwise you'll get eye strain."

"I only wear them when I *have* eye strain, and since I haven't had much to look at for the past two days, my eyes are fine." He turned his head on the sofa arm to study her more fully. "You're pretty nosy. Did you look through my wallet, too?"

"Of course not! I was cleaning, not snooping. I've never liked living in a pigpen."

"Could've fooled me, what with the way you've been dropping clothes around."

"That was only the first night, and I was exhausted." She noticed a strange light in his eyes and suspected he was enjoying the sparring. It occurred to her that she was, too. "What's in your wallet, anyway? Something dark and sinister? Something I shouldn't see?"

He shrugged. "Nothing extraordinary."

"Wads of money?"

"Not quite."

"A membership card to a slinky men's club?"

"Not quite."

"A picture of your sweetheart?"

"Not…quite."

"Who is she, anyway—the one who burned you?"

The day before he wouldn't have wanted to talk about Nancy. Now, suddenly, it seemed less threatening. "She's someone I was seeing, whom I'm not seeing now."

"Obviously," Deirdre drawled. "What happened?"

Neil pursed his lips and thought of the best way to answer. He finally settled on the most general explanation. "She decided I didn't have enough potential."

"What was she looking for? An empire builder?"

"Probably."

"You don't sound terribly upset that she's gone."

"I'm getting over it," he said easily.

"Couldn't have been all that strong a relationship, then."

"It wasn't."

Deirdre settled her book against her stomach and tipped her head to the side. "Have you ever been married?"

"Where did that come from?"

"I'm curious. You asked me. Now I'm asking you."

"No. I've never been married."

"Why not?"

He arched a brow. "I never asked you that. It's impolite."

"It's impolite to ask a woman that, because traditionally she's the one who has to wait for the proposal. A man can do the proposing. Why haven't you?"

It occurred to Neil that there was something endearing about the way Deirdre's mind worked. It was quick, unpretentious, oddly refreshing. He smiled. "Would you believe me if I said I've been too busy?"

"No."

"It is true, in a way. I've spent the past fifteen years devoted to my career. She's a very demanding mistress."

"Then she's never had the right competition, which means that the old cliché is more the case. You haven't met the right woman yet."

He didn't need to ponder that to agree. "I have very

special needs," he said, grinning. "Only a very special woman can satisfy them."

Deirdre could have sworn she saw mischief in his grin. She tried her best to sound scornful. "That I can believe. Any woman who'd put up with a face full of whiskers has to be special. Do you have any idea how…how grungy that looks?"

The insult fell flat. To her dismay, he simply grinned more broadly as he stroked his jaw. "It does look kinda grungy. Nice, huh?"

"Nice?"

"Yeah. I've never grown a beard in my life. From the time I was fifteen I shaved every blessed morning. And why? So I'd look clean. And neat. And acceptable. Well, hell, it's nice to look grungy for a change, and as for acceptability—" He searched for the words he wanted, finally thrust out his chin in defiance. "Screw it!"

Deirdre considered what he'd said. He didn't look unclean, or unneat, or unacceptable, but rather…dashing. Particularly with that look of triumph on his face. Helpless against it, she smiled. "That felt good, didn't it?"

"Sure did."

"You're much more controlled when you work."

"Always. There's a certain, uh, decorum demanded when you're dealing with corporate clients."

"Tell me about it," she drawled, bending her right leg up and hugging it to her chest.

Once before, he'd taken her up on the offer. This time he let it ride, because he didn't really want to talk about corporate clients. He wanted to talk about Deirdre Joyce.

"What about you, Deirdre? Why have you never married?"

"I've never been asked."

He laughed. "I should have expected you'd answer that way. But it's a cop-out, you know," he chided, then frowned and tucked in his chin. "Why are you looking at me that way?"

"Do you know that that's the first time I've heard you laugh, I mean, laugh, as in relaxed and content?"

His smile mellowed into something very gentle, and his eyes bound hers with sudden warmth. "Do you know that's the first time I've heard such a soft tone from you. Soft tone, as in amiable." As in womanly, he might have added, but he didn't. He'd let down enough defenses for one day.

For a minute Deirdre couldn't speak. Her total awareness centered on Neil and the way he was looking at her. He made her feel feminine in a way she'd never felt before.

Awkward, she dropped her gaze to her lap. "You're trying to butter me up, being nice and all. I think you're looking for someone to do the laundry."

Laundry was the last thing on his mind. "I don't think I've ever seen you blush before."

The blush deepened. She didn't look up. She didn't trust the little tricks her hormones were playing on her. She felt she was being toasted from the inside out. It was a new and unsettling sensation. Why *Neil*?

Lips turning down in a pout, she glared at him.

"Aw, come on," he teased. "I liked you the other way."

"Well, I didn't." It smacked of vulnerability, and Deirdre didn't like to think of herself as vulnerable. "I'm not the submissive type."

His laugh was gruffer this time. "I never thought you were. In fact, submissive is the last word I'd use to describe you. You prickle at the slightest thing. I'd almost think that *you'd* been burned."

The directness of her gaze held warning. "I have. I was used once, and I didn't like the feeling."

"No one does," he said softly. "What happened?"

She debated cutting off the discussion, but sensed he'd only raise it another time. So she crossed her right leg over her cast and slid lower in the chair in a pose meant to be nonchalant. "I let myself be a doormat for a fellow who had nothing better to do with his life at the time. The minute he sensed a demand on my part, he was gone."

"You demanded marriage?"

"Oh, no. It was nothing like that. Though I suppose he imagined that coming. My family would like to see me married. They don't think much of my...lifestyle."

"You're a swinger?"

She slanted him a disparaging glance. "Just the opposite. I avoid parties. I can't stand phony relationships. I hate pretense of any kind."

"What does pretense have to do with marriage?"

"If it's marriage for the sake of marriage alone, pretense is a given."

Neil couldn't argue with that. "Do you want to have children?"

"Someday. How about you?"

"Someday."

They looked at each other for a minute longer, then simultaneously returned to their books. Deirdre, for one, was surprised that she was talking about these things with Neil. She asked herself what it was about him that inspired her to speak, and finally concluded that it was the situation, more than the man, that had brought her out. Hadn't she come here to soul-search, to ponder the direction her life was taking?

Neil was brooding about his own life, his own direction, and for the first time that brooding was on a personal bent. Yes, he'd like to be married, but only to the right person. He was as averse to pretense as Deirdre was. Nancy—for that matter, most of the women he'd dated over the years—had epitomized pretense. One part of him very much wanted to put his law practice in its proper perspective, to focus, instead, on a relationship with a woman, a relationship that was intimate, emotionally as well as physically, and rewarding. And yes, he'd like to have children.

Absently he turned a page, then turned it back when he realized he hadn't read a word. He darted a glance at Deirdre and found her curled in the chair, engrossed in her book. She was honest; he admired her for that. She didn't have any more answers than he did, but at least she was honest.

Settling more comfortably on the sofa, Neil refocused on his book and disciplined himself to read. It came easier as the morning passed. The rain beat a steady accompaniment to the quiet activity, and he had to admit that it was almost peaceful.

Setting the book down at last, he stood. "I'm making sandwiches. Want one?"

Deirdre looked up. "What kind?"

His mouth turned down at the corner. "That's gratitude for you, when someone is offering to make you lunch."

"I can make my own," she pointed out, needing to remind him—and herself—that she wasn't helpless.

"Is that what you'd rather?"

"It depends on what kind of sandwiches you know how to make."

"I know how to make most anything. The question is what have we got to work with?" He crossed into the kitchen, opened the refrigerator and rummaged through the supplies. Straightening, he called over his shoulder, "You can have ham and cheese, bologna and cheese, grilled cheese, grilled cheese and tomato, grilled cheese and tuna, a BLT, egg salad, peanut butter and jelly, cream cheese and jelly—" he sucked in a badly needed breath "—or any of the above taken separately."

Any of the above sounded fine to Deirdre, who'd never been a picky eater. She tried not to grin. "That's quite a list. Could you run through it one more time?"

The refrigerator door swung shut and Neil entered her line of vision. His hands were hooked low on his hips and his stance was one of self-assurance. "You heard it the first time, Deirdre."

"But there are so many things to choose from…and it's a big decision." She pressed her lips together, feigning concentration. "A big decision…"

"Deirdre…"

"I'll have turkey with mustard."

"Turkey wasn't on the list."

"No? I thought for sure it was."

"We don't have any turkey."

"Why not? Thomas should have known to pick some up. Turkey's far better for you than ham or cheese or peanut butter."

Hands falling to his sides, Neil drew himself up, shoulders back. He spoke slowly and clearly. "Do you, or do you not, want a sandwich?"

"I do."

"What kind?"

"Grilled cheese and tuna."

He sighed. "Thank you." He'd no sooner returned to the refrigerator, when he heard her call.

"Can I have it on rye?"

"No, you cannot have it on rye," he called back through gritted teeth.

"How about a roll?"

"If a hamburg roll will do."

"It won't."

"Then it's white bread or nothing. Take it or leave it."

"I'll take it."

He waited a minute longer to see if she had anything else to add. When she remained silent, he tugged open the refrigerator and removed everything he'd need. He'd barely closed the door again, when Deirdre entered the kitchen.

"If you've changed your mind," he warned, "that's tough. Your order's already gone to the cook. It's too late to change."

She was settling herself on the counter stool. "Grilled cheese and tuna's fine." Folding her hands in her lap, she watched him set to work.

He opened a can of tuna, dumped its contents into a bowl and shot her a glance as he reached for the mayonnaise. A glob of the creamy white stuff went the way of the tuna. He was in the process of mixing it all together with a fork, when he darted her another glance. "Anything wrong?"

"No, no. Just watching. You don't mind, do you? I'm fascinated. You're very domestic for a man."

"Men have to eat."

"They usually take every shortcut in the book, but grilled cheese and tuna...I'm impressed."

"It's not terribly difficult," he scoffed.

"But it takes more time than peanut butter and jelly."

"Tastes better, too."

"I *love* peanut butter and jelly."

"Then why'd you ask for grilled cheese and tuna?"

She arched a brow, goading him on. "Maybe I wanted to see what you could do."

Neil, who'd been slathering tuna on slices of bread, stopped midstroke, put down the knife and slowly turned. "You mean you purposely picked what you thought was the hardest thing on the menu?"

Deirdre knew when to back off. "I was only teasing. I really do feel like having grilled cheese and tuna."

With deliberate steps, he closed the small distance between them. "I don't believe you. I think you did it on purpose, just like you asked for turkey when you knew damn well we didn't have it."

She would have backed up if there'd been anywhere to go, but the counter was already digging into her ribs. "Really, Neil." She held up a hand. "There's no need to get upset. Unless you're having ego problems with my being in the kitchen this way—"

The last word barely made it from her mouth, when Neil scooped her up from the stool, cast and all, and into his arms.

"What are you doing?" she cried.

He was striding through the living room. "Removing you from my presence. You wanted to get my goat. Well, you got it. Picking the most complicated sandwich. *Ego* problems." They were in the hall and moving steadily. "If you want to talk, you can do it to your heart's content in here." He entered the bedroom and went straight to the bed, his intent abundantly clear to Deirdre, who was clutching the crew neckline of his jersey.

"Don't drop me! My cast!"

Neil held her suspended for a minute, enjoying the fact of his advantage over her. Then, in a single heartbeat, his awareness changed. No longer was he thinking that she'd goaded him once too often. Rather, he was suddenly aware that her thigh was slender and strong beneath one of his hands, and that the fingertips of the other were pressed into an unexpectedly feminine breast. He was thinking that her eyes were luminous, her lips moist, her cheeks a newly acquired pale pink.

Deirdre, too, had caught her breath. She was looking up at Neil, realizing that his eyes, like his hair, weren't black at all, but a shade of charcoal brown, and that his mouth was strong, well formed and very male. She was realizing that he held her with ease, and that he smelled clean, and that the backs of her fingers were touching the hot, hair-shaded surface of his chest and he felt good.

Slowly he lowered her to the bed, but didn't retreat. Instead he planted his hands on either side of her. "I don't know what in the hell is going on here," he breathed thickly. "It must be cabin fever." His gaze fell from her eyes to her lips, declaring his intent even before he lowered his head.

CHAPTER SIX

HIS MOUTH TOUCHED hers lightly at first, brushing her lips, sampling their shape and texture. Then he intensified the kiss, deepening it by bold degrees until it had become something positively breathtaking.

Deirdre could barely think, much less respond. She'd known Neil was going to kiss her, but she'd never expected such force in the simple communion of mouths. He drank from her like a man who was dying of thirst, stumbling unexpectedly upon an oasis in the desert. From time to time his lips gentled to a whisper, touching hers almost timidly in reassurance that what he'd found wasn't a mirage.

His hands framed her face, moving her inches away when his mouth would have resisted even that much. "Kiss me, Deirdre," he breathed, studying her through lambent eyes.

His hoarse command was enough to free her from the spell she'd been under. When he brought her mouth back to his, her lips were parted, curious, eager, and she returned his kiss with growing fervor. She discovered the firmness of his lips, the evenness of his teeth, the texture of his tongue. She tasted his taste and breathed his breath, and every cell in her that was woman came alive.

"Deirdre," he whispered, once again inching her face from his. He pressed his warm forehead to hers and worked at catching his breath. "Why did you *do* that?"

Deirdre, who was having breathing difficulties of her own, struggled to understand. "What?"

"Why did you do that?"

"Do what?"

"Kiss me!"

The haze in her head began to clear, and she drew farther away. "You told me to kiss you."

His brows were drawn together, his features taut. "Not like that. I expected just a little kiss. Not…not that!"

He was angry. She couldn't believe it. "And who was kissing whom first like that?"

His breath came roughly, nostrils flaring. "You didn't have to do it back!" Shoving his large frame from the bed, he stormed from the room, leaving Deirdre unsure and bewildered and, very quickly, angry.

She sat up to glare in the direction he'd gone, then closed her eyes and tried to understand his reaction. Though she'd never, never kissed or been kissed that way, she wasn't so inexperienced that she couldn't see when a man was aroused. Neil Hersey had been aroused, and he'd resented it.

Which meant he didn't want involvement any more than she did.

Which meant they had a problem.

She'd enjoyed his kiss. More than that. It had taken her places she'd never been before. Kissing Neil had been like sampling a rich chocolate with a brandy center, sweet and dissolving—yet potent. He went straight to her head.

She touched her swollen lips, then her tingling chin. Even his beard had excited her, its roughness a contrast to the smoothness of his mouth. Yes, he was smooth. Smooth and virile and stimulating, damn him!

Dropping her chin to her chest, she took several long, steadying breaths. With the fresh intake of oxygen came the strength she needed. Yes, they were stuck under the same roof. They were even stuck, thanks to a matching stubbornness, in the same bed. She was simply going to have to remember that she had problems enough of her own, that *he* had problems enough of his own. And that he could be a very disagreeable man.

Unfortunately Neil chose that moment to return to the bedroom. He carried her crutches and wore an expression of uncertainty. After a moment's hesitation on the threshold, he started slowly toward the bed.

"Here," he said, quietly offering the crutches. "The sandwiches are under the broiler. They'll be ready in a minute."

Deirdre met his gaze, then averted her own, looking to the crutches. She reached for them, wrapped her hands around the rubber handles and studied them for a minute before raising her eyes again.

The corners of his mouth curved into the briefest, most tentative of smiles before he turned and left the room.

Leaning forward, Deirdre rested her head against the crutches. Oh, yes, Neil was a very disagreeable man. He also had his moments of sweetness and understanding, which, ironically, was going to make living with him that much more of a trial.

She sighed. It had to be done. Unless she was prepared to capitulate and leave the island by choice. Which she wasn't.

Struggling to her feet, she secured the crutches under her arms and, resigned, headed for the kitchen.

Lunch was a quiet, somewhat awkward affair. Neil avoided looking at Deirdre, which she had no way of knowing, since she avoided looking at him. She complimented him on the sandwiches. He thanked her. When they were done, he made a fresh pot of coffee—medium thick—and carried a cup to the living room for her. She thanked him. And all the while she was thinking of that kiss, as he was. All the while she was wondering where it might have led, as he was. All the while she was asking herself why, as was he.

Knowing she'd never be able to concentrate on her book, she brought her knitting bag from the bedroom, opened the instruction booklet and forced her attention to the directions.

Neil, who was in a chair drinking his second cup of coffee, was as averse to reading as she was, but could think of nothing else he wanted to do. "What are you making?" he asked in a bored tone.

She didn't look up. "A sweater."

"For you?"

"Hopefully." She reached for a neatly wound skein of yarn, freed its end and pulled out a considerable length. Casting on—that sounded simple enough.

Neil noted the thick lavender strand. "Nice color."

"Thank you." With the book open on her lap, she took one of the needles and lay the strand against it.

"That's a big needle."

She sighed. Concentration was difficult, knowing he was watching. "Big needle for a big sweater."

"For you?"

Her eyes met his. "It's going to be a bulky sweater."

"Ah. As in ski sweater?"

She pressed her lips together in angry restraint. "As in warm sweater, since it looks like I won't be skiing in the near future."

"Do you ski?"

"Yes."

"Are you good?"

She dropped the needle to her lap and stared at him. "I told you I was athletic. I exercise, play tennis, swim, ski... At least, I used to do all of those things. Neil, I can't concentrate if you keep talking."

"I thought knitting was an automatic thing."

"Not when you're learning how."

One side of his mouth twitched. "You haven't done it before?"

"No, I haven't."

"Was it the broken leg that inspired you?"

"I bought the yarn several months ago. This is the first chance I've had to work with it."

He nodded. She lifted the needle again, studied the

book again, brought the yarn up and wound it properly for the first stitch. It took several attempts before she'd made the second, but once she'd caught on, she moved right ahead. Before long she had enough stitches cast on to experiment with the actual knitting.

When Neil finished his coffee, he returned the cup to the kitchen and started wandering around the house. At last, all else having failed to divert him, he picked up his book again.

By this time Deirdre was painstakingly working one knit stitch after another. The needles were awkward in her hands, and she continually dropped the yarn that was supposed to be wrapped around her forefinger. Periodically she glanced up to make sure Neil wasn't witnessing her clumsiness, and each time she was frowning when she returned to her work. Simply looking at him turned her inside out.

He was stretched full length on the couch...so long...so lean. The sleeves of his jersey were pushed back to reveal forearms matted with the same dark hair she'd felt on his chest. *Felt*. Soft, but strong and crinkly. The texture was permanently etched in her memory.

From his position on the sofa, Neil was also suffering distractions. His curiosity as to what Deirdre hid beneath her bulky sweatshirt had never been greater. He'd felt the edge of her breast. *Felt*. Strong and pert, but yielding beneath his fingertips. He'd carried her; she was light as thistledown and every bit as warm. He'd tasted her. That was his worst mistake, because there'd been a honeyed sweetness to her that he never would have imagined. Did the rest of his imaginings pale by comparison to the real thing?

From beneath half-lidded eyes he slanted her a look. Her hands gripped the needles, the forefinger of each extended. She was struggling, he saw, but even then the sweep of her fingers was graceful. Athletic? Perhaps. But if so, in a most healthy, most fitting, most feminine way.

Slapping the book shut, he sat bolt upright. Deirdre's questioning eyes shot to him.

"I can't read with that clicking," he grumbled. "Can't you be any quieter?"

"I'm having trouble as it is. Do you want miracles?"

"Not miracles. Just peace and quiet." Dropping the book on the sofa, he began to prowl the room.

"Book didn't grab you?"

"No." He ran a hand through his hair. "How about playing a game? Victoria has a bunch of them in the other room."

The knitting fell to Deirdre's lap. She wasn't sure she was up to playing games with Neil. "What did you have in mind?" she asked warily.

"I don't know. Maybe Monopoly?"

"I hate Monopoly. There's no skill involved."

"What about Trivial Pursuit?"

"I'm no good at history and geography. They make me lose."

"You make you lose," he argued. "The game doesn't do it."

"Whatever. The result's the same."

"Okay. Forget Trivial Pursuit. How about chess?"

"I don't know how."

"Checkers."

She scrunched up her nose in rejection.

"Forget a game," he mumbled.

"How about a movie?" she asked. It was a rainy day; the idea held merit. Her fingers were cramped, anyway.

"Okay."

"What do we have to choose from?"

In answer he started off toward the den. Deirdre levered herself up and followed, finding him bent over a low shelf in contemplation of the videotapes. She came closer, trying not to notice how snugly his jeans molded his buttocks, how they were slightly faded at the spot where he sat.

"*Magnum Force?*" he suggested.

"Too violent."

"*North by Northwest?*"

"Too intense." Leaning over beside him, she studied the lineup. "How about *Against All Odds?*"

"That's a romance."

"So?"

"Forget it."

"Then *The Sting.* Unromantic, but amusing."

"And boring. The best part's the music."

Her gaze moved across the cassettes, eyes suddenly widening. "*Body Heat.* That's a super movie. William Hurt, Kathleen Turner, intrigue and—"

"—Sex." Neil's head was turned, eyes boring into her. "I don't think we need that."

He was right, of course. She couldn't believe she'd been so impulsive as to suggest that particular movie.

"Ah." He drew one box out. "Here we go. *The Eye of the Needle.* Now that was a good flick."

It had action, intrigue, and yes, a bit of sex, but Deirdre felt she could take it. "Okay. Put it on." She set her crutches against the wall and hopped to the leather couch.

Removing the cassette from its box, Neil inserted it in the VCR, pressed several buttons, then took the remote control and sank onto the couch an arm's length from Deirdre. The first of the credits had begun to roll, when he snapped it off and jumped up.

"What's wrong?" she asked.

"We need popcorn. I saw some in the kitchen cabinet."

"But it takes time to make popcorn, and we're all set to watch."

"We've got time. Besides, it doesn't take more than a couple of minutes in the microwave." He rubbed his hands together. "With lots of nice melted butter poured on top—"

"Not butter! It's greasy, and awful for you."

"What's popcorn without butter?" he protested.

"Healthier."

"Then I'll put butter on mine. You can have yours without."

"Fine." She crossed her arms over her chest and sat back while he went to make the popcorn. Gradually her frown softened. It was rather nice being waited on, and Neil wasn't complaining. She supposed that if she'd had to be marooned with a man, she could have done worse. She *knew* she could have done worse. She could have been stuck with a real egomaniac. True, Neil had his moments. It occurred to her that while she'd given him a clue as to what caused her own mood swings, as yet she had no clue to his motivation. She'd have to work on that, she decided, merely for the sake of satisfying her curiosity. Nothing else.

Neil entered the room carrying popcorn still in its cooking bag. He resumed his seat, turned the movie back on and positioned the bag at a spot midway between them.

"Did you add butter?" she asked cautiously.

"No. You're right. I don't need it."

"Ah. Common sense prevails."

"Shh. I want to watch the movie."

She glanced at the screen. "I'm only disturbing the credits."

"You're disturbing me. Now keep still."

Deirdre kept still. She reached for a handful of popcorn and put one piece, then another in her mouth. The movie progressed. She tried to get into it but failed.

"It's not the same watching movies at home," she remarked. "A theater's dark. It's easier to forget your surroundings and become part of the story."

"Shh." Neil was having trouble of his own concentrating. It wasn't the movie, although as he'd seen it before, it held no mystery. What distracted him was Deirdre sitting so close. Only popcorn separated them. Once, when he reached into the bag, his hand met hers. They both retreated. And waited.

"You go first," he said.

She kept her eyes on the small screen. "No. That's okay. I'll wait."

"I've already had more. Go ahead."

"I don't need it. I'll get fat."

"You won't get fat." From what he'd seen, she wasn't a big eater; as for getting fat, from what he'd felt she was slender enough. Still, he couldn't resist a gibe. "On second thought, maybe you're right. You will get fat. You're smaller than I am, and I'm the one who's getting all the exercise around here. I'll wear it off easier."

He reached for the popcorn, but Deirdre already had her hand in the bag. She withdrew a full fist, sent him a smug grin and with deliberate nonchalance popped several pieces into her mouth.

Neil, who'd almost expected she'd do just that, wasn't sure whether to laugh or scream. Deirdre was impetuous in a way that was adorable, and adorable in a way that was bad for his heart. She had only to look at him with those luminous brown eyes and his pulse raced. He never should have kissed her. Damn it, he never should have kissed her!

But he had, and that fact didn't ease his watching of the rest of the movie. He was constantly aware of her—aware when she shifted on the couch, aware when she dropped her head back and watched the screen through half-closed eyes, aware when she began to massage her thigh absently.

"Leg hurt?" he asked.

She looked sharply his way, then shrugged and looked back at the screen.

"Want some aspirin?"

"No."

"Some Ben-Gay?"

"There is no Ben-Gay."

His lips twitched. "I'd run to the island drugstore for some if you'd let me rub it on."

She glared at the movie, but carried on the farce. "The island drugstore's out. I checked."

"Oh. Too bad."

Deirdre clamped her lips tightly, silently cursing Neil for his suggestion. *Let me rub it on.* Her insides tingled with a heat that, unfortunately, didn't do a whit to help her thigh.

Neil, too, cursed the suggestion, because his imagination had picked up from there, and he'd begun to think of rubbing far more than her thigh. He wondered whether her breasts would fit his hand, whether the skin of her belly would be soft....

He shifted away from her on the couch, and made no further comments, suggestive or otherwise. The movie was ruined for him. He was too distracted to follow the dialogue; the intrigue left him cold; the sex left him hot. The only thing that brought him any relief from the build-up of need in his body was the thought of Hartford, of work, of Wittnauer-Douglass. And because that upset him all the more, he was truly between a rock and a very hard place, where he remained throughout the evening.

He and Deirdre ate dinner together. They sat together before the fire. They pretended to read, but from the way Deirdre's eyes were more often on the flames than her book, he suspected that she was accomplishing as little as he was. He also suspected that her thoughts were running along similar lines, if the occasional nervous glances she cast him were any indication.

There was an element of fear in her. He'd seen it before; he could see it now. And it disturbed him. Was she afraid of sex? Was she afraid of feeling feminine and heated and out of control?

Even as he asked himself those questions, his body tightened. What in the hell was *he* afraid of? Certainly not sex. But there was something holding him back, even when every nerve in his body was driving him on.

He sat up by the fire long after Deirdre had taken refuge in bed. When at last he joined her, he was tired enough to fall asleep quickly. By the time the new day dawned, though, he was wondering whether he should relent and sleep in another room. Twice during the night he'd awoken to find their bodies touching—his outstretched arm draped over hers, the sole of her foot nestled against his calf.

What *was* it that made them gravitate toward each other? Each had come to Maine in search of solitude, so he'd have thought they'd have chosen to pass the time in opposite corners of the house. That hadn't been the case. Spitting and arguing—be it in the bedroom, the kitchen, the living room or den—they'd been together. And now... still...the bed.

He saw Deirdre look over her shoulder at him, then curl up more tightly on her side. Rolling to his back, he stared up at the ceiling, but the image there was of a disorderly mop of wheat-colored hair, soft brown eyes still misty with sleep, soft cheeks bearing a bed-warmed flush and lips that were slightly parted, unsure, questioning.

He had to get out. Though there was still the intermittent patter of rain and the air beyond the window was thick with mist, he had to get out. Without another glance at Deirdre, he flew from the bed, pulled on the dirty clothes he'd been planning to wash that day, laced on the sneakers that still bore a crust of mud from the day of his arrival on the island, threw his Windbreaker over his shoulders and fled the room, then the house.

Surrounded by the silence left in his wake, Deirdre slowly sat up. Being closed in had finally gotten to him, she mused. It had gotten to her, too. Or was it Neil who'd gotten to her? She'd never spent as uncomfortable an evening or night as those immediately past, her senses sharpened, sensitized, focused in on every nuance of Neil's physical presence. He breathed; she heard it. He turned; she felt it. Once, when she'd awoken in the middle of the night to find her hand tucked under his arm, she'd nearly jumped out of her skin, and not from fear of the dark.

Her body was a coiled spring, taut with frustration. She wanted to run six miles, but couldn't run at all. She wanted to swim seventy-two laps, but couldn't set foot in a pool, much less the ocean. She wanted to exercise until she was hot and tired and dripping with sweat, but…but… Damn it, yes, she could!

Shoving back the covers, she grabbed her crutches, took a tank top and exercise shorts from the dresser drawer and quickly pulled them on. She sat on the bed to put on her one sock and sneaker and both leg warmers, then pushed herself back up, tucked her cassette player and several tapes under one arm and her crutch under the other, and hobbled into one of the spare bedrooms. Within minutes the sounds of Barry Manilow filled the house.

Deirdre took a deep breath and smiled, then closed her eyes and began her familiar flexibility exercises. Her crutches lay on the spare bed; she discovered she could stand perfectly well without them. And the fact that various parts of the routine had to be altered in deference to her leg didn't bother her. She was moving.

In time with the music, she did body twists and side bends. She stretched the calf and ankle muscles of her right leg, and the inner thigh muscles of both legs. It felt good, so good to be feeling her body again. She took her time, relaxed, let the music take her where it would.

After several minutes, she moved into a warm-up, improvising as she went to accommodate her limited mobility. The music changed; the beat picked up, and she ventured into an actual dance routine. Though she couldn't dance in the true sense of the word, her movements were fluid and involved her entire upper torso as well as her good leg. By the time she'd slowed to do a cool-down routine, she'd broken into a healthy sweat and felt better than she had in days.

So immersed was she in the exercise that she didn't hear the open and closing of the front door. Neil, though, heard her music the minute he stepped into the house. He was incensed; it was loud and far heavier than the music he preferred. Without bothering to remove his wet jacket, he strode directly toward the sound, intent on informing Deirdre that as long as they were sharing the house, she had no right to be so thoughtless.

He came to an abrupt halt on the threshold of the spare bedroom, immobilized by the sight that met him. Eyes closed, seeming almost in a trance, Deirdre was moving in time to the music with a grace that was remarkable given her one casted leg. But it wasn't the movement that lodged his breath in his throat. It was her. Her body.

If he'd wondered what she'd been hiding beneath her oversized clothes, he didn't have to wonder any longer. She wore a skimpy tank top that revealed slender arms and well-toned shoulders. Her breasts pushed pertly at the thin fabric, their soft side swells clearly visible when she moved her arms. Her waist was small, snugly molded by the elasticized band of her shorts, and the shorts themselves were brief, offering an exaggerated view of silken thighs.

He gave a convulsive swallow when she bent over, his eyes glued to crescents of pale flesh. Then she straightened and stretched, arms high over her head, dipping low and slow from one side to the other. He swallowed again, transfixed by the firmness of her breasts, which rose with the movement.

Neil realized then that Deirdre's shapelessness had belonged solely to her bulky sweat clothes. Deirdre Joyce was shapely and lithe. With her hair damp around her face, her skin gleaming under a sheen of perspiration, with her arms flexing lyrically, her breasts bobbing, her hips rocking, she looked sultry, sexy and feminine.

He was in agony. His own body was taut, and his breath came raggedly. Turning, he all but ran down the hall, through the master bedroom, directly into the bathroom. He was tugging at his clothes, fumbling in his haste, knowing only that if he didn't hit a cold shower soon he'd explode.

His clothing littered the floor, but he was oblivious to

the mess. Stepping into the shower, he turned on the cold tap full force, put his head directly beneath the spray, propped his fists against the tile wall and stood there, trembling, until the chill of the water had taken the edge of fever from his body. He thought of Hartford, of Wittnauer-Douglass, of his uncle who'd died the year before, of basketball—anything to get his mind off Deirdre. Only when he felt he'd gained a modicum of control did he adjust the water temperature to a more comfortable level for bathing.

Deirdre, who was totally unaware of the trial Neil had been through, finished her cool-down exercises and did several final stretches before allowing herself to relax in a nearby chair. Feeling tired but exhilarated, she left the music on; it was familiar, comfortable and reassuring.

At length she sat forward and reached for her crutches, knowing that if she didn't dry off and change clothes, her perspiration-dampened body would soon be chilled.

She turned off the music and listened. The house was still silent, which meant, she reasoned, that Neil was still outside, which meant, she reasoned further, that she could have the bathroom to herself without fear of intrusion. A warm bath sounded very, very appealing.

The smile she wore as she swung her way down the hall was self-congratulatory. She was proud of herself. She'd exercised, and in so doing had not only proved that she could do it, but had worked off the awful tension she'd awoken with that morning. So much for Neil Hersey and his virility, she mused. She could handle it.

Intending to fill the tub while she undressed, she passed straight through the master bedroom to the bathroom. The door was closed. Without a thought, she shouldered it open and let the rhythm of her limp carry her several feet into the room. There she came to a jarring halt.

Neil stood at the sink. His head was bowed and he was bent slightly at the waist, his large hands curving around the edges of the porcelain fixture. He was stark naked.

The breath had left her lungs the instant she'd seen him,

and Deirdre could do no more than stare, even when he slowly raised his head and looked at her. He had a more beautifully male body than she'd ever have dreamed. His back was broad and smooth, his flanks lean, his buttocks tight. Seen in profile, his abdomen was flat, his pelvic bones just visible beneath a casement of flesh, his sex heavy and distinct.

"Deirdre?" His voice was husky. Her eyes flew to his when, without apparent modesty, he straightened and turned to face her. Two slow steps brought him close enough to touch. He repeated her name, this time in a whisper.

She was rooted to the spot, barely able to breathe, much less speak. Her eyes were wide and riveted to his.

He brought up a hand to brush the dots of moisture from her nose, then let his thumb trail down her cheek, over her jaw to her neck and on to the quivering flesh that bordered the thin upper hem of her tank top. Her breath was suddenly coming in tiny spurts that grew even tinier when he slipped his hand beneath her shoulder strap and brushed the backs of his fingers lower, then lower. She bit her lip to stifle a cry when he touched the upper swell of her breast, and though she kept her eyes on his, she was aware of the gradual change in his lower body.

"I didn't know you looked like this," he said hoarsely. "You've kept it all hidden."

Deirdre didn't know what to say. She couldn't quite believe he was complimenting her, not when he was so superbly formed himself. Surely the other women who'd seen him this way had been far more desirable than she. And though she knew he was aroused, her insecurities crowded in on her.

The backs of his fingers were gently rubbing her, dipping ever deeper into her bra. "Take off your clothes," he urged in a rough murmur, eyes flaming with restrained heat. "Let me see you."

She shook her head.

"Why not?"

She swallowed hard and managed a shaky whisper. "I'm sweaty."

"Take a shower with me." His baby finger had reached the sensitive skin just above her nipple, coaxing.

Pressing her lips together to hold in a moan, she shook her head again. "I can't take a shower." Her voice was small, pleading.

"Then a bath. Let me bathe you."

She wasn't sure if it was the sensuality of his words, or the fact that his finger had just grazed the hard nub of her nipple, but her good knee buckled, and she would have fallen had not her crutches been under her arms. His finger moved again, then again, sending live currents through her body. This time she couldn't contain the soft moan that slipped from her throat.

"Feel good?" he whispered against her temple, his own breath coming quicker.

"I don't want it to," she cried.

"Neither do I, but it does, doesn't it?"

It felt heavenly—his touching her, his being so near, so naked. She wanted to be naked beside him, too, but she was frightened. He'd be disappointed. She was sure of it. She was an athlete, "boyish" by her family's definition, and that description had haunted her doggedly over the years. She wasn't soft and fragile and willowy.

And even if Neil wasn't disappointed looking at her, he'd be let down by what would come after that. She felt the ache, the emptiness crying out inside of her, and knew she'd want to make love. And then he'd be disappointed, and the illusion would be broken.

She hobbled back a step, dislodging his hand. "I have to go. I have to go, Neil." Without waiting for his reply, she turned and fled from the bathroom, taking refuge in the bedroom where she'd exercised, collapsing in the chair and cursing her failings. *So much for handling Neil's virility.* Hah!

She didn't know how long she sat there, but the sweat had long since dried from her skin and she was feeling chilled when Neil appeared at the door. He wore a fresh pair of jeans and a sweater, and was barefoot, as usual. She wished she could believe that things were back to normal between them, but she knew better.

Neil felt neither anger nor frustration as he looked at her, but rather a tenderness that stunned him. Padding slowly into the room, he took an afghan from the end of the bed, gently draped it over her shoulders, then came down on his haunches beside her chair. "What frightens you, Deirdre?" he asked in a tone that would have melted her if the sight of him hadn't already done so.

It was a minute before she could speak, and then only brokenly. "You. Me. I don't know."

"I'd never hurt you."

"I know."

"Then what is it? You respond to me. I can feel it in your body. Your breath catches, and you begin to tremble. Is that fear, too?"

"Not all of it."

"You do want me."

"Yes."

"Why don't you give in and let go? It'd be good between us."

She looked down at her hands, which were tightly entwined in her lap. "Maybe for me, but I'm not sure for you."

"Why don't you let me be the judge of that?"

"I'm an athlete, not soft and cuddly like some women."

"Just because you're athletic doesn't mean you're not soft and cuddly. Besides, if it was a cushiony round ball I wanted, I'd go to bed with a teddy bear."

As he'd intended, his comment brought a smile to her face. But it was a tentative smile, a nervous one. "Somehow I can't picture that."

"Neither can I, but, then, I can't picture myself being

disappointed if you let me hold you...touch you...make love to you."

His words sent a ripple of excitement through her, and there was clear longing in her gaze as she surveyed his face. "I'm scared" was all she could manage to say.

Neil studied her a minute longer, then leaned forward and kissed her lightly. "I'd never hurt you. Just remember that." Standing, he left the room.

His words were in Deirdre's mind constantly as the day progressed. She believed that he'd meant what he'd said, but she knew that there were different kinds of hurt. Physical hurt was out of the question; Neil was far too gentle for that. But emotional hurt was something else. If their relationship should take the quantum leap that love-making would entail...and he should be let down...she'd be hurt. How it had happened, she didn't know, particularly since they'd spent most of their time together fighting, but Neil had come to mean something to her. She wasn't up to analyzing the exact nature of that something; all she knew was that she was terrified of endangering it.

If he'd thought long and hard, Neil couldn't have come up with a better way to goad Deirdre that day than by being kind, soft-spoken and agreeable. Without a word he prepared their meals. Without a word he did the laundry. He was indulgent when she tackled her knitting again, abiding the noise without complaint. He was perfectly amenable to watching her choice of movie on the VCR. He didn't start a single argument, but, then, neither did she. It was the quietest day they'd spent on the island.

Deirdre was as aware as he of that fact. She was also aware that, by denying her any cause to bicker, Neil was allowing her time to think about what he'd said and what she was going to do about it. If the issue had been entirely cerebral, she might have had a chance to resist him. But her senses refused to be reasoned with and were constantly attuned to his presence. That side of her she'd never paid much heed to was suddenly clamoring for attention.

Though all was peaceful on the outside, inside she was a mass of cells crying for release from a tension that radiated through her body in ever-undulating waves.

By the time they'd finished dinner and had spent a quiet hour before the fire, she had her answer. Yes, she was frightened and very, very nervous, but she'd decided that if Neil approached her again, she wouldn't refuse him. The sensual side of her nature wouldn't allow her to deny herself.

Head bowed, she quietly got to her feet, secured her crutches under her arms and left the living room. Once in the bedroom, she slowly changed into her pajamas, then sat on the side of the bed and reviewed her decision. She was taking a chance, she knew. A big one. If things didn't go well, the atmosphere in the house would be worse than ever. Then again, maybe not. They might be able to settle into a platonic relationship for the rest of their time here. Then again, Neil might not even come to her....

Even as she pondered that possibility, she sensed his presence in the room. Her head swiveled toward the door, eyes following his silent approach. Every one of her insecurities found expression in her face. Her back was straight. Her hands clutched the rounded edge of the bed.

More than anything at that moment, Neil wanted to alleviate her fear. It tore at him, because he knew he was its cause, just as he knew that her fear was unfounded. If she worried that she wouldn't please him, she worried needlessly. Deirdre turned him on as no other woman had, turned him on physically and in a myriad of other ways he'd only begun to identify.

Hunkering down, he raised his eyes to hers. He wanted to ask, but couldn't find the words. One part of him was frightened, too—frightened of being turned down when the one thing he wanted, the one thing he needed just then, was to be accepted, to be welcomed. So his question was a wordless one, gently and soulfully phrased.

Deirdre's insides were trembling, but she wasn't so

wrapped up in apprehension that she didn't hear his silent request. It was a plea that held its share of unsureness, and that fact, more than anything, gave her the courage she needed.

Of its own accord, her hand came up, touching his cheek, inching back until her fingers wove gently into his hair. Tentatively, nervously, she let her lips soften into the beginnings of a smile.

Neil had never seen anything as sweet. He felt relief, and a kind of victory. But more, a well of affection rose inside, spreading warmth through him. Whatever Deirdre's fears were, she was willing to trust him. That knowledge pleased him every bit as much as the prospect of what was to come.

Holding her gaze, he brought his hands up to frame her face. His thumbs stroked her lips for a minute before he came forward and replaced them with his mouth. His kiss was sure and strong, the sealing of a pact, but it was every bit as gentle in promise, and Deirdre was lost in it. It was almost a shock when he set her back and she remembered that there was more to lovemaking than kisses alone. Her expression reflected her qualms, and Neil was quick to reassure her.

"Don't be frightened," he whispered. "We'll take it slow." Sitting back on his haunches, he slid his hands to her neck, then lower to the first button of her pajamas, which he released. He moved on to the second button, working in such a way that some part of his hand constantly touched her flesh. For him, the touch point reflected sheer greed; for Deirdre it was a sensually electric connection that served as a counterpoint to her apprehension.

Only when the last of the buttons was released did Neil lower his gaze. With hands that trembled slightly, he drew back the voluminous pajama fabric, rolling it outward until her breasts were fully exposed. The sight of them, small and high, but well rounded, shook him deeply. He'd been right; imagination did pale against reality. Or maybe it was that he hadn't dared dream....

The cool air of the bedroom hit Deirdre simultaneously with trepidation, but when her arms would have moved inward, he gently held them still.

"You're beautiful, Deirdre," he breathed. "What could ever have made you think that you wouldn't be right for me?"

She didn't answer, because the light in his eyes was so special, so precious, that she was afraid of distracting him lest his fascination fade. So she watched, mesmerized, as he brought both hands to her breasts. Long fingers circled them, tracing only their contours before growing bolder. A soft sigh slipped through her lips when he began to knead her fullness, and the feeling was so right and so good that she momentarily forgot her fears.

When the pads of his fingers brushed her nipples, she stiffened her back, but it was a movement in response to the surge of heat, not a protest. She had to clutch his shoulders then, because he had leaned forward and opened his mouth over one tight nub, and the sensation was jolting her to her core.

His tongue dabbed the pebbled tip. His teeth toyed with it. And all the while his hand occupied her other breast, caressing it with such finesse that she bit her lip to keep from crying out.

At last, when she simply couldn't help herself, she began to whimper. "Neil...I don't think I can stand this...."

"If I can, you can," he rasped against her skin.

"I feel like I'm on fire...."

"You are."

"I can't sit still...."

"Sure you can. Let it build."

"It's been building for three days!"

"But it has to be slow, has to be right."

He drew back only long enough to whip the sweater over his head. Then he came up to sit beside her and take her in his arms. That first touch, flesh to flesh, was cataclysmic. Deirdre's entire body shook when her breasts made contact with his chest. Her arms went around him, holding him tightly, as though otherwise she'd simply shatter.

Neil's grip on her was no less definitive. His large body shuddered at the feel of her softness pressing into it. His breath came raggedly by her ear, while his hands hungrily charted every inch of her bare back, from her shoulders, over her ribs, to the dimpled hollows below her waist. Her pajama bottoms hung around her hips; he took advantage of their looseness to explore the creamy smoothness of her belly, the flare of her hips, the conditioned firmness of her bottom.

Deirdre, whose body all but hummed its pleasure, was finding a second heaven touching Neil. She loved the broad sweep of his back, the textured hollows of his collarbone, the sinewed swells of his chest. Slipping her hands between their bodies, she savored his front as she'd done his back. It was hairier, enticingly so, and his nipples were every bit as taut, if smaller, than hers were.

"What you do to me, Deirdre," he murmured dazedly, recapturing her face with his hands and taking her lips in a fevered kiss. "I think I agree with you. I'm not sure how much more I can stand, either."

She'd been right, he realized. Though they hadn't known it at the time, they'd endured three days of foreplay. From the very first there'd been curiosity. And it had grown more intense, despite every argument they'd had, despite every scathing comment they'd exchanged. Later he would wonder how much of the fighting had been caused by that basic attraction between them, but for now all he could think about was that their mutual desire was on the verge of culmination.

Coming up on one knee, he grasped her under the arms and raised her gently to the pillow. He eased the quilt from under her until she was lying on the bare sheet, then, unsnapping her pajama bottoms, he worked them down her legs and over her cast, finally dropping them to the floor.

Deirdre experienced a resurgence of anxiety when he sat back and looked at her, but his gaze was filled with such reverence that those fears receded once again. The hand he skimmed up her leg was worshipful, and when he reached the nest of pale hair at the juncture of her thighs, he touched her with care that bordered on awe.

She felt totally exposed, yet treasured. Looking at Neil, seeing the way his large frame quivered with restrained desire, she marveled that fate had brought him to her.

"Neil...please..." she begged in a shaky whisper. "I want you."

He needed no more urging. Sitting back, he unsnapped his jeans and thrust them down his legs along with his briefs. Within seconds he was sliding over her, finding a place for himself between her thighs, threading his fingers through hers and anchoring them by her shoulders.

Bearing his weight on his elbows, he rubbed his hot body back and forth over hers. He made no attempt to penetrate her, simply sought the pleasure of his new level of touching. But the pleasure was galvanic, causing them both to breathe quickly and unevenly.

Deirdre had never before known such anticipation. She wasn't thinking about her fears, wasn't thinking about what would happen if Neil didn't find her lovemaking adequate. She was only thinking of the burning deep within her, knowing that she needed his possession now.

Eyes closed, she arched upward, hips straining toward his in a silent plea that dashed the last of his resistance. Nudging her legs farther apart, he positioned himself, then tightened his fingers around hers.

"Look at me, Deirdre," he whispered. "Look at me, babe."

Her eyes opened, then grew wider when, ever so slowly, he entered her. She felt him clearly, sliding deeper and deeper; it was as though each individual cell inside her responded to his presence, transmitting one heady message after another to her brain. By the time he filled her completely, she knew that she'd never, never be the same again.

Neil closed his eyes and let out a long and tremulous sigh. Satisfaction was so clearly etched on his features that Deirdre would have breathed a sigh of relief, too, had she been able to. But he'd begun to move inside her, and breathing became increasingly difficult. All she could do was to give herself up to the spiral of passion he created.

The heat built steadily. Neil set a pace that maximized her pleasure, knowing precisely when to slow, precisely when to speed up. She moved to his rhythm, following his lead with a flair of her own that drove him on and up.

Then, when the fire within her became too hot for containment, she arched her back a final time, caught a sudden deep breath and dissolved into a seemingly endless series of spasms. Somewhere in the middle, Neil joined her, holding himself at the very entrance of her womb while his body pulsed and quivered.

It was a long time before either of them could speak, a long time during which the only sounds in the room were the harsh gasping for air and the softer, more gentle patter of the rain. Only when they'd begun to breath more normally did Neil slide to the side, but he brought her with him, settling them face to face on the pillow.

"Well," he asked softly, "what do you think?"

For an instant, Deirdre's old fears crowded in on her. "What do *you* think?" she whispered.

"I think," he said slowly, reining in a smug smile, "that for a lady with a sharp tongue and a questionable disposition, you're one hell of a lover."

CHAPTER SEVEN

RELIEF WASHED OVER HER, this time thoroughly wiping away whatever lingering doubts she'd had. A smile lit her face, unwaveringly, even as she raised her voice in mock protest.

"Sharp tongue? Questionable disposition? It was all because of you, Neil Hersey. You were the one who wasn't supposed to be here!"

Neil was undaunted. His own euphoria was too great. "And if I hadn't been," he ventured naughtily, "just think of all we'd have missed."

Deirdre had no suitable answer for that, so she simply continued to smile, and he was content to bask in her sunshine. After a time, he tenderly brushed a damp wisp of hair from her cheek.

"You're looking happy."

"I am...happy...satisfied...relieved."

"Was it that awful—the thought of our making love?" he chided.

"Oh, no, Neil," she answered quickly. "It was exciting. But you knew I was frightened."

"I'm still not sure why. It couldn't have been the athletic thing alone. Did it have something to do with the fellow who burned you once?"

She thought about that. "Indirectly, I suppose." Her gaze dropped. "Things were okay between us...sexually. It's just that when he got the urge to leave, he up and left, like there really wasn't anything worth sticking around for.

On a subconscious level, I may have taken it more personally than I should have." She lapsed into silence as she considered why that had been. Her fingers moved lightly over the hair on Neil's chest in a reminder of what had just passed between them, and it gave her the courage to go on.

"I think it relates more to my family than Seth. I've always been the black sheep, the one who didn't fit in. My mother is the epitome of good manners, good looks and feminine poise. My sister takes after her. I've always been different, and they've made no secret of their opinion of me."

He cupped her throat in the vee of his hand, while his thumb drew circles on her collarbone. "They don't think you're feminine enough?"

"No."

His laugh was a cocky one. "Shows how much they know."

She rewarded him with a shy smile. "You're talking sex, which is only one part of it, but you're good for my ego, anyway."

"And you're good for mine. I don't think I've ever had a woman want me as much as you did just now. I know damn well that sex was the last thing on your mind when you got here, and that makes your desire so precious. I'd like to think it wasn't just any man who could turn you on like that."

"It wasn't!" she exclaimed, then lowered her voice. "There's only been one man, and that was Seth. I'm not very experienced."

"Experienced women are a dime a dozen. You're worth far more."

"I've never been driven by sexual need. I've never seen myself as a sexual being."

"We're all sexual beings."

"To one degree or another, but those degrees can vary widely." She moved her thigh between his, finding pleasure in the textural contrast of their bodies. "I guess what I'm saying is that I've always assumed myself to be at the lower end of the scale."

"Do you still?" he asked softly.

The look she gave him was every bit as soft. "With you? No."

He ran his hand down her spine, covered her bottom and pressed her hips intimately close. "That's good," he said, and sucked in a loud breath. "Because I think I'm needing you again."

Deirdre couldn't have been more delighted. Not only was he proving once again that her fears had been unfounded, but he was mirroring the state of her own reawakening desire. She followed the progress of her hand as it inched its way down his chest. "I think the needing is mutual."

"Any regrets?" he asked thickly.

"Only that I can't wrap both legs around you."

"It is a challenge with your cast. I didn't hurt you before, did I?"

She was fascinated by the whorl of hair around his navel. "Did I sound like I was in pain?" she asked distractedly.

"Dire pain."

"It had nothing to do with my leg." Her hand crept lower, tangling in the dark curls above his sex.

"Deirdre?" He was having trouble breathing again.

She was too engrossed in her exploration to take pity on him. "You have a beautiful body," she whispered. Her fingers grazed his tumescence. "I didn't have time to touch you before."

"Oh, God," he breathed when she took him fully into her grasp. His hand tightened on her shoulder, and he pressed his lips to her forehead. "Oh…"

"Do you like that?" she asked, cautiously stroking him.

"Oh, yes…harder…you can do it harder." His body was straining for her touch; when she strengthened it, he gave a moan of ecstasy. "Almost heaven—that's what it is."

"Almost?"

He opened his eyes and gazed at her then. "True heaven is when I'm inside." Inserting his leg between hers, he brought her thigh even higher. "You're hot and moist and tight, so tight. The way I slip in—" he put action to words "—shows how perfectly you...ummmmmm...how perfectly you were made...for me."

It was Deirdre's turn to gasp, then moan. He was lodged deeply within her, while his hand was caressing the rest of her with consummate expertise. When he withdrew, then surged back, she thought she'd explode.

The explosion wasn't long in coming. His mouth covered hers and he filled her with his tongue, as his manhood already filled her. One bold thrust echoed the other in a rhythm that repeated itself until all rhythm was suspended in a climactic surge.

This time when they tumbled back from that pyrotechnic plane, they had neither the strength nor the need to talk. Fitting Deirdre snugly into the curve of his body, Neil held her until her breathing was long and even. Soon after, he, too, was asleep.

THE NEXT DAY was the most glorious one Deirdre had ever known. She awoke in Neil's arms with a smile on her face, and if the smile ever faded, it was never for long. He instructed her to stay in bed while he showered, then he returned and carried her in for a bath. By the time he'd washed her to his satisfaction, they were both in need of satisfaction of another sort. So he carried her back to bed, where he proceeded to adore every bare inch of her body.

He taught her things about herself she'd never known, banishing any modesty she might have had and reaping the benefits. With deft fingers, an agile tongue and pulsing sex, he brought her to climax after climax, until she pleaded for mercy.

"A sex fiend!" she cried. "I'm stranded on an island with a sex fiend!"

"Look who's talking!" was all he had to say. Not only had she been as hungry as he, but she'd taken every one of the liberties with his body that he had with hers.

They didn't bother to get dressed that day. It seemed a waste of time and effort. The weather was as ominous as the thought of putting clothing between them. When they left the bedroom, they shared Deirdre's pajamas—the top was hers, the bottom his. He teased her, claiming that she'd brought along men's pajamas with precisely that goal in mind, but he wasn't about to complain when he knew all he had to do—whether in the kitchen, the living room or the den—was to raise her top, lower his bottom, and enter her with a fluid thrust.

Deirdre let his presence fill her, both body and mind. She knew they were living a dream, that reality lurked just beyond, waiting to pounce. But she refused to be distracted by other, more somber thoughts when she was feeling so complete. Neil accepted her. He'd seen her at her worst, yet he accepted her. His attraction to her wasn't based on who she was, what she did for a living, or what she wore; he liked her as the person she was.

Neil was similarly content. The realization that he was avoiding reality did nothing to temper his feelings about Deirdre. He refused to dwell on the fact that she didn't know about the downturn his life in Hartford had taken, because it didn't seem to matter. She was happy; he'd made her happy. She didn't care about his financial prospects or his reputation. She was satisfied to accept him as he was.

And so they didn't think about the future. One day melded into the next, each filled with relaxation, leisure activity, lovemaking. Deirdre finished one book and started a second. She got the hang of knitting well enough to begin work on the actual sweater, and made commendable headway on it. She exercised each day but made no attempt to devise new routines, loath to do something that might start her brooding on whether she'd be able to teach again.

Neil did his share of reading. He continued to take responsibility for most of the household chores, and it was his pleasure to do so. From time to time Deirdre tried to help, but he saw the frustration she suffered with her cast, and it was enough to tell him that he wasn't being used.

The bickering they'd done during those first three days was, for all intents and purposes, over. This was not to say that they agreed on everything, but compromise became the mode. Neil accepted the loud beat of Deirdre's music, while she accepted the drone of his radio-transmitted Celtics games. She subjected herself to a clobbering at Trivial Pursuit, while he endured the gyrations in *Saturday Night Fever*.

One night, when he was feeling particularly buoyant, he took a Havana cigar from his bag, lit it and sat back on the sofa in bliss. Deirdre, who'd watched in horror his elaborate ceremony of nipping off the end of the cigar, then moistening the tip, simply sat with one finger unobtrusively blocking her nose. It was an example of how far they'd come; as disgusting as she found the smell, she wasn't about to dampen his obvious pleasure.

He'd been smoking for several minutes before he cast her a glance and saw her pose. "Uh-oh. Bad?"

She shrugged. "Are't dose tings illegal in dis country?" she asked, careful to breathe through her mouth.

"It's illegal to import them. But if a foreigner brings them in for his own personal use and shares them with his friends, it's okay."

"Is dat how you got it?"

"I have a client from Jordan who has business interests here. He gave me a box several months ago." Neil eyed the long cigar with reverence. "I'm not usually a smoker, but I have to admit that if you want to smoke a cigar, this is the way to go."

"Da Mercedes of cigars?"

"Yup." Eyes slitted in pleasure, he put the cigar to his mouth, drew on it, then blew out a narrow stream of thick smoke. "Should I put it out?"

"Dot on my accou't. But do't ask me to kiss you later, commie breath."

His lips quirked at the corners. Leaning forward, he carefully placed the cigar in an ashtray, then stood and advanced on her.

She held up a hand. "Do't come closer. I dow what you're goi'g to do."

He propped his hands on the arm of her chair and bent so that his face was inches from hers. He was grinning. "I'll kiss you if I want to, and you'll like it, commie breath and all."

"Deil, I'm warding you—"

Her warning was cut short by his mouth, which took hers in a way that was at once familiar and new. After the initial capture, his lips softened and grew persuasive, coaxing hers into a response she was helpless to withhold.

When at last he ended the kiss, he murmured softly, "You can breathe now."

Deirdre's eyes were closed, and the hand that had protected her nose had long since abandoned that post and moved from the rich texture of his beard up into his thick, brown hair. "How can I do that…when you take my breath away…." When she pulled him back to her, he was more than willing to accede to her demands.

As time passed the cigar burned itself out, but neither of them noticed.

EARLY IN THE MORNING of their one-week anniversary on the island, Thomas called them from shore. Neil was the one to talk to him, but Deirdre, standing by, heard every word.

"How're you folks making out?"

Neil grinned, but made sure his voice was suitably sober. "Okay."

"I got your messages, but I've been away most of the week. I figured that you'd keep trying if there was any kind of emergency."

"He feels guilty," Deirdre whispered mischievously. "Serves him right."

Neil collared her with a playful arm as he spoke grimly back into the receiver. "We'll live."

"Deirdre's doing all right with that leg of hers?"

Neil hesitated before answering. Meanwhile, he toyed gently with Deirdre's earlobe. "The house has taken a beating. She's not very good with her crutches."

Deirdre kicked at his shin with her cast. He sidestepped her deftly.

"Oh," Thomas said. "Well, that's Victoria's problem. Are you two getting along?"

"Getting along?" Deirdre whispered. She slid her hand over Neil's ribs and tucked her fingers in the waistband of his jeans.

Neil cleared his throat and pulled a straight face. "We're still alive."

"You'll drive him crazy," she whispered. "He's dying of curiosity."

"Let him die," Neil whispered back, eyes dancing.

During the brief interlude, Thomas had apparently decided that what was happening between Neil and Deirdre was Victoria's problem, too. "Well," came his staticky voice, "I just wanted to let you know that you've got a store of fresh supplies on the dock."

"On the dock?" Neil looked at his watch. It was barely nine. "You must have been up before dawn."

"I left them last night."

"Coward."

"What's that?" came the static. "I didn't get that last word?"

Deirdre snickered noisily. Neil clamped a hand on her mouth. "I said, thank you," he yelled more loudly than necessary into the handset.

"Oh. Okay. I'll be out next week to pick you up, then. If there's any change in plans, give me a call."

For the first time, Neil's hesitation was legitimate.

Looking down, he saw that Deirdre's too, was suddenly more serious. His fingers grew tighter on the handset.

"Will do" was all he said before switching off the instrument and replacing it on its stand. He stood silent for a minute with his arm still around Deirdre. Then, with a squeeze of her shoulder, he took a fast breath. "Hey, do you see what I see?"

She was ready for a diversion. Any diversion. Thomas's last comment had been a depressant. "I don't know. What do you see?"

He raised his eyes to the window. "The sun. Well, maybe not the sun itself, but it's brighter out there than it's been in a week, and it hasn't rained since yesterday, which means that the paths will have begun to dry out, which means that I can get the things in from the dock pretty quick, which means—" he gave her shoulder another squeeze "—that we can take a walk."

Deirdre followed his gaze, then looked back up at him. "I'd like that," she said softly. "I'd like it a lot."

THE BREAK IN THE WEATHER offered new realms of adventure for them. As though determined to restake its claim after a long absence, the sun grew stronger from one day to the next. The air remained cool, and Deirdre's mobility was limited by her crutches, but she and Neil managed to explore most of the small island. When they weren't wandering in one direction or another, they were perched atop high boulders overlooking the sea. They watched the sun rise one morning, watched the sun set one evening, and in between they agreed that neither of them had ever visited as serene a place.

Unfortunately, with greater frequency as the days passed, their serenity was disturbed by the memory of Thomas's parting words. He'd be by to pick them up at the end of a week, and that week seemed far too short. Deirdre began to brood more and more about Providence, Neil about Hartford, and though the making up was always breathtaking, they began to bicker again.

Finally, three days before they were to leave, things came to a head. They'd finished dinner and were seated side by side in the den, ostensibly watching *Raiders of the Lost Ark*, but in truth paying it little heed. With an abruptness that mirrored his mood, Neil switched off the set.

Deirdre shot him a scowl. She'd been thinking about leaving the island, and the prospect left her cold. "What did you do that for?"

"You're picking your fingernail again. The sound drives me crazy!" What really drove him crazy was the thought of returning to Hartford, but Deirdre's nail picking was as good a scapegoat as any.

"But I wanted to watch the movie."

"How can you watch the movie when you're totally engrossed in your nail?"

"Maybe if you weren't rubbing that damned beard of yours, I'd be able to concentrate."

His eyes darkened. "You haven't complained about my beard for days." In fact, she'd complimented him on it. It was filling in well, she'd said, and looked good. He'd agreed with her assessment. "And maybe I'm rubbing it to drown out the sound of your picking! Why do you *do* that?"

"It's a nervous habit, Neil. I can't help it."

"So why are you nervous? I thought you were supposed to be calm and relaxed."

"I am!" she cried, then, hearing herself, dropped both her gaze and her voice. "I'm not."

Silence hung in the air between them. When Deirdre looked up at last, she found Neil studying her with a pained expression on his face.

"We have to talk," he said quietly.

"I know."

"Thomas will be here soon."

"I know."

"You'll go back to Providence. I'll go back to Hartford."

"I *know*."

"So what are we going to do about it?"

She shrugged, then slanted him a pleading glance. "Tell him we're staying for another week?" Even more frightening to her than the prospect of returning to Providence was the prospect of leaving Neil.

He snorted and pushed himself from the sofa, pacing to the far side of the room before turning on his heel. "I can't do that, Deirdre. Much as I wish it, I can't."

"Then what do you suggest?"

He stood with one hand on his hip, the other rubbing the back of his neck. His gaze was unfocused, alternately shifting from the wall to the floor and back. "I don't know, damn it. I've been trying to think of solutions— No, that's wrong. I've avoided thinking about going back since I arrived, and as a result, I have no solutions. Then there's *this* complication."

Deirdre didn't like the sound of his voice. "What complication?"

He looked her in the eye. "Us."

It was like a blow to her stomach. Though she knew he was right, she couldn't bear to think of what they'd shared in negative terms. "Look," she argued, holding up a hand in immediate self-defense. "*We* don't have to be a complication. You can go your way, I can go mine. *Fini.*"

"Is that how you want it?"

"No."

"How do you want it?"

"I don't know," she cried in frustration. "You're not the only one who's avoided thinking about going back. I haven't found any more solutions than you have."

"But we do agree that we want to keep on seeing each other."

"Yes!"

His shoulders sagged in defeat. "Then it is a complication, Deirdre. On top of everything else, what we have is very definitely a complication." He turned to stare out the window.

Deirdre, in turn, stared at him. "Okay, Neil," she began softly. "You're right. We have to talk. About everything." When he didn't move, she continued. "When we first came here, you were as bad-tempered as I was. I know my reasons, but I've never really known yours. At first I didn't want to know, because I have enough problems of my own. Then, when things got...better between us, I didn't want to ask for fear of upsetting the apple cart." She was sitting forward on the couch, a hand spread palm down on each thigh. "But I'm asking now. If we're going to figure anything out, I have to know. What happened, Neil? What happened in Hartford that brought you up here in such a temper? Why did you need to escape?"

Neil dropped his chin to his chest, her questions echoing in his brain. The moment of truth had come. He gnawed on the inside of his cheek, as though even doing something so pointless would be an excuse for not answering. But it wasn't. Deirdre was curious, and intelligent. As much as he wished he didn't have to tell her, she more than anyone deserved to know.

He turned to face her but made no move to close the distance between them. "I have," he said with a resigned sigh, "a major problem back home. It involves one of my principal clients—strike that, one of my principal *ex*-clients, a very large corporation based in Hartford." He hesitated.

"Go on," she urged softly. "I'm with you."

"I've been chief counsel for the corporation for three years, and during that time I've come to be increasingly familiar with various aspects of the business. Last summer, quite inadvertently, I stumbled onto a corruption scheme involving the president of the corporation."

Deirdre held her breath and watched him with growing apprehension. She refused to believe that he'd knowingly condone corruption, yet, as corporate counsel, his job was to side with his client.

"No," he said, reading her fear, "I didn't demand a cut—"

"I never thought you would! But you must have been put in an awful position."

He was relieved by her obvious sincerity, but in some ways that made his task all the more difficult. He would have liked to be able to tell her that his practice was successful and growing even more so. He would have liked to have shone in her eyes. But the facts were against him.

Deirdre didn't deserve this. Hell, *he* didn't deserve it!

"Awful is putting it mildly," he declared. "I could have chosen to look the other way, but it went against every principle I'd ever held. So I took the matter before the board of directors. That was when things fell apart."

"What do you mean?"

"They were involved! All of them! They knew exactly what was going on, and their only regret was that I'd found out!"

Deirdre felt her anger rising on his behalf. "What did you do?"

"I resigned. I had no other choice. There was no way I'd sit back and watch them pad their own pockets at the expense of not only their stockholders but their employees. Their employees! The last people who could afford to be gypped!"

"But I don't understand, Neil. If you resigned, isn't it all over? You may have lost one client, but you have others, don't you?"

"Oh, yes," he ground out with more than a little sarcasm. "But those others have dwindled with a suddenness that can't possibly be coincidental." His jaw was tight. "It seems that Wittnauer-Douglass wasn't satisfied simply with my resignation. The executive board wanted to make sure I wouldn't do anything to rock a very lucrative boat."

She was appalled. "They blackballed you."

"Worse. They passed word around that I'd been the mastermind behind the corruption scheme. According to the chairman of the board—and I got this from a reliable source—if I hadn't left, they'd have leveled charges against me."

"But they can't say that!"

"They can say anything they damn well please!"

"Then they can't *do* it!"

"I'm not so sure. There's a helluva lot of murky paperwork in the archives of any large corporation. That paperwork can be easily doctored if the right people give the go-ahead."

"But why would the board at Wittnauer-Douglass want to even mention corruption? Wouldn't it spoil their own scheme?"

"Not by a long shot. They simply reorganize, shift outlets, juggle a few more documents. When you've got power, you've got power. It's as simple as that."

"And you can't fight them." It was a statement, a straight follow-up to Neil's. Unfortunately it touched a nerve in him that was all too raw.

"What in the hell can I do?" he exploded, every muscle in his body rigid. "They've spread word so far and so fast that it's become virtually impossible for me to practice law in Hartford! The major corporations won't touch me. The medium-sized ones are leery. And it's gone way beyond my profession. Nancy—the woman I was seeing—quickly opted out, which was okay, because it was only a matter of time before we'd have split, anyway. But before I knew what had happened, I'd been replaced as chairman of the hospital fund-raising drive. That did hurt. Word is that I'm a crook, and even if some people believe in my innocence, there are still appearances to uphold. Hell, I can't even find a squash partner these days. I've become a regular pariah!"

"They can't do that!"

"They've done it," he lashed back. His anger was compounding itself, taking on even greater force than it had held in Hartford, mainly because he detested having to dump this on Deirdre. "I've worked my tail off to build a successful practice, and they've swept it away without a care in the world. And do you know what the worst part is?" He was livid now, furious with himself. "I didn't see it coming! I was naive...stupid!"

Deirdre was on her feet, limping toward him. "It wasn't your fault—"

He interrupted, barely hearing her argument over the internal din of his self-reproach. "How could I have possibly spent so much time working with those people and not have seen them for what they are? I'm too trusting! I've always been too trusting! Good guys finish last, isn't that what they say? Well, it's true!"

She took his arm. "But trusting is a good way to be, Neil," she argued with quiet force. "The alternative is to be an eternal skeptic, or worse, paranoid, and you couldn't live that way."

"My friends. They even got to my *friends*."

"A real friend wouldn't be gotten to."

"Then I've been a poor judge of character on that score, too."

"You're being too harsh on yourself—"

"And it's about time! Someone should have kicked me in the pants years ago. Maybe if they had, I wouldn't have been such a damned optimist. Maybe I would have seen all this coming. Maybe I wouldn't be in such a completely untenable position now."

"You can find new clients," she ventured cautiously.

"Not the kind I want. My expertise is in dealing with large corporations, and those won't come near me now."

"Maybe not in Hartford—"

"Which means relocating. Damn it, I don't want to relocate. At least, not for that reason."

"But things aren't hopeless, Neil. You have a profession that you're skilled in—"

"And look where it's gotten me," he seethed. "I have a great office, two capable associates and a steadily diminishing clientele. I have a condominium, which the people I once called friends won't deign to visit. I have a record for charity work that's come to a dead halt. I have squash gear and no partner."

Deirdre dropped her hand from his stiff arm. "You also

BARBARA DELINSKY

159

think you have a monopoly on self-pity. Well, you don't, Neil. You're not the only one who has problems. You're not the only one who's frustrated."

"Frustrated?" He raked rigid fingers through his hair. "Now *that's* the understatement of the year. And while we're at it, you can add guilt to the list of my transgressions. I came up here and took every one of those frustrations out on you!"

"But you weren't the only one to do it! I used you for that too, Neil, so I'm as guilty as you are."

"Yeah." His voice was calm now. "Only difference is that your problem has a solution in sight. Once the cast is off—"

"It's not only my leg," Deirdre snapped, turning away from him. "I wouldn't have been in such a lousy mood if it was simply a question of my leg. There's a whole other story to my life, and if you think that in its own way my situation isn't as frustrating as yours, you can add egotistical to that list you're drawing up."

There was silence behind her. For the first time since he'd begun his tirade, Neil's thoughts took a tangent. *A whole other story to my life,* she'd said. He was suddenly more nervous than he'd been angry moments before, inexplicably fearful that his world was about to collapse completely.

"What is it—that other story?"

Head down, she hobbled over to rest her hip against the desk. A dry laugh slipped from her throat. "It's ironic. There you are, without a corporation to represent. Here I am, with a corporation I don't want."

"What are you talking about?"

Slowly she raised her head. Almost reluctantly she replied, "Joyce Enterprises. Have you ever heard of it?"

"I've heard of it. It's based in…" The light dawned. "Providence. You're that Joyce? It's yours?"

"Actually, my family's. My father died six months ago, and my sister took over the helm."

Neil frowned. "I didn't make the connection…I never…it doesn't fit."

"With who I am?" She smiled sadly. "You're right. It doesn't fit. I don't fit, and that's the problem. My parents always intended that the business stay in the family. Sandra—my sister—just can't handle it. I have two uncles who are involved, but they're as ill-equipped to run things as my mother is."

Neil had come to stand before her. "So they want you in."

"Right."

"But you don't want in."

"Right again. I tried it once and hated it. I'm just not the type to dress up all day and entertain, which is largely what the head of a business like that has to do. I don't take to diplomatic small talk, and I don't take to being a pretty little thing on display."

"That I can believe," he quipped.

Deirdre responded to his teasing with a scowl. "I wish my family could believe it, but they won't. They keep insisting that I'm their only hope, and maybe I would be able to handle the management end of the business, but the political end would drive me up a tree! For six months now they've been after me, and while I was busy doing my own thing I had an excuse. At least, it was one I could grasp at. I've always known that sooner or later, as I got older, I'd slow down, but I thought I had time to find a substitute. Now I don't. Suddenly I can't do my own thing, and they've started hounding me to do theirs. Even before I left the hospital they were on me." She paused for a breath, then continued.

"They think I'm selfish, and maybe I am, because I want to be happy, and I know I won't be if I'm forced to be involved in the business. It's really a joke—their pushing me this way. I've always been odd in their minds. I'm a failure. They look down their noses at the work I do. And even beyond that, I don't have a husband, or children, which compounds my sin. What good am I? Nothing I do is right, so they say. Yet they stand over me and insist that I help run Joyce." She rubbed a throbbing spot on her forehead, then looked up at Neil.

"The family needs me. The business needs me. Can I stand by and let it all go down the tubes? Because it will, Neil. I keep telling them to bring in outside help, but they refuse, and if they continue to do that, the whole thing is doomed. Oh, it may take a while. The corporation is like a huge piece of machinery. It's showing signs of wear and tear right now, but the gears are still turning. When it comes time to oil them, though, and there's no one capable of doing the job, things will slow down, then eventually grind to a halt."

She gave a quick, little headshake, more of a shiver. "Talk of guilt, I've got it in spades. I have a *responsibility*, my mother keeps reminding me. And that's the worst part, because as much as I can't bear the thought of having anything to do with the business, I do feel the responsibility. I deny it to them. I've denied it to myself. But it's there." She looked down at her fingers and repeated more softly, "It's there."

Neil wrapped his hand around her neck and kneaded it gently. "We're a fine twosome, you and I. Between us, we've got a pack of ills and no medicine."

She gave a meek laugh. "Maybe the island drugstore has something?"

He sighed. "The island drugstore filled the prescription for two souls who needed a break, but I'm afraid it doesn't have anything for curing the ills back home."

"So," she breathed, discouraged. "We're back where we started. What are we going to do?"

He looked at her intently, then dipped his head and took her lips with a sweetness that wrenched at her heart. "We are going to spend the next three days enjoying each other. That is, if you don't mind dallying with a man who has a very dubious future…"

It was at that moment, with Neil standing close, looking at her as though her answer were more important to him than anything else in the world, that Deirdre knew she loved him.

She smiled softly. "If you don't mind dallying with a woman who would rather spend the rest of her life on this island than go back to the mainland and face up to her responsibilities…"

His answer was a broad smile and another kiss, this one deeper and more soul reaching than anything that had come before. It was followed by a third, then a fourth, and before long, neither Neil nor Deirdre could think of the future.

THEIR FINAL DAYS on the island were spent much as the preceding ones had been, though now there was direction to their thoughts, rather than a random moodiness. For his part, Neil was relieved to have told Deirdre everything, even if the telling hadn't solved a thing. She'd accepted his quandary without criticism, and her affection—yes, he was sure it was that—for him seemed, if anything, to have deepened.

For her part, Deirdre was relieved to have shared her burden with an understanding soul. Neil hadn't jumped on her for her failings; if anything, his affection—yes she was sure it was that—for her seemed stronger than ever.

If that affection took on a frantic quality at times, each attributed it to the fact that the clock was running out.

Thomas had arranged to pick them up at eight o'clock in the morning on that last day. So the night before they found themselves cleaning the house, making sure that everything was as it had been when they'd arrived two weeks before. Tension suddenly surrounded them, reducing them to nearly the same testy state they'd been in when they'd arrived.

Neil did a final round of laundry, inadvertently tossing Deirdre's teal-green sweatshirt into the wash with the

towels, half of which were an electric blue not far different from her sweatshirt, half of which were pure white.
When the white towels emerged with a distinct green tinge,
he swore loudly.

"Goddamn it! I thought you'd packed this thing
already!"

"I haven't packed anything yet." She'd been putting
that particular chore off for as long as possible. Now,
studying the once-white towels, she scowled. "Didn't you
see the sweatshirt when you put the towels in?"

"How could I see it in with these blue ones?"

"The sweatshirt's green!"

"That's close enough."

"You must be color-blind."

"I am not color-blind."

They were glaring at each other over the washing
machine. Deirdre was the first to look away. "Okay," she
said, sighing. "We can put the white towels through again,
this time with bleach."

"The little tag says not to use bleach."

Fiery eyes met his. "I've used bleach on towels before,
and it does the trick. If you don't want to take the risk, you
find a solution." Turning, she swung back to her cleaning
of the refrigerator, leaving Neil to grudgingly add bleach
to a second load.

Not long after, intent on doing the packing she'd put off,
Deirdre was headed for the bedroom, when her crutch
caught on the edge of the area rug in the living room. She
stumbled and fell, crying out in annoyance as well as
surprise.

"Who put that stupid rug there?" she screamed.

Neil was quickly by her side, his voice tense. "That
'stupid' rug has been in exactly the same spot since we got
here. Weren't you watching where you were going?"

"It's the damned rubber tips on these crutches!" She
kicked at them with her good foot. "They catch on everything!"

Rescuing the crutches, he put an arm across her back and helped her up. "They haven't bothered you before. Are you okay?"

"I'm fine," she snarled, rubbing her hip.

"Then you're lucky. Damn it, Deirdre, are you trying to kill yourself? Why don't you watch where you're going next time?"

"Watch where I'm going? I was watching!"

"Then you were going too fast!"

"I wasn't going any faster than I ever go!"

"Which is too fast!"

Deirdre, who had returned the crutches to their rightful place, backed away from him, incensed. "I don't need advice from you! I've taken care of myself for years, and I'll do it again! Just because you've helped me out this week doesn't give you the right to order me around. If you really wanted to help me, you'd offer to take that damned corporation off my back!"

"If you really wanted to help *me*, you'd *give* me the damned corporation!" he roared back.

For long minutes they stood glaring at each other. Both pairs of eyes flashed; both pairs of nostrils flared. Gradually both chests stopped heaving, and their anger dissipated.

"It's yours," Deirdre said quietly, her eyes glued to his.

"I'll take it," he countered, but his voice, too, was quiet.

"It's a bizarre idea."

"Totally off the wall."

"But it could offer an out for both of us."

"That's right."

They stood where they were for another long minute. Then, resting a hand lightly on her back, Neil urged her toward the sofa. When they were both seated, he crossed one leg over his knee, propped his elbow on the arm of the sofa and chafed his lower lip with his thumb.

"I've done a lot of thinking since we talked the other night," he began, hesitating at first, then gaining momentum. "I've been over and over the problem, trying to decide what I want to do. There are times when I get angry, when the only thing that makes any sense to me is revenge. Then the anger fades, and I realize how absurd that is. It's also self-defeating, when what I really want to do is to practice law." He paused, lowered his hand to his lap and looked at her. "You have a corporation that you don't want. I could make good use of it."

Nervously she searched his features. "For revenge?"

"No. Maybe it'd be a sort of reprisal, but that wouldn't be my main objective. I need something, Deirdre. It kills me to have to say that, especially to you. It's hard for a man—for anyone, I suppose—to admit that he's short on options. But I'm trying to face facts, and the sole fact in this case is that Hartford is no longer a viable place for me to work."

"You said you didn't want to relocate."

"I said I didn't want to relocate because of Wittnauer-Douglass. Maybe it's convoluted logic, but I'm beginning to think that Joyce Enterprises would have attracted me regardless of the problems in Hartford. No matter what you see happening now within the company, Joyce has a solid reputation. I wouldn't be afraid to put my stock in it. And it may be the highest form of conceit, but I do think that I have something to offer. I'm a good lawyer. I'm intimately familiar with the workings of large corporations. I may not be an entrepreneur, but I know people who are. And I know of a headhunter who could help me find the best ones to work with.

"Unfortunately—" he took a breath and his eyes widened as he broached the next problem "—that would mean bringing in an outsider. From what you say, your family has been against that from the start, which raises the even more immediate issue of whether or not they'd even accept me."

Deirdre tipped up her chin in a gesture of defiance. "I hold an equal amount of stock to my mother and sister. If you were to enter the corporation alongside me, they wouldn't dare fight."

"But you don't want to enter the corporation. Wasn't that the point?"

"Yes, but if we were…" She faltered, struggling to find the least presumptive words. "If we were together… I mean, if I made it clear that we were…involved…"

"That we were a steady couple, as in lovers?"

"Yes."

He gave his head a quick shake. "Not good enough. It'll have to be marriage."

"Marriage?" She'd wanted to think that they'd be tied somehow, but marriage was the ultimate in ties. "Isn't that a little radical?"

Neil shrugged, but nonchalance was the last thing he felt. He'd been searching for a way to bind Deirdre to him. He loved her. Somewhere along the line that realization had dawned, and it had fit him so comfortably that he hadn't thought of questioning it. He couldn't say the words yet; he felt too vulnerable. Marriage might be sudden, but it served his purposes well. "Radical only in that we've known each other for such a short time. We get along, don't we?"

"We fight constantly!" she argued, playing the devil's advocate. If she knew that Neil loved her she wouldn't have had an argument in the world. But he hadn't said those words, and she didn't have the courage to lay herself bare by saying them herself, so she felt obligated to resist.

"Not constantly. Only when we're frustrated by problems that seem beyond our control. We've had our smooth times, haven't we?"

"Yes," she admitted, albeit reluctantly.

"And if this whole plan solves our problems, we won't have cause to fight, will we?"

"Every married couple fights."

"Then we wouldn't be any different. Look at it objectively, Deirdre. We have similar values and interests. We've already proved that we can live with each other. If we survived these past two weeks, being together twenty-four hours a day, we've got one foot up on many other couples who marry."

She didn't want to look at it objectively. Love wasn't objective. "But we've known each other in such a limited sphere. This isn't the real world. It's possible that we could return to Providence and find that we *hate* each other."

"That's your insecurity talking."

"Okay, maybe it is. I don't think I'm cut out to be a corporate wife any more than I'm cut out to head that corporation." She waved a hand back and forth. "I'm not the prissy little hostess. I'm not the adorable little lady who always wears and says the right things."

"I'm not complaining about who you are. And I wouldn't ask you to do anything you're uncomfortable with. If we entertain—and I assume there'd be some of that—you'd look as beautiful as any woman in the room. And rather than having you cook we could take people out or have something catered."

"In my modest town house?" she squeaked.

"In the house I'd buy for us." He sat forward, determination strong in the gaze he sent her. "I'm not a gigolo, Deirdre. I wouldn't go into this if I felt I was getting a free ride. You may not know it yet, but I do have my pride. If we agree to go ahead with this scheme, I'll work my tail off in the business. I'll be the one to support us, and that means providing the kind of home for you that I think you deserve. I guess I'm old-fashioned in that way."

"Does that mean I can't work or do whatever else I want?"

"You can do anything you want. I'm not *that* old-fashioned. And if you think I'm bothered by the thought of your teaching aerobics, think again. I adore your athletic body. Don't you know that by now?"

She simply slanted him a wry glance.

"Exercise is the way to go nowadays," he continued. "I'll be proud to have a wife who keeps her body toned."

"If I can," she muttered. "Whether I teach or not is still a big question."

"You'll teach. I told you that. When the cast comes off, you'll have physical therapy or whatever else it takes to get that leg working right."

"But…even if that happens, many of my classes are evening ones. How will you feel when you come home to an empty house after a hard day's work and there isn't even a hot meal ready?"

"I can cook. You know that. I'll be proud of you, Deirdre. My wife will be doing something that's constructive, something she enjoys." He paused for a breath, sobering. "And while we're talking of pride, if you agree to marry me, I'll insist on a prenuptial agreement."

Deirdre couldn't conceal a quick flare of hurt. "I don't want your money!"

"You've got it backside-to. It's you I want to protect. If you agree to marry me, I'll draw up a paper stating that your holdings in Joyce Enterprises—and anything else you now have to your name—will remain solely yours. If you should decide, at any point, that you want out of the marriage, you'll have everything you had when you entered into it. And if, at any point, you decide that I'm a detriment to Joyce Enterprises, you'll have the full right to can me."

She couldn't imagine that ever happening. For that matter, she couldn't imagine ever wanting out of a marriage to Neil. Unless he wanted it. "But what about your interests? They won't be protected if you sign a document like that. You thought you'd been naive regarding Wittnauer-Douglass. Isn't your plan now equally short-sighted?"

"I'd rather think of it as a challenge, one I'm approaching with my eyes wide open. I think I can make a go of running Joyce Enterprises, and if I do that, you won't have any cause to let me go. Like I said before, I'm not looking for a handout. I'm prepared to do the job. Yes, you'd be doing me a favor by giving me the chance, but I'd be doing you every bit as big a favor by relieving you of a responsibility you don't want."

He took her hand and studied the shape of her slender fingers. "You'd have a husband, which would please your family. And don't you think it's about time, anyway? I know it is for me. I'm not getting any younger. I'm more than ready to settle down."

But love? What about love? Deirdre pleaded silently. "Somehow it seems very…calculated."

"Sometimes the best things are."

"You don't have to marry me. We could still work all of this out."

"I'm sure we could, but marriage will be expedient when it comes to your family. They don't have to know about any agreement we sign. As far as they're concerned, what is yours is mine. I'll be a member of your family. The 'family business' will stay intact." He curved his fingers around hers and lowered his voice. "And I *want* to marry you. I wouldn't be suggesting it if that weren't the case."

But why do you want to marry me? she ached to ask, but didn't. He could give her the answer she craved, which would thrill her, or he could repeat the practical reasons he'd listed earlier, which would distress her. Rather than take the risk, she simply accepted his statement without prodding.

"Will you marry me, Deirdre?" he asked softly.

She met his gaze, knowing that love shone in her own with a strength she was helpless to dim. Silently she nodded, and closed her fingers around his.

CHAPTER EIGHT

AS HE'D PROMISED, Thomas was at the dock bright and early the next morning to pick them up. His curiosity was evident in the surreptitious glances he cast toward Deirdre, then Neil, at well-spaced intervals. They simply smiled at each other, feeling smug, but more than that, pleased with what lay ahead. If they'd dreaded the day they'd have to leave their island refuge, the knowledge that they were going to be together reduced that dread to a small twinge of sentimentality as the island faded behind them.

Neil had wanted to drive Deirdre back to Providence, but she insisted, with reason, he finally agreed, that it made no sense for her to leave her car in Maine when she'd want to use it at home. So he followed her on the highway, making sure she stopped periodically to stretch, then later, eat lunch.

It was mid-afternoon when they pulled up at Deirdre's mother's house. They'd discussed that, too, agreeing that the sooner they broke the news of their impending marriage to Maria Joyce the better. And, anticipating that the woman might give Deirdre a hard time, given her history of doing just that, Neil was vehement that he be present.

Maria was in the library when Deirdre called out from the front door. She came quickly, exclaiming loudly even before she entered the hall, "Deirdre! It's about time! I've been worried sick about where you were and how you were making out. If I hadn't thought to call Victoria—"

She stopped short when she caught sight of her daughter, leaning on her crutches, beside a tall, bearded man in jeans. "Good Lord," she whispered, staring at the pair, "what have you brought home this time?"

Deirdre felt a movement by her elbow and knew that Neil was trying not to laugh. For that matter, so was she. In her eyes, Neil looked positively gorgeous, but she knew that her mother was wondering what the cat had dragged in.

"Mother, I'd like you to meet Neil Hersey. Neil, Maria Joyce."

Neil stepped forward and extended a firm hand, which Maria had no choice but to meet. "It's my pleasure, Mrs. Joyce. Deirdre has told me a lot about you."

Maria didn't take the time to wonder about the nature of that telling. She was too concerned about retrieving her hand from what was a far-too-confident grip. She nodded at Neil, but her focus was quickly on Deirdre.

"Victoria finally admitted that you'd gone to Maine. I can't believe you did that, Deirdre. The place is totally isolated, and in your condition—"

"My condition is fine. And Neil was there with me." Before her mother could pounce on that, she rushed on. "Neil is a friend of Victoria's, too. Now he's a friend of mine. Furthermore—" she looked at Neil "—we're going to be married. We wanted you to be the first to know." She took perverse delight in her mother's stunned expression.

For a minute the older woman was speechless. Then, pressing a hand to her heart, she revived.

"You can't be serious."

"We are. Very."

"Deirdre, you don't know this man!" She gave Neil a once-over that was disapproving at best.

"You'd be surprised, mother. Two weeks on an island, with no one else around—you can get to know a man pretty well."

Neil rolled his eyes at her smug tone and quickly sought

to make amends to Maria. "What Deirdre means is that we had a chance to talk more than many people do in months. We shared responsibility for the house and everything to do with our daily lives. We feel that our marriage would be a good one."

Maria, who'd been eyeing him warily during his brief speech, closed her fingers around the single strand of pearls she was wearing with her very proper silk dress. "I think I need a drink," she said, and turned toward the living room.

Deirdre took off after her, with Neil following in her wake. "It's the middle of the afternoon! You don't need a drink in the middle of the afternoon!"

"Oh, yes, I do," came Maria's voice. She was already at the elegant cherrywood bar, fishing ice from a bucket. "When a woman hears that, after years of nagging, her daughter has decided on the spur of the moment to get married—and to a man she thinks she knows, but can't possibly, since she met him a mere two weeks ago—she needs a drink, *regardless* of the time of day!"

Deirdre took a deep breath and sent Neil a helpless glance before lowering herself to a nearby ottoman. "I think you ought to listen to the rest of what I have to tell you before you pass judgment. You may say something you'll later regret."

"I doubt that," Maria stated. She'd poured a healthy dose of bourbon into the glass and was standing stiffly by the bar. "I don't know where I failed with you, Deirdre, but I very definitely have failed. I've tried to instill in you certain values, and you've rejected every one of them. I tried to raise a lady, but you insist on running around in leo-tards—"

"Not leotards, mother. A tank top and running shorts. Leotards cut off my circulation."

She waved that aside. "Whatever. The point's the same. I tried to raise you with a sense of family, but you've insisted in going your own way. I've tried to make you see that you have an obligation to the business, but you won't hear of that. And now, when you've got nothing better to do with your time, instead of giving us a hand, you run off, meet up with a passing...hippie, and decide to marry him."

Neil, who'd been standing quietly at Deirdre's shoulder, felt that he'd heard enough. He didn't mind the insults to him, but they were a smaller part of insults to Deirdre, and he wouldn't have that. "I don't think you understand the situation, Mrs. Joyce," he said with such authority that Maria was forced to listen. "I am not a hippie, nor am I passing. If you've formed an opinion of me based on the way I look, I think you should remember that I've just come from a two-week vacation. The bulk of my life is spent in tailored suits, suits that would hold their own—" he looked at the bench before the grand piano "—with that Dunhill tapestry." He shifted his gaze to the small painting to the left of the bar. "Or that Modigliani." He dropped his eyes to the marble coffee table by Deirdre's knees. "Or that Baccarat vase."

Deirdre looked up at him. "I'm impressed," she mouthed.

He nudged her hip with his knee, shushing her with a frown.

Maria arched a well-shaped brow, but she wasn't about to be fully appeased. "The slickest of con men pick up a wealth of knowledge about fine accessories, Mr. Hersey. What is it you do for a living?"

"I'm a lawyer. I head my own firm in Hartford, specializing in corporate work. I can give you a full list of my credits, starting with law review at Harvard, but I don't think that's necessary. Suffice it to say that in recent years I've done work for Jennings and Lange, KronTech, and the Holder Foundation, as well as the Faulkner Company here in Providence." He was confident that the corporations he'd named would give him solid recommendations. He was equally confident that Maria Joyce had heard of them. She would have also heard of Wittnauer-Douglass. There was always the possibility that if the woman ran a check on him, she'd come across that problem, but it was a risk he'd have to take. And besides, by the time she learned anything, his marriage to Deirdre would be a fait accompli.

Maria dipped her head in reluctant acknowledgment of his credentials. "All right. I'll admit that my judgment may have been premature, but the fact remains that this marriage is very sudden. When was it going to take place?"

Deirdre opened her mouth, but Neil spoke first. "As soon as the law will allow. I believe there's a three-day waiting period once the license has been taken out and the blood tests done. I know a judge here in Providence who might cut even that down."

Maria studied her bourbon, pressing her lips together as she ingested that information. "Is there a rush?" She sent Deirdre a meaningful glance. "I know that there are home tests on the market that can give instant results—"

"I am not pregnant, mother," Deirdre interrupted. "And even if I were, I'd have thought you'd be pleased. You've been harping on having grandchildren since I was old enough to vote."

"Every woman wants grandchildren," Maria countered in self-defense.

"So you've said many times. And here's your chance. I don't know why you're complaining. Even if I *were* pregnant, Neil and I will be married before anyone is the wiser. At most, the baby would be born two weeks early, so to speak, which no one would think twice about. You wouldn't have any cause for embarrassment."

Maria scowled at her daughter. "All right," she said crossly. "Forget a pregnancy." Her annoyance broadened to include Neil. "You'll get married and take off for Hartford, leaving Joyce Enterprises in the lurch yet again. Honestly, Deirdre, is that fair?"

Neil answered. "We won't be living in Hartford. We'll be living here."

Maria arched a skeptical brow. "You'd walk away from that successful law practice?"

"I can practice law anywhere," he returned, tamping down a moment's discomfort. "Providence is as good a place as any."

"The fact is, Mother," Deirdre spoke up, "that we are going to bail you out, after all. Neil has agreed to help me with Joyce Enterprises."

For the second time in a very short period, Maria Joyce was speechless. She looked from Deirdre to Neil and back, then raised her glass and took a bolstering drink. By the time she'd lowered the glass, she'd regained a small measure of her composure, though not enough to keep the glass from shaking in her hand. She set it carefully on the bar.

"That," she began slowly, "is an unexpected turn."

"So is our wedding," Deirdre pointed out, "but it all makes sense. You've been after me for years to help with the business. I've been convinced that I'm not right for the job, but I'm equally convinced that Neil is." And she was. She had no doubts but that Neil could handle Joyce Enterprises. "You've wanted to keep things in the family. Neil will be in the family. What more could Dad have asked for than a son-in-law who could take over where his daughters left off?"

"But he's a lawyer," Maria argued, though more meekly this time. "He's not trained in this type of work."

"Neither am I—nor Sandra, for that matter."

Neil joined in. "I've worked closely with large corporations like Joyce for years, so I'm starting with a definite advantage. And I've had the benefit of seeing how other corporations function, which means that I can take the best of the systems and strategies I've seen and implement them at Joyce." He paused. "I think it could work out well for all of us, Mrs. Joyce. I assure you that I wouldn't be putting my career on the line if I didn't feel that the odds were in my favor."

Maria appeared to have run out of arguments. She raised both brows and nervously fingered her pearls. "I...it looks like you've thought things out."

"We have," Deirdre said.

The older woman shook her head, for the first time seeming almost confused. "I don't know, Deirdre. It's so sudden.... I was hoping that when my daughters got married they'd have big weddings, with lots of flowers and music and people."

Deirdre's shoulders rose with the deep breath she took. "I've never wanted that, Mother. I'll be perfectly happy with something small and private."

Maria looked at them both. "You will be happy? This is what you truly want?" They knew she wasn't referring to the wedding, but to the marriage itself.

Neil's hand met Deirdre's at her shoulder. "It is," Deirdre said softly.

Neil echoed the sentiment. "We'll be happy, Mrs. Joyce. You can take my word for it."

FEELING AS THOUGH they'd overcome their first hurdle, they left Maria, stopped for their marriage license and blood tests, then went to Deirdre's town house. Though Neil agreed that it was on the small side, he was charmed with the way she'd decorated it. Whereas old-world elegance had been the word at her mother's house, here everything was light and airy. The furniture was modern, low and cushiony. One room opened into another with barely a break. There were no Dunhill tapestries, no Modiglianis, no pieces of Baccarat crystal, but a small and carefully chosen selection of work by local artists and artisans.

"I feel very much at home here," Neil said to Deirdre as they lay in bed that night.

Chin propped on his chest, she smiled at him. "I'm glad."

"It's pretty and bright, uncluttered and unpretentious. Like you."

She tugged at his beard. "I think you want something. What is it?"

He smiled back and wrapped an arm around her waist.

"Just that when we find the right home, you do it like this. I don't want to live in a museum or…or in a shrine to a decorator."

Deirdre narrowed her eyes. "Is that what your place is like?"

"A shrine to a decorator? Yes, it is, and I never thought twice about it until now, but I don't want that, Deirdre. There's a sophistication in the simplicity here. That's what I want. Okay?"

"Okay."

"No argument?"

"No argument."

"Good."

THEY HEADED for Hartford the next day. Neil had a long list of things to take care of, the most pressing and difficult of which was informing his associates that he'd be leaving. Both men were talented lawyers, but being young they hadn't yet developed reputations that would attract new business. Neil gave them the choice of joining other firms or taking over his practice themselves. When they opted for the latter, he assured them that he'd do everything he could to help them out, which included drawing up a letter to send his clients, telling them of the change and assuring them that they'd be in good hands if they remained with the firm.

The second order of business was putting his condominium on the market. The real estate agent, who had a list of people waiting for openings in that particular building, was delighted.

"Are you sure you want to sell it?" Deirdre asked timidly.

"Why not? I won't be living here."

"But if you find that you don't like Providence…or that things don't go well…"

He took her firmly by the shoulders. "I will like Providence, and things will go well. I'm making a commitment, Deirdre. There's no point in doing it halfway."

She didn't argue further, particularly since his confidence buoyed her. So they returned to Providence and went house hunting. Once again luck was on their side. They found a charming colonial on the outskirts of the city, not far from Deirdre's mother's house ironically, but in a younger neighborhood. The property encompassed three acres of land, with a wealth of trees and lush shrubbery, and though the house needed work, the previous owners had vacated several weeks before, and the work could begin immediately.

Three days after they arrived back from Maine, Deirdre and Neil were married in the church Deirdre had attended as a child. Her mother had made the arrangements—Deirdre felt it was as good a consolation prize as any—and there were more people, more flowers, more food than Deirdre might have chosen herself. But she was too happy that day to mind anything.

Neil looked breathtaking in his dark suit, white shirt, striped tie and cordovans. He'd had his beard professionally trimmed, along with his hair, and she decided that he looked far more like a successful businessman than a conservative corporate lawyer.

Deirdre, who'd had a walking cast put on to replace the original, wore a long white dress, the simplicity of which was a perfect foil for her natural good looks. She'd applied a minimum of makeup—touches each of blusher, mascara, eyeliner and shadow—and though never one to lean heavily toward jewelry, she'd taken pride in wearing the pearl earrings and matching necklace that her father had given her for her twenty-first birthday.

The ceremony was short and sweet, and Deirdre was all smiles as she circulated through the luncheon reception on the arm of her new husband. He'd given her a stunning gold wedding band, as simple as her gown, with a tracing of diamond chips forming a central circle, but she would have been happy with something from the five-and-dime, as long as it told her they were married. Though he still hadn't said the words, she was sure she'd seen love in his eyes throughout that day, and it was the proverbial frosting on the cake.

THE NEXT FEW WEEKS were hectic ones. Neil threw himself fully into Joyce Enterprises, determined to familiarize himself with every aspect of the business. Sandra readily accepted him; not only was she relieved to have the brunt of the load taken from her shoulders, but Deirdre suspected that she was enthralled by Neil. And rightly so. He exuded confidence and was charming not only to Sandra, but to the uncles, as well. If he came home exhausted at night, Deirdre was more than willing to understand. She was also more than willing to make a challenge out of reviving him, which she did with notable success.

He kept her abreast with what was happening at work, sharing his observations, discussing his plans. And he was even eager to hear about the progress at the house, the redecorating of which she was orchestrating with an enthusiasm that surprised her. She'd never seen herself as a decorator. When she'd moved into her town house she'd simply papered and carpeted to suit herself. Knowing that Neil approved of her taste was a major stimulant—that and knowing the house she now decorated was for the two of them.

By the time they moved in three weeks after the wedding, Deirdre was reeling with confidence. A week later her cast came off, and if that confidence faltered when she experienced a fair amount of pain, Neil was the one to offer encouragement. He personally helped her with the exercises the doctor had outlined, and when those exercise sessions ended more often than not in lovemaking, Deirdre wasn't about to complain. In lieu of verbally professing their love for each other, this physical bonding was crucial to her.

Deirdre put off returning to work, knowing that her leg wasn't ready. Strangely, she didn't miss it as much as she'd thought she would, but, then, between setting up the house and joining Neil for those social engagements he'd warned her would be inevitable, she had little time to miss much of anything.

Strangely, she didn't mind the social engagements, either. But, then, she was with Neil. He never failed to compliment her on the way she looked; as a result, she found that dressing up wasn't as odious as it had been in the past. Moreover, he was the perfect host, drawing her into conversations with their guests such that she experienced far less pain on that score than she'd anticipated.

Neil was exceedingly satisfied with the way things had worked out. Deirdre was as wonderful a wife as she'd been a lover, and as they'd left most of the bickering behind in Maine, he found her to be a thoroughly amiable companion. The only thing that bothered him from time to time was his awareness of the agreement they'd struck. He wanted to think that they were together out of love, not simply taking advantage of a mutually beneficial arrangement. Since the latter was what had brought about this marriage, he went through passing periods of doubt regarding Deirdre's feelings for him.

He had no such self-doubt when it came to Joyce Enterprises. The work was interesting and challenging, and he seemed to have a natural affinity for it. As he'd intended, he brought in a highly experienced executive from a Midwest corporation. Together they mapped out a strategy for keeping Joyce Enterprises not only running smoothly but growing, as well. Between them, they provided the vision that had been lacking since Deirdre's father's death.

Deirdre was thrilled. Her faith in Neil had been justified.

Maria Joyce was likewise pleased, though she made sure Deirdre knew of the risks involved. "I checked up on Neil," she informed her daughter when the two were having lunch at a downtown restaurant one day. "Neither of you was fully honest with me about his past."

Deirdre, who'd been savoring her victory, paused. "We were honest."

"You didn't tell me about Wittnauer-Douglass."

"There wasn't anything to tell. He had a bad experience with one client and was forced to terminate that particular relationship, but it was an isolated incident. He did the same kind of quality work for Wittnauer-Douglass that he did for the rest of his clients."

"According to my friend Bess Hamilton, whose husband is on the board at Wittnauer-Douglass, Neil took part in some unethical dealings."

Deirdre's anger was quick to rise. "If Bess Hamilton's husband was on the board, *he* was involved in the unethical dealings. Neil resigned because he wouldn't have anything to do with it!"

"That wasn't what Bess said."

"And who do you choose to believe, your friend or your son-in-law?"

Maria's gaze didn't waver. "I don't have much choice, do I? Neil is firmly entrenched in the running of our business—"

"And he's doing an excellent job. You can't deny it."

"But I have to wonder what his motives are. From what Bess said, he was washed out in Hartford."

"He wasn't *washed out*. His two associates are doing fantastically well with the business he left them, and if it hadn't been for his own urgings, those clients would have left in a minute and gone elsewhere. They had faith in Neil, which is why they followed his recommendation and stayed with the firm."

Maria wasn't about to be fully convinced. "Still, he got a good thing going for him when he married you. It was a shrewd move."

"What are you trying to say, Mother?" Deirdre asked through gritted teeth.

"Just that I think you ought to be careful. I think we all ought to be careful. He may be trying to take over Joyce Enterprises and sweep it away from us."

"Neil wouldn't do that."

"How do you know?"

"Because I'm *married* to him. Because I *know* him."

"You love him, and love sometimes clouds people's judgment."

"Not in this case. I trust him." She also knew of the papers she'd signed before she and Neil had been married, but she didn't feel that was any of her mother's business. "And I'd think that if you can't find it in yourself to trust him, as well, the least you can do is appreciate him. He's taken a load off all our backs, and what he's doing with Joyce Enterprises would have made Dad proud."

Maria had nothing to say on that score, so she changed the subject. Her words, however, lingered for a long time in Deirdre's mind.

Deirdre had meant what she'd said—that she trusted Neil. There were times, though, when she wondered about the energy he was pouring into the business. Rarely did a night pass when he didn't bring a project of some form home from the office with him. The enthusiasm he had for his work seemed boundless....

Perhaps, Deirdre mused, she was simply jealous. She recalled the days they'd spent in Maine, and there were times when she wished for them again. Neil had been totally devoted to her there; here she had to share him with a very demanding job. She recalled his saying that he'd never married before because the law was such a demanding mistress. At the time she'd argued that the right woman had simply never come along.

Now she wondered if *she* was the right woman, and let her insecurities suggest that she might not be. Yes, Neil was warm and affectionate. Yes, he put aside his work when she came to talk with him. Yes, he was patient with her frustration when her leg seemed to take inordinately long in healing.

But he went off to work quite happily each morning. And he never said that he loved her.

Then again, she realized, maybe her unease was reflec-

tive of nothing more than the changes her life had under-
gone in a few short months. The work on the house was
now finished. It was furnished to their mutual satisfaction
in the style of understated sophistication that Deirdre had
never before thought of as a style; it was merely the way
she wanted to live. She wasn't one to spend hours simply
looking at the finished product or wandering from one
room to another, and the demands Neil made on her for
evening engagements weren't enough to occupy her time.

As time passed she grew restless.

She started going to the health club. Though she
probably could have taught, she didn't want to. She felt
tired. Her leg, though better, still bothered her. She began
to wonder whether her compulsion to teach had been
directly tied to her need to escape Joyce Enterprises. Since
that need was no longer there the compulsion had faded.

She sat at home for long hours, missing Neil, wondering what to do with herself. She lunched with friends, but
that brought no lasting relief from her malaise. She took
part in the planning of a ten-kilometer charity run, but that
occupied far too little of her time.

Finally, on impulse one day, she flew down to meet
Victoria for lunch. They hadn't seen each other since the
wedding, which Victoria had proudly and delightedly
attended, and Deirdre was counting on her friend to bolster
her morale.

"How long have you know Neil?" Deirdre asked,
broaching the topic as soon as the waiter had left with their
order.

"Three years," Victoria answered, cocking her head to
the side. "Why do you ask?"

"Did you know him well during that time?"

"We didn't see each other often, but if I were to judge
from the quality of the time we spent together, I'd say we
were close." She pursed her lips. "Something's up, Dee.
Spill it."

Deirdre shrugged, absently playing with the moisture

on the outside of her water glass. "I don't know. It's just that everything between us happened so fast. I sometimes wonder if we rushed things."

"You have doubts about Neil?"

"No. Well, maybe once in a while. My mother said something a few weeks ago that bothered me, something about Neil—"

"Your mother," Victoria scoffed. "Your mother is a good friend of mine, but that doesn't mean I can't see her faults. She's one of those people who are never satisfied. You take her too seriously, Dee. I've told you that before."

"I know. But I can't help hearing her little 'words of wisdom.'"

"You may have to hear them. You don't have to heed them."

"But it's like they niggle in the back of my mind and they refuse to go away." She raised beseeching eyes to her friend. "Victoria, do you think Neil is ambitious?"

"I should hope so. No one is successful if he isn't ambitious."

"Ruthlessly so? Would you call Neil ruthlessly ambitious?"

Victoria didn't have to think about that. "No. Unequivocably. Neil is not a ruthless person. If anything, the opposite is true. If he had a little more of the bastard in him, he might not have had that problem with Wittnauer-Douglass."

"If he hadn't had that," Deirdre pointed out with a lopsided grin, "he'd never have run off to Maine and I'd never have met him, so I can't be sorry about Wittnauer-Douglass." Her grin faded. "It's just that my mother learned about all that, and she suggested that Neil might be out for himself when it comes to Joyce Enterprises."

"Is that what you think?"

"No. At least, I want to think that it isn't so. But he's taken to his work with such…such *glee*, and there are times when I wish he showered more of that glee on me."

"You can't have it both ways, Dee. If he's to turn Joyce Enterprises around, he's going to have to put in the hours. Take my word for it, though. Neil Hersey has nothing but the most upstanding intentions when it comes to your business. I don't think there's a selfish bone in that man's body. Did he ever tell you what he did for my niece?"

Deirdre frowned. "No. He never mentioned your niece."

"He wouldn't. That's his way."

"Well? What did he do?"

"A while ago, my niece got involved in a criminal matter. The girl was only nineteen at the time, and her mother—my sister—was frantic. They live in a small town in western Connecticut and aren't very well off, and they didn't know where to turn for help. I called Neil, knowing that criminal law wasn't his specialty but hoping that he'd be able to refer us to a capable person. Not only did he do that, but he personally involved himself in the case, and then, when the other lawyer would have given him a referral fee, he insisted that the man deduct it from the fee he charged my sister—a fee, mind you, that was on the low side, anyway, considering that my niece got away with nothing but probation. Now—" she tipped up her chin "—if Neil were only out for himself, would he have done all that for my niece?"

Deirdre felt a rush of pride in her husband. "No. And I know that he's always done charity work. It's just that the situation with us is so different. There's so much at stake for him now."

"I doubt he'd consider anything more important than your love."

Deirdre held her breath.

"Dee? You do love him, don't you?"

"Oh, yes!"

"But…?"

"I'm not sure he loves me."

"Are you kidding?"

Deirdre responded defensively. "No, I'm not kidding.

He's never told me he loved me. Our marriage was… was…expedient, and that was his own word."

Victoria pressed a calming hand on her arm. "Look, sweetheart, I know enough about each of your situations to realize that your getting married solved certain problems for you both. But I saw Neil at your wedding, and if that man wasn't in love, I'll turn in my matchmaker badge." She paused. "What does he say when you tell him that you love him?"

Deirdre didn't have to answer. Guilt was written all over her face.

"My Lord, Dee. Why not? You're no wilting pansy!"

"But I don't want to pressure him. Worse, I don't want to say it and not have him say it back. And anyway, when he's home there's so much else we talk about, and then we don't want to talk at all…."

Victoria shot her a knowing grin. "That's more like it." She raised her eyes when the waiter approached with their plates, and waited until he'd deposited the meal and gone. "So, Neil is very busy with work, and you're feeling lonesome."

"Yes."

"Have you told him that?"

"No."

Victoria cast pleading eyes toward the ornate ceiling high overhead. "I know I shouldn't ask this, but why not?"

"Because in the first place, I don't want to sound like a complainer. When we first got to Maine, that was all I did—bitch at him, and everything else in sight. Then our relationship gelled, and I stopped griping. I liked myself a lot more then. I don't want to go back to that other way." She paused for an exaggerated breath. "And in the second place, there's nothing he can do about it."

"He can reassure you, maybe help find something to keep you busy."

Deirdre shook her head sadly. "I don't know, Victoria. I look at you and I'm envious. When you finish one thing you start another. I used to have a million and one things to do with my day, but now I can't seem to find anything that tempts me."

"You want to be with Neil. Everything else is…blah. So why don't you work part-time at the office?"

"That'd be tantamount to surrender. I swore I'd never work there."

"And you're so rigid that you can't reconsider, particularly knowing that working there now would be out of choice, rather than need?"

Deirdre didn't respond immediately; she sat absently nudging her cold salmon with a fork. "Put that way, I sound pretty childish."

"If the shoe fits…"

"I don't know, Victoria. I'm not sure that's what I want, either."

"Do me a favor, Dee, and talk with Neil? He's a patient man. Really, he is. And he's resourceful. Most important, he's your husband. He wants you to be happy." She speared a firm green bean and held it over her plate. "Will you?"

"I'll try."

"Don't try. *Do* it!"

DEIRDRE WOULD HAVE done it that night, had Neil not offered her a solution before she'd been able to utter a word. He'd come home particularly tired, and they were relaxing in the living room, sharing a glass of wine.

"I need your help, Deirdre," he announced in a business-like tone.

"There's a problem at the office?"

He nodded. "In personnel. Art Brickner, our man there, is giving us flack about hiring people to fill in certain gaps. He wanted to bring people up from the ranks, and I agree with him in theory, except that in several of these cases there simply is no one to bring up from the ranks. Most of his resistance is to new blood, and I fall prominently in that category. Art was one of your father's original men."

"I know… But how can I help?"

"Work with him. Ease him through the transition. He's a good man—"

"He's stodgy."

Neil chuckled. "Yes, he's stodgy, but his instincts are good, and your presence in his office might just remind him that, contrary to what he fears, all is not going down the tubes at Joyce Enterprises."

"Oh, Neil…what do I know about personnel?"

"You have common sense, and a feel for the company. Art will take care of the mechanics, while you handle the, uh, the spiritual end. What do you think?"

"I think," she said, studying the features she adored so much, "that you look exhausted. You're working too hard, Neil."

Loosening his necktie, he sank deeper into the sofa. "You're right. But it has to be done." His eyes narrowed. "You look exhausted, too. Was it running down to New York to have lunch with Victoria?"

"Uh-uh. I'm tired from having too much time on my hands."

"Then helping Art could be just the thing."

"Neil—"

"You wouldn't have to work full-time, only twenty hours a week or so."

"But I—"

"You could wear whatever you wanted, since you wouldn't be in the limelight."

"But what—"

"I'd even pay you." He grinned broadly. "How does that sound?"

She sighed, stared at him in exasperation for a minute, then took his silent offer and settled under the arm he held out. "When you smile at me like that, Neil Hersey, I'm a goner. But you know that, don't you, which is why you do it! I'm a sucker. That's all. A real sucker."

"Then you will work?"

"Yes, I will work."

"And you'll tell me if it turns out to be too much?"

"It won't turn out to be too much. I'm young. I'm full of energy. I'm brimming with enthusiasm…."

BUT IT DID TURN OUT to be too much—or rather, it put a strain on Deirdre that she hadn't expected. She worked from nine to two every day, and was positively drained. After a week of mornings when she couldn't seem to get going, she began coming in at ten. Even then she was dragging by the time Neil arrived home at night.

Witnessing her struggle, Neil grew more and more tense. He waited for her to come to him, to broach the subject, but she didn't. Finally, after two weeks of help-lessness, he took matters into his own hands.

Arriving home early from work, he found Deirdre curled beneath an afghan on their king-size bed, sound asleep. He sat on the bed beside her, leaned down and kissed her cheek.

Her lashes fluttered, then rose. "Neil!" she whispered, pushing herself up. "I'm sorry. I never dreamed you'd be home this early!"

He pulled a bouquet of flowers—actually, three roses and an assortment of greens—from behind him. "For you."

Groggy still, she looked from him to the roses and back, smiling at last. "They're lovely. Any special occasion?"

"Mmm-hmm. Today's the day we admit that you're pregnant."

Deirdre's smile vanished, as did what little color had been on her cheeks. She lay back on the bed, closed her eyes and spoke in a very small voice. "How did you guess?"

Neil was stricken by the unhappiness he saw on Deirdre's face. He'd assumed that she'd been afraid to tell him—though he didn't know why—but apparently there was more than fear involved. He answered her quietly. "We've been married for nearly three months, and during that time you haven't had a single period."

"I'm an athlete," she pointed out. "That can do strange things to a woman's system."

"You're constantly tired. Even the slightest activity exhausts you."

"It's everything that's happened in the past few months. I'm on emotional overload."

"And the greater fullness of your breasts?" he asked, his voice deep and low. "And the slight thickening of your waist? Things that nobody else sees, I do. Come on, Deirdre. Let's face the facts. You're pregnant. Is it so awful?"

She focused tired eyes on him. "I feel so lousy right now that, yes, it's awful."

"Then you agree that it's true?"

"It's true."

"But you haven't been to a doctor."

"No."

"Why, Deirdre? Don't you want to have a baby?"

"I do!" she cried, then lowered her voice. "It's just that, on top of everything else, it's so sudden…."

"We weren't using any birth control. You had to know there was a possibility this would happen."

"How did you know I wasn't using birth control?" she countered, being contrary.

"Deirdre, I was with you constantly. I would have known."

"Not if I'd had an IUD."

"But you didn't have one, and you're pregnant now!"

"Thanks to you. If you knew I wasn't using anything, why didn't *you* use something?"

"Deirdre, I do not pack prophylactics as a matter of habit. The last thing I expected when I went up to Maine was that I'd be with a woman."

"So neither of us was prepared, and both of us knew it, and we did nothing, and look what happened."

"I don't think it's such a horrible situation, Deirdre."

"You don't?"

"Of course not."

"You don't feel that it's just another burden on your shoulders?"

"Have I ever talked of burdens?"

"No. But they're there."

"This one's a nice one. I told you I wanted children."

"'Someday,' you said."

"Then 'someday' is now. And the more I think about it, the happier I am." Scooping her up, he tucked her against him. "I know you're not feeling great, Deirdre, but once you see a doctor and he gives you vitamins, and once you pass the initial few months, you'll feel better."

To Deirdre's dismay, she began to cry. Her fingers closed around the lapel of his suit jacket, and she buried her face in his shirt.

"I'll be…be fat."

"You'll be beautiful."

"You'll…you'll be stuck with me."

"I'm not complaining."

"You're being so…kind."

"You're being such a ninny." He hugged her, trying his best to absorb whatever pain she was feeling. He knew she'd been through a lot, and that having a baby at a later time would probably have been better for her, but he wasn't sorry. It bound her all the closer to him.

Weeping softly, Deirdre was thinking similar thoughts. Oh, yes, she wanted the baby, but because it was Neil's, more than for any other reason. When she thought of it, having his baby made the tie between them even more permanent than marriage. It was both a reassuring and a frightening thought, because if something went wrong and Neil decided he'd had enough, a wholly innocent child would be affected.

The scent of roses by her nose interrupted her sniffles. She opened her eyes and saw Neil touch each bloom.

"One for you, one for me, one for baby. A nice bunch, don't you think?"

His sweetness brought a helpless smile to Deirdre's wet face. "A very nice bunch."

Later, she told herself, she'd watch for the thorns. For now, she was too tired to do anything but relax in Neil's arms.

CHAPTER NINE

ONCE DEIRDRE accepted the fact of her pregnancy, she was better able to cope. She saw a doctor and began a regimen of vitamins that compensated for what the baby demanded of her body. She continued working with Art Brickner, adjusting her hours to accommodate her need for sleep.

Neil seemed legitimately pleased about the baby, and that relieved her most of all. In turn, she made up her mind to do everything in her power to make their marriage work.

When she was at the office, she dressed accordingly, intent on making Neil proud. When she was at home she planned their meals and coordinated the various cleaning efforts so that the house was always immaculate should Neil decide to bring people home at the last minute. At Neil's insistence, though, they'd hired a maid to help. She resumed her visits to the health club—the doctor had okayed that—and though she didn't teach, she took part in classes. She swam. She diligently kept herself in shape—as much as a woman with a slowly growing belly could.

And she never argued with Neil. She didn't complain when he was delayed for several hours at the office and dinner was held up. She didn't say a word when he had to go away on a business trip. She didn't nag him to take time off from work to play tennis with her. She graciously attended cocktail parties and dinners, and when she and Neil were finally alone at night, she did her very best to satisfy him, both physically and emotionally.

But because she refused to give him any cause for displeasure, the frustration that had built within her had nowhere to go. She wished he didn't work so hard, but she didn't say so. She yearned for time alone with him—even their weekends revolved around business demands—but she didn't say so. She ached, positively ached to hear him say that he loved her, but she didn't say so, and he didn't tell her what she wanted to hear. She felt as if she were walking a tightrope.

The tightrope began to fray when her mother dropped in one morning. Deirdre was getting ready to leave for work.

"Have you heard his latest scheme?" Maria asked with an arrogance Deirdre found all too familiar. They were standing in the front hall; Deirdre knew enough not to invite her mother to sit, or she'd be in for an even longer siege.

"That depends on which scheme it is," Deirdre countered with confidence. "Neil's had a lot of them lately, and they're all very promising."

"This one isn't."

"Which one?"

"He's bidding on a government contract for the electronics division."

Deirdre had known that. "Is there a problem?" she asked blandly.

"We've never bid for government contracts. We've always devoted ourselves to the private sector."

"That doesn't mean we can't change now, if doing so will be good for the company."

"But will it? That's the question. Is Neil bidding for that contract because it will be good for the company or for him?"

"Aren't they one and the same?" Deirdre asked, ignoring her mother's barely veiled reference to the earlier accusation she'd made.

"Not by a long shot. You may not know it, but one of the other bidders is Wittnauer-Douglass."

Deirdre hadn't known it. She ignored the frisson of anxiety that shivered through her. "I'm sure there are many other bidders—"

"None Neil holds a grudge against."

"Neil doesn't hold a grudge against Wittnauer-Douglass," Deirdre insisted. "What happened there is done. He is very successful in what he's doing now. I think you're way off base."

"You've thought that from the start, when I told you to be careful, but this is the evidence I need."

"Evidence? What evidence?"

"Your husband is involving Joyce Enterprises in something solely for the sake of avenging himself. He would never be bidding for a government contract if it weren't for that. Think about it. Isn't it awfully suspicious that the first time we do anything of this sort, a major competitor is the very one Neil has a gripe against?"

Deirdre set her purse down on the table. "Do you know the details, Mother? Who submitted a bid first, Wittnauer-Douglass or Joyce Enterprises?"

Maria fumbled with the collar of her sable coat. "I don't know that. How could I possibly know that!"

"If it's evidence you're looking for, that'd be a place to start. If Neil submitted his bid first, without ever knowing that Wittnauer-Douglass would be a competitor, his innocence would be obvious."

"The rest of the evidence is against him."

Deirdre was losing her patience. "What evidence?"

"Deirdre," her mother said, sighing. "Think. Neil met you at a time when he needed a change of location and occupation."

"He did not need—"

"He latched onto what you had to offer, married you as quickly as possible and set about implementing his plans."

"The plans he implemented were for the resurgence of Joyce Enterprises, and he's done a remarkable job! He's done us a favor!"

"He's done himself a favor. Look at it objectively. He's at the helm of a successful corporation. He's become so well respected in the community that the two of you are in demand at all the parties that matter—"

"If you had any sense of appreciation, Mother, you'd spend your time tallying all he's done for *you*. He's married the more undesirable of your two daughters and is about to give you a grandchild. He's taken responsibility for the family business—and even gotten *me* involved in it. What more do you want?"

"I want Joyce Enterprises to remain in the black."

"And you think that bidding on a government contract will prevent that?" Deirdre asked in disbelief. "He's just bidding."

"If he wants that contract badly enough, he'll bid low enough to undercut Wittnauer-Douglass, and if he does that, he could jeopardize our financial status."

"And if he does that," Deirdre pointed out angrily, "he'll be jeopardizing the very position he's built for himself. It doesn't make sense, Mother. You're being illogical."

"It's a risk—his bidding for that contract."

"There's always a risk if the prize is worth anything. If Neil only stuck with what was safe, the business would be at a standstill."

"He's being rash. I think you should talk with him."

Deirdre had had enough. "I don't have to listen to this." She snatched up her purse, took her coat from the nearby chair and headed for the door. "You can stay if you like. I have to get to work."

Deirdre might have been fine had the conversation she'd had with her mother been the only one of its kind. But several days later, Art Brickner raised the issue, complaining that Neil had spoken with him about hiring an enlarged cadre of workers if the government contract came through. Art questioned both the logistics and the wisdom of what Neil proposed, and all Deirdre could do was to support Neil and insist that his plan was sound.

Several days after that, she was approached by one of the long-standing vice presidents of the company, who, too, had doubts as to the direction in which Joyce was headed. Again Deirdre expressed her support for Neil, sensing that what she was hearing was simply a resistance to change, but she grew increasingly uncomfortable.

She didn't tell Neil about any of the three discussions. She didn't want to anger him by suggesting that she had doubts, when, in fact, she had no qualms about the viability of winning and working through a government contract. What bothered her was the possibility that his motives weren't entirely pure, that, as her mother had suggested, he was being driven by a desire for revenge. She tried to ignore such thoughts, but they wouldn't leave her.

At the root of the matter were the doubts she had regarding their relationship. Oh, they were close. They said all the right things, did all the right things. To the outside world—and to themselves, on one level—they were a loving couple. If she recalled the original reasons for their marriage, though, as she did with increasing frequency, she couldn't help but question what it was that drove Neil. His questionable motives bothered her far more than the prospect of any contract, government or otherwise.

So she walked the tightrope. On one end was what she wanted; on the other what she thought Neil wanted. The rope frayed. It finally snapped when he arrived home unexpectedly one afternoon. She was instantly pleased, delighted by the thought of spending stolen time with him. The sight of him—ruggedly handsome, with his beard offsetting his more formal suit—never failed to excite her, as did the inevitable kiss with which he greeted her.

Threading his arm through hers, he led her into the den. When he held her back, though, the look of tension on his face told her something was amiss.

"I need a favor, Deirdre. I have to run to Washington for a meeting tonight. Do you think you could handle the dinner party on your own?"

They'd long ago invited three couples to join them at a restaurant in town. Deirdre knew the couples. They weren't her favorite people.

Her face fell. "Oh, Neil…do you have to go?"

"I do. It's important." He felt like a heel, but there was no way around it.

"But so sudden. You were planning to go down for the presentation tomorrow morning, anyway. Can't you have this meeting then?"

"Not if I want the presentation to be the best it can be."

"It will be. You've been working on it for weeks."

"I want that contract," he stated, then coaxed her more gently. "Come on. You can handle things at the restaurant."

"You know how I hate dinners like that."

"I know that you manage them beautifully." She'd proved it in the past weeks, and he'd been proud of her.

"With you by my side. But you won't be, which makes the whole thing that much more distasteful."

"I'm asking for your help. I can't be two places at once."

Annoyances, past and present, rose within her. She left his side, grabbed a throw pillow from the sofa and began to fluff it with a vengeance. "And you choose to be in Washington. If you wanted to be here, you could send someone else to Washington. Why can't Ben go?" Ben Tillotson was the executive Neil had brought in from the Midwest.

"Ben's daughter is visiting from Seattle. He feels badly enough that he has to leave her tomorrow."

"Well, what about me? You have to leave me tomorrow, too." She dropped the first pillow and started on another.

"It's my responsibility before it's Ben's."

"Then if Ben can't make it, why don't you let Thor go?" Thor VanNess headed the electronics division. In Deirdre's mind, he'd be the perfect one to attend the meeting.

"Thor is fantastic at what he does, but he is not a diplomat, and the meeting tonight is going to involve a fair share of diplomacy."

"And you're the only diplomat at Joyce?"

Her sarcasm was a sharp prod, poking holes in Neil's patience. "Deirdre," he said, sighing, "you're making too much out of a single meeting. If you want, I can have my secretary call and cancel the dinner party, but I'd hoped that wouldn't be necessary. Believe me, I've looked for other outs. I've tried to think of someone else who can get the job done tonight in Washington, but there is no one else. It's *my responsibility*."

She tossed the second pillow on the sofa and leaned forward to straighten a small watercolor that hung on the wall. "Then you take too much on your own shoulders. I was under the assumption that delegation was critical to the smooth functioning of a corporation this size." She lowered her voice in an attempt to curb her temper. Yes, she was making too much out of a single meeting, but it had become a matter of principle. She faced him head-on. "Send someone else. Anyone else."

"I can't, Deirdre. It's as simple as that."

"No, it's not," she declared, unable to hold it in any longer. "It's not simple at all. You put your work before every other thing in our lives, which shows where *your* priorities lie."

Neil bowed his head and rubbed the back of his neck. "You're being unfair," he said quietly.

"Unfair? Or selfish? Well, maybe it's about time!" She stalked to the large ship's clock that hung on another wall, took a tool from its side, opened it and angrily began to wind it.

"Take it easy, babe. You're making a mountain out of—"

"I am not!"

"You're getting upset." His gaze fell to the tiny swell just visible in profile beneath her oversized sweater. "It's not good for you *or* the baby."

She turned to glare at him. "That's where you're wrong. It's the *best* thing for me, and therefore for the baby, because I can't pretend anymore. I'm being torn apart inside."

Neil stiffened. "What are you talking about?"

"I can't stand this, Neil. I've tried to be the perfect wife for you. I've done all the things I swore I'd never do, and I've done them without argument because I wanted to please you. I wanted to make this marriage work."

"I thought it was working. Do you mean to tell me you were faking it all?"

She scrunched up her face in frustration. "I wasn't faking it. On one level the marriage does work. But there has to be more. There has to be total communication. You discuss the business with me, but I don't know what you're really thinking or feeling. There are times when I feel totally left out of what's happening."

"You could ask more."

"You could offer more."

"Damn it, Deirdre, how do I know what you want if you don't ask?"

"Don't you know me well enough to know what I want without my having to ask?"

"No!" he exploded, angry now himself. "I thought you wanted me to make a go of your damned business, but it looks like I was wrong. I've been busting my ass in the office racking my brain, dipping into resources I didn't know I had, looking for one way, then another to make Joyce Enterprises stronger."

For an instant she was taken back. "I thought you enjoyed the work."

"I do enjoy the work, but that's because I've been successful. I've felt good knowing that I was carrying out my part of the bargain, knowing that I had the business moving again. Every bit of my satisfaction relates directly or indirectly to you."

Deirdre eyed him skeptically. "Are you sure? Isn't there a little satisfaction that relates solely to you?"

"I suppose," he answered, rubbing his bearded cheek.

"If I stand back and look at what I've been able to do in a few short months, yes, I'm proud of myself. I'm a lawyer by training, not a businessman, yet I've taken on entrepreneurial tasks that two, four, six years ago I'd never have dared tackle."

"But you have now. Why?"

Neil was still for a moment, his tone almost puzzled when he spoke. "It was part of the agreement we made."

"No. Go back further." Her hand tightened around the clock tool. "Why did we make that agreement?"

"Because you needed me and I needed you."

"That's right. And I guess it's one of the things that's been eating at me. You needed a means of reestablishing yourself after what happened in Hartford. You came in here, took over the reins, and you've done more with this company than anyone else—including my father—has done in years. You've done everything I expected, and more. Why, Neil? Why so much?"

"That's an absurd question," he snapped. "If there are things to be done, I believe in doing them. Yes, I could have stopped thinking a while ago, and Joyce Enterprises still would have been in far better shape than it had been. But I've seen potential in the company. I'm trying to realize it."

Replacing the clock tool, Deirdre moved to a plant hanging by the window and began to pick dried leaves from it. "Or are you trying to prove to Wittnauer-Douglass that you can beat them at their own game?"

"What?" He tipped his head and narrowed one eye. "What are you talking about?"

"This government contract. You've told me all about your end of it, and I've been in favor of it. What you didn't tell me was that Wittnauer-Douglass is bidding for the same contract." She crushed the dried leaves in her hand. "My *mother* had to tell me that, and at the same time she leveled a pretty harsh accusation."

"Your mother's leveled accusations before, and they've proved unfounded." He was staring hard at Deirdre. When she reached toward the plant again, he bellowed, "Leave the damn plant alone, Deirdre. I want your full attention right now."

Slowly she turned to face him, but she didn't say a word, because his expression was suddenly one of fury, reminiscent of their first days in Maine, but worse.

His lips were thinned; tension radiated from the bridge of his nose. "You think that I'm going for this contract to get even with Wittnauer-Douglass!" he spat, his eyes widening. "You actually think that I'm out for revenge, that everything I've done since we've been married has been with this in mind! I don't believe you, Deirdre! Where have you *been* all these weeks?"

She grew defensive. "I didn't say I thought that. I said my mother thought that."

"But you're raising it with me now, which means that you have your own doubts."

"Yes, I have my doubts! I've stood behind you one hundred percent, defending you before my mother, before Art Brickner, before others of my father's people who've approached me with questions. I've been as strong an advocate as I can possibly be, but after a while all I can think of is that our marriage was *expedient*." She covered her face with one rigid hand and spoke into her palm. "I hate that word. God, do I hate that word."

"Then why do you use it?" he yelled back.

She dropped her hand. "Because *you* used it, and it's stuck in my mind like glue, and I try to shake it off, but it won't let go! We married for the wrong reasons, Neil, and it's about time we faced it. I can't go on this way. It's driving me nuts!"

Neil thrust a hand through his hair. "Driving *you* nuts! Do you think it's any different for me? I've tried my best to make things work, and I thought they were working. Now I find out that every one of my efforts has been in vain. I thought you trusted me, but maybe all you wanted was someone to bail you out. Now that I've done that, I'm expendable. Is that it?"

"No! I never said that!"

"Then what are you saying? What in the hell do you want?"

She was shaking—in anger, in frustration, in heartache. Clenching her fists by her sides, she cried, "I want it *all*! I don't want an expedient marriage! I never did! I want *love*, Neil! Damn it, *I want the real thing*!"

Neil was far from steady himself. Equal parts of tension, fear and anguish thrummed through his body, clouding his mind, robbing him of the thoughts, much less the words to fight her. Feeling more impotent than he'd ever felt in his life, he turned and stormed from the room.

Deirdre wrapped her arms around her middle and tried to control the wild hammering of her heart. She heard the front door slam, then, moments later, the angry rev of the LeBaron. It had long since faded into silence before she began to move in small, dazed steps, working her way slowly toward her favorite room, the loft above the garage.

Late-afternoon sun filtered in across the polished wood floor, splashing on bare stucco walls with a cheeriness that eluded her at the moment. Her cassette player and a pile of tapes lay in one corner. She'd often used the room for exercise, though what she'd really hoped was that one day it would be a playroom for their children.

Now all that seemed in doubt.

Carefully easing herself down onto the cushioned sill of the arched window, she tucked her knees up, pressed her forehead to them and began to cry.

Neil didn't love her. If he had, he'd have said so. She'd given him the opening; she'd told him what she wanted. And he'd left her. He didn't love her.

And their future? A big, fat question mark. In some respects they were back where they'd started when they'd first arrived on Victoria's island.

What had she wanted, really wanted then? Love. She hadn't realized it at the time, but in the weeks since, she realized that everything else would have fallen into place

if she'd found love. She could teach, or not. She could
work at Joyce Enterprises, or not. The one thing that held
meaning was love.

NEIL DROVE AROUND for hours. He stopped at a pay phone
to call the office, but he had no desire to show up there.
He had no desire to go to Washington. He had no desire
to bid for, much less win, that government contract he'd
sought. He had no desire to do anything…but return to
Deirdre.

That was the one thing that became eminently clear
with the miles he put on his odometer. Deirdre was all that
mattered in his life.

He relived their meeting in Maine, their arguments,
their eventual coming to terms with each other. He
reviewed the months they'd been married and all that had
happened, both personally and professionally, during that
time. But mostly he replayed the scene he'd had with
Deirdre that day. He heard her words, pondered them,
analyzed them.

And it occurred to him that he was possibly on the
verge of making the biggest mistake of his life.

Stopping the car in the middle of the street, he ignored
the honking of horns, made a U-turn and mentally mapped
the fastest route back to the house. When he arrived, it was
nearly ten o'clock. The house was every bit as dark as the
night was, and for a minute he feared he was too late.
Then his headlights illumined Deirdre's car, parked as unobtrusively as she'd left it beneath the huge maple tree.
Pulling up behind it, he jumped from his own and ran
inside.

"Deirdre?" he called, flipping lights on in each of the
ground floor rooms. "Deirdre!" There was no anger in his
voice, simply worry. With the irrational fear of a man in
love, he conjured up every one of the dreadful things that
might have happened to her during his absence. She was
upset. She was pregnant. Oh, God…

Taking the stairs two at a time, he searched their bedroom, then the others. Only when there was still no sign of her did he stop to think. Then, praying that he'd find her there, he headed for the loft.

"Deirdre?" Fearfully he said her name as he switched on the light, then caught his breath when he saw her curled on the window seat, her head having fallen against the windowpane. In the seconds it took him to cross to her, he added even more dreadful things to his list of fears.

Lowering himself by her side, he brushed her cheek with his thumb. Dried tears streaked her skin, but her color was good and she was warm.

"Deirdre?" His voice was soft and shaky. "Wake up, sweetheart. There's something I have to tell you." He smoothed the hair from her forehead, leaned forward to kiss her wheat-hued crown, framed her face with both hands. "Deirdre?"

She took in a hiccuping breath and, frowning, raised heavy lids. Disoriented, she stared at him for a minute, then her eyes opened fully and she pushed herself up against the window frame. "You're back," she whispered.

He smiled gently. "Yes."

"What…what happened to Washington?"

"It's not important."

"But the contract—"

"Isn't important."

"But you wanted it—"

"Not as much as I want you." When her eyes filled with confusion and disbelief, he explained. "I've driven around for hours thinking about things, and when I went back over what you said earlier, I realized that I may have got things wrong. I was so convinced that you wanted out of the marriage, that you'd gotten tired of me and it, that I took your words one way, when they could have been taken another." His hands were cupping her head, thumbs stroking the short, smooth strands of hair behind her ears. "I may be wrong again, but I think it's worth the risk."

He took a deep breath. Once there might have been pride involved, but he'd gone well beyond that. Still, he was nervous. His words came out in a rush. "I love you, Deirdre. *That* was why I wanted to marry you in the first place. Anything else that came along with the marriage was nice, but purely secondary. Maybe I've had my guard up, because I never knew for sure why, deep down inside, you agreed to marry me. And I was afraid to ask outright, because I didn't want to know…if you'd married me simply because of our bargain. But what you said earlier set me to thinking. What you said, and the anguish in it, would make sense if you love me and fear that I don't love you back." His eyes grew moist, and his voice shook again. "Do you, Deirdre? Do you love me?"

Tears welled on her lower lids, and her chin quivered. "Very much," she whispered, which was all she could manage because emotion clogged her throat, making further sound impossible.

Neil closed his eyes in relief and hauled her against him. "Oh, Deirdre," he rasped, "we've been so foolish." His arms wound fully around her; hers had found their way beneath his jacket and held him every bit as tightly. "So foolish," he whispered against her hair. "We never said the words. The only words that mattered, and we never said them."

Deirdre's heart was near to bursting. "I love you…love you so much," she whispered brokenly, and raised her eyes to his. "We had so much going for us, and we nearly blew it."

A shudder passed through him. He took her mouth in a fierce kiss, gentling only when he reminded himself that she wasn't going to leave. "When I think of everything else I've had in my life, things I've risked, things I've lost, they seem so unimportant now. You're what matters. This is where you belong, in my arms. And I belong in yours."

"I know," she said, and buried her face against his neck. The scent of him was familiar and dear; it was an aphrodisiac in times of passion, a soothing balm in times of emotional need. She breathed deeply of it, and her face blossomed into a smile. Then the smile faded, replaced by a look of horror. "Neil!" She pushed back from his arms. "The dinner party! They'll have gone to the restaurant and we've stood them up!"

He chuckled. "Not to worry. I called my secretary and had her cancel on our behalf. We'll make it another time. Together."

Deirdre wrinkled her nose. "I don't like the Emerys. He is an arrogant bore, and she has bad breath." Neil laughed aloud, but she hadn't finished. "And Donald Lutz is always checking out the room, on the lookout for someone important to greet, while that wife of his can't take her hand off the chunky emerald ring she wears. And as for the Spellmans, they're—"

Neil put a hand over her mouth, but he was grinning. "They're important clients. Once in a while we have to sacrifice our own personal preferences for the sake of the corporation."

"Speaking of which…" She mumbled into his hand, then spoke more clearly, if softly when he removed it. "I don't distrust you, Neil. Everything you've done at Joyce has been good. And I *am* in favor of the government project if it comes through."

"I didn't do it because of Wittnauer-Douglass, Deirdre. I didn't even know they were bidding for the same project."

"That was what I suggested to my mother," Deirdre said, feeling faintly smug. "She's a troublemaker. Do you know that? The woman is a born troublemaker! I never realized it, because I always assumed that she was right and that everything was my fault, but she's been dead wrong about us from the start. Victoria had her pegged. My mother is one of those people who are never satisfied. It may be a little late, but I actually feel sorry for my father. No wonder he poured so much of his time and energy into the business. He was running away from her!"

Hearing her evaluation of her parents' relationship gave Deirdre a moment's pause. Her confidence wavered. "Were you doing that, Neil? Were you running away from me, spending every minute thinking about the business?"

"A good many of those minutes you thought I was thinking about the business, I was thinking about you," he said with a crooked smile. Then the smile vanished. "I wanted to please you. I felt that if I couldn't win your heart, I'd at least win your respect."

"You've had that from the start. And I admire—no, I stand in awe of—what you've done with the business." She sharpened her gaze on him. "But I meant what I said about delegating authority. I want more of your time, Neil! I want to do things with you. I want to go out to romantic little lunches every so often, or play tennis, or take off for the weekend and go…wherever!"

His eyes twinkled. "I think I can manage that."

"And I want to go to Washington with you tomorrow."

"No."

"Why not?"

"Because I'm not going."

She stared at him for a minute. "You're not?"

"No. Ben can handle it."

"But you're the best one for the job! You know it, and I know it."

"But there is a question of conflict of interest."

"I don't believe that! I was angry, or I'd never have even suggested it!"

"Now you're being diplomatic," he teased.

"I am not!"

He grew serious. "I thought a lot about that situation, too, while I was out driving. No, I didn't originally know that we'd be competing against Wittnauer-Douglass for that contract, but I have to admit that when I found out, there was intense satisfaction in it. I mean, we may not get the contract. The bids are sealed, and I have no way of knowing who bid what. The contract may go to Wittnauer-

Douglass, or it may go to one of the other bidders. But I did get an inordinate amount of pleasure knowing that Joyce is right up there in the Wittnauer-Douglass league."

"There's nothing wrong with that—"

"But the point is that I have already avenged myself."

"Yes, but through honest hard work and talent. Not just anyone could have done what you've done, Neil. Joyce Enterprises was marking time. You have it moving forward. If you won't take the credit, then I'll take it for you!"

Her pride in him gave him a thrill. "You will, will you?"

"Uh-huh." She thought for a minute. "But what about practicing law. That was what you really wanted to do. Don't you miss it?"

"I've been practicing law at Joyce, but with lots of other things thrown in. I do think it's time Ben and I switch places, though. I want to maintain a position of power, because I've enjoyed having a say in what we do when, but I don't need a fancy title, and I *don't* need the full burden of responsibility I've been carrying." He paused. "But what about you? You haven't been teaching, and that was what you really wanted to do. Don't you miss it?"

"No," she said firmly, then grew pensive. "Maybe I've outgrown it. Maybe the need just isn't there anymore. It filled a void in my life, but the void is gone. Being a helpmate to you is far more satisfying than teaching ever was."

He hugged her. "The things you mentioned before— things we could do together—I want to do them, too, Deirdre. We never did take a honeymoon."

"We had that before we were married."

"But I want another one. A *real* one. You know, a luxurious cottage someplace warm, champagne at sunset, hours lying on the beach in the sun, maid service and laundry service and room service."

Deirdre slanted him a mischievous grin. "What happened to the man who could do it all himself?"

"He wants to be able to concentrate solely on his wife. Is that a crime?"

"You're the lawyer. You tell me."

He never did. Rather, he kissed her with such sweet conviction that she didn't care if they broke every law in the book.

SECRET OF THE STONE

CHAPTER ONE

"WHAT DO YOU think, Jesse?"

"Not bad. Not bad at all."

"Kinda pale?"

"May just be the lights. They're geared for sculpture, not skin."

"She does look sculpted."

"Nicely."

"Reedy."

"Hmm, no. Slender, maybe. But there are curves."

"You're searching."

"Aren't you, Ben? Isn't that why the two of us are standing here gawking at her, rather than at her artwork?"

"I suppose. Want to know what Margie says?"

"What does Margie say?"

"Margie says she's a loner. Cool and unattached. Reputed to be untouchable, almost like her work."

"I don't know. Her work is sensual in its way."

"Sensual? Are you kidding? Cold rock?"

"Come on, Ben. Where's your appreciation of art? She's done amazing things with marble. It may have been cold, hard stone once, but she's wrung something very warm from it."

"Hmph. Maybe so. But I think Margie might be right. Look at her. It's like she's insulated somehow from all this."

"And to her credit. How would *you* like to have two hundred people milling around scrutinizing you?"

"They're scrutinizing her work, Jesse, not *her*."

"Wanna bet? The exhibit's going to be on for the next four weeks. This is the only night the sculptress will be here. Don't tell me these people always choose to dress up in monkey suits in ninety-degree weather to go to a crowded gallery. Hell, I wouldn't be here myself if you hadn't dragged me."

"It's good for you."

"It's good for *you*. You're the guy who has to go places on the chance that you might pick up a client or two. You just want me along to add class. Whew, it's warm in here."

"It's air-conditioned."

"Yeah. But it's crowded, and besides, we had to go outside to get here. So did everyone else. Which proves my point. They're here to see *her*. No other reason."

"Hell, Jesse. This is the cream of New York society. These people dress up all the time. Besides, it's not *too* rough moving from an air-conditioned penthouse to an air-conditioned limo to an air-conditioned gallery. They don't suffer."

"Come to think of it, there were an awful lot of limousines out there."

"It's a narrow street."

"Man, she looks cool as a cuke."

"That's what I said."

"No. Cool as in composed…in control… polished."

"Just like that alabaster figurine over there."

"It looks alive."

"But it's stone. So's she."

"That's where you're wrong, Ben. There's feeling in her work. It may have a hard, shiny finish, but there's feeling in it. I'd guess there's plenty of feeling in *her*."

"You're nuts. She's hard. Look at her—like porcelain."

"Mmm. Fragile. Very lovely."

"But inert. Dead."

"Nope. I'd say deep down inside she's a passionate woman."

"Passionate? That's funny. Even if Margie hadn't tipped me off, I'd have judged her to be frigid."

"Frigidity is relative, my friend. To you or me, a raw piece of marble is frigid. To *her*, it has feeling...which she has the skill to bring out. If she is reputedly untouchable, it may be because a man has never come along who's skillful enough to chip through the outer shell to find the warmth beneath. Mmm, I'd say she's a very passionate woman."

"Is that smugness I hear? Come on, Jesse. You may be the master of seduction, but she's not your type."

"No?"

"No. You like fast women. Glossy, sexy women."

"Umm. And after the act they leave me cold as ice."

"I'm telling you. That one'd be cold before, during *and* after the act."

"Wanna bet?"

"Yeah, I'll bet. I'll bet you can't get to first base with her."

"He-ey, you underestimate the master."

"What'll you bet?"

"Hmm. Nice arms. Graceful. Too bad her legs are covered by that damned gown—they're probably the same."

"She may have sausage thighs."

"I doubt it. Look at her breasts—just suggestive enough beneath that silk..."

"Tickets to the play-offs?"

"Hmm?"

"I'll bet you a pair of tickets to the play-offs."

"The play-offs? Look who's talking speculation. You don't even know if the Knicks'll make it to the finals."

"They'll make it. I doubt you will."

"You're very sure of yourself."

"And you're not? Well, is it a bet?"

"I don't know, Ben. Good Knicks tickets are hard enough to get during the season."

"What's the matter, Jesse? Getting cold feet? Is the master having second thoughts?"

"Not on your life. She's penetrable. It just may take time. That kind of woman needs to be wooed."

"*Wooed*? Geez, you're going soft. Since when have you had to *woo* a woman?"

"This one's different. If I'm gonna do it, I'll have to do it right."

"You're chicken."

"No way."

"Two tickets to the play-offs?"

"The play-offs—*if* the Knicks are in them—will be only a week from now."

"A week is a long time…unless you're losing your touch."

"Not on your life."

"Two tickets?"

"Come to think of it, I would like to see the Knicks whip L.A. Wonder if the sculptress likes basketball."

"I'll be the one to win the tickets, pal."

"You won't win."

"Wanna bet?"

"You're on."

PAIGE MATTHESON stood serenely amid a cluster of admirers. She smiled and nodded, speaking softly when questioned about one piece or another that was on display. When the group shifted and several new faces approached, she began the ritual again. Franco Roget, the gallery owner, stayed close by her elbow and introduced her to everyone.

Her composure was exquisite. No one meeting her had the slightest inkling that she'd rather be elsewhere. No one meeting her would have imagined the convincing it had taken to get her here. She seemed perfectly at ease, if the slightest bit shy. But the shyness was appealing, adding to the alabaster beauty that was so much in keeping with her art.

"So you work exclusively in stone?" one patron asked.

"No. I also enjoy working with wood."

"I don't see any of those pieces here tonight," a second guest remarked.

"They're on display at other galleries around the city. We decided to limit this exhibit."

"Wood, stone—they're not the usual for a contemporary artist, are they?"

She smiled. "Many sculptors today work with newer media—metals, plastics, synthetics. But I think there's a slow but growing movement back to more traditional materials. The challenge is in taking the traditional and sculpting it into something thoroughly modern."

"You've done it well." This from a man who'd been introduced to her as Christopher Wright III. Though slightly shorter than she was—perhaps the same height had she been barefoot—he was reasonably good-looking. "Are you as modern as your work?"

"I'm as traditional." It was her stock line for men who were fishing, and Christopher Wright III was fishing. If the heavy scent of his cologne hadn't warned her, his proprietorial stance by her side would have.

"How about a traditional dinner?" he murmured, leaning closer. "I understand you're going to be in the city for several days."

Her poise didn't waver. "Just one more, and it's booked up from start to finish. If all goes well, I'll be on my way home the day after tomorrow. I'm afraid I just won't have time, Mr. Wright—"

"Christopher. Do you get to New York often?" he asked.

She shook her head, then turned as another of the group asked where she lived. "I'm from New England. Not far away, but far enough. I don't think I'd ever get any work done if I lived in a city like this. The pace is mind-boggling." If she sounded like a small-town girl, it was by design. The fact was, she'd cut her teeth on Manhattan. From the time she'd been old enough to walk more than a block without complaining, her parents had taken her and her brothers on visits to the city. She'd always been glad to go home again.

As new people joined the group, others drifted away. In her quiet, understated way, Paige made impressions on each just as she was expected to do. She graciously handled small talk and discussed her work, deftly parried personal questions by smoothly shifting the conversation back to the moment.

At all times she appeared to give her full attention to the person to whom she was speaking, yet she was attuned to bits and snatches of conversations around her. Her work was being well received, and she was pleased. She also knew that, though her shyness was sometimes taken as aloofness, the group of patrons present had seemed to warm to her. As for the occasional derogatory comment, breathed behind her back by the Christopher Wright IIIs of the crowd after they'd made their play and failed, she shunted the hurt aside. Oh, yes, she knew what they thought. "Ice maiden" was a term she'd heard more than once. She didn't know if the label was true, only knew that she hadn't yet laid eyes on the man with whom she cared to put it to a test.

IT WAS LATE THAT NIGHT when the crowd finally dispersed. Soon after, Paige found herself in a small restaurant with her agent Marjory Goodwin, and Marjory's assistant, Carolyn Pook.

Marjory twirled her wineglass, sat back in her seat with an exaggerated sigh and grinned broadly. "We did it, ladies. That was quite a success. Of course, a third of the pieces on display are on loan from private collections, but if the queries pan out, we may have sold fully half of the rest."

"You're kidding," Paige said. Surprise and pleasure were quick antidotes for her fatigue. "That many?"

"Yup. That many...*if* the queries pan out."

"They should," Carolyn interjected. "At least, if the enthusiasm of the people I spoke with is any indication. They loved your stuff, Paige. Congratulations."

Paige smiled warmly. "Thanks. I hope they did. I don't think I can manage these trips often."

"You look bushed," Marjory observed.

"I couldn't sleep last night. The city keys me up."

"The town house is comfortable, isn't it? Sylvia said to make yourself at home."

"Oh, it's lovely. And it was kind of your friend to offer it. But making oneself at home is one thing. Being at home is another. I miss the ocean."

"You've only been gone a day."

"I know. But it's soothing there. The endless roll of the surf is very different from the eternal ruckus here. You've been to my house, Margie. You know how peaceful it is."

"Hmph. I'm a city girl. The ocean is a nice place to visit, but to live there? The peace would drive me mad."

"Don't you get lonesome?" Carolyn asked. "You live there all alone."

"It's the only way I can work. And I like living alone. Besides, there's always the surf. When I wake up in the middle of the night I go out on the deck. I can't imagine a sedative more effective than that soothing rhythm."

"I can," Marjory drawled, arching her brows suggestively. "Another rhythm. One as timeless."

Carolyn laughed. "Marjory Goodwin, you have a one-track mind."

"It's a wild track, isn't it? Let me tell you, there were some good-looking men there tonight. If I hadn't been so busy trying to sell your work, Paige, I might have been tempted to make use of Franco's private room at the back of the gallery."

"It was in use," Carolyn informed her blithely. "I saw Craig Hutchinson go in there with his date. Craig must wield some clout with Franco."

"I thought they wielded it together," Marjory remarked

dryly. "Unless Craig's suddenly gone straight. In which case Franco should have been distraught."

"Franco was as preoccupied as you were," Paige pointed out. "He was really wonderful, staying so close beside me all night."

Carolyn laughed. "Maybe he was trying to make Craig jealous. But again that doesn't fit. By rights, if he wanted to make Craig jealous, he should have hung on the arm of some gorgeous guy." She frowned. "Unless we've really screwed up this analysis."

Paige sipped her wine, then set it down as her companions continued to discuss the relationship between Franco and Craig. "Poor Franco. How does he ever put up with you two?"

"He loves us," Marjory answered. "That's one of the things that's so great about him. He's not threatened by women as many men are." She lowered her voice. "Did you get a chance to meet Tom Chester? Big guy, but all muscle, no fat?"

"How would you know it's muscle?" Carolyn teased.

Marjory grinned. "I managed to put my arm around his waist. You know how agents can be when they're trying to sell something. And that waist was lean." Again she lowered her voice. "I gave him my card. Just in case he wants...anything."

Paige laughed aloud. If she didn't know Marjory Goodwin as well as she did, she'd have been offended by the definitely unprofessional turn of the conversation. But she did know her. Marjory happened to be wonderfully kind and solicitous to her. Marjory happened to be utterly effective, a whiz at selling her work. Marjory also happened, at the age of forty, to be man hungry. "You're incorrigible, Margie. What happened to David?"

"David? Oh, David's fine. He said to send his regrets. He had a business meeting tonight or he would have been at the gallery."

"Wouldn't he mind if you just picked up and had an affair with another man?"

"Sure he would."

"Then…why all this talk?"

Leaning forward, Marjory patted Paige's hand. "Because it's talk. And it's fun. And David, for all those boring business meetings of his, still happens to be a fantastic lover. I'm telling you, Paige, you really should get yourself a man. It'd open all kinds of new horizons."

Paige sat back and gave her friend a self-confident smile. "My horizons are plenty wide, thank you. I like my life just the way it is."

It was Carolyn's turn to lean forward. "But think of how much more exciting it could be." Her eyes widened. "You could fly off for the weekend every now and again with some handsome prince. There were several there tonight."

"Princes?" Paige laughed. "Carolyn, Carolyn, I think you've spent too much time with Margie. Either that or you're still hung up on fairy tales, which, since you're nearly my age, I doubt. Margie, what are you doing to this poor girl?"

"This poor girl," Marjory scoffed, "has had the time of her life these past few months escorting some of our most attractive clients around town. She's got Walter Emerson calling her twice a week."

"The cartoonist? But I thought he was in his fifties!"

"Careful, dear," Marjory said. "To some of us, fifty doesn't sound that old."

"You're off by a decade, anyway," Carolyn corrected Paige. "People make the mistake all the time. It's because of his name—"

"And that gray hair—"

"Prematurely gray. More like thick, gleaming silver." Carolyn's grin told far more than her words. "He's a nice guy."

"And has he whisked you away to— Doesn't he live in some huge plantation house in South Carolina?"

"Georgia. And it's beautiful. But we're getting off the subject."

"Which is?"

"Finding you a man."

Paige turned from Carolyn to Marjory. "Tell her, Margie."

"Tell her what?" Marjory countered innocently.

"That I'm not interested."

Eyeing Paige's placid smile, Marjory scowled. "Well, you should be. You're twenty-nine years old and it's about time you *experienced* life."

"I've experienced plenty."

Her protest was ignored. Marjory narrowed her gaze on Carolyn. "How about Jon Whitley? He's a runner. He's in great shape."

Carolyn tipped her head, thoughtfully looking at Paige. "Hmm. Maybe. But I dunno—his hair's just her color. I think we need some contrast here."

"I'm not interested," Paige stated.

"Bill Shaeffer," Carolyn counteroffered. "The coloring's right, and the guy's newly divorced—"

"For the third time. Chalk him."

"I'm not interested," Paige repeated, though for all the good it did she might have been the only one to hear the three small words.

Just then Marjory's eyes lit up. "I know. Donovan Greene!"

Paige sent a gaze heavenward. "Spare me, Lord. I've done no wrong—"

"That's just the point, Paige," Marjory stated. "You're *too* good. It's about time you break out and do something—" she struggled for the words "—something daring." She gave a vicarious shiver of delight. "What you need is to find a terrific-looking guy and have a hot, bone-melting, blood-pumping affair. It's good for the soul, Paige. Good for the soul."

Paige sincerely doubted it. Her indulgent smile said as eloquently as anything could that she didn't for a minute take Marjory seriously. And by the time the chauffeured limousine finally dropped her back at the borrowed town house and she was alone at last, she was too tired to give much thought to anything but showering and falling into bed.

AWAKENING RELUCTANTLY to the sound of her alarm, Paige struggled to roll out of bed the next morning. Exhaustion had overcome urban insomnia; she'd been dead to the world for hours. Though usually a morning person, she felt less than chipper. She was not looking forward to the day, one in which she would be hopping from one gallery to another, visiting the dealers who sold her work.

She showered again, more to shake the morning muzzies and relax herself than to clean the body that had been thoroughly cleaned the night before. Wearing a soft silk teddy, she sat at the dressing table and brushed her thick, dark hair before gathering and pinning it into a shiny knot at her nape. This, too, was a reluctant move. At home she let her hair fall loose, enjoying the sensual feel of the gentle waves at her shoulders. Here in New York, though, her hairstyle reflected her city image—sleek, controlled, elegantly poised. She needed to look older, sophisticated. She knew that of the people she'd be seeing today there would be those who might resent the fact that she'd found success at the tender age of twenty-nine.

In keeping with this purpose, she carefully applied makeup to cover the faint sprinkling of freckles across the bridge of her nose. The sun had brought them out in early spring, and had later deepened them. Given her habit of taking daily walks on the beach, freckles had been unavoidable. Not that she normally minded them; she felt they added spice to her face, giving her a natural, healthy look. Unfortunately, it wasn't the look she wanted today.

Finishing off her makeup with graded shades of lavender eye shadow, then dark liner and mascara, she feathered a shadow of blusher on her cheeks, then stood. Staring at herself in the mirror, she had to admit her success. She did look mature, quite sophisticated. Her preference for no makeup could wait. One more day, that was all. One more day.

Wearing a summer suit of white linen with a black silk blouse beneath, she made a final analysis of her appearance in the bedroom's full-length mirror. *Not bad, Paige,* she thought. *Mother would be pleased.* Not only had she attained the overall effect she'd wanted, but she did feel properly dressed for the city. It was something that had been ingrained in her from the earliest age. She remembered the discussions vividly.

"No, Paige, you may *not* wear jeans."

"But the boys are wearing them."

"The boys are different. And they'll be wearing blazers, which will dress them up. A young lady does not wear dungarees in Manhattan. That's all there is to it."

So it had been decreed; so it was. Paige smiled fondly at the thought of her very elegant, very proper mother. They'd always gotten along well, partly because, for all her elegance, her mother loved her dearly. That fact had never been disguised. And Paige had quickly learned to compromise. Indeed, she probably wouldn't feel comfortable wearing slacks in the city now, though so many women did. Dressing up was something of a novelty for her, anyway, since at home she wore what she wanted when she wanted. And by the following evening she'd be free....

If only there weren't this odious business of forcing smiles for ofttimes boring gallery owners!

Glancing at the slim gold watch on her wrist, she saw that her driver was due in twenty minutes. She headed downstairs to the kitchen, then brewed herself a cup of coffee, perching on a high stool at the counter to drink it. If she were at home, she mused, she'd have coffee on the deck, then disappear into her studio for several hours' work before emerging for breakfast. Today there wouldn't be such a lovely midmorning break, and it occurred to her that she ought to scramble an egg. But her stomach rebelled. She simply could not eat at eight forty-five in the morning. She'd have to wait for lunch—wherever and whenever that would be.

Returning to the upstairs bedroom with coffee cup in hand, she sprayed cologne on her neck, her wrists, then into the air, promptly walking through the fragrant cloud. Carrying both her purse and the coffee, she descended the two flights to the living room to await the limousine.

She still had five minutes to spare. As always, she was early. With the painfully slow passing of seconds, she began to curse the habit. Idleness bred contemplation, and contemplation this day centered on the meetings ahead.

"Margie, you know how I hate those things," she'd protested over the phone the week before.

"I know, which is why I haven't told you about them until now. The less time you have to brood, the better off you'll be. But Paige, they want to see you, especially the gallery owners who are handling your work for the first time."

"Why can't they just come to the opening?"

"They can, and many of them will be there. But the opening is mostly for patrons and those dealers who can make it in from out of town. The local dealers take pride in their own galleries, and you really can't blame them. It'll be a feather in their caps to have you there, even for an hour. And you make such a good impression."

"At great cost. By the end of the day, my mouth will be stiff from smiling and my legs will ache from all that standing."

"So ask them for a chair."

"Won't you be with me?"

"No. Not that day. The limousine will pick you up. The driver will have your schedule. At the end of the day he'll sweep by to collect me and we'll have dinner together. You'll be able to tell me how everything went."

"Coward."

"Now, now, none of that. You'll do better on your own, Paige. The owners will be very proprietorial."

"That's what I'm afraid of. Really, Margie, I wish you hadn't planned a full day."

"Once a year…is that too much to ask? It's for a good cause, Paige. Your career's flourishing. This will give it an added boost."

"I'd rather let my work stand on its own."

"I know you would, and it does. But a little back-scratching now and again doesn't hurt."

A little back-scratching. Just what Paige hated. There was a phoniness about it that rankled her. If she had to stay in New York another day, she'd much rather have spent it going to museums or even shopping. Of course, her preference would have been to drive home that very morning.

Feeling uncharacteristically testy, and resenting the cause of her mood, she downed the last of her coffee just as the front doorbell rang. Nine o'clock. Felix was always on time…damn him.

Snatching her purse from the cushion beside her, she pushed herself up, telling herself that she shouldn't take her sour mood out on the poor man whose job was to shuttle her from gallery to gallery for the next ten hours. A quick glance out the window revealed the familiar lines of the long, black limousine. Assured that the bell indeed announced her driver, she opened the door with a flourish, only to catch her breath when she saw that the man awaiting her was most definitely not Felix. Felix was a small man with sparse gray hair. The man before her, though he wore a similar dark suit, white shirt and tie, was tall, broad-shouldered and lean. His skin was faintly tanned, his sandy hair obviously full beneath his very proper chauffeur's cap. But it was his eyes that drew and held Paige's gaze. They were blue, crystal-clear and strangely refreshing.

"Ms. Mattheson?" he asked in a deep voice that was a bit gravelly.

"Yes?" She was aware of a rush of warmth and wondered if it was going to be another scorching day.

"My name is Dallas. I'll be your driver for the day."

His eyes danced; she couldn't look away. With great effort she controlled a sudden breathlessness. "I...is Felix ill?"

"The agency needed him for something else today. I have a complete list of your stops." He glanced past her toward the living room, freeing Paige's eyes from his own compelling ones. "Is there anything you need to bring with you?"

"Just my purse." Unnecessarily, she held it up. "I'm all set."

"Then I'd suggest we start out. The traffic's pretty heavy." He reached to close the door behind her as she passed him.

At the close contact, Paige realized just how large he was. At five foot five—more, given her heels—she'd never thought of herself as being short. This man, she decided, was six-two at least. Six-two, and built. *So there, Marjory Goodwin, I did notice!*

"It's going to be pretty hot again," came the voice by her side. "Unusual for the first of June."

"It is," she said softly as she climbed the few stairs that led up to the street. Dallas was instantly before her, opening the rear door of the limousine. She thanked him and settled herself into the seat while he slid behind the wheel. He checked what had to be her schedule on the seat beside him, then started the car.

"You've got a busy day," he commented, sparing her a glance in his rearview mirror moments before he pulled away from the curb.

"Mmm. I'll say." But her voice held little of the annoyance she'd felt moments before. The appearance of this man had broken the momentum of her ill mood; she felt decidedly better than she had before he'd come.

They drove in silence. Paige removed her own copy of her schedule from her purse and studied it in preparation for her first stop. When they arrived at the small East Side gallery, Dallas pulled over to the curb, hopped out and opened the door for her.

"I'll be right here waiting for you," he said as he accompanied her to the gallery door and held it open.

She tipped up her head and smiled. Moments later she was being effusively greeted by the first of those whose backs she'd come to scratch.

When she emerged from the gallery an hour later, Dallas was lounging against the side of the limousine. At the sight of her, he immediately straightened and jumped to open the door.

"How did it go?" he asked, his rough voice soothing. Again Paige had the sensation of a breath of fresh air.

She rolled her eyes and said nothing, but the corners of her lips twitched as she slid into the back of the car.

"Sorry about the heat," he said. "I started the car to cool it off every so often, but it's a losing battle on a day like this." He switched the air conditioner to high.

"This is fine." Paige felt simple relief at being away from the cloying atmosphere of the gallery. As the car headed off, she studied her driver. His hair was neatly trimmed at his neck, shorter at the sideburns as was the style. She couldn't help wondering if he wouldn't be cooler without the hat; it seemed a shame to imprison such thick hair in any way.

Redirecting her wayward thoughts, she reviewed the past hour. It hadn't been all that bad. Henry Thistle had enthusiastically shown her how her pieces had been set out for display. He had gone into detailed discourse on the sales he'd made in the past few months and the homes he'd found for her work. In turn, she had exhibited due appreciation and gratitude, stroking the man with gentle praise, admiring the works of other artists in his shop. No, it hadn't been all that bad, but eight more such stops before the day was done?

"Here we go." Dallas tossed his head toward the gallery they approached.

"Already?" She was cool and comfortable and would have preferred to drive around for a while.

"'Fraid so," he returned. There was something mischievous in the gaze he sent back to her, something that underscored his insightfulness. She had little time to ponder it, though, for he had parked and was helping her out, again assuring her that he'd be waiting.

He was. This time she simply nodded and sank into the back seat to recover from her second appointment. This one had been downright boring. The gallery owner had been a quiet, dignified man who had handled only two of her pieces. After fifteen minutes she hadn't known quite what to say to him. It had been a relief that Marjory, wisely, had only allotted him forty-five minutes. As it was, she'd made her escape after forty.

"Are you okay?"

She looked up to find that, rather than shutting her door, Dallas was leaning in, his blue eyes strangely clouded. "I'm okay," she said quietly, then took a deep breath and steeled herself. "I'm okay."

Though he looked doubtful, he returned to his place behind the wheel and started off again. "Are you sure you'll make it through seven more stops?" he called gently over his shoulder when they had stopped at a light.

"I'd better or Margie will have my head."

"Margie?"

"My agent. She's the one who set up these meetings for me."

The light turned green and the limousine moved forward. "Do you have work in all of these galleries?"

She chuckled. "I'm not *that* prolific. I've got things in five of the nine. The other four are future possibilities."

Nodding, Dallas gave full attention to guiding the car smoothly through the crowded streets. Paige had the sudden impulse to ask him about himself, but she curbed it, knowing that a certain distance was traditionally kept between driver and passenger in limousines of this length.

Besides, it was enough that she felt his touch each time he glanced in the rearview mirror, that her hand tingled each time he helped her out of the car, that the sight of him when she emerged from an appointment was instant resuscitation. She didn't need to breach *too* many boundaries.

After the third gallery had been visited, Paige sagged back against the seat. The owner she'd spoken with had been a woman, polite enough but with an aggressiveness that made Paige uncomfortable. Her own manner was so much more easygoing, yet she'd left that gallery feeling that she had to rush home to work round the clock for the next few months to provide the pieces that the woman insisted she already had buyers for. Such confidence should have been encouraging, but it served only to make Paige tense. Once again she realized that she could never, never live in the city.

"How about a cold drink?" Dallas offered. "The next stop is nearby. We've got a few minutes to spare."

Lifting her head from where it lolled against the seat, Paige brightened. "That's the best offer I've had all morning." She saw the bunching of Dallas's cheek and knew he was smiling.

"Done."

Within minutes he'd pulled up at an umbrella-shaded stand at the corner. Leaning across his seat, he studied the billboard.

"Looks like it's all in cans. What'll it be—Coke, 7 UP, orange soda?"

"Coke will be fine." *Anything* to soothe her dry throat and give her a bit of energy. She reached to take money from her purse, but Dallas was out of the car before she could press the bills in his hand. Through the dark glass of the limousine windows, she watched him speak to the vendor, then dig into his pocket. The movement brushed his jacket aside and pulled the fabric of his slacks smoothly across a thigh that was firm and well formed.

Paige blushed, unable to fathom where her sudden

interest in the male physique had come from. Dallas was her driver, for heaven's sake! Her *chauffeur*!

By the time he returned, she'd recomposed herself. He slid into the driver's seat and twisted to hand her the drink. She noted that he'd bought one for himself and felt a twinge of guilt that he had to wait out in the heat while she went from one air-conditioned gallery to another. He looked cool enough, however, with only a faint sheen of dampness on his neck to suggest that he might be warm.

She thrust the money forward. "Here." At his blank look, she explained. "For the drinks. Both of them."

For a split second he seemed almost angry. His brows lowered, his mouth settled into a firm line. Then he relaxed his features. "Thank you, but it'll be taken care of by the agency." His eyes met hers with that same devastating lure that could capture her, sweep her up and set her on a brighter plane.

She forced herself to nod and lowered her head to return the money to her purse, then accepted the cold drink and settled back in her seat. Dallas pulled around one corner, then another until he found a shady spot to stop the car. Only then did he snap open the tab of his Coke. Lifting the can to his mouth, he tipped his head back and took a long swallow. From her perch behind him, slightly to his right, Paige followed the path of the liquid, watching the muscles of his throat constrict to carry it down. His sudden "Oh!" snapped her to attention. Reaching into the pocket of his jacket, he pulled out a straw and passed it to her.

His sheepish expression was thoroughly endearing, making her smile. "Thanks. I think you had the right idea the first time."

But she accepted the straw. If she were at home, she would never have bothered with it. Unfortunately, she wasn't at home. She was in the middle of Manhattan, ensconced in the roomy hollow of a sleek limousine. So instead she carefully peeled off the wrapper and inserted the straw into the flip-top opening of the can. When she looked up she saw Dallas studying her, faint amusement in his eyes. With a shrug, she began to sip her drink.

Moments later she sighed. "Ahhhh, that's better."

"Don't they offer refreshments at your meetings?"

"Hot coffee. Or tea, equally hot. Not terribly creative, or welcome on a day like this. I think there must be something etched in the gallery owner's manual to the extent that boiling water is a must. It doesn't impress *me* terribly much, but then…" She let her voice trail off, realizing that Dallas might think her less sophisticated than her image.

But he smiled and turned to the front, saying nothing at all to reveal his opinion of her. As she thought about it, she was surprised—though pleased—that he'd gotten himself a drink. Somehow chauffeurs always seemed immune to the needs of mortals. She was relieved that Dallas was not.

All too soon they'd finished their drinks and she was headed for her fourth appointment. It and the fifth were a repeat of the earlier ones, with the exception of several collectors of her work being present at each. Paige wore her most composed expression, conversed as smoothly as she had the night before and was drained once again when she finally relaxed in the limousine. It was nearly two o'clock.

"You look tired," Dallas remarked, turning in his seat to study her pale features before starting the car. "I hope they fed you."

She shook her head, then wearily laid the back of her hand against her warm brow. "Each assumed I'd been fed elsewhere. Evidently gallery owners' manuals don't go into ensuring an artist's survival."

Instead of smiling at her humor, Dallas continued to examine her closely. There was a grim set to his lips, not unlike earlier, when she'd offered to pay for their drinks. Then he turned and started the car. "We'll have to remedy that." Maneuvering the long limousine out into the traffic, he followed the flow, making one deft turn then another before finally pulling up before a small restaurant. "I'll be right back," he said abruptly. Warm as it was with the car turned off, Paige was grateful to simply sit and rest.

When he returned, he carried a large brown bag. Bidden by hunger and an enthusiasm sparked by promise of its assuagement, she flipped down one of the folding chairs and slid forward onto it. "What have you got?"

He headed out into the traffic again. "This 'n' that. Any objection to the park? If there's any breeze it'll be there, and we can at least get some shade and a little quiet for you."

Touched by his concern, she smiled. "The park sounds wonderful. But I didn't think there were places to stop."

"Not to the uninitiated, perhaps," he drawled in such exaggerated fashion that she had to laugh. A far cry from the eminently controlled Felix. She was glad Dallas was with her today. Propping a forearm against the back of the front seat, she watched him drive. It didn't occur to her to return to her own place.

"You're a native New Yorker?" she asked.

"No. But I've been here long enough to find little ins and outs that many people miss."

"Of course. Your job. You must know these streets like the back of your hand."

He didn't answer for a minute. Then he spoke in a pensive tone. "Perhaps it's in spite of my job. There are times when I feel I'm stuck here and I need a reminder that there are, in fact, open spaces in the world. Central Park is far from what I crave, but when one is desperate and without recourse, second best will do."

There was such sincerity in his voice that Paige knew he was speaking person-to-person rather than chauffeur-to-passenger. He spoke well. She wondered where he'd come from, what he'd done in life, why he'd chosen to become a chauffeur. He looked to be in his late thirties. There were tiny lines around his eyes—whether from laughing or squinting, she didn't know—and the ghost of creases by the corners of his mouth. She remembered how he'd frowned when he'd been studying her earlier, and realized that those creases had perfectly fit the frown. He was a man who had many a sober moment, she sensed, and she continued to wonder about him as they approached the park. To her amazement, he found a small turnoff from one of the park roads and crept along it for just a minute before pulling to a halt beneath a stand of trees.

"This is terrific," she exclaimed as he helped her from the back. He held her hand firmly in his as he too surveyed the bit of peace they'd found, then slowly released it.

"Let me get the things." Ducking into the car, he picked up the bag, tossing his hat onto the seat in exchange. He had only half straightened when he cast a hesitant look her way. "You don't mind, do you?"

"Of course not. I was wondering if you were hot wearing it."

Tucking the bag under his arm, he raked his hair from his forehead with his free hand. Paige could see that it was damp, also that it had been shaped by a fine barber. It fell promptly into place, full and vibrant.

Realizing she was staring, she averted her gaze under the pretense of finding a place to sit. Dallas appeared to be doing the same, for moments later he gestured to a spot where the grass was thick and soft.

"There. That should do just fine." He glanced back at Paige, dropping his gaze to her white skirt. "Uh, on second thought, we may have a problem here. You look so pretty and neat. Grass stains would never do." Then he gave her a slow, lazy grin. Before she could begin to imagine what solution he had in mind, he'd thrust the bag containing their lunch at her and had shrugged out of his jacket. Covering the distance to the chosen spot with three long strides, he spread the jacket on the ground with a gallant flourish. His smile was broad when he straightened and extended his hand.

Paige felt strangely reckless, as though she was breaking a rule being here with her chauffeur this way. But

Dallas was more relaxing than anyone she'd been with in the past two days. And although an air-conditioned restaurant might certainly have been cooler, this spot promised to be more quiet. Besides, if she went to a restaurant, Dallas would wait in the car. It struck her that for the first time in recent memory she wanted the company.

CHAPTER TWO

SEATED COMFORTABLY ON Dallas's jacket, Paige watched him unpack their lunch.

"Crabmeat. Chilled shrimp. Fresh fruit salad. Pita bread." He identified the contents of each container as he set it on the grass. "And lemonade with extra ice." He drew paper plates, plastic forks and a wad of napkins from the bag and was about to uncover the first container when he paused. "Tell me you're allergic to fish."

She laughed, feeling oddly lighthearted. "Living on the water the way I do? I play games with myself. If I accomplish what I want on a particular day, the reward is a quick ride into town to pick up fresh fish from the dock. Lobster, shrimp, cod—whatever they've got, I eat."

Prying the lid off the crabmeat salad, he scooped healthy dollops onto each plate. "You live on the water?"

"Uh-huh. Marblehead Neck. It's on the north shore of Massachusetts."

"Near Gloucester."

Her eyes brightened. "You're familiar with the area?"

"I have friends there." He divided the shrimp evenly between them. "I try to get up whenever I can. It's a beautiful area."

"I know. I love it."

"Have you always lived there?"

"No. My family's from Connecticut. But I'd visited Marblehead as a child and when it came to finding a place of my own I knew just where I wanted to go."

He sat back to study her for a minute, then reached for the fresh fruit and doled it out. "It's an inspiring area. Must be conducive to working, if the number of artists there is any indication."

"It's perfect. The Sausalito of the East Coast." For the first time she glanced down at her plate. "Hey, that's enough. I'm not sure I can eat all you've given me."

His gaze was knowing. "When was the last time you ate?"

"Last night."

"Then you'll eat it all." His lips twitched. "And anything you can't, I'll help you with. I have a passion for shrimp. In fact, you'd better start. I've been known to snitch from other people's plates even *before* they've had their fill."

She glanced at her watch, then, her expression sobering, reached for her plate. "Hmm. We haven't got all that much time anyway." Within seconds a twinkle returned to her eye. "I think I'll start on the shrimp." Picking one up, she dipped it into the sauce Dallas presented. "Mmmmmm. Not bad...for New York."

"I'll have you know we get the best of fresh fish here."

"Not as fresh as my dock."

He dipped into the cocktail sauce himself. "You're prejudiced. If you were to close your eyes right now and picture yourself on that dock surrounded by the salty air and the sounds of fishermen unloading their catch, I doubt you'd taste a difference in the shrimp."

She knew he was right. Even without closing her eyes and transporting herself to the seaside, she found the shrimp to be delicious. It had to be the atmosphere here, she decided, tipping her head back to scan the greenery overhead.

"There is a little breeze. I didn't think there was any." Realizing that she still wore her linen jacket, she wiped her fingers on a napkin, slipped out of the jacket and laid it neatly on the grass beside her before reaching for her lemonade. "This is nice. I didn't expect to have any break at all." Her eyes sought his. "Thank you."

But his eyes weren't on hers. They were focused on the strand of pearls that burrowed against the folds of her black silk blouse. "Those are beautiful," he said softly.

Self-conscious, she peered down at the pearls. "My city beads. I never wear them at home."

"You don't dress up there?"

"Oh, occasionally, I suppose. To go into Boston from time to time. But I much prefer to live casually."

"And you weren't thrilled about making this trip into the city." He'd obviously put two and two together.

"No." Her voice was soft, almost apologetic.

"I'd think it would be exciting for you. I…understand you're a very successful sculptress."

"My works are selling, yes. But the business side of it all doesn't thrill me. These trips are tedious." She watched him take a forkful of crabmeat. His hands were strong, fingers well formed, slightly tanned, thoroughly masculine. She reached for another shrimp. "If I had my way, I'd simply stay at home and let Margie do that selling on her own. For that matter," she thought aloud, "I wouldn't care if my pieces *ever* sold. It's the work itself that I love."

"But if you didn't sell, you wouldn't be able to support yourself. Uh, unless there's a man in the picture…."

"No man. And my needs aren't great." It was the truth, though not fully revealing. The fact was that she had a handsome inheritance from her parents, which would easily support her whether she sold her work or not. She knew how fortunate she was. It had occurred to her more than once, as her career had taken off, that the freedom she felt toward her work, the lack of monetary worry, might be in itself responsible for her artistic blossoming. Her life was tension free, so her work flowed.

"Don't you get lonesome up there all by yourself?" Dallas asked, repeating Carolyn's question of the night before almost verbatim. All too well, Paige recalled the aspects of that conversation dealing with men and sex. Looking at her chauffeur, so very handsome here beneath the oaks of Central Park, she felt a renewed twinge of the sensual awareness that had hit her from time to time since she'd opened her door that morning to gaze into the bluest of blue eyes. Stunned, she returned her attention to her lunch and gave Dallas the same answer she'd given Carolyn.

"I like being alone. It's the best way to work."

"But to play? What do you do for fun?"

She speared a cantaloupe cube. "My work is fun. And I have friends. There are parties sometimes. Small get-togethers." She raised her eyes to deny the defensiveness she'd heard in her own voice. "I walk the beach a lot. That's play. It's fun and relaxing. I read. I window-shop in town. I take long drives along the coast. I may be alone, but I'm not lonely."

For a split second Paige caught the glint of skepticism in his gaze and thought he would argue. Seeming to curb the impulse, though, he took a bite of pita bread and lounged back on his elbows, crossing his long legs before him.

"This is nice," he mused, closing his eyes and breathing deeply.

Looking at him was so pleasant that she felt light-headed once more. "Mmm," she teased. "You do know the right spots, though I can't imagine that it'd be as charming at night."

His grin was crooked. He didn't open his eyes. "If you're suggesting that I bring my dates here to neck, you're wrong."

"I wouldn't suggest something like that," she drawled, knowing that was exactly what she'd done. "But now that you've mentioned it…"

"I come here myself. My dates prefer greater comfort."

"Then you're not married."

"No."

"Have you been driving long?"

"Since I was sixteen."

"I mean..." She gestured toward the limousine, slightly disconcerted that Dallas had stopped eating and was looking at her. She felt vulnerable to his gaze. Vulnerable...and almost as if she were being physically touched. Long, soothing fingers on her cheeks, her lips. A palm against the sensitive cord on the side of her neck.

"Oh, that," Dallas said. It took Paige a minute to recall that she'd asked him about his job. "No, not for very long. But it's proving to be an adventure. One way to meet interesting people."

"Tell me about them...the others you've driven around."

He sucked in a deep breath and sat up straight again. "I think we'd be better to concentrate on eating. You've got another appointment in twenty minutes."

At the reminder, she crinkled her nose. He seemed mesmerized by the gesture. "You've got freckles."

"Uh-oh. They were supposed to be covered up."

"Whatever for?"

"To make me look older."

"What are you, anyway?" His eyes were dancing again. "Thirty-three, thirty-four?"

A husky laugh rumbled from her throat. "I'm not sure whether to be thrilled or hurt. I'm twenty-nine."

"Imagine that," he said in mock wonder.

She shot him a quelling glance and stabbed a piece of honeydew with her fork. They ate in silence for a bit. Paige couldn't help but reflect on how comfortable she felt. There was something totally unhurried about Dallas, something about his relaxed manner that set her at ease. She knew full well that he was being paid for every minute of his time, but she didn't care. Even taken at face value, his solicitousness was good for her peace of mind.

As he'd predicted, she managed to do a respectable job on the food he'd dished out. It was with reluctance that she drained the last of her lemonade.

"I'm done, I guess." When she began to gather the plates together, the strong hand she'd admired moments before shot forward to rescue the lone shrimp that remained on her plate. As he dipped it in cocktail sauce and popped it into his mouth, he winked. Paige thought she'd melt. To control the sensation, she worked harder at cleaning up their impromptu picnic. But Dallas removed the plates from her hand, insisting on doing the dirty work himself while she stood, straightened her skirt and donned her jacket once more. That done, she picked up his jacket, shook it out, then draped it over her arm as she watched him walk to a rusty trash can and execute a graceful dropshot.

"Not bad," she teased. "Tell me you're an off-season basketball player."

"Off-season? But the season's not done."

"No?"

"No." He reached for the jacket she held out and shrugged into it. "The play-offs are still in progress. If I were a Knick, I'd be beating my tail up and down the court, praying for a chance to meet the Lakers in the finals." Placing a light hand at her waist, he guided her toward the car.

"Would you make it?" she asked in a breathy tone. Looking up, she caught his arched brows and a hint of amusement they gave his expression.

"I might. I just might at that."

THE NEXT FOUR HOURS, with one stop apiece, were even more exhausting for Paige than the earlier ones had been, for there was a strange restlessness in her that set patience at a premium. Overall she was pleased with the way she handled herself; she certainly had to be pleased with the reception she was given at each of the galleries she visited.

The brightest moments, though, came when she returned to the car. Dallas was her guardian angel, handing her in with care, making sure she was comfortable before he headed off. He was concerned by her fatigue and purposely took roundabout routes to prolong the drive from one stop to the next, sensing that she'd welcome the rest, which she did. She welcomed his frequent glances in the mirror, feeling strangely protected. She welcomed his intermittent discussion, which tapered off as soon as he sensed she needed a moment of quiet. She welcomed the ice-cream bar he thrust into her hand when she was almost wilting.

Increasingly, as the afternoon wore on, she found herself reacting to him. He had simply to approach her and she felt her insides tingle. And that was *before* he touched her arm or took her hand. Outside one of the galleries, her heel had caught in a sidewalk grate; he'd been there to catch her when she'd wobbled, and she'd clung to his strength for a long, precious moment.

He might have been her chauffeur, but he somehow seemed more like a friend. It was as though they shared an understanding of the day's ordeal, exchanging wry glances when a new gallery owner would greet her ebulliently. They might have been co-conspirators, stealing off to the park for lunch, clandestinely licking chocolate-covered ice-cream bars behind the shade of the limousine's dark glass.

Was she truly physically attracted to him? She tried to deny it, blaming the rush of warmth through her veins on the heat of the day. She tried to attribute her hormonal activity to the power of suggestion; having spent several hours the night before in the company of two such lecherous females as Marjory Goodwin and Carolyn Pook, it would be understandable if some of the hunger wore off.

Hunger? Paige Mattheson had never known sexual hunger before. She wasn't a virgin, though her one experience with a man, a fellow artist named Tyler Walsh, who'd been as young as she at the time, had ended with a total absence of satisfaction on her part. She'd never been inclined to try again. But then, she'd never, even that first time, felt the kind of inner excitement she felt now. It was as though hidden parts of her had suddenly come to life, as though the pulsing of her body demanded she recognize those heretofore ignored nooks and crannies.

Marjory's words came back to her and, for the first time, Paige wondered what it *would* be like to have a hot, bone-melting, blood-pumping affair. Would it be good for the soul? She wondered...

"Miss Goodwin said she'd be waiting at the door of her building at eight," Dallas announced as he turned onto Third Avenue, then cast a sharp glance in the mirror at Paige's face. "Are you sure you're up to this?"

"The worst is over," she answered quietly. "Margie will want a full rundown. I've got one more appointment tomorrow morning, then," she said, sighing, "I'll be on my way home."

"You're taking the shuttle to Boston?"

"No. I, uh, I have this thing about flying. It was one of the conditions I made when I agreed to come to the city. Felix drove me down the other day. I assume he'll be driving me back tomorrow."

Dallas said nothing as he pulled up at a modern structure fronted by smoky glass. Marjory breezed out almost simultaneously, jumping into the back seat with a sigh of relief.

"It is hot!" she exclaimed as she settled into the cool interior of the limousine. "I mean, it's not that everything isn't air-conditioned, but I've been running in and out all day and the constant switch is enervating." Rummaging in her voluminous bag, she extracted a tiny pillbox, tossed two aspirin into her mouth and swallowed.

Paige winced. "You can do that without water?"

"Since we have no water and I have a splitting headache, yes." She directed her voice toward Dallas. "I've made reservations at the World Trade Center."

He nodded and pulled away from the curb.

"Not bad," Marjory murmured more quietly to Paige, tossing her head toward Dallas.

Paige simply smiled. "So we're doing it up big tonight?"

"I figured I had to do something super after what I put you through today. Do you hate me?"

"I have to admit that there have been moments..."

"Tell me. I want to hear everything."

Paige began to detail her day. Marjory interrupted her regularly to ask questions, trying to read between the lines of the gallery owners' chatter. They reached their destination before Paige had even finished telling of the morning's appointments.

Dallas dutifully opened the door and helped each woman out in turn. His hand was just releasing Paige's—reluctantly?—when Marjory spoke.

"Give us several hours. We should be fortified by then." She moved forward with her customary confidence.

Paige lingered for a minute to look up at Dallas. "You'll get something to eat?" she asked in a whisper.

His lips twitched. "Beer and a sandwich sound mighty good. Not quite your champagne and caviar, but it'll do."

"I feel guilty."

"Nonsense." His hand slipped up her back and he gave her a gentle nudge forward. "Go on, and enjoy yourself. You deserve it."

She was about to argue that he did too when she saw that Marjory had stopped and was waiting for her. "Thanks," she murmured with a shy smile, then trotted ahead. Marjory promptly slipped an arm through the crook of her elbow and propelled her on.

"What was *that* all about?"

"What?"

"Soft whispers to your chauffeur."

Paige was grateful that the revolving door took them momentarily apart. By the time they were together again inside the building, she had her composure intact. "He's a nice guy."

"I'm glad of that. When the agency called this morning to say that Felix wouldn't be driving you, I was a little worried. They assured me that this fellow was capable."

"Capable…and patient." Among other things. "If you and I found the heat to be oppressive today, think of what he must have felt."

"That's his job. He's paid well."

"Still…"

They stood at the elevator bank, waiting for a car to arrive to whisk them effortlessly to the one-hundred-and-seventh floor. Marjory eyed her cautiously. "Am I really seeing what I'm seeing?"

Paige schooled her expression to one of blankness. "What?"

"If I didn't know better, I'd think you like the guy."

"I told you. He's nice."

"No. I mean, *like* the guy. As in *being soft on.*" She enunciated each word.

Paige's poise held. "Margie, he's my *driver.*"

"He's also gorgeous. You didn't notice?"

"He is pleasant to look at."

"Aha! We're getting somewhere."

"Now, just a minute." Paige feigned annoyance. "I don't think I like what you're suggesting."

"I'm suggesting that every little admission is a small victory with you. Honestly, Paige. You're a woman. I know you to be warm and giving. But for some reason you insist on sublimating."

The elevator arrived and their discussion was momentarily curtailed as others entered the car. Paige didn't forget Marjory's comment, though. She felt strangely annoyed. It wasn't until they'd been seated at a table with a spectacular view of the city that she was able to pursue it.

"Explain how you think I sublimate."

"You pour your passion into your work, leaving none for the male of our species. Do you have something against men?"

Paige might have been further annoyed had it not been for Marjory's gentle tone. "Of course not."

"Then why do you avoid them? Really. There were at

least a dozen eligible bachelors at the party last night, but you didn't notice one. I suppose it's none of my business, and you could tell me to shut up. But I care about you, Paige. You'd make someone a wonderful, loving wife."

Paige simply smiled with a return of her characteristic serenity. "Maybe. Someday. For now I'm just happy sculpting."

"Then you haven't ruled it out?"

"Marriage? Of course not. Come the day I meet the right man, I'll get married. I'm young. There's no rush."

Her utter composure told Marjory that it would be pointless to argue. Taking a deep breath, followed by a long sip of the martini the waiter had just delivered, Marjory returned the conversation to business.

By the time the elevator carried them back down to the ground floor, Paige had grown strangely edgy. She was tired, anxious to return to the limousine that had come to represent a haven of sorts. As always, the sight of Dallas waiting beside the car gave her a burst of energy.

Since Marjory's apartment was in the East Village not far from the World Trade Center, it made sense to drop her first. The two women wouldn't be seeing each other again before Paige left the following noontime for home. Warm hugs punctuated their parting.

"You'll call me when you get home and let me know how it went with Groeffling?" Marjory demanded.

"I will. Thanks for everything, Margie. You've done a super job."

"Have to earn my commission, don't I?" Margie teased with a final squeeze before slipping from the car and waving as it started off.

Paige's thoughts had nothing to do with either the man she'd be meeting the next morning or her agent's commission as Dallas headed the limousine uptown. Her thoughts were on Dallas himself. She wanted to ask if he'd gotten his beer and sandwich but found herself tongue-tied. She wondered where he'd go after he dropped her off, who he'd be driving tomorrow, whether he affected all of his female charges this way.

His head, formally capped, was a dark silhouette. She would have given far more than a penny for his thoughts at that moment, but he seemed as disinclined to speak as she.

As Twenty-third Street became Thirty-fourth, then Forty-fifth, she felt a gnawing tension in her body that grew and spread until it radiated around her. Through a sprinkling of traffic the limousine cruised up Sixth Avenue to Central Park, turned east, then north again. All too soon it approached the Seventies, where her borrowed town house stood.

When Dallas turned onto her street, she shifted in her seat. She wanted something…didn't dare put it into words…felt a curiosity, a heat….

Pulling the car into a parking space, he stilled the engine, then sat for just a moment while Paige held her breath. When he slowly opened his door and climbed out, she took her lower lip between her teeth. Tightly clutching her purse, she waited while he opened her door. If his hand closed more tightly than usual around hers, she attributed it to her imagination. No way, though, was she imagining the quickness of her own breath or the jumping of her stomach. Those things were too real, as was the fact that he didn't release her hand as they walked slowly toward the steps.

The glow from the streetlights dimmed as they descended the steps. When they stood in the small hollow before her front door, Paige slipped her hand from his so that she could reach into her purse for the key. Head bent, she closed her fingers around the hard metal and faltered. She wanted to say something, do something….

A strong forefinger touched her skin, curving under her chin to very gently raise her head. Dallas was looking at her, his tall, sturdy form a mere breath away. She couldn't make out his expression, but his touch bore the unmistakable tension she thought had been hers alone. When he lowered his head she didn't move.

His lips brushed hers lightly once, then again. She knew he was giving her time to demur, to refuse him, to put him in his place. She could do nothing, though, but stand before him, entranced by the pleasure of his touch. Her eyes closed; she floated. He was slow, so slow, whispering the faintest of kisses against her lips until they opened with a will of their own in a soft blend of curiosity and desire.

Only then did he deepen the kiss. Only then did Paige learn what a real kiss was. It was warm. It was delicious. It was a moist caress that seared a fiery path through her bloodstream. It was increasingly hungry, caused increasing hunger. It was exciting, powerful and, in its way, frightening.

Stunned by the intensity of the pleasure she felt, she pulled back to look up at him. The shadows kept his expression a mystery, but the city sounds couldn't muffle the faint unevenness of his breathing.

"Have you got your key?" he murmured hoarsely. Nodding, she pulled it from her purse. He took it, turned it in the lock and pushed the door open.

Paige continued to study the dim outline of his features, half-afraid to believe that a man could make her feel so...so feminine. Not *a* man. *This* man. One she'd known for less than a day, one who was a virtual stranger to her by every reasonable measure. He was her driver...*her driver*. But it didn't matter. Nothing mattered but that he seemed to have the key to unlock feelings in her she'd feared had been frozen.

Turning to her now, he slid his fingers to the back of her neck and caressed the line of her jaw with his thumb. Its pad was faintly abrasive, broadcasting masculinity in the gentlest of ways. When he kissed her this time, her lips were open and waiting.

She had never known such delight; there was no way she could possibly turn from it. Instinct guided her...or was it Dallas himself? She only knew that what was happening, the response she felt and gave, was the most natural, the most exhilarating thing she'd ever experienced. Her lips yielded to his, then demanded in turn. Even her tongue found new purpose as it cavorted with his.

A shudder passed through Dallas and he raised his head. "Should I come in?" he asked, a definite thickness in his voice.

A shock of excitement ricocheted through her body at his words, his tone. She couldn't speak, simply nodded.

"Are you sure?"

Again she nodded. She held no illusions. Dallas wanted nothing more than what she wanted—a few moments' pleasure. The difference was that while this was surely nothing new to him, it was new to her. She wanted to know where the inner heat she felt would lead. If the night ended in failure, she had nothing to lose. She'd be leaving tomorrow, would never see Dallas again. If, on the other hand, the night ended in the ecstasy she'd only heard about, she'd have memories and the certain knowledge that she was a woman in every sense of the word. If that proved to be the case, Dallas would have no idea of the true service he'd performed this day.

Slipping his arm around her back, he guided her into the apartment and kicked the door shut. Then he turned her to him and, taking her face in his large hands, kissed her deeply. Every recess of her mouth was touched and explored. Her knees shook so wildly that she might have fallen had she not wound her arms around his neck. But there was discovery in that, too. His shoulders felt as broad, as strong as they looked. His neck was warm, firmly corded. The hair at his nape was crisp, then soft and exquisitely enticing to her touch.

Releasing her face, he tossed his hat to the sofa and, wrapping his arms around her back, crushed her to him. Feeling his full strength for the first time, she might have been intimidated had it not been for the thrill of excitement the nearness brought.

His arms loosened and he ran his hands up and down her back. His head dipped. He buried his face against her neck while he gently eased off her jacket and dropped it to the side. When his hands moved on her again, the silk of her blouse was a sensual conduit. His fingers traced her spine, then spread around her middle, thumbs paving the way, burning her as they inched up her ribs.

She felt the swelling of her breasts moments before he covered them, and couldn't stifle the gasp that slipped from her lips when his fingers shaped her fullness and kneaded gently.

"Shh," he soothed, catching her lips with his as his thumbs zeroed in on the tight buds straining against the fabric. Back and forth he stroked. Paige had to gasp for breath. Her entire body seemed on fire, as though her veins were wicks carrying a spark from the spots he touched to her every extremity. She hadn't dreamed it could be like this, so flagrant, so all-consuming. She hadn't *dared* dream. But now she knew. And she wanted more. More of this phenomenal rapture that Dallas's touch inspired.

His breathing was as ragged as hers when he dragged his mouth away. Forehead resting against hers, he worked carefully at the buttons of her blouse. She wasn't sure if she could breathe, so great was the sense of anticipation, of excitement, of apprehension. She waited for something within her to still, to die, but nothing did. When her blouse lay completely open and his hands smoothed the silk from her shoulders, she felt more inflamed than ever.

The feeling only intensified when he began to caress her bare flesh. Her neck, her back, her ribs—every inch was covered in turn by his seeking hands. Her mouth opened widely beneath his, welcoming him with an abandon that might have stunned her had she been aware of it. But she only knew that what she felt was right and good and devastatingly healthy.

Within minutes he'd slipped his fingers beneath the thin straps of her teddy and eased them down her arms, pushing the fabric and her skirt low on her hips, leaving her torso bare to his gaze. The only light in the room was that which filtered in from the street through the gauzy drapes. It was enough. He held her back for a minute to admire what he'd uncovered, but the discovery was largely Paige's. She should have been shy at his blatant study of her nakedness; no man had ever examined her with quite such thoroughness. But what she felt was pride and hunger. She stood still as long as she could.

"Touch me," she whispered. Even her voice sounded foreign, its husky tone new to her ears but fully in keeping with the moment. "Please?"

He needed no more encouragement. His hands were warm against her flesh, exploring her curves with barely restrained eagerness. "You're very beautiful," he rasped, his fingers less steady than they'd been before.

Paige grasped his shoulders for support, not releasing them even when he knelt to free the rest of her body from the confines that seemed suddenly so restrictive. Skirt, teddy, nylons—each was tossed aside. When she was completely naked, he sat back on his heels, hands curved behind her thighs, to look at her again. She couldn't believe how her arousal was fueled by his gaze alone, but it was. Another discovery. She half wanted to call it off at this point if only to always remember the divine sensation of being worshiped in all her naked glory by a man. For he did worship her. His eyes, his expression, his subservient stance—she felt desirable, precious, powerful in her way.

But it wasn't enough. She grew conscious of the tight knot that had formed low in her belly and knew that, however glorious the moment was, there was still more to discover. She was on a voyage with a stranger and she was loving every minute of it.

Dallas swallowed audibly, then inched his hands slowly down her legs. He circled her ankles and began to climb back over her shins, but his gaze moved faster, coming to rest at the dark apex of her thighs. His hands reached her knees, which began to wobble with embarrassing instability. The message wasn't lost on him. With an abrupt glance at her face, as though he'd momentarily forgotten that part of her, he stood and began to quickly shed his clothes.

Paige watched, mesmerized, as each span of flesh was revealed. With the dispensing of his jacket, tie and shirt, she saw that his chest was firm, lightly haired in an erotic pattern that channeled her eyes to the belt he was unbuckling. He released the fastening of his trousers, lowered his zipper, thrust everything from his hips as he stepped out of his shoes. Then he was before her, as naked and aroused as she, and once again she was awed by the excitement of merely looking.

But Dallas had passed that point. He swept her into his arms and pressed her willing flesh to his. Chest to chest, belly to belly, thigh to thigh, they reveled in the intimate contact. Paige moaned. Dallas sighed. Winding their arms around the other's back, each held tightly as if to preserve that which could be so fleeting.

Then Paige was being lowered to the plush carpet and Dallas was looming over her. He kissed her, stroked her with a fever that might have been contagious had she not already been thoroughly afflicted. Foreplay was unnecessary; the day itself had been one long, taunting session. She was ready to explode even as she felt his first prodding touch. Her only thought of caution was one of a most practical nature.

"Dallas," she whispered urgently, "I don't...I haven't got anything..."

Arms trembling, he paused on the brink of penetration. "Oh, God."

"I'm sorry. I'm sorry. But I didn't plan..."

"Shh." He kissed her lightly and began to ease himself away.

Paige was suddenly frantic, imagining that her one chance at ultimate glory was being denied her by her own practicality. She clutched at his shoulders, willing him back. "It's okay…I'll take the chance…I think it's safe…."

"Shh, love. I have something." Sitting on his heels, still framed by her legs, he reached for his pants, rummaged in a pocket, found a condom and applied it. Then, as though hypnotized by the sight of her open and waiting for him, he lingered for a minute. Slipping his hands up her legs, he touched her gently, rotating his thumbs in ever-encroaching circles that revealed quite plainly her readiness for him.

"Please! Now!" she cried.

Surging forward, he propped his hands beneath her arms, bowed his back and thrust upward, bringing Paige such abrupt bliss that she feared she'd die of delight. She felt filled and fulfilled, but only until he began to move more steadily; then her desire left one plane and moved on to the next. A look of wonder gave a glow to her features. She was as astonished by her own sexuality as she was by the myriad ecstatic sensations the male form could generate. The excitement compounded itself, leaving her little control. Swept up in a dizzying twister of passion, she whirled round and round, higher and higher until, arching her back, she lay suspended for a long, pulsing moment before finally exploding into a series of rapturous spasms that left her gasping for air, clinging to Dallas, whispering his name in awe.

With the slow return of consciousness, she realized that he was still inside her, as hard and full as ever. She opened her eyes to find him smiling gently above her.

"You haven't…"

"I haven't come. I know. I was sidetracked watching you. That was something to behold."

She squeezed her eyes shut and turned her face aside with a moan. But Dallas's lips were sprinkling warm kisses on her cheek, then her nose and mouth.

"Don't be embarrassed," he breathed, his voice exquisitely gentle in its rough way. "You have no idea how arousing it is for a man to witness the pleasure he brings a woman. I had no idea, for that matter. So by rights I'm the one who should be embarrassed. I didn't know. It makes it all that much more wonderful. Don't you see?"

With a moment's thought, she did see. Further, she saw that he'd said what she needed to hear. She wasn't quite prepared for his next words, though, or for the twinkle in his eye that even the room's dimness couldn't hide.

"Besides, it makes this next part that much more of a challenge."

"A challenge?" she whispered.

"Uh-huh. Now I want to see if I can make it happen again."

"Oh, Dallas…I don't know…I feel…"

"Spent? That's why we're resting right now. You'll get your second wind. Just watch."

She hadn't expected the first wind and was still marveling at the incomparable joy of it. Second wind? If it never came, she'd still be in heaven. She'd done it! There was nothing wrong with her after all! To hell with Tyler and his inept fumblings so many years ago! To hell with all those who'd called her an ice maiden!

"I want to please you, Dallas," she whispered. "Tell me what to do."

"You do please me. You don't need instruction."

"But I want you to feel what I felt. I want to see it, too." She tightened herself around him and found, to her amazement, that she wasn't as drained as she'd thought. The feel of him deep inside her sent reborn tingles through her veins. When he slowly withdrew, then returned once again, she gasped in surprise.

"Feel good?"

His smugness was merited. "Oh, yes," she breathed.

He began to move steadily, then with increasing speed. She felt his arms tremble. Her wandering hands charted the tightening of his body. As the fire grew hotter, he closed his eyes, but she saw nothing beyond that, since her own eyes had closed under the force of renewed passion.

This time they climbed together, gasping in turn, kissing wildly until they needed every breath to surge with the growing delirium.

Moments before she reattained that newly discovered precipice, she cried his name. "Dallas!"

"Jesse," he panted hoarsely. "My…first name…is Jesse."

She never had a chance to say it. When he gave a deep moan and thrust a final time, wave after wave of ecstasy burst upon her, perfectly coinciding with the thunderous climax that shook his large frame.

It seemed an eternity before either of them could think, much less breathe. Dallas collapsed over her, then slid his slick body to the side. He left a limp arm draped across her waist, a long leg lying lethargically between hers. He pressed his lips to her bare shoulder and left them there, as though he had neither the strength nor the wish to move away.

Paige felt weak, totally drained. She was also unbelievably satisfied. Eyes closed, she dropped her head to rest against Dallas's hair. Her lips curved into a broad smile. Without intending to, she fell asleep.

Several hours later Dallas awakened her with a light kiss. She opened her eyes slowly. Only after a moment's disorientation did she remember where she was, who she was with, what they'd done together. Then, helplessly, her lips split into that same broad smile.

"You seem pleased with yourself."

He should only know, she thought. Very softly, she said, "I am."

"Do I take it everything was…satisfactory?"

Her eyes met his then and, rather than finding a smug expression on his face, she saw a glimmer of unsureness. "It was," she assured him quickly.

"No second thoughts? No regrets? After all, I am your... chauffeur."

"Are all chauffeurs such wonderful lovers?"

"I don't know. I've never made love to a chauffeur, myself."

His unsureness seemed to have eased. Tipping his head, he began to nibble on her ear. The moisture of his touch was infinitely pleasing. She slid her fingers into his hair, delighting in the vitality of the sandy shock.

His voice was muffled against the lobe of her ear when he spoke. "Do you do this often?"

"Nope."

"You seemed...stunned."

She knew exactly what he was referring to. It had nothing to do with his being a chauffeur and everything to do with the pleasure she'd felt. "I was."

"Why?"

"I...it was very strong."

"You've never felt it quite that way before?"

She hesitated for a minute, then whispered, "No."

Dallas appeared to be more than content with her simple answer. A low growl emerged from his throat, his breath tingling her shoulder bone, to which his lips had moved. He seemed intent on exploring and tasting, something neither of them had had time or patience for earlier.

Paige quickly discovered the pleasure of this, too. His mouth moved in leisurely progression, leaving no inch of her untouched. At times she was embarrassed, but her rising ardor quickly overcame that emotion—that, and the lilting words of encouragement and praise that Dallas lavished on her throughout his journey. If the heat built slowly, it was no less searing when he finally eased into her. And the pleasure she found was, if anything, all the more intense for the buildup.

It was a cycle that repeated itself throughout the night. They made love, slept, then woke up and made love again. For Paige, one discovery followed another. She learned ways to make love she'd never imagined, learned that her own participation, indeed, her initiative, was not only desirable to Dallas but infinitely rewarding to herself. At some point, he carried her upstairs to the cushioning softness of the bed, where, remarkably, their tired bodies found new strength.

The last thought she had when she drifted back to sleep shortly before dawn was that she would never, never forget the night that had been.

It was a good thing. When her alarm wrenched her from a blissfully deep sleep at nine, she was alone.

CHAPTER THREE

PAIGE SMILED. SHE REMEMBERED more, and her smile widened. With a feline stretch, she grew aware of myriad unfamiliar muscles and chuckled softly. She took a deep breath and turned onto her side, facing that half of the bed where her lover had lain.

Dallas. What a wonderful man. He'd been gently forceful, tenderly fierce. Feeling irrepressibly buoyant, she laughed aloud, threw back the sheet that covered her and bounded from bed. She'd spent the night in the arms of her chauffeur. In theory, it was deliciously scandalous, decidedly decadent. In reality, it was the most wonderful thing that had ever happened to her.

Knowing that she was to be picked up at ten for her last appointment of the trip, she showered, dressed, packed her bag and set it neatly by the front door, then made herself a cup of coffee. All the while her thoughts were on the night that had been. She had no regrets—she'd done what she'd wanted to do. Now she could return to her house by the sea, to the skylit studio she loved so much and to her work, knowing for the first time in her life that she was complete. Whether or not she ever again found the passion to which Dallas had introduced her, she would be always grateful for the night now past. Because of it she could rest assured that, sexually, she was lacking in no way, shape or form. With this knowledge, she felt she could bring to her work an even greater sensitivity. She couldn't wait to sculpt again.

Promptly at ten the doorbell rang. Its peal spawned a strange inkling of self-doubt. She assumed that Felix would be back today. But if he wasn't? If it was Dallas at the door? How would she act? How would he?

Having already washed her coffee cup and checked that there was no lingering trace of her presence in the borrowed town house, she headed for the window. Yes, that was the limousine outside. But who had driven it here?

Stilling the tiny butterflies that flitted through her stomach, she opened the door and found—to her relief, or disappointment?—that Felix had indeed returned.

"Good morning, Miss Mattheson," the small and very proper chauffeur said. "How are you today?"

"Just fine, Felix." She gave a last, perhaps wistful glance around the room, then sighed. "I do believe I'm ready."

Having already lifted her suitcase, Felix stood aside for her to pass, then closed the door firmly. If Paige heard the solid thud as symbolic of the end of a very brief, very brilliant moment in her life, she was quickly consoled by the knowledge she'd attained from it. She felt as though she were a different woman from the one who had left Marblehead three days before. And, she reasoned, it was probably better that she not see Dallas again. After all, he had his life—whatever it was—and she had hers.

She wasn't sure how many times she repeated that litany during the drive to her appointment, or how often she thought of it during the meeting itself. She knew that her mind was not on the rotund gallery keeper before her, or on the handful of collectors he'd invited for midmorning tea. By the time she finally emerged into the city heat once more, her thoughts were fully directed toward home.

That was before she caught sight of Dallas pushing off from the side of the limousine to stand straight and tall, awaiting her.

Ignoring a sudden weakness in her knees, she walked steadily forward. He touched the visor of his cap in a mute greeting, only the searing blue of his eyes bearing hint that there'd ever been anything other than total formality between them.

She came to a halt at the car door that he'd opened and gave a shy smile. "I...didn't expect you." Her body hadn't either, but that didn't stop the leaping and bounding that had already commenced therein. Once again she marveled at the effect the simple sight of this man had on her, though now there was far more than his looks to stimulate her. There were memories, mental images of naked bodies enmeshed with each other, of hands and lips and tongues exploring and caressing, of backs arching, hips thrusting.

"I didn't expect me either," Dallas murmured soberly.

For an instant Paige feared he'd been pressed into a service he clearly didn't want. Her stomach knotted. "I'm sorry," she whispered, then ducked her head and slid into the limousine.

Dallas leaned in after her. "I'm not. That wasn't what I meant."

"It's all right." She forced a smile. "It'll be pretty boring for you driving all the way to Marblehead and back. I don't blame you." She frowned. "Uh, unless I've misunderstood. Felix was to drive me home. Where is he?"

"Back at the agency. I'll be driving you home."

After having reconciled herself to never seeing him again, she wasn't sure how she felt about the change in plans. With the firm shutting of her door and Dallas's sliding into the driver's seat, though, it appeared that she had no choice.

Settling back, she concentrated on the buildings they passed, on the bustle of city life she was leaving at last. Only three days she'd been here, yet it seemed longer. So much had happened—so much of it centering around the man in front of her.

Quite helplessly, she smiled. She felt good, better and better as they sped along the East River then crossed over the Triborough Bridge. She was going home with her memories, an even brighter outlook on life, *and* the man who had made it all possible.

Dallas's feelings were far more mixed. Time and again he asked himself what he was up to. He'd won his bet, though he hadn't thought to call Ben with the news. By the time he'd returned to the brownstone he owned, a short two blocks from where he'd left Paige sleeping so blissfully, he'd been so confused that he'd been able to do nothing but shower and shave, then sit in a chair wondering what in the devil to do next.

He'd been right—Paige Mattheson was passionate to the core. Innocent and without guile, she'd been an incredible lover. Far from leaving him cold, as every other woman in recent memory had done, she'd left him aching for more. He'd taken her again and again, finding joys in lovemaking that he, for all his experience, had never known before.

He should have left it at that. But he couldn't. He'd picked up the phone no less than three times before he'd finally done what he knew he had to do. He had to see Paige again, learn where she lived, spend just that little bit more time with her. There was something about her that went far beyond one night's interest and, much as he resented it, he was helpless to deny his fascination.

The agency had been as agreeable in granting his request that he drive Paige home today as it had been when he'd wangled his way into driving her around the city. The fact that the owner of the agency was an old acquaintance of his hadn't hurt. Neither had the fact that Jesse Dallas was a respected member of the media community, perhaps not as flashy or powerful as some, but respected nonetheless.

What Jesse didn't understand was why he was chasing after a woman this way. He never chased women. He used them, discarded them. So why was he here, masquerading as a chauffeur, no less? And what did he expect was going to happen when they finally arrived in Marblehead at the seaside home that this woman loved so much?

A dry smile toyed at the corners of his mouth. Oh, he

knew what he wanted to happen. Even now he felt a telltale tightening in his groin. Man, was he sore! He'd worked his body—or had it worked him?—in inspiring and inspired ways last night. *She* had done that to him. Paige Mattheson. Frigid? Not by a long shot! He didn't know about her, but aches and all, he was ready for another go-round right now.

Daring a glance in the rearview mirror, he saw that her head lay against the back of the seat. Her eyes were closed. She wore a serene expression that was almost disturbing in its beauty. He wondered if she was thinking of their lovemaking, too, but didn't have the courage to ask. Didn't have the courage? Since when had he not had the courage to speak his mind before a woman? Bastard, many had called him when he'd been his usual blunt self. Perhaps he was a bastard. Certainly he was a loner, a man who prized his independence. He had a good job, one that demanded his every waking hour from the moment he began an assignment to its completion.

Fortunately he was on R and R right now. Otherwise he'd never have been able to come in pursuit of Paige this way.

He winced at his own choice of words. And the cycle of equivocation began again.

For better than two hours they drove in relative silence. They were approaching Hartford, their halfway point, when at last Dallas spoke. "Hungry?"

Paige raised her head and looked around. She'd been so buried in her own thoughts that she hadn't charted the progress of the car as she might otherwise have done. "A little," she answered quietly.

"There's a super place at the Civic Center. Continentaltype food. Interested?"

"Very." In point of fact, hunger was secondary. She'd been wondering if Dallas was ever going to talk to her again. Lunch at a continental-type restaurant in the Civic Center sounded promising.

Obviously familiar with the city, Dallas knew just which exit to take, which way to turn after that. Paige wasn't at all surprised when, rather than dropping her at the front of the restaurant as Felix might have done, he drove into the huge parking garage adjacent to the center and parked.

She didn't think of Dallas as her chauffeur. When he tossed his cap onto the seat and helped her out, he was her escort. Her tall, handsome, breathtakingly sexy escort. When he took her hand in his, it seemed the most natural thing in the world. Without words he confirmed that the night before had been no dream, as she'd half begun to wonder during the silent drive north.

He handled himself smoothly, speaking in quiet tones to the maître d', gesturing toward the table he wanted, a quiet one by a large potted palm. By the time they'd been seated, Paige was feeling surprisingly happy, if vaguely shy. She waited for him to speak to her, which he did only after he'd ordered a bottle of what she recognized to be a very fine white wine. It occurred to her that the agency might not be thrilled.

"This is on me," he said quietly, finding it a matter of pride that she know he was no parasite. Despite what he'd so blithely said when she'd offered to pay for their cold drinks yesterday, he refused to bill the agency for anything, least of all his time. Even beyond the issue of pride, he felt less…devious doing it this way.

"I was wondering," she answered as softly, a hint of teasing in the eyes he saw now to be the prettiest of jade. He wondered why he hadn't noticed them before, realized he'd been distracted by…other aspects of the intriguing woman before him.

For long moments he simply stared at those eyes, trying to understand why they fascinated him so. They were shy without being coy, warm without being suggestive. He found himself decidedly content staring into their depths. It was this very contentment that struck a note of annoyance in him.

"How do you feel?" he asked.

"Fine."

"No…regrets the morning after?"

"It's the afternoon." The shyness she'd felt was slowly burning off, as a fog beneath the sun, leaving a lightheartedness shining from her face. He was the one who was awkward, she realized. The knowledge made him that much more endearing.

"You know what I mean."

"Yes. And no, I have no regrets." Her soft smile supported her claim.

"Are you surprised that I'm here?"

"A little. I didn't expect to see you again."

"Did you want to?"

"I wasn't sure."

If he had hoped to unsettle her with his bluntness, he was failing badly. Despite her words, she seemed very sure of herself. And she seemed unbothered by the arrogance that he knew shadowed his questions.

"What were you thinking?" he prodded, driven by ego as much as by anything else.

"I was thinking that even if I never saw you again, I'd remember last night. It was very special."

"Glad to hear it. You shouldn't have hoped I'd come today, though. I'm unreliable in that way."

"I wasn't hoping. Just wondering."

"You weren't hoping? Not just a little?"

She looked down and stifled a grin. "I think I'm denting your armor."

"Of course not. Well, maybe a little. Every man likes to think that once he's made a woman his, she can't wait to see him again."

Raising her head, she looked at him. Her gaze held if not smugness then at least full command of the moment. "Is that what you did…made me yours?"

His cheeks burned. And he thought *he* was direct!

"Well, euphemistically speaking, I suppose. Some men feel possessive toward the woman they've made love to."

"Do you?"

"No. I don't believe in ties like that."

"You've got nothing to fear from me," she said.

Her utter sincerity set him back again. For an instant he wondered if perhaps Ben had been right. There was passion, and there was passion. Paige now seemed so calm, so self-assured that he had to force himself to remember how she'd been last night. "You don't believe in ties?"

"I don't need to belong to someone—" She raised her eyes and stopped speaking when the waiter brought their wine. He made a ceremony of uncorking it, poured a sample for Dallas to taste, then, with his approval, filled their glasses. When Dallas promptly ordered for both himself and Paige, she indulged him. She was secure enough of her individuality not to be threatened by his gesture of dominance.

"A toast," he said, lifting his glass as soon as the waiter had gone. "To us."

Looking deep into his eyes, Paige nodded once, then took a sip of her wine. How did one respond to such a toast? To agree was to suggest some future relationship, yet she held no pretense on that score. To disagree, on the other hand, was rude. And perhaps a lie. Though she had no designs on Dallas's future, she couldn't rule out the possibility that they might see each other from time to time.

"You were saying?" he drawled, setting down his glass, placing his forearms on the table and interlacing his fingers.

Though, as always, Paige was affected by his nearness, she was undaunted by his taunting tone. "I was saying," she resumed on the same soft note, "that I like my life as it is. I enjoy living by myself. I enjoy my independence."

"But you enjoyed last night, didn't you?"

"I told you, I did. That doesn't mean that I need it tonight. I'm not a hanger-on, Dallas—"

"Jesse," he whispered, then paused. "Say it."

His whisper stirred all those things in her that she'd felt

the day before. Where his curtness couldn't stir her, his softness did.

"Jesse," she whispered back, then lowered her eyes self-consciously and laughed. "I think I'll always think of you as Dallas. Jesse feels...strange."

"Strange as in personal? Intimate? Will you always think of me as your chauffeur?"

"But I don't," she argued quickly, knowing it was true. Though she'd said the words in her mind, even voiced them to Marjory, she'd never in her heart believed them, not in the truest of senses, certainly not by way of conde-scension. To her, Dallas's occupation had been incidental, and more than a little mystifying, given his obvious social grace. Sitting across from her as he was, wearing his tailored navy suit and an air of thorough comfort in as high-priced a restaurant as this was, he might have been a lawyer or a stockbroker or a playboy who'd inherited millions. Maybe that was it, she mused. Maybe he worked as a chauffeur for kicks. But kicks...suffering boredom and the heat as he'd done yesterday? Of course, the results had been well worth his while. Perhaps he'd simply devised a new way to combat the singles' scene, guaran-teeing himself wealthy women, to boot. *There* was a thought that *did* bother her. It made her feel used. Dirty.

"Do you do this often?" she heard herself ask. The need to know was suddenly very great.

"Do what?"

"Pick up women this way?"

For the first time that afternoon, he seemed amused. "You mean, do I often seduce my passengers?" When she gave a hesitant nod, his smile broadened. "No. This was a first."

"Why did you do it?"

"That's a naive question." Even as he said it, he felt the slightest bit guilty. For one thing, there was the matter of the deception he practiced. For another, there was the bet he'd made with Ben. But neither of those facts touched at the root of the matter. "The attraction was there from the beginning," he said more quietly.

"Did it…bother you?"

"Should it have?"

She shrugged, not quite sure what she was getting at, herself. "I don't know."

"Look, Paige," he offered, feeling a sudden need to put her at ease. "The attraction I feel for you is as natural as that which you feel for me. There's nothing wrong with it, and I refuse to apologize. No, I don't make a practice of picking up women that way, but I'm not sorry things happened as they did. You're a very special lover."

It was Paige's turn to blush then, which she did with uncommon innocence. But she was pleased. She'd never dared think that any man might call her what Dallas just had. It boggled her mind.

"That's pretty," he murmured, brushing the back of his fingers against her cheek.

"What is?" she whispered.

"Your blush. I couldn't see it last night in the dark. Were you blushing then, too?"

Her color deepened all the more. When he was like this, his voice so gentle and gravelly, her insides tickled. "At times."

"Surely there've been other men."

"Obviously."

"Many?"

"One."

"Only one?" He couldn't curb his surprise, though it helped explain the wonder he'd seen on her face at various times during the night. "Why is that, Paige? You're a beautiful woman. You obviously feel the right things at the right times."

"It wasn't always that way."

"What do you mean?"

She studied him with gentle eyes, abundantly a̶w̶ the intimacies they'd shared. One more see̶n̶

She saw no point in being evasive, and she had nothing to be ashamed of now that she *knew*. "There was an artist a long time ago. We were both very young. He assumed I was frigid. I was never quite sure...until last night."

If Dallas's ego had been shaky, her words set it on firm ground. It was a heady thought—that he'd been able to draw from her what no other man had. "No wonder you look so pleased with yourself."

"I am." Here, with Dallas, she felt feminine through and through. It was a new image of herself. She rather liked it.

"Then—" Dallas frowned, trying to put the pieces of the puzzle together "—you've avoided men over the years out of fear?"

"Oh, no. I just wasn't interested." At the narrowing of his eyes, she came to her own defense. "I wasn't. Honestly. My life is very full, what with my work. It's not as if I've been aware of any great void. I'm not aware of any now, for that matter. Last night taught me something about myself, but it won't necessarily change the way I live."

"You don't want a husband...or children?"

"By all means. But there's no rush. Why are you looking at me that way? I'm not unusual in this day and age."

"You're unusual," Dallas stated, swirling the wine in his glass, then draining it. When he set the glass down, he looked her in the eye. "I'm still not sure I believe it. You have a kind of self-containment that's remarkable. I can't remember when I've met anyone as sure of herself."

"Oh, I have my moments of insecurity."

"When?"

"When I'm sculpting. Or rather, when I finish. I may l⟨...⟩what I've done. After all, there's a little bit of myself ⟨...⟩ I do. Unfortunately, more often than not, I ⟨...⟩nd the piece to one gallery or another. It's ⟨...⟩ to the world. I'm not all that secure until ⟨...⟩hat the piece has been well received." ⟨...⟩e what they think of you?"

"Not of me. Of my work. I'd be less than human if I didn't."

"But you said you didn't care if you ever sold—"

"Selling is one thing, and I don't care about that. But—" she struggled for the words to express what she felt "—sculpting is creating. It's taking something ostensibly without form and shaping it into an object with meaning. If my meaning doesn't get across, I'm crushed."

"Has that ever happened?"

"Several times."

"What do you do then?"

She grinned. "I keep clay on hand. It's therapeutic. Several hours of slapping it on the bench, giving it shape then slapping it into a blob again usually does the trick."

"A little temper tantrum, eh?"

"You could say."

"And then you feel better?"

"*Then* I have the courage to call Margie back. She's great for consolation. By that time she's usually been able to shift the piece to another gallery. I suppose it must be like having a child. You pour sweat and tears into its rearing and send it off into the world only to find that it's found a niche that isn't right. Things like that can be remedied, though it's plenty painful until they are."

Dallas was shaking his head, sighing deeply. "You'd probably be devastated as a mother when another kid on the block called yours names."

"I'm sure I would be."

"And that doesn't discourage you from ever having children?"

He wasn't just making conversation. Paige sensed there was deep feeling in his words. She wondered where his streak of pessimism came from. For some reason she couldn't ask.

"I'm not discouraged. My work is basically strong. Often it's simply a question of finding the right home for it. I assume the same is true of children. You instill in them certain values, build certain strengths. If you've done it right, they find their place, regardless of what trials they may have getting there."

"Is that what happened to you?"

"No. I've been lucky. Life's been kind all along. But I've seen others who've gone through hard times. They survived." She was thinking, most specifically, of one of her brothers. She'd always viewed him as the most creative of the three Mattheson boys, yet somehow he'd been channeled into a mathematical career where his creativity stagnated. He'd moved from one high-tech corporation to another, and was increasingly miserable, until at last he'd thrown caution to the winds and had signed on to write computer programs for a fledgling software manufacturer. Though his income was nowhere near where it had been, he was finally happy.

"Tell me about yourself, Paige," Dallas asked softly.

"Isn't that what I've been doing?"

"No. I mean, about what you were like as a child. What your family's like. How you got to be so lucky."

The arrival of their lunch gave Paige several minutes to compose her thoughts. It was only after they'd sampled and approved their cold duck salads that she spoke.

"I grew up in Connecticut."

"Whereabouts?"

"Westport."

"Ahh. That says a lot."

She knew it did, which was why she usually didn't volunteer that particular bit of information. She wasn't sure why she had done so now, only she knew that something in Dallas's intense gaze wouldn't permit less than the full truth. "Yes. That's one of the ways in which I was lucky. My father was—is—a bank executive. We grew up—"

"We?"

"I have three older brothers." When Dallas nodded, she went on, "We grew up with many of the things that others never have. Not only material things, but good health… and love."

"Do your parents still live in Westport?" She nodded. "Are you close?"

"Very."

"Were they at the party the other night?"

"No. I didn't want them there." She pushed a cherry tomato around her plate. "I...shows like that are hard for me. I'd rather see my parents in more relaxed times."

"Hard for you? You looked totally in control." When her head came up and she eyed him strangely, Dallas realized his error. To her knowledge, he hadn't been at that party. "What I mean is that you always seem so cool and self-assured. I can't imagine your having trouble anywhere."

This time her gaze was lightly chiding. "You, more than anyone, should know better. If it hadn't been for you yesterday, I might never have made it."

"You'd have made it," he said gruffly, then softened his tone. "But it was fun, wasn't it?"

She smiled, shyly, and nodded. It *had* been fun—a picnic in the park, gentle conversation, a companion. Then, of course, there had been last night. The memory stirred her as she looked into the blue eyes sparkling before her. She felt lured, drawn in. Suddenly she wanted to reach out and touch him, those lean, faintly shadowed cheeks, that mouth. She took a deep breath, then let it out in a long, unsteady sigh, and finally smiled. "You are inspiring, Dallas. Has anyone ever told you that before?"

DALLAS REPEATED those words time and again in his mind during the rest of the drive. Not only the words, but their attendant expression. He'd been giving her his guaranteed-to-knock-'em-dead stare, and she'd simply absorbed it, taken a deep breath and smiled. The master was slipping, that's all there was to it. By rights she should have already invited him to spend the night.

But she hadn't. In fact, she seemed perfectly content with the notion that last night had happened and was done. He had to believe she still wanted him. There had been the unevenness of her breath, the faint tremor of the pulse at her neck.

But she was in control. Cool, firm control. And he? He wanted her more than ever. Perhaps it was the challenge that appealed to him. Yes, that was enough of an excuse to try to seduce her a second time. As soon as they reached her beachfront home, he'd simply take her in his arms and she'd melt. He knew it.

It would be too easy. Too quick. No, for Paige he'd have to come up with a more cunning approach. After all, where would the fun be otherwise?

THE JOKE WAS ON HIM. Sitting alone in the huge limousine, parked on the shoulder of the road, Dallas stared moodily across the water at the darkening horizon. He was as taut as a wire, as frustrated as if he'd been bound by one with no hope of escape. He'd miscalculated somewhere. Trying to understand what had happened, he reviewed the events of the hours now past.

After leaving the restaurant, they'd returned to the highway. Conversation had been intermittent and light. Paige had been as calm, as self-possessed as ever, even more so as they'd neared her home. It had been as though she approached Shangri-la. She'd relaxed fully, kicking her shoes off and stretching out on the seat. When at last they'd left the highway, she'd rolled down her window and deeply breathed in the fresh sea air.

If he'd thought Paige beautiful before, he hadn't seen her on her home turf. She'd grown happier by the minute, almost as though she were a child seeing the ocean for the first time. Her cheeks pinkened. Her eyes brightened. When she'd reached up and pulled the pins from her hair, letting it fall gracefully behind her shoulders, she'd looked like that child...yet every bit a woman. He'd actually adjusted the rearview mirror to more easily see her. She'd been a vision.

He'd barely pulled the long limousine to a halt when she

had her shoes back on and was out the door. She'd stood still then, shoulders back, head up to the breeze. She'd inhaled once, and again. Then, as if fortified by the most potent drug in the world, she'd turned to him with the most brilliant of smiles.

"Great, isn't it?" she'd said, but hadn't given him time to answer, for she'd run up the pebbled walk and entered the house before he'd barely climbed from the car.

After opening the trunk and removing her suitcase, he'd taken a minute to admire the home she loved. He had to admit that it was magnificent. Contemporary, and sprawling over its own minipeninsula, it combined fieldstone and shingle to create a distinctly natural effect. With a steep sloped roof, it backed onto the sea. Even before he entered the large open living room he'd guessed what he'd find. Glass facing the sea. Walls and walls of glass. Living room, dining room, kitchen, bedrooms—she'd given him the grand tour, enjoying every minute of it herself. Her pride had been boundless, most evident in the studio, which stood in one wing.

"Did you have it built yourself?" he'd asked, sensing that the house was her, through and through. It fit her perfectly.

"Oh, no. I lucked out here, too. The man who built it— an architect—was moving south. He'd put it on the market the very day I came looking. Houses go fast here, particularly ones overlooking the ocean."

How long they'd stood in that living room, staring out over the weathered deck toward the sea, Dallas didn't know. The waves had mesmerized him almost as much as they mesmerized Paige, who stood beside him. Almost, but not quite. He'd been aware of her every breath, of the way her lips curved into a dreamy smile, of the way her heart beat.

He'd taken her in his arms then and kissed her with every bit of the tenderness she inspired. And tenderness had yielded to hunger as he'd known it would. Her lips had been warm and moist, her body arching into his.

Only when he'd sensed her total surrender—when her hands had begun to roam his back in silent invitation, when her lips had begun to demand on their own—had he set her back.

"Take care," he'd whispered. Pressing a final kiss on her forehead, he'd turned and left.

She'd wanted him, just as he'd known she would. And unless she truly was hard as stone, she'd have plenty to think about that night. Unfortunately, so would Dallas. He hadn't counted on the toll his cleverness would take on his own body.

Climbing from the car, he walked around to lean against its hood and face the sea. The air was refreshing, its evening coolness some relief on his fevered skin. The rustle of the high grasses behind him soothed. The surf lulled. He could see why she'd been so anxious to return. What he didn't see was what *he* was going to do about the ache that lingered.

Then he stood straight and knew what he was going to do. He was going to drive straight back to New York, return the fool limousine, put in a random call to one of the names in his little black book and forget that Paige Mattheson existed.

Perhaps he'd even call Ben and gloat. After all, he'd won the bet, hadn't he?

AS IT TURNED OUT, the only thing he did that night was return the limousine. By the time he reached home, he was thoroughly exhausted. Wandering from room to room, he felt strange, displaced. He ran his finger along things as he ambled—the back of the long leather sofa in the living room, the thick oak banister leading upstairs, the bookshelves that lined both the bedroom and den on the second floor, the edge of the metal table in his workroom on the third. He stared distractedly at the two TV monitors atop the table, then at the leader that fed film from one screen to the other. These were the tools of his trade. He knew them as intimately as he'd known any woman, and Lord knew he spent much more time with them.

Why, then, did he feel unsettled? By rights he should be very much at home and content. The Kem machine was his closest friend, the nearest thing he had to a long-standing mistress. Had he lost interest in her, too? Why was it she suddenly seemed so cold and unappealing? Was it simply that he wasn't working, that there was no film now flowing through the mazes connecting screen to screen?

Without even bothering to flip on his answering machine and find out if anyone had called, he retraced his steps to the bottom floor, poured himself a healthy glassful of Scotch and sagged down onto the sofa.

The next thing he knew, it was morning. Late morning. The empty glass lay on its side on the floor. His muscles were cramped from confinement on the sofa all night. Sitting up, he propped his elbows on spread knees and dropped his face into his hands. His head ached. His neck was stiff. He felt as he did when he worked round the clock on a tight deadline, except that this morning he had nothing to show for his time. Nothing whatsoever.

A glance at his watch told him it was nearly noon. Pushing himself from the sofa, he went into the kitchen, poured himself a cold glass of milk, then drank it slouched against the counter. A police siren screamed in the distance. Scowling, he wondered where it was headed, what it would find when it got there. Forced entry? Robbery? Perhaps a little murder? Depressing.

Setting the glass none too gently in the sink, he climbed to his third-floor workroom and turned on the answering machine to find that his agent had called the day before. Urgent, he'd said. With a sigh, Dallas dialed his number. The secretary put him right through.

"John?"

"It's about time you got back to me!"

"I just got the message." He was in no mood to argue. "What's up?"

"Wagner called. He wants you to edit the piece he did in Nicaragua."

"I didn't know he was doing anything in Nicaragua."

"Neither did he. It was pretty last minute. He didn't think he'd be able to get into the country. When the okay finally came, he grabbed cameras and crew and ran."

"Nice."

"Well? Will you do it?"

"No."

"Why not?"

"I'm on vacation."

"Come on, Jesse. This is a great opportunity. We're talking hot film."

"I'm on vacation."

"You're there, aren't you? How long could this take—a week, maybe two? So you'll take your vacation then."

"I want it now."

"The money's good."

"The money was good on the prison piece I just finished, which is why I don't need to work for a while."

"Hey, where's your ambition? Wagner's the best, and he wants *you*."

Dallas ran a hand through his already-disheveled hair and sighed. "Another time, okay, John?" he coaxed wearily. "I'm just not up for it now. It'd be far worse to take the job and do it poorly than to simply explain that the timing's not right. Wagner will understand. You'll handle it well. Diplomacy's your specialty."

"Hmph. Thanks to you I get plenty of practice. Sure you won't reconsider? It's a plum."

"I'm sure."

"Are you all right?"

"Sure."

"You sound down."

"Naw. Just tired. Nothing a few weeks' rest won't cure."

A few weeks' rest. He thought about it as he hung up the phone. He did need a few weeks' rest. And not here. The city was about as restful as an army of ants.

He could fly up to the Gaspé. The small inn he'd stayed

at two years ago had been restful enough. Boring, but restful. Or out to the Rockies. Of course, there wouldn't be any skiing this time of year. The Caribbean? But it'd be hot as hell.

In that instant he knew that he might name a hundred spots and find something wrong with each. There was one spot, though, that interested him. It'd be cool and refreshing, what with the steady breeze off the ocean. It'd be interesting, doubtlessly stimulating. He could take his time, sate his curiosity, get her out from under his skin once and for all.

Without further deliberation, he trotted downstairs, shaved and showered, then pulled out his duffel bag and filled it with the clothes he'd need. His headache had miraculously eased, as had the stiffness of his limbs. In fact, he felt remarkably peppy.

Within the hour he was on his way north.

CHAPTER FOUR

PARKING HIS CAR IN THE driveway of the rambling house, Dallas climbed out, stretched, breathed deeply of the salty air much as Paige had done when they'd arrived here nearly twenty-four hours before. It was late in the afternoon, still warm, though the breeze was welcome relief from the heat he'd left behind in the city.

He started up the front path, then changed his mind and veered off onto a smaller path that led around the house toward the sea. The roar of the surf lured him on. He passed low-growing shrubs and trees that miraculously withstood the coastal elements. At a low stone wall he stopped. Beyond him was a sloping hill of rock, beyond that the sea. For long moments he stared at it, feeling more refreshed by the minute.

Then he glanced up toward the deck extending high on his left and caught his breath. Paige stood there, so absorbed in her thoughts that she was oblivious to his presence.

It had been an odd day for her. She'd been up early, had walked the beach feeling strangely unsure as to what she wanted to do. She'd known what she *should* do; she should get to work on a stupendous piece, the first to send to one of the galleries she'd visited. She'd already sent thank-you notes—last night when she'd been unable to fall asleep—to those who'd hosted her. But in the morning light she'd still felt restless, unable to settle down. Perhaps she needed a day to unwind, she'd told herself.

Then she'd spotted a stone on the beach. She'd picked

it up, turned it in her hand, studied it, read its heart. And she'd known what she wanted to do. It was something personal, something she'd never sell. But working on it all day as she'd done, she felt more at peace than she had since…since Dallas had left.

Mesmerized, Dallas stared at her. She wore a red blouse, knotted at midriff, and white shorts. Her hair blew free in the breeze. Arms wrapped around her waist, she seemed in a world of her own, a world she shared with her house and the sea.

For the first time he stopped to consider that he was intruding. She was a woman of solitude. She might not want him here.

But his needs at that moment were too great to allow for his turning and leaving as he'd done yesterday. He had to see her. He had to hold her.

At his first movement toward the plank steps leading from ocean to deck, Paige looked around sharply. Heart racing, she watched Dallas swing himself from the low stone wall to a midway point on the stairs. He boldly loped the rest of the way, slowing only when he'd reached the deck, halting only when he stood before her.

He tried to judge her reaction by her expression. Round-eyed, she was startled, as obviously a woman would be who had suddenly and unexpectedly found a man making his way to her deck. She was unsure—the way she bit her lower lip attested to that. And she was vulnerable; it was written all over her face.

This vulnerability was something he hadn't seen in her before and it had a strange effect on him. Rather than sweeping her into his arms and promptly picking up where he'd left off the day before, he lifted a hand to her cheek and caressed her softness with his thumb. She seemed suddenly like porcelain, fragile, delicate, but not at all cold and untouchable. Rather, she inspired tenderness and a protectiveness that would have stunned him had he not been so entranced by the spell she cast.

"Hi," he breathed softly.

She smiled, still uncertain. She hadn't expected him, had assumed, after yesterday, that he'd gone for good. She didn't know what to expect now, only knew that, some-where deep inside, she was pleased to see him.

He cleared his throat and cast a quick glance down at his shirt and jeans. "I, uh, I figured I'd better go home and change. A suit just isn't right for the ocean."

She laughed, a soft laugh that was half whisper, and lowered her eyes. His jeans were clean but worn, fitting his hips well. His shirt, neatly starched, was plaid, the top two buttons open. Arms bare below his short sleeves, his skin was firm, lightly haired, exuding warmth.

"You look fine now," she whispered, finding her breath in short supply.

"I feel better." He kept his thumb busy at her cheek while he gently spread his other fingers into her hair. "You looked so pretty standing here. A beautiful statue."

Her eyes met his then with a message that went beyond her words. "I'm no statue."

"I know," he murmured shakily, then lowered his head and opened his mouth over hers. His lips barely touched at first but coasted lightly as, eyes closed, he savored the fact that he was here again, at last. She seemed unreal, far too precious for him. He knew he should stop himself. He knew he should never have come. He'd only hurt her, as he had so many women in the past. But none of those others lured him as Paige did with her self-assurance, her poise, the vulnerability that had seeped through her veneer for that very short time. He knew he should leave, but he couldn't. He needed her too badly.

Only when he felt her lips part beneath his did he kiss her fully, and even then it was with a care that was novel for him. She tasted warm and sweet, very special. And she returned his kiss with the same kind of care. There was a softness to her—her lips, her tongue, the moist inner recesses of her mouth—that branded her different, and he found himself trembling under the responsibility he'd taken upon himself.

He drew back to find that her eyes were closed. She seemed in a trance, her expression dreamlike. He traced her lips with the tip of his tongue. When her own tongue crept out to meet it, he gasped. Hugging her fully to him, he buried his face in her hair.

"Paige…Paige…" he rasped, knowing that, for all the gentleness she inspired, he had to have her now. His hands roamed steadily and widely, exploring her shoulders, her back, her hips and thighs before returning to her bottom and crushing her hips to his. "I need you, Paige. God help me, but I need you!"

She nodded against his shoulder, her hands clutching at the corded muscles of his back. She couldn't think beyond the moment, beyond the heavenly state of pleasure Dallas created. She was attuned to her body, and its every sense ached for him. Only now did she admit how disturbed she'd been last night when he'd kissed her so enticingly and then left. Sexual frustration was new to her; she wasn't sure she liked it.

But Dallas was here now, promising the same bliss he'd shown her that sultry night in New York. But she knew so little about him. Would he arouse her again, then leave before bringing her the fulfillment her body craved?

Hands on his shoulders, she held him back. "Dallas, don't start if…if…"

He read the fear in her eyes and it turned his insides to jelly. "I won't, love," he murmured, smoothing the hair back from her face. "I won't leave. Is that what's got you worried?" When she nodded, he brought her back into his embrace. His limbs trembled under the self-restraint he imposed. His breath was warm in her hair. "I'm sorry for last night. I was a bastard. If it's any consolation, I was in agony all the way to New York. I should have turned around before I'd ever reached the highway and come back, but I'm dumb sometimes. Really dumb." Holding her back, he framed her face with his hands. His voice was little more than a breath. "So special. So very special."

He kissed her softly, then raised his head to watch the slow movement of his hands on her neck. Ever downward they crept, trembling slightly, fingers inching under the open tabs of her shirt, gliding downward still. The swell of her breasts inflamed him, but he continued his progress until he reached the knot at her ribs and released it. He spread the soft fabric to the side, easing it wider and wider until her bare breasts were open to his gaze. Holding his breath, he touched her, first the creamy outer contours and soft undersides, then the nipples, taut and puckered. He brushed the pads of his thumbs over them, watched them tighten more as her breath came faster. A tiny sound came from her throat and he raised his eyes to her look of desire.

"Do you want me?" he whispered, needing to hear the words.

"Oh, yes."

Abandoning her breasts abruptly, he took her hand in his. This time his voice came out in a growl. "I don't think I can tease and play. Come on."

She didn't have to ask where he was leading her. She knew, and she wanted to go. Her pulse raced as she let herself be led through the living room, then down the long hall and into her bedroom. There he caught her in his arms and kissed her fiercely.

Her shirt fell easy prey to his marauding fingers, drifting to the floor, already forgotten. He sank back on the bed and drew her between his knees, his lips closing over one breast with such precision that she cried out in stunned delight. It felt so right, his mouth suckling her while his hands slid hungrily up and down her back. The tip of his tongue darted against her nipple, his teeth gently closed and tugged. A ripple of heat seared through her and settled in her womb, and she clutched his shoulders to hold herself upright. When he took her other nipple between his thumb and forefinger and rolled it around, she muffled a moan against his hair.

Suddenly time was of the essence. Dallas's hands were in her shorts, pushing them and her panties over her hips. He continued to kiss her breasts while he worked blindly at the buttons of his shirt, then his belt, shifting her to lie on the bed for only as long as it took him to shuck his clothes. Then he was back beside her, on her, in her, thrusting powerfully.

Paige welcomed the force. She needed it, if for no other reason than to assure herself she wasn't dreaming. She thrived on it, rose to meet it, found the fireball inside glowing, growing, bursting. Long orgasmic shudders shook her then. She panted, cried raggedly in release. Seconds later Dallas stiffened and moaned, gasping for air as raggedly as she.

He murmured her name brokenly and collapsed over her. "Paige…Paige…how good it is with you…."

She could do nothing but smile. Where last time she'd been overjoyed simply to reach that exploding pinnacle, this time she took pleasure just as much in Dallas's. To know that he'd wanted her enough to come back, to know that she'd been able to satisfy him again was another feather in her cap. She ran her hands over his damp body and beamed her pride.

"I'm crushing you," he grunted. "God, I don't think I can move."

"Don't. I'm all right."

But he forced himself to his side, turning his head to bask in her satisfaction. The sounds of their labored breathing filled the air, slowing gradually to coincide with the rhythmic pound of the surf beyond the open sliding door. He moved his head on the pillow, then realized that it wasn't linen beneath his ear. "We didn't even pull the spread back. Man, I couldn't think straight." Not then. But now he could. He bolted up on an elbow. "Oh, my God."

Paige raised her head, eyes filled with concern. "What is it?"

"Oh, my God. Paige, I couldn't think straight. It was so fast. I didn't use anything…."

She grasped his shoulder then, gently kneading the tense muscle. "It's all right, Dallas," she said softly. "It'll be okay."

He eyed her strangely. "Don't tell me you rushed out to a doctor this morning."

"I won't. I didn't." She hadn't anticipated the need.

"Then how could it be okay? If I've gotten you pregnant—"

"We'll worry about it then. I told you the other night. The timing's okay for me."

He scowled. "You really think the rhythm method works? Talk about naiveté!" Thrusting a hand through his hair, he sagged back to the bed. "Dumb is dumb. I take the cake when I'm with you. Damn it, if I hadn't wanted you so badly..."

"Dallas—"

"It's *Jesse*, damn it! I'm not your chauffeur anymore!"

Gathering her composure, Paige sat up quietly on the bed. "What are you?"

He glowered. "Your lover! Or hadn't you noticed?"

She eyed him steadily. "What are you?"

He stared at her angrily, then bounded up and reached for his jeans. "What in the hell are you talking about?"

"I'm talking about you, Jesse. I want to know who you are, what you do, why you're here."

With an impatient tug he zipped his jeans. "You want to know? You really want to know?"

"Yes."

He gritted his teeth. "Well, I'm sure as hell not a chauffeur!"

"I think I knew that," she stated calmly. "Now tell me something I don't know."

"I was at the party the other night."

For the first time her composure wavered. She wasn't sure what she'd expected to hear him say, but it wasn't this. "My show?"

"Yes. Your show. I was there with all the others, dragged

along by a friend of mine, a high-priced lawyer who picks up clients at bashes like those."

"I see," she said softly and lowered her head, only to jerk it back up when he exploded.

"No, you don't see! We were standing around, the two of us, drinking the champagne that your host so graciously provided, and we were studying you. My friend had heard rumors." She winced, but he went on. "I told him they were wrong. We made a bet."

Paige swallowed hard. Her insides were trembling in a way totally unrelated to the passion she'd known moments before. "A bet?" she asked, her voice thin.

Dallas had come too far to turn back, not that he was thinking of doing so at the moment. He was angry at the emotions Paige generated. He went on, aiming to hurt. "A bet that I could make it with you. Looks like I won."

He didn't feel like a winner. He felt like a snake. Unable to stand himself for a minute longer in the confines of the room, he whirled on his bare heel and stormed out.

Paige shook all over. Creeping jerkily to the edge of the bed, she strained down for her blouse, then held it to her breasts and slowly rocked back and forth. She stared at the door, then the floor. She took several deep, shuddering breaths.

Out on the deck, Dallas was in no better shape. He hated himself, hated her for causing it. No, he corrected, he didn't hate her. It was what he felt that he hated. Tender. Possessive. And aching to soothe the hurt he'd caused.

She hadn't asked for him. Not once had she been the seducer. She was happy with her life. Who was he to mess it up? Oh, sure, he'd taught her something about herself. She knew now that she was capable of true passion. So what in the devil was she supposed to do with it?

Bending over, he propped his hands on the wood railing. The sea looked stormy, or was it simply a reflection of the turbulence within himself? He didn't know what to do, whether to leave or stay, whether to apologize or forget he'd ever said a word. The most compassionate thing he could do now was to get out of her life. She'd forget him. She'd find someone who was warm enough, caring enough, man enough to give her the love she deserved. He couldn't. Love wasn't part of his vocabulary. He didn't want the responsibility of a wife, much less children. If she was pregnant, he didn't know what he'd do!

For a long time he stood there brooding. The air cooled with the lowering of the sun, but he welcomed the chill on his bare chest as a reminder of the coldhearted soul that he was. They'd all been right. He was a bastard. In *every* sense of the word.

He jumped when he felt a hand on his shoulder and whirled to find Paige with his shirt. She'd dressed, this time wearing a crewneck sweater and high socks with her shorts. Her face was pale. He could see remnants of moisture on her lower lids.

"You'll catch cold," she murmured, reaching to drape the shirt across his shoulders. Taking the shirt from her, he put it on, buying time as he carefully secured the four lower buttons.

"After what I've done, I'd have thought you'd be pleased if I caught pneumonia."

"I wouldn't."

"You should. I'm a lout. You deserve someone better."

"I'm not looking for someone. And you couldn't catch pneumonia. It's too warm and you're too strong."

Her beneficence ate at him. He took her shoulders, tempted to try to shake some sense into her. She should scream at him, kick him out. But she didn't. And he couldn't shake her, not when he felt suddenly so very tired. "Paige," he said, sighing quietly, "didn't any of what I said bother you?"

"Of course it bothered me. I'm human. No one likes to feel cheap."

He winced. "God, don't use that word." His fingers bit into her shoulders. "It wasn't like that. I swear. It may have started with a bet, but I'd never have made the bet in the first place if you hadn't appealed to me from the start. Bet or no, I'd probably have sought you out. It was the air of challenge surrounding the bet that made me pose as your chauffeur. I'm usually more direct."

"I'm sure."

"Damn it, how can you be so calm! Yell at me, Paige! Tell me what a jackass I am!"

"That's not my way. Of course, if you insist on a tantrum, I could probably muster a feeble one. Should I try?" The corners of her lips were twitching. She was trying her best not to smile. Yes, Dallas had hurt her, but she didn't have it in her heart to carry on. It was as though she sensed that an inner demon was eating him, that he didn't want to be this way, that he didn't *have* to be this way. And, in spite of everything, he did make her feel like a woman. She couldn't find fault with that.

He scowled at her, closed his eyes and shook his head, then gently enfolded her in his arms and held her against him. He felt her catch her breath and resist for an instant, but only an instant. Slowly she relaxed. The faint shudder that passed through her suggested that she was more sensitive than she let on. Once again he told himself to leave, but his arms wouldn't listen. They simply held her tighter, rocking her gently.

"Paige, Paige, Paige. What am I going to do with you? You're a fool to put up with someone like me."

"I'm not 'putting up' with you. You're just…here."

"Same difference. I don't want to hurt you, really I don't, it's just that I don't have much experience with gentleness."

She drew her head back and looked up at him. "What do you do, Jesse, when you're not masquerading as a chauffeur?"

He smiled. It was nice, holding her like this, passion spent, simply…close. He couldn't remember ever having done anything like it. "I'm a film editor."

"Feature films?"

"Documentaries, mostly."

"Are you between jobs?"

"You could say that. I'm on vacation. When I work, it's pretty intensive. I finished something a week ago and I need a break."

"What was it that you finished?"

"A documentary on prison reform. Pretty depressing considering the footage I had to leave on the floor in order to keep the tone the producer wanted."

"Not much reform, huh?"

His features tightened. He focused unseeing on the ribbing of her sweater. "Not much. I mean, they're working at it, but it's like trying to plug a three-foot leak with a toothpick. Conditions inside this country's prisons are terrifying and getting worse."

"They're better than in many other countries."

"That doesn't excuse it. This is America. We pride ourselves on being progressive. Let me tell you, the stuff on that film was discouraging."

"Do you feel that the finished product is deceptive?"

"No. Not deceptive. It told the truth. Maybe not the whole truth—" he met her gaze "—but then, many of us are guilty of that from time to time." He took a measured breath. "I never lied to you at any point, Paige. I mean, when you asked me about driving and all, I never lied."

"I know," she said softly. "Don't worry about it. You've told me the whole truth now, haven't you?"

It was his chance. Holding her slightly away, he rubbed her upper arms for a minute. Then he dropped them and pressed his palms to the wood rail behind him. There was a fierceness underlying the quiet in his tone. "I'm a loner, Paige. I don't want you or any other woman tying up my life. I can't be expected to give. I don't have it in me. For as many times as we're together, one day I'll pick up and be gone. I can promise you nothing."

In an uncharacteristic burst of anger, she tipped up her

chin. "I thought I told you that I didn't want anything. Weren't you listening? Or did you simply chalk off my words to female nonsense? Well, I was serious, Dallas. I'm not asking a *thing* of you. I didn't ask you to drive me around New York, or to kiss me outside my front door." She held up a hand to ward off a retort. "I know, I know. I kissed you back, but I only took what was offered. I didn't ask for a thing. I never have. I never will. I have my pride, too. And my house, my life, my career. I'm perfectly capable of taking care of myself with or without you!"

Throwing her hands in the air, she half turned, muttering, "Of all the egotistical—" Then she caught herself and whirled back, hair flying. "And if you're so worried about demands I might make, why don't you climb back into that grotesque limousine—" she pointed toward the front of the house with a shaking hand "—and race back to New York." She shook her head and began muttering again. "God, I've never seen anything like it. Must be urban insanity. Why is it that city people think life revolves around them? There is more to life than *you*, Jesse Dallas." She stared at him for another minute, then, wearing a look of exasperation, stalked to the far side of the deck and faced the darkening sea.

Jesse came up quietly beside her. "I wasn't sure you could do that."

"Do what?"

"Let loose."

"Now you know."

"Mmm, so I do."

"I don't do it often," she cautioned, calming almost miraculously. She'd blown up and was done. That was all there was to it. "You've been treated to a rare show."

"Then I'll treasure it all the more."

Feeling very much herself again, she slanted him a look. "Are you hungry?"

"Where did *that* come from?"

"I haven't eaten since ten."

"See what happens when you don't have a chauffeur to look after you."

"I always do it this way. Brunch at ten, dinner at six. Two meals. Very healthy."

He arched a brow. "I wonder. You must be starved."

"I've got some fresh sole in the refrigerator. I thought I'd broil it in lemon butter. Sound okay?"

"You're inviting me to dinner?"

"Unless you have other plans. You did mention you had friends in the area."

"They're in Gloucester and they don't know I'm here."

"You were going to surprise them, too?"

Her smug tone goaded him. "I hadn't even thought of them," he growled. "I came to see you. You know that."

"If that's the case, why not join me for dinner?"

"I'd rather take you out."

"Afraid of my cooking? I'm pretty good."

"I'm sure you are. But I didn't come here to put you to work."

They were back to square one. "Why *did* you come, Jesse?" she asked, teasing forgotten. Even the dimming light couldn't hide the urgency on her face.

He took a deep breath, then let it slowly out and raised his eyes to the sky. "I'm not quite sure." His gaze leveled. "I needed to see you, to be with you. I needed a vacation from—" he gestured vaguely southward "—from all that. It was an impulse, I suppose. Hell, I'm not sure why I came!"

"Do you want to spend the night?"

"Of course I want to spend the night!"

"Are you good with your hands?"

He stared at her in disbelief for a minute, then abruptly shifted gears. "You *know* I'm good with my hands."

Unfazed by his innuendo, she plugged on. "Can you fix things?"

The drawl receded. "That depends on what they are."

"Wood planks. Several of the lower ones near the beach

are loose. Several others need to be replaced. There's also a faucet that drips in the kitchen, and the bathroom door sticks."

"You need a handyman."

"If I had one, I wouldn't be asking you, would I?"

"No."

"Well? Can you make yourself useful while I work tomorrow?"

"You're gonna work? I was hoping we could drive along the coast, maybe stop at a little place for lobster—"

"I'm gonna work. You're the one who's on vacation, not me."

"All work and no play—"

"Do you want the sole? It won't be fresh much longer, and—"

"You're starved. I know. All right. Broil your damned sole." He watched her start across the deck. "But I'll get that lobster with you one day." He spoke louder as she disappeared through the doorway. "You can't carve stone all the time…!"

THEY ATE at the lacquered table in the dining room, seated comfortably in contemporary armchairs opposite each other. It wasn't a heavily romantic dinner; there were no candles, no fresh flowers. But it was pleasant, companionable. When Jesse wanted to know more about Marblehead, Paige indulged him. In turn, when she wanted to hear more about his work, he opened up.

"It's a lonely job, high on pressure. But it's fascinating. Challenging."

"How did you get into it?"

"Actually, I was a photographer. Straight out of high school. I'd been freelancing to support the habit, but I didn't have enough money for college, so I decided to work for a couple of years. I guess I did okay. Enough of my pictures were picked up by the Associated Press for them to eventually take me on staff. From there things seemed to never stop." He snorted. "I wanted to see the world. I sure did. All the hot spots—Iran, Rhodesia, Vietnam, the Philippines. I was young and energetic. Anywhere the other photographers didn't want to go, I went."

"It must have been enlightening."

"To say the least. Oh, there were pleasant stops on the tour. I saw most of Europe and places in this country that I'd never seen. But for the most part I was sent to trouble spots. Enlightening? That's one word for it. Poverty, squalor, repression, revolution—it's frightening what goes on in the world."

"I'd think you'd burn out after a while."

"I did, though at the time I refused to admit it. I told myself that it was simply time to go back to school."

"College?"

"Mmm. I had enough money saved and, though I'd always been an avid reader, something inside me insisted on a formal education."

"What was it...that something?"

He thought for a while before answering. "Pride, I suppose. I came from nothing, but I wanted to be as good if not better than the next guy, and a college education seemed one step toward that."

"How old were you?"

"Twenty-seven and a hell of a lot older than most of my classmates, I can tell you. If I hadn't been so determined, I think I'd have dropped out after the first semester. It was hard going back to it cold."

"But you made it."

"Uh-huh. And I discovered film editing in the process." His thoughts tripped back and he smiled. "I had this fantastic professor. Very bright guy. Real dry wit. We hit it off from the start. He got me my first job."

"He must be proud that you've continued in the field."

The smile faded. "He's dead. Had a heart attack one day and—" he snapped his fingers "—he was gone."

"I'm sorry."

Jesse shrugged. "That's the way it is. Anyway, he's left his legacy. And my career has soared."

Listening to him talk, studying the changing expressions on his face, Paige saw that Jesse was an expert at denying pain. She guessed that he'd been very fond of this professor, but that to say that he missed him would have been to acknowledge the sorrow of his death. Jesse was hard; the things he'd seen in his days as a photographer must have trained him all too well, she mused.

"What are some of the other films you've edited?" she asked, hoping to spark his enthusiasm again. Her ploy didn't quite work.

He frowned wryly. "Let's see. There was a documentary on child abuse, one on kiddie porn. I did a super thing on suicide. And the elderly—chronicling their plight in a society that thrives on youthfulness was interesting. Then there was a thing on political corruption that turned a lot of heads."

"If it was anything like *Follow the Leader*, I can imagine."

"You saw *Follow the Leader*?"

"Uh-huh. Last winter."

"What did you think?"

"It was riveting. Fascinating like a good horror flick, all the more terrifying because it wasn't. I thought it was well-done. Totally effective."

"Thank you."

Her eyes widened. "It was yours?" She smiled in delight at discovering now just how talented he was. "Oh, dear, what if I'd said it was terrible?"

"If that had been your honest opinion, I'd have accepted it."

"You accept a lot, don't you?"

"What choice have I got?"

She knew that he was right in a way. One couldn't fight things one couldn't change. But she was sorry to see the matter-of-factness his words implied. There was such a thing as feeling—feeling happy or sad, relieved or disappointed. Dallas felt; she knew he did. The faint smile that had touched his lips when he'd thanked her for praising *Follow the Leader* told her that he'd been pleased.

Concentrating on other feelings she was sure existed, she jumped back to the enumeration he'd given her of his work. She'd heard the sarcasm in his voice. "Do you have a choice as to what films you work on?"

"I can always say no."

"You sounded cynical before. Does it depress you when you work on films like those?"

"What depresses me is that the conditions exposed in those films exist. The work itself is great. I like what I do."

"You mentioned pressure. Where does it come in?"

"The producer may want one thing, the director may get another. I've got to work my tail off to try to please them both *and* produce something that doesn't look like it's been edited. It's worse with feature films, technically speaking. Between special effects and places where the viewer has to be tricked into believing something happened that really didn't—"

"Like what?" Enrapt, Paige propped her elbow on the table, her chin in her palm.

For the first time in the discussion, Jesse's eyes twinkled. "Like when the heroine is supposed to be swinging across an open gorge on a vine. She doesn't really, y'know. She'll be shown pulling back to leap with vine in hand, holding her breath, looking terrified. Then the frame will switch to a companion or a pursuer. By the time the audience sees the heroine again, she's falling in a heap, safe but shaky, on the other side of the gorge."

"That's sneaky."

"That's often the way it works."

"How can you bear to go to the movies, knowing all that's probably gone on in the cutting room? Isn't it disillusioning?"

He grinned. "Not necessarily. I do what the rest of the audience does. I choose to believe. That's what entertainment's all about. Take singing. You've got this beautiful gal belting out a soulful ballad. She's oozing love or anger or heartbreak. You know damn well it's just a song, but you believe she's in agony. You also know that she's practiced singing the song this way a thousand times and that she'll sing it this way a thousand more times. And that if one song's sad, the next one will probably be happy."

"Isn't it possible she's singing from the heart?"

"Not likely. And she sure as hell's not singing to you like it seems."

"I think you wish she were," Paige said, a daring smile on her face.

"Me? Are you kidding? Not me!"

"I'm not so sure," she mused, standing to gather the dishes. As she headed for the kitchen she added a teasing note to her voice. "I think you might like to have a woman so in love with you that she'd pour out her heart and soul that way."

She heard a low grumble, that was all. Smiling to herself, she decided that it might be good for him to have a woman like that. He struck her as a man who'd been alone too long, who'd seen too much of the dark side of life. He'd been right when he'd said that he needed a break from all that. Perhaps a few days here at her beach house might brighten his outlook.

When she returned with a tray bearing coffee and healthy slabs of blueberry pie, she cocked her head toward the deck. Jesse quickly took the tray and she led the way. Moments later they were seated at the small table there, sheltered from the sea breeze by the wide overhang. A porch light behind them cast a warm glow. The full moon did the rest. In the background the surf serenaded.

Jesse sat back in his chair and inhaled deeply. "It's lovely here."

"Relaxing?"

"Mmm."

"Vacationlike?"

Rather than agreeing a second time, he found himself staring at her. "You like living alone. Won't my being here cramp your style?"

"It'll be a novelty. Besides, you won't be here very long."

His gaze narrowed. "How do you know?"

"You've already told me you'll pick up one day and be gone."

"But if that day comes later rather than sooner?"

"Then…it'll be an experience. If worse comes to worst and you get on my nerves, I'll send you packing."

He leaned forward and spoke in a very low, very sober voice. "Do you realize what you're doing, Paige? You're inviting me to spend my vacation here."

"I'm not inviting. You showed up and you seem to like the place. I'm simply saying that you can stay if you'd like. I'm not so selfish that I can't share for a little while. It's a big place."

"You're generous."

"What're friends for?"

"We're lovers, Paige. You haven't forgotten that, have you?"

She spoke more softly. "No."

"And if I stay here I won't be sleeping in the guest room."

"I didn't expect that you would."

He sat back then, his expression grim. "Why are you doing this?"

"Offering my house—"

"And yourself—"

"Because I like you. Does there have to be another reason?"

"There usually is."

"Oh, look," she said, sighing, "I'd get all huffy again but one show of high spirits a day is all I can manage. The fact is that you're welcome to stay here if you want. If you don't, you can leave. The decision's yours. It's no big thing."

For what seemed an eternity to Paige, he pondered her words. When she could stand no more of his silence, she taunted, "What's the matter, Jesse? Are you afraid of my feelings, or your own?"

"I'm not afraid."

"Then why the dilemma? There aren't any strings attached to my offer. Take it or leave it."

"You're a cool cookie."

"So are you."

"Which means that we might actually survive in each other's presence for more than a day? I've never lived with anyone before."

"You're not *living* with me. You're just…staying in my house."

"And you're playing with words."

She sighed again, this time with fatigue. "Maybe so. But not anymore. I intend to eat my pie, drink my coffee, clean up the mess in the kitchen, then sit down with a book. Okay?"

Jesse couldn't help but smile at the question she'd tacked on at the end, as if she were asking his permission when he knew very well that she'd do what she wanted. It was, indeed, her house, her life.

Yes, she could eat her pie, drink her coffee, clean up the mess in the kitchen, then sit down with a book. And, yes, he would stay for a time, if for no other reason than to prove to them both that he could handle it, then leave, as he'd promised.

CHAPTER FIVE

JESSE WAS THE ONE WHO SAT WITH a book, but it was the following afternoon, and he wasn't reading. He was staring out over the deck, thinking of the night before. For all the indifference she showed at times, Paige had been as impassioned as ever in bed. It was as though the softest side of her came out then, softest and wildest. For a woman who'd never known the fullness of lovemaking, she was a marvel. Making up for lost time, perhaps. Perhaps simply high on new discoveries. Whatever, he was pleased. And so he sat there with no desire to leave.

Oh, yes, he'd begun work on the chores she'd suggested. Early that morning—well, it had seemed early to him, since it was soon after he'd awoken, though Paige had been in her studio for hours—they'd gone into town to pick up the tools and materials he'd needed. He grinned, remembering the pseudoargument they'd had before they'd left.

"I'll drive," she'd proclaimed, slipping her car keys from their hook.

"You will not. I won't have a woman toting me around. *I'll* drive."

"I'm sorry. That limousine may have been fine for the city, but I won't be seen in it around here. Besides, there'd be nowhere to park. It's too big."

"I'll drive," he'd insisted, taking her arm and all but dragging her out of the house.

"My car, then," she'd grumbled, pressing her keys into

his hand. He'd promptly pocketed them in exchange for his own. On the front walk moments later she'd dug in her heels. And stared. Then slanted him a dry gaze. "No limousine. Cute."

"The limousine went back the other night. I do have wheels of my own."

"So I see. Not bad, for an MG. A little old, perhaps, but not bad."

"Not old. Vintage."

She'd shrugged. "If you say so."

"Would you bad-mouth Victoria?"

"Oh, Lord, it's got a name."

"Of course it does. And I won't have it taken in vain."

"You should have told me you drove your own car up here."

"But then we wouldn't be standing here arguing. I love it when you get worked up. Your freckles stand out."

She'd stared at him, then finally thrown up her hands in a gesture of helplessness. "You're impossible."

"Mmm. That's what I've been trying to tell you. Come on. I thought you had work to do. If we don't get these errands done— Listen, I really can go myself."

"You don't know the way. I'll show you this time, then next time you'll be on your own."

"What did I ever do without you?" he'd muttered, tongue-in-cheek, as he'd pressed her into the MG.

They'd stopped at the hardware store, the lumberyard, the supermarket and the dock. Fortunately she'd only given him momentary argument when he insisted on paying for everything they bought. He wouldn't be a kept man—he felt strongly about that. She must have sensed it.

At Paige's insistence, they'd made one other stop. Jesse had argued that he'd be more than willing to take the responsibility for birth control, but she'd been firm. She didn't trust him, she'd teased, eyes twinkling. So, leaving him to wait—by choice—in the car, she ran in to see her doctor.

At least she'd be protected, he mused now. He didn't care how it happened, but he wanted her safe. Unwanted pregnancies were high on his list of prohibitions. There were far too many children born into the world to parents who either lacked the desire or capacity to give them what they needed. He knew all about that. He knew about it all too well.

Frustrated with the turn of his thoughts, he stood up on the deck and stretched, then on impulse headed for Paige's studio. He'd only seen it once, that first night when she'd given him a quick tour of the house. He wanted to see it again now.

The door was open. He came to a halt on its threshold, as though barred by an invisible gate. This room, like the others on the ocean side of the house, was fully skylit. The outer walls were glass. On a summer day such as this the sliding doors were open, allowing large screens to admit the breeze. Though there was central air-conditioning in the house, Jesse suspected that Paige rarely used it. She didn't have to. The ocean air was more than adequate.

It wasn't the airiness of the room that held him still. It was the emotional atmosphere. There was a serenity here, a sense of peace. His eye roamed, touching on tools and raw materials, workbenches, pedestals, a wide desk. An occasional poster, well framed, hung on white plastered walls. A large bulletin board bearing miscellaneous drawings and notes held on with pushpins hung over the desk.

Inevitably, though, his gaze came to rest on Paige. She sat on a stool at the far end of the room. A large piece of burlap fully covered her lap. Atop it lay a piece of wood, cushioned securely in the notch between her thighs. She wore a face shield, a piece of clear plastic that hung from a headpiece and extended beyond her chin. In one hand she held a mallet, in the other a gouge. Putting mallet to gouge to wood, she hammered gently, rhythmically. After several moments she stopped, lifted the piece to study what she'd done, replaced it on her lap, turning it slightly, and began to hammer again.

So engrossed was she in her work, so obviously content, that he couldn't disturb her. He turned and was about to leave when she caught sight of him and slid her mask back to the top of her head.

"Don't go."

"I didn't mean to bother you."

"You're no bother. I need a break, anyway."

"What are you working on?" He didn't budge from the door. It seemed he'd be trespassing otherwise.

She glanced down at the wood in her lap and ran her hand over it. "It's the first of a group of sandpipers."

"A group. Mmm, you did have several groups of other kinds of things in your show, didn't you?"

"So you did see something besides me that night," she teased. He simply arched his brows and tipped his head sideways in confirmation. She hesitated for just a minute. "What did you think?"

"Your work is beautiful. Filled with feeling. That was one of the reasons I was so convinced you weren't... well, you know."

"Yes," she admitted quietly. "Jesse?"

"Hmm?"

Her eyes twinkled. "You can come in."

"In? Oh. Sure." The invisible gate opened. He took several steps forward. He still felt like an intruder encroaching on a very private, serene world, but she'd made the offer, and the peace of it was too good to pass up. Planting his hands in the pockets of his jeans, he rocked back on his bare heels and made a quick sweep of the room. "This is a nice place to work. Very bright... pleasant."

She followed the path of his gaze. "Actually, it's the master bedroom. Or was. But from the first time I saw the house, this room struck me as an ideal studio. It's large and has plenty of work space. The walk-in closet is terrific for storage. And the bathroom supplies all the running water I need." She glanced toward the alcove in question. "I had the door taken off so it becomes part of the room." The bathroom itself was huge and multifaceted. What was now open held two sinks and abundant counter space. The bath, shower and commode were behind separate doors.

Jesse began to move quietly around the room, studying more closely those things he'd glimpsed from the door. He paused at the workbench, above which were mounted a mind-boggling assortment of tools. "You use all these?"

"At one point or another."

"They look alike." Reaching out, he ran his hand across a neat lineup of metal somethings.

"Those are rasps. Each one is just a little different from the next. When it comes to the fine work on a piece, the small differences are critical."

He moved on to a cluster of what looked to be cloth strips.

"Abrasives," she explained before he could ask. "They can be kept wide or cut thinner. I use them for smoothing and finishing when I'm working in wood."

"I'd have thought you'd use sandpaper."

"Perhaps once in a while. But those strips are more sensitive, more gentle."

Nodding, he left the bench and approached her. His gaze was on her lap. "What kind of wood is that?"

She lifted the roughly carved chunk and turned it slowly. "Walnut."

"Will the other sandpipers be walnut, too?"

"Uh-huh. Each one will be slightly different, though. No two pieces of wood—or stone—are identical. For that matter, no single piece is entirely predictable."

Considering her words, he looked back toward the desk. "You make sketches beforehand?"

"Uh-huh. Go look. The sandpipers are right on top."

Crossing to the desk, he studied the drawings. On a large single sheet were solo birds, then clusters. Far from detailed, they merely outlined the general shapes she sought. "Very pretty. Light."

"That's what I'm hoping for. Sandpipers always look like little imps scurrying along the sand. I'd like to catch some of that movement."

"In a stationary form?"

"Sure. It's all in the shape of the bird, its attitude, the placement of its feet."

He nodded, intrigued. "What will you mount them on?"

"Sand, I hope. Glue does wonders for immobilizing tiny grains."

"Should be very effective." He walked back to her. "Most of the things on exhibit the other night were larger. Are you changing your style?"

"Just varying it. I'd like the sandpipers to be life-size."

"But not in exact detail." None of her things were fully realistic; he'd learned that at the show. It was the interpretation she brought to seemingly common objects that made her work unique.

"No. It's the general form I want, a fluidity to enhance that sense of movement. The eye follows lines, curves, changes in tone and color. It's the rhythm of this eye movement that brings the piece to life." She paused, thinking aloud. "I may blend two birds together. I'm not sure. It depends on how the wood responds."

"So you play it by ear?"

"Uh-huh. Spontaneity can be exciting."

"Then you don't always know what you're going to do when you get started?"

"I have vague ideas. But I have to be flexible. Every piece of wood, every slab of stone has flaws. If I suddenly find a weak spot, I've got to work around it. Compensate, so to speak."

Stepping back to lean against the workbench, Jesse crossed his arms over his chest. "Do you ever run into a problem and have to chuck the whole thing?"

"Once in a while. Fortunately the worst flaws usually

show up in the early stages. It'd be heartbreaking to do all the work only to find, at the end, that the piece was hopelessly weak."

"I can imagine." He found himself studying the mask atop her head. It pulled her hair back from her face so that even at work she looked pretty. "Do you always wear that plastic shield when you work?"

"At this stage in the piece, yes. It'd be too easy for chips of wood to come flying up at me. By the time I get past roughing out and shaping, it's not necessary. The finishing work is safer. At least with wood. When it comes to stone and I'm using hand drills for refinement, there's a whole lot of dust. If it's really bad I wear a respirator." She glanced around her. "That's one of the reasons this room is so perfect. The ventilation's great."

Jesse took it all in, his gaze returning time and again to Paige. She looked so...content sitting there cradling her work. She seemed perfectly willing to answer his questions, and there were more he wanted to ask. But she had to work. Much as he'd like it if she quit for the day and spent time with him, he couldn't ask. He knew how he resented interruptions when he worked, and he didn't want to risk being the object of *her* eventual resentment.

Good intentions intact, he straightened and was walking toward the door when a small stone piece caught his eye. It lay on one of the auxiliary worktables to one side of the room. He stopped, picked it up, stared at it.

"What's this?"

"It's...it's just something I was fooling around with," she offered a bit too quickly.

He sent her a curious glance, then looked back at the stone. It was slightly larger than his hand, longer than it was wide or tall. One part of the top had been carved; it was this portion that held his attention. He scrutinized it cautiously, looked down at his own hand, then again at the stone. He saw them clearly—two fingers, with a third on the way. They were masculine.

Wondering when she'd started the piece but half-afraid to ask, he set down the stone and walked thoughtfully from the studio. Barefoot, he moved silently through the house, across the deck and down the wood stairs to the beach. The tide was high. He skirted its lacy edge, picking his way over stones and seaweed, through random rock clusters. When he reached a large boulder, he rested against it.

That was where Paige found him moments later.

"I thought you might be here," she said, approaching with considerable hesitance. "Can I…can I join you?"

The gaze that searched her features conveyed far greater intensity than the shrug he gave. "It's your beach."

"I won't disturb you if you'd rather be alone." When he shrugged a second time, she averted her eyes. "I wanted to explain," she said quietly, looking toward the horizon. "That was…your hand."

"I wondered."

"I started it yesterday."

"Why?"

It was her turn to shrug. She looked down at the pebbles underfoot. "I don't know. I was walking out here and saw the stone. The vision just came."

"Is that how it happens?"

"Not always. Sometimes I have an idea and spend months searching for the right piece to carve it from." Her eyes lit up. "Other times the piece itself generates the idea. It's like…" Self-consciously she let her words trail off.

"Like what?"

When she still hesitated, Jesse smiled softly and gave her a coaxing nod. She resumed in a shy murmur, "It's like the stone speaks to me." Her cheeks grew pink. She knew she probably sounded overly esoteric, but she desperately wanted to share her feelings with Jesse. "Like it's got a…a secret just waiting, waiting in there." She lowered her voice to a near-whisper. "The secret's often very special, very private. There are times when I hesitate to carve it out, almost feeling as if I'm betraying something the stone might not want revealed."

"Then why do you do it?" he asked gently.

"I don't know. Compulsion maybe. Maybe for the satisfaction of proving that what I saw was there. Maybe just because it is there and it's too beautiful to keep hidden."

"My hand's here in real life. Why replicate it in stone?"

"Because it *is* beautiful. And...because there's something to be said for the continuity of nature."

He reached out then and, curling his fingers around her neck, brought her closer. He slipped his arm around her shoulders, pulling her down to sit by his side against the boulder.

"Does that mean you'd carve other parts of my body?"

"It'd be a challenge."

His breath teased her brow. "For me, too. I'm not sure I could take it—your hands on me like that."

"My hands would be on the stone."

"Yeah, and the stone would be like a voodoo doll. I'd feel everything."

She grinned. "What if I just stuck with something innocent, like your shoulders."

"You'd sculpt a pair of shoulders? Boo-hiss."

"Then...a torso." She touched his chest, drew her hand down to his waist. "It's very fit."

"You're getting hotter. So am I."

She saw the direction of his thoughts, "Jesse Dallas, I wouldn't sculpt that!"

"Why not? Michelangelo did it any number of times."

"You were the one who spoke of voodoo dolls. How would you feel if I did what you're suggesting?"

"Just like stone. Damned...hard."

Chuckling, she turned to him and buried her face against his shirt. He'd begun to gently caress her back. It felt good. "That's one of the reasons I wouldn't do it."

"And the other?"

She tipped her head back and met his gaze. "Some

secrets really are too private. Some I just don't want to share."

He growled deeply, as though he was in pain, and swung her from her seat and around until she stood between his spread knees, her slender body arched, her arms circling his back.

Her lips were soft and moist. Unable to resist their silent invitation, he lowered his own in a kiss filled with magic. At least Paige thought it was magic, because suddenly and fully every one of her senses came alive.

Similarly affected, Jesse dug his fingers into her bottom and pressed her intimately to his hips. "What do you think of *that*?" he drawled.

"Just like stone. Damned…hard."

He laughed, a deep rumbling laugh. She didn't hear him laugh often, certainly not like that. It was a good sound, a healthy sound filled with pleasure and appreciation. It made her feel very glad that he was here.

When he lowered his mouth to murmur in her ear, his voice came out more gravelly than ever. "How about if we go in and try out that toy the doctor gave you this morning?"

"I'm working," she teased, knowing full well she'd do no more sculpting today, knowing full well she didn't want to.

"I'll give you plenty to work on. You can touch everything. Y'know, memorize shapes and textures and—"

"I get the idea. But we'd better hurry or you'll have to carry me all the way up to the house. My legs don't do well under this kind of strain." The strain she spoke of was heady. Her breasts were already swelling against the firmness of his chest. Her ribs felt every breath he took. She couldn't help but respond to the slow undulation of his hips. Her insides were molten.

Before she could do more than catch her breath, Jesse swung her up into his arms.

"Hey!" She squirmed. "I'm not incapacitated yet!"

He grinned. "It's my machismo seeping out. Indulge me."

She indulged him everything, but the indulgence was far from one-sided, for he was as giving a lover as ever.

Much later, after they'd showered and dressed and dined on sautéed scallops, fresh broccoli and potatoes, they sat down in the living room to read. Paige couldn't remember spending a more relaxed evening. She was doing nothing that she wouldn't normally do, yet it was different. She felt warm and content, and wondered if it had anything to do with the man sitting at his own end of the sofa engrossed in a book he'd chosen from her shelf. How incredibly comfortable it had been having Jesse around.

She enjoyed telling him about her work, voicing feelings she'd previously held private. She enjoyed the banter that sparked easily between them, even that of a sexual nature, so new to her yet such fun. She enjoyed the way he held her, the way he touched her with exquisite tenderness one time, with fiery need another. Whether protectively gentle or wild with demand, he made her feel that she was the only woman in the world.

Of course, it wasn't true. He'd had women before and he'd have them again. She knew that; she accepted it. But when he gave of himself, he gave fully. And he was giving to her now. So what if he'd leave one day? She'd simply return to the life she'd had before and be all the fuller for what she and Jesse had shared. She was lucky, very lucky. Life continued to treat her well.

THE NEXT TWO WEEKS were unbelievably wonderful. Having lived so long alone, Paige was astonished at how easily she adapted to having Jesse around. He took care of everything around the house, freeing her to work so that they'd have more time to spend together, which they did.

They ate out often, at Jesse's insistence and expense, and he continued to pay for all of the groceries that entered the house. Paige teased that he was buying her off so she'd let him watch the basketball play-offs on television, but she knew that his pride would allow him no other course.

They drove south to Boston, north to the quaint coastal towns of Maine. They took in a movie one evening, rented a boat and went sailing another. They even attended a party given by one of Paige's friends, where Jesse blended in beautifully and enjoyed himself, to boot. Paige felt particularly happy that night, happy and proud and complete.

But the times she most treasured were when she and Jesse were alone at home, sitting together in the living room or on the deck, often at sunset when the sky was indigo and the sea reflected burnished golds from the west.

Those were the times when they talked, when she was able to indulge her curiosity about the man who'd fit into her life with such ease. She wanted to hear more about his work, and she listened, fascinated, as he related anecdotes and adventures.

He had a streak of cynicism. She'd learned that early on, and it emerged regularly during these storytelling sessions. But increasingly, as the days passed, she was aware that he said nothing about his family or childhood. And she began to wonder. It was only natural that, one evening on the deck, she asked him directly.

"Tell me about your family, Jesse."

He looked at her sharply, then curbed what appeared to be censure. But he didn't speak, simply stared across the deck.

"You never mention them," she coaxed in her most gentle tone. "I want to know what it was like for you growing up."

"Why?"

"I'm curious." When he shot her a quelling stare, she refused to be cowed. "Blame it on the artist in me. I'm forever looking beneath the surface of things. God only knows I've talked about myself enough. I mean, you've heard all the little stories about my childhood, you've seen the way I live day-to-day, you've met my friends. It's only fair that you give me a glimpse of you."

"I thought I was doing that," he said coolly, and for the first time Paige felt a twinge of apprehension. He'd been dispassionate before, back when he'd felt called upon to convince her that he had nothing to offer but one day at a time. Then it hadn't bothered her. Now it did. She cared for him, cared deeply. And the more resistant he was to talking about himself, the more badly she wanted to know.

"You let me see Jesse the adult," she reasoned softly. "You tell me about your work. But it's as though from high school back there's nothing. Well, there has to be something. A person doesn't suddenly become eighteen without living through the years before." When she saw that he remained silent, she stood up and waved him away. "Okay, don't tell me. It must be some secret you're keeping. Either that or you're ashamed—" She'd started to walk toward the house when he caught her wrist and held it firmly.

"It's no secret. And I'm not ashamed. It's just…difficult to talk about, y'know?"

The chill in his voice had eased. Paige let herself be drawn down onto the lounge beside him. It was a tight fit, but she welcomed the closeness. It was as though he needed it at that particular moment, and his need was a statement in itself.

"I didn't have quite the life you had."

"That's okay. I told you, I was lucky. Where did you grow up?"

"On the wrong side of the tracks."

"Where were the tracks?"

"Delaware. Outside Wilmington. My mother was a hooker. My father wasn't there to watch. There was just my older brother—half brother, actually—and me. He left as soon as he could and then I was alone."

Paige struggled to contain her dismay. "Your mother must have been there sometimes."

"Why 'must'?" he asked, cynicism narrowing to pure bitterness. "As far as she was concerned, bringing me into the world was enough. I never heard the end of it. She told me how she'd hated being pregnant, how her labor had been long and hard. Nine months she'd given me. In her book that was the supreme sacrifice."

"But when you were an infant *someone* had to take care of you."

"Someone did. I don't know who, but someone did. By the time I was old enough to remember, I was being passed from one sitter to the next. My mother showed up from time to time to grudgingly pay the bill, but she was more than happy to leave again. I cramped her style. She told me *that* more than once."

"Didn't your father do something?"

"How innocent you are, Paige. You assume that a parent has to care. Well, he doesn't. And mine didn't...*neither* of them. My father was off somewhere doing his own thing. I never knew him."

"Oh, Jesse, I'm sorry...."

"I don't need your pity," he grated. "I survived."

"How? What happened?"

"It was a great relief for my mother when I got old enough to go to school. Fewer sitters to pay. She splurged once a year and bought me clothes. Of course, it didn't matter that there were holes in the knees by Christmas or that by April the pants were inches too short. She felt she was being very generous. Once in a while I got hand-me-downs from neighbors. They still had holes in the knees but at least they fit."

He paused and shifted his arms around her; she suspected he'd momentarily forgotten her presence. "When I was ten I got this one jacket that I loved. She found it on sale. It was a winter jacket and had a furry lining. I used to stick my hands inside the zipper—I told the other kids it was to keep them warm, which made sense since I didn't have mittens, but it was the fur I loved. So soft and warm. I used to sleep with that jacket beside me, turned inside out. It was my teddy bear, my security blanket. I used to imagine being in a world completely surrounded by that fur." He gave a deep, unsteady sigh. Then, with the blink of an eye, he was back in the present.

"I don't know why in the hell I'm telling you this," he growled, but he didn't let her go. "You must think I'm crazy. A ten-year-old hugging an inside-out jacket to fall asleep—"

"Is that what she told you? That it was crazy?"

"The word she used was babyish, but she only started in on that when I outgrew the jacket and she wanted to throw it out. I cried. I really cried over a stupid jacket."

"It wasn't stupid. It represented something you needed."

"It was a jacket, for God's sake, a cheap little jacket! What kind of kid has a love affair with a jacket? Anyway, I made such a stink about the thing that not only did she steal it away from me and have it burned, but she made sure that the next jacket she bought had no fur on it. It was an abrasive woolen thing. I hated it. I hated her."

"You didn't really."

"I did really," he stated with such calmness that Paige almost believed him. "She made my life miserable. It was like she had to constantly punish me for my existence. I felt totally alone in the world."

"But you had your brother, for a time at least. Didn't that help?"

"It was a different situation for my brother. His father may never have been around, but at least he sent gifts from time to time and money for clothes. Brian could dream that someone cared. I didn't have even that luxury."

Again Paige wanted to say how sorry she was, but loath to rile him, she held her tongue. Her heart ached for the little boy who'd never known love, for the man who had steeled himself against that kind of vulnerability. She rubbed her cheek against his shoulder and tightened her arm about his waist, wanting nothing more than to give him that which he'd never had. But she wasn't his mother, and she couldn't make up for what he'd lost. And there was still more that she wanted to hear.

"How was it during your teenage years?"

"Better. My brother had left by then, but I was old enough to take care of myself so at least there weren't strangers pushing me around. I went to school with a key in my pocket. I came home to an empty house. When I got hungry I scrounged around for whatever happened to be in the refrigerator. My mother would usually stop in at dinnertime, then again around dawn. She was always sleeping when I got up in the morning, so it was no big thing when she didn't make it home some days. By the time I got to high school, I was the envy of every kid around. I was free-wheeling and independent, just like they wanted to be." He snorted. "They should have only known."

"Were you a good student?"

The snort was a dry laugh this time. "Not particularly. I resented authority. I still do, which is why my work suits me. I take jobs when I want. When I don't, I lie low."

"But you do work to please."

"That's the name of the game. This particular one, at least. I get in my shots, though. Believe me." He took a deep breath and his arms loosened. "I haven't seen my relatives for years and I don't care. So now you've heard *the* story. Fascinating, huh?"

What Paige felt just then wasn't fascination, it was frustration. She wanted him to keep holding her. She wanted to hug him back. But the moment was seeping away.

"It helps to explain lots of things," she said softly.

His arms fell away completely, until he was grasping the sides of the lounge chair. "What things?"

"Your view of the world. It's hard, y'know."

"Damned right, it's hard!" he boomed, dragging his arm from under her and quickly rising. "That's a mean world out there." He stalked to the edge of the deck.

Behind him, Paige sat up. "You've said that before, but I don't agree with you."

"Why should you? You've had it easy. You were never twelve and sick and struggling to clean up the mess you'd made when you'd thrown up all over the floor!" He whirled around, every muscle tense. "Do you have any idea what that's like, Paige? You're burning up with fever, your entire body is shaking, you're scared 'cause you feel like you're dying…and you feel guilty, guilty for the whole thing!"

She quickly rose and went to him. "No, Jesse, I've never had that experience, but that doesn't mean I can't imagine how horrible it must have been. It doesn't have to be that way, though. Your situation was unique—"

"Like hell it was! I've seen similar things time and again in the course of my work!"

"All right. Not unique. But one-sided. There's another side, the side I saw, the side you can just as easily have now if you choose to."

His tone grew stony. "What are you talking about?"

"Happiness. Security, warmth, comfort. Just because you didn't have those things as a child doesn't mean that they're not yours for the taking. You opt for the role of the cynic, you choose to see the negative side of life. You surround yourself with it, almost as if you want reassurance that there's no point in taking a risk for anything else. And that's where I disagree. All those good things are out there right alongside the bad. It's a matter of ambition. As long as you tell yourself that the world's a crummy place, you're content to live with the crumbs. On the other hand, if you dare to strive for something better, you might be surprised just how attainable that something better might be."

Jesse stared at her, eyes dark in anger. "I don't believe this discussion. Have you become a preacher now, Paige, a sermonizer? Or a psychologist bent on straightening my crooked outlook?"

"No."

"Then what?" he growled, hands in fists by his sides. "What's the point of all this? Here I tell you things I've never told another person, and you turn them on me."

"I'm not turning anything on you," she argued, trying to keep her voice steady. He was slipping away, slipping away. She felt helpless and inept. "I'm saying that I'm sorry you had to live with what you did for all those years, but that the scars won't fade unless you turn them to the sun."

He raked a hand through his hair. "God save me from the poetic mind. That I can very *well* live without."

"Then maybe you'd better leave," she stated quietly, "because I'm not about to change. You know, there are many people who have *everything*, but who keep themselves miserable wondering whether it's going to last. They become paranoid and suspicious. They're afraid to spend a dime for fear something's going to happen to the rest of their wealth. Well," she said angrily, "that may be their choice, but it's not mine. I refuse to sit here worrying about a day something terrible may happen. The odds are against me. No one goes through life without a little heartache. But I choose to be positive. It's the only way I can be."

When Jesse continued to stare at her through the darkness that now surrounded them, she badgered. "Well, haven't you got a retort?"

"I think you covered just about everything," he gritted.

If she'd hoped to impress him with what she'd said, it appeared that she'd failed. But then, she *wasn't* a psychologist, and even if she were she sensed it would take days, weeks, months to help him work through his anger. For it was anger. Masked behind cynicism, perhaps couched in bitterness, it was anger nonetheless. Anger at the mother who didn't care, at the father who hadn't been around, at the brother who had that little bit more and took the first road out, at the world that had allowed it all to happen.

He was missing so much in life that she wanted to cry for him. And after that, she mused, she'd cry for herself. Because she was falling in love with him. And it seemed hopeless.

Knowing that tears would do neither of them any good,

she turned to leave. Her shoulders were hunched, her limbs weary. "I'm going in," she murmured sadly as she walked toward the house.

She hadn't expected him to follow, and he didn't. For a long, long time she lay in bed with an unopened book, wishing he'd come back fighting if for no other reason than to give her another shot. But he wouldn't. By choice he was a man alone in the world. All along he'd told her what to expect; she'd had no idea then how hard accepting that might be.

It was very late when he finally came to bed. Paige was still awake, wondering if he'd ever come, if perhaps he'd follow the suggestion she'd so blithely made that he leave. When she heard the rustle of clothing, she held her breath. He might be packing, in which case she had no one but herself to blame. The past two weeks had been almost idyllic; she should have left well enough alone.

Moments later he slipped under the covers, and she felt weak with relief. Oh, he'd leave sometime; she was sure of it. But each additional day would be another to treasure. She wasn't ready to lose him yet.

Jesse lay quietly for a time, staring at the ceiling. He was hurting her. He'd known he would, but he couldn't help himself. He also knew that he should leave, but that seemed somehow impossible, too. He was selfish, wanting one more day, always one more day. It stunned him that he continued to find her company so pleasant—barring, of course, the discussion they'd just had. Even now he wasn't quite sure how that talk had gotten out of hand. Even now he wasn't quite sure why he'd told her all those things. Perhaps it had been because she'd asked, or because she had shared so much of herself with him. Perhaps, just perhaps, he'd needed to voice it all after living so long with it buried inside. Why, then, did he feel an even greater burden on his shoulders? If he'd been counting on her to simply listen and accept, he'd miscalculated once again. Come to think of it, she'd done a similar thing the night that she'd first conned him into staying here. She'd parried his arguments—half-baked as even he knew they were— with aplomb, speaking up to him, expressing her opinions with eloquence. She wasn't a yes-person, not by a long shot, and the way she could so calmly and quietly inject her personal feelings into a discussion fascinated him. As always, she seemed so very sure of herself. It was enough to make a man wonder.

Turning his head on the pillow, he saw that her eyes were open. Looking at him in…fear? He began to ache.

"Paige?" he whispered. She blinked. "You okay?" She bobbed her head twice. "What are you thinking?"

She didn't say anything for a minute and when she did it was in a barely audible whisper. "I feel cold."

He groaned and turned to her. "Come 'ere." Sliding an arm under her, he pulled her to his warmth. She was as naked as he and, he sensed, as disinclined to make love. Something else was needed after what they'd just been through. Closeness. Simple, comforting closeness.

He heard her let out a breath and felt her snuggle even closer. She draped an arm around his ribs and burrowed her hand between his body and the sheet. Strangely, he didn't mind the gentle shackle, or the blanket of her hair on his chest, or the gentle weight of her leg over his. Rather, he found it all reassuring.

The last image that flitted through his mind moments before he fell asleep was of the soft jacket that had been his lone friend long ago.

CHAPTER SIX

WHEN THEY AWOKE THE NEXT morning, neither Jesse nor
Paige made reference to the discussion they'd had the
night before. In unspoken agreement they resumed the
pattern they'd established over the past two weeks. Paige
spent the morning working, stopping to breakfast with
Jesse at ten before returning to her studio to sculpt until
midafternoon. He did any chores that needed to be done,
ran any errands, then relaxed, sitting down with a book,
perhaps lying out on the deck in the sun.

Outwardly things were the same. They talked softly
with each other, smiled, joked. Each new day brought
something new to admire; Paige found herself increasingly
enthralled with Jesse and, since he made no move to return
to New York, she assumed that at least he wasn't bored.

But there was something else now, something that had
taken root in that heartrending talk they'd had and was a
tiny ripple marring an otherwise smooth sea. It was subtle,
very subtle, a fine undercurrent of tension that appeared
from time to time in a look, a glance, a stare. On Jesse's
part, it came from an effort to understand just what it was
about Paige that kept him here. On her part, it stemmed
from an attempt to cope with her growing love.

Increasingly Jesse found himself deep in thought on the
beach, tossing pebbles across the water in frustration. He'd
never known a woman like Paige, one as poised and undemanding. But those very qualities, he found, could be
unbelievably demanding.

Increasingly Paige found herself staring blindly at the work in her lap, seeing varying images of Jesse's face. Sometimes he was calm and absorbed, and intelligence marked his features. Sometimes he was angry, and his eyes darkened to midnight blue, the bridge of his nose tensed, his lips thinned. Sometimes he was gentle, and his gaze worshiped her and his concern for her well-being was boundless. And sometimes he was vulnerable.

The last didn't happen often. He seemed forever on his guard, as though he regretted having told her about his childhood and didn't want to make the same mistake twice. He saw himself as being strong, self-contained, she realized, and he'd actually been ashamed by the show of emotion he'd let slip out that night.

One thing Paige knew with growing sureness as the days passed. Jesse Dallas, for all his proclamations to the contrary, was a sensitive man. Just as he'd anticipated her needs that long hot day in New York, so he continued to do here. He'd materialize behind her in the studio just when her shoulders were beginning to ache and he'd massage them in silence until her energy returned. When he sensed she was tired he'd suggest an early night. He knew just when she'd had enough of one activity or another.

He was sensitive, too, in what he felt himself, though this he diligently sought to deny. Nonetheless Paige had seen the moistness in his eyes when he'd been reading a particularly moving piece of nonfiction, and she knew the pain he felt for the underprivileged of the world. She'd seen the way she took to the locals, inquiring with concern about the fisherman who'd broken his leg and was relegated to mind the dock. She'd seen the way he stopped to shoot baskets with a group of children on a local basketball court. On one such occasion he even ran up and down the court with a delighted six-year-old in his arms, letting the child slam-dunk his share to the playful chagrin of their opponents. And she'd seen the way he reached for *her*, seeking comfort from time to time.

For a man who was supposedly hard and callous, he had a remarkable capacity for warmth. Paige wondered if he'd always been that way, or if the past weeks had done something to release what had lain dormant all along. She knew that he'd never been anything but gentle with her. Oh, yes, they argued at times and he scowled and snapped and said things that hurt. But in the wake of such incidents he was all the more solicitous and caring. If she didn't know better, she might suspect he was falling in love with her.

She did know better, however. Rather, she knew she'd be foolish to read something into his softer side. He'd set out his terms at the start: no strings, no promises, no future. She had agreed; she did agree. After all, she'd been alone for years and she liked her life. The only thing she couldn't quite reason away was the chill she felt at the thought, the knowledge, that one day he'd be gone.

IT DIDN'T GET EASIER as the days passed. Despite the intense concentration that seemed to absorb more and more of Jesse's private time, there were light moments to share, moments when it seemed that they were made for each other, moments when their inevitable parting seemed absurd.

One morning, a drizzly day when outside activity was of necessity put on hold, Paige sat perched on a kitchen stool talking to her mother on the phone. She'd told her about Jesse the previous week, that she'd met him in New York and that he was spending his vacation at her home. When her mother had asked detailed questions about him—as mothers from tight-knit homes were wont to do— Paige had answered as many as she'd felt were pertinent and had deftly fielded the rest.

As it stood, her mother knew Paige liked the man; the simple fact that he was there was proof of that. Paige had never dated any man for long or with much interest, let alone invited him to share her home. Laura Mattheson knew that her daughter enjoyed living where she did, as she did. She also knew that, at twenty-nine years of age, Paige had a right to live with a man if she so chose, and though she might worry about her only daughter's future, she could only interfere so much.

So it was that on this particular day they were discussing not Jesse or the nature of Paige's feelings for him, but the upcoming annual golf tournament that was the highlight of Paige's father's summer.

"Is Daddy all set?"

"He's been on the course every afternoon for the past two weeks. I should hope he's all set. Funny, when he was working full-time in the city, I used to dream about the day when he'd retire and we'd have more time to spend together." She sighed wistfully across the telephone line. "Well, he's semiretired now and he's *still* gone all day. A woman can't win, it seems."

"Don't give me that, Mother," Paige chided with a smile, looking up to find Jesse coming to lean against the kitchen arch. Her smile broadened to one of welcome. "You were never one to be idle for long. You're still playing bridge twice a week, aren't you?"

"Of course. The girls send their best, by the way. Elizabeth's daughter had another baby. A girl this time, or have I already told you?"

"No, you haven't," Paige teased, arcing a mischievous look toward Jesse, who had left his post and was slinking toward the counter on which she rested her elbow. "How many grandchildren is it for Liz now?"

There was a running competition between the bridge friends to see who had the greatest number of grandchildren. For a time Laura had all but pleaded with her daughter to help out her side—among Paige's three brothers, the Mattheson tally was at five—but she'd long since learned that such pleading fell on deaf ears.

"Seven," Laura moaned. "She's not quite up to Vivie's eight, but she's getting there."

"Vivie has five children of her own," Paige replied.

"Seems to me that's a distinct advantage. Shouldn't there be handicaps given in this thing like there are in golf?" When Jesse arched his brows, questioning the content of the conversation, she simply winked at him. This particular discussion he didn't need to hear; it'd make him nervous indeed.

"Handicaps!" Laura's voice brightened, as though she was actually considering the possibility. "That's not a bad idea. I'll have to mention it to the girls. Did I tell you about the garden-club meeting we had the other day?"

"No…"

Jesse was twisting a lock of Paige's hair around his finger, tugging gently from time to time. It wasn't the tugging she minded. It was the way his thumb brushed her neck. And "minded" wasn't really the word. It was more a matter of being distracted.

"It was marvelous!" Laura went on, unaware of her daughter's momentary preoccupation. "The fellow who spoke to us is one of the foremost iris breeders in the country."

"Iris breeders," Paige repeated. Jesse had pushed aside her hair and, leaning around her, was nibbling at her nape. His lips were warm, the moisture from his tongue cooling where the air then passed. She shivered, trying to concentrate on what her mother was saying.

"He's introduced the most amazing iris hybrids. He brought slides and as many plants with him as he could. They were beautiful. Coral and lime and…"

Paige sucked in her breath, then bit her lip to contain her delight when Jesse's mouth slid around to her collarbone. His fingers were paving the way, parting her shirt, brushing her skin in a manner that was seductive to say the least.

"Velvety texture in addition to being larger and richer in color," Laura rambled. "Unfortunately the newest things he's done won't reveal themselves in bloom for another three years. I told your father about them, and he said I should give the fellow a call. We're thinking of enlarging the greenhouse and…"

Paige's free arm now curved around Jesse's broad back. Her blouse lay open, mysteriously unbuttoned, and Jesse's lips were at her breast, setting fire to her swelling flesh. Moments later, his tongue dabbed sweet moisture on her nipple with devastating effect. She closed her eyes and let her head fall back. The hand that clutched the phone seemed to contain the only strength in her body.

Her mother's voice came at her from a distance. "I've already called the caterers and…"

Greenhouse…caterers… Through a haze Paige realized that she'd missed something. Clutching at Jesse's shoulder to hold him away, she lowered her head and muffled the phone against her neck. "Please, Jesse," she whispered frantically. "I can't follow what she's saying!" Returning the phone to her mouth, she managed a slightly shaky "Uh-huh" at what she thought might be an appropriate spot.

Jesse grinned and proceeded to slip a hand between her legs. She squeezed them together, succeeding only in heightening the red-hot sensation.

"Not that they weren't well recommended," her mother continued buoyantly, "but the salmon had bones and your father didn't think that there were enough hors d'oeuvres. So this time we'll try Georgia's people. She's been raving about them, and I do want this party to be a success." She paused, then went on, apparently not hearing the change in Paige's breathing. "Do you think you'll be able to make it, dear? Everyone wants to see you, and I'd love to be able to show you off."

An answer. Her mother wanted an answer. Paige tried to remember the question, but it was difficult with Jesse's hand stroking her that way. Something about a party, she thought, but when?

Taking a handful of Jesse's hair, she tugged sharply.

Much as she adored what he was doing, she needed a breather long enough for her to end the conversation and get off the phone.

Dazed as her senses were by smoldering desire, she misjudged the force she used. Jesse yelped. Paige winced in silent apology. And Laura Mattheson finally caught wind of something happening.

"Paige, darling, what was that?" she asked cautiously.

"That? Oh, uh, that was Jesse, Mom. He's having trouble with something. I think I'd better give him a hand. Can I call you back another time? You'll give my love to Daddy, won't you?"

"Of course…to both," Laura said, seeming to accept Paige's hurried explanation and departure. "Take care, dear. I love you."

"Love you too, Mom," Paige said more quietly, feeling strangely sensitive about Jesse's overhearing those particular words. Bridge groups and garden clubs and caterers were one thing. But those last few words represented, in a nutshell, all he'd needed and had never had.

Straining forward to replace the receiver on its hook, she was hampered by the tight press of Jesse's face to her chest. She wondered if they'd bothered him, those words, and, wanting to comfort him, she began to stroke his hair.

"What did your mother have to say?" His voice was muffled, its tone almost indistinguishable.

"I don't know," she murmured. "I couldn't concentrate 'cause some sexy guy was making love to me. On the other hand—" she feigned a frown "—it might have been a bad connection. The weather's pretty lousy—"

Her teasing was cut off by a deep growl accompanied by hands sinking into her bottom, lifting her off the stool as Jesse stood. Whatever he intended to do, though, was put off by the ring of the phone.

"Not again," he moaned.

"Still. She's probably forgotten something she feels is positively urgent." Paige reached for the phone, fully expecting her mother to be on the other end of the line. "Hello?" she said in a singsong tone.

"Is this the Mattheson residence?" asked a male voice she didn't recognize.

She straightened, laying a restraining hand on Jesse's arm. "Yes."

"This is Benjamin Waite. I'm a friend of Jesse Dallas."

She recognized the name. Indeed so. "Yes?"

"I was told I might find him there."

She paused. "You might." As a matter of pride, she had no intention of making things easy.

"Is he, uh, available?"

She hesitated. "Yes."

"Can you call him to the phone?"

She waited. "Possibly." She was beginning to feel pleased with herself. The thought of that bet and the macho smugness that had been behind it challenged her to some form of retaliation.

"Uh…would you?"

This time she let him sit for a full five seconds. "If you say 'please.'"

Jesse, who'd been observing the one-sided exchange with a look of puzzlement, put his ear to hers in hopes of recognizing a voice. What he heard was a long pause, then an indulgent "Please?" in a voice he did, indeed, know well. With a chuckle, he took the phone from Paige.

"The woman's got this thing about our little bet, Ben," he began without preliminary, his eyes on Paige. "I think she was offended."

Paige raised both brows and pointed to herself in an innocent who-me gesture. Then she slid her hands around his neck and, standing on her toes, touched the tip of her tongue to his free ear. Her retaliation had just begun.

"Not so offended that she hasn't forgiven you, it appears," Ben remarked, unaware of the shudder that shook his friend. "Or is she holding you hostage up there? Man, I was beginning to wonder when I didn't hear from you. There was no answer at your place, aside from that asinine machine of yours. I know your message by heart, I called so many times."

"Touching, Ben," Jesse murmured. When Paige lightly nipped his earlobe, he cleared his throat. "You called John?" His agent was the only one who'd known where he was. They'd talked on the phone several times in the past weeks; though Jesse wasn't ready to work, he wanted his options open.

"Yeah, and he wasn't thrilled about passing on the number."

"Confidentiality. It makes him feel important." If there was a husky timbre to Jesse's voice, it had nothing to do with the sarcasm of his words. Paige had lowered her hands and was tracing large circles on his chest. When he sent her a warning glance, she simply shifted tactics, using strategically placed thumbs as center points for the tracings.

"Whatever. Speaking of our bet, I take it you won."

"Yup," Jesse said, though again he wondered. To win implied dominance. Yet at that moment Paige seemed fully in charge.

"But you missed the play-offs."

"That's okay. I had better things to do." If he couldn't beat her, he'd have to join her. Slipping his hand around her, he ran his fingers slowly down her spine. She leaned forward and pressed an openmouthed kiss to his freshly shaved jaw while her hands began a descent of their own.

"Tell me she's teaching you to sculpt."

He cleared his throat again. "Not exactly."

"Then she's a great cook."

Her hands had reached the buckle of his belt. He felt like butter in a hot frying pan. Great cook? "Among other things."

Ben chuckled. "You must be mellowing, Jess. All this time with one woman. Are you sure you're feeling okay?"

"Feeling okay?" he echoed in a somewhat strangled

tone. Having released the buckle of his belt, Paige had lowered his zipper and was in the process of invading his briefs. "Uh, I'm fine. Just fine." He closed his eyes and swayed, completely forgetting that he was supposed to be doing his share of the petting. He clutched Paige's hip, but only to support himself. His blood raced; his muscles twitched. It was always like this, this instantaneous desire. Paige's nearness was a potent aphrodisiac. Either that, or he'd taught her too well, he mused in a moment's lucidity. But Ben had said something else.

"Hmm?"

"Uh, forget it. Why is it I get the feeling that I'm interrupting something?"

Ben was a bit more astute than Paige's mother had been, but then he was a man, and he also knew Jesse well. Jesse grinned and mustered the strength to deliver the longest sentence he had to date in the conversation. Of course, his voice wasn't smooth; his breathing had grown suspiciously choppy. "You will be if…you keep me on much longer. Unless, of course, you…get your kicks listening to the sounds of—"

"No way," Ben asserted quickly. It was bad enough that Jesse Dallas got any woman he wanted, but to rub salt in the wound? "I'm going. Glad to hear you're okay, though. Any idea when you'll be back?"

"Uh…can't answer that right now." He burst out laughing, knowing it was a choice between that or screeching. The situation was truly ludicrous. How Paige expected him to think straight when she was rubbing him that way, he didn't know. But then, she'd gotten him back, hadn't she? He had to hand it to her. When it came down to it, his laugh was as much in pride and delight as in anything else.

"I read you loud and clear," Ben announced. "Listen, Jess, take it easy. You're not a kid anymore."

"Thanks," Jesse growled, but the growl was directed at Paige, who'd sunk to her knees and was about to… "I gotta go. Talk with ya later. 'Bye."

From that day on, it became a joke with them. When one was on the phone, the other played the distracter. It was as though neither wanted the interruptions that would remind them of the world beyond.

MANY OF THEIR lightest moments took place on the beach. When the sun was hot they played in the surf, splashing and dodging each other, drifting apart only to meet again atop a cresting wave. Paige discovered that Jesse was not only a powerful swimmer, he also—incidentally, of course—did marvelous things for the otherwise shapeless Lycra nothing he wore. His body, lightly bronzed when she'd first met him, had taken on a deep golden hue from the time he'd spent in the sun. His sandy hair had grown lighter; the soft hair on his arms, legs and chest positively glowed. He was the embodiment of health and the source of a constant attraction for Paige.

One afternoon Paige stood in the shallows, watching Jesse stroke smoothly away from shore, turn and swim back. His arms arced with graceful strength, and sunlight sparkled on his wet flesh. When he turned to swim out again, she was hit by an idea. Running quickly across the beach and up the steps to the house, she returned in time to see him emerge from the waves. Lifting her camera to her eye, she snapped one picture, then another as he approached.

"What are you doing?" he growled, scooping his towel from the sand as he advanced on her.

Click. Whir. Click. "Capturing Poseidon."

"Poseidon, huh?"

"Yup." Click. From his waist up. Whir. Click. Head and shoulders.

"Is this another one of your talents?"

"Talents? I don't know." Click. Head only. He was directly before her. She lowered the camera and met his gaze. His hair dripped wetly on his forehead. His skin gleamed. "I've been known to take pictures of things I want to sculpt. I'm surprised I didn't think of this sooner."

He mopped his face, then his hair. "Come on, Paige. You're not on to that again, are you?"

"Sculpting you? Why not?"

The towel seesawed around his neck. "Because my body's private, remember? And besides, I thought you were working on something else."

Having finished the grouping of sandpipers, she had indeed begun on a new piece. It was of limestone and she wasn't sure what it was—a new experience for her—but some compulsion kept her going. She was in the earliest stages of roughing out and was as fascinated by the shape taking form as she was mystified.

"I am, which is precisely why pictures of you might be nice. By the time I get around to doing anything with them, you might not be around. What would I use as a model then?"

Jesse's gaze grew harder. He was searching, she knew, trying to see if any emotion existed beneath her blithely worded explanation. She kept her expression light, but as he turned in silence and began to walk toward the steps, she had the sinking sensation that time was running out.

Deep down inside she wanted those pictures. To sculpt from, perhaps. To cherish, without a doubt. It was only a matter of days now before he'd be leaving. Every sign pointed that way.

In some respects, she felt as though she was living on borrowed time. She wasn't pregnant; she'd known that for nearly ten days. She'd half feared that Jesse would leave as soon as he knew. The fact that he hadn't was like a small gift, painful in its impermanence but precious nonetheless.

Wishing only to savor the gift while it lasted, she shouldered her camera and followed him up the steps.

PAIGE CONTINUED to photograph Jesse and, as much as he protested that he preferred being on the other side of the lens, he indulged her. It seemed a small thing, with so many larger ones on his mind.

With each passing day he grew more moody. Yes, he was getting the itch to work at last; he'd never taken a vacation quite as long as this. But what really bothered him was the fact that he felt so comfortable here. Being with Paige day and night evoked emotions in him that he had neither the will nor the ability to handle.

Paige was aware that he was now in closer touch with his agent. She sensed his restlessness. When he began to spend more and more time on the beach, she respected his need for solitude and left him alone. Time and again she'd put down her work and walk to the glass wall of her studio to catch sight of his sandy hair, his downcast head as he walked the sand. And she knew that all she could do was to make things as warm, as comforting, as loving as she could for him when he returned.

Though she had the luxury of her work to keep her occupied, the occupation seemed more often than not limited to her hands alone, another reason why her new piece was a mystery. Her thoughts were still on Jesse. And though she told herself that the time she spent alone was good for her, that she'd better get used to solitude once more, doing so was harder than she'd ever dreamed.

BY THE TIME the seventh week approached, things had grown strained between them. The lighter times were fewer and far between. The inevitable seemed upon them.

It was Saturday. As she tried to do unless working on a deadline, Paige had steered clear of her studio. She'd slept late with Jesse and had made a hearty brunch. They'd driven to the small craft shops in Rockport and had returned. Silence had dominated the trip.

When Jesse suggested that they go out for dinner at one of the more elegant local restaurants, Paige had had a premonition of what was to come. When, dressed in their finery that night, they'd said more to the waiter than to each other, she'd known.

They'd returned to the house and were having brandy

in the living room when she finally took the bull by the horns. "When are you leaving?" she asked quietly.

He glanced up from an intense study of the amber liquid in his snifter. There was neither surprise nor confusion on his face.

"Tomorrow." He held her gaze. "I'll be starting work on a new film on Monday."

Paige wondered how long he'd known, but knew that a show of indignation would do nothing but spoil their final hours together. She nodded. "What...uh, what is it on?"

"The CIA."

"Oh?"

He shrugged. "The CIA can be pretty depressing, but, yes, I think it'll be easier to take. The producer wants something that plays like an adventure. It might even be fun."

She smiled. "I'm glad." When he reached over and tugged at her shoulder, she slid the short distance on the sofa until she rested against him.

"You look pretty tonight," he said in the gruff tone she'd come to know so well but had missed in recent days.

Resting her hand on his thigh, she toyed with the crease of his trousers. "So do you."

"Pretty?"

"Handsome."

"Ah, that's better." Setting his snifter on the nearby table, he fingered the pearls that nestled in the vee of her teal-blue silk dress. "Very nice. You were made for pearls, or have I already told you that?"

Her skin warmed where he touched and she was suddenly overcome by the urge to throw herself into his arms and hold him until tomorrow passed. One more day she wanted. Then another. And another. Letting him go was going to be the hardest thing she'd ever done but, loving him as she did, she knew she had no choice. He was free, an adult. She couldn't hold him against his will. And evidently his will was to return to New York.

"Will you be okay?" he asked, suddenly sounding less sure of himself than she'd ever heard him sound. Where once she might have given an indignant retort, saying something to the effect that she'd lived alone for years and could very well do so again, she was struck by his concern and answered with it in mind.

"Sure. I'll be fine. You've fixed everything that needs to be fixed, so the house won't fall apart on me. I may even get some work done," she teased.

"You have been working."

"Not as much as usual. You're a distraction, or hadn't you noticed?"

"Then it's just as well that I'm leaving," he stated, grasping on the excuse as though it eased his guilt.

She tipped her head back and looked up at him. "I'll miss you, Jesse."

His eyes darkened, his voice grew more gruff. But he didn't push her away or stand up in a huff. Rather, his fingers tightened on her shoulder and he held her closer. "Don't say that. I told you the day would come. I never planned to stay as long as this."

"I know. Why did you?"

"It's been...nice," he said more gently. "You're not bad for a roommate."

She saw the softening of his gaze and knew then that if they had one night left it would be a night to remember. Easing her own snifter to the floor, she put her hand to his face, tracing each of the features she now had indelibly etched both on film and in her mind. Well-shaped eyebrows, tiny crow's-feet at the corners of those soul-reaching blue eyes, lean cheeks faintly roughened by the beard that had begun growing the instant he'd shaved, a strong, firm jaw...she could touch forever and never tire.

"Neither are you...bad for a roommate," she breathed. "I'm surprised at how easy it was."

His gaze was touching her as her hand was touching him. The light in his eyes was warm, sad, intense. Catching her fingers, he drew them to his lips, taking one after another into his mouth, sucking gently on each. Rather than a gesture of studied seduction, it seemed one of need, a need that Paige was more than willing to meet. With fingers moist from his lips she brushed his cheeks, then leaned up and blew lightly on the streaks before wetting them again with her own tongue. She'd give him anything and everything he needed this night. That was what love was about, and she brimmed with it.

He kissed her then, lowering his lips to hers. What his mouth did, hers mirrored. The wetness of the open kiss only strengthened the bond.

Jesse pressed a long finger to her throbbing lips. "I'll take care of the glasses. Why don't you run ahead to the bathroom. I'll be right in."

"Let's do it here," she whispered, reluctant to let him go for an instant. But he was dragging her arms from his neck and pushing himself to his feet. He knelt for her glass and looked up at her.

"We're gonna do it right," he said hoarsely. "Long and thorough. For what I have in mind, this sofa is not the place."

The promise in his eyes set her blood racing in heated currents through her veins. She watched as Jesse stood, reached down and drew her to her feet.

"The bathroom?" he reminded her, a crooked smile on his face.

"The bathroom," she muttered, willing her knees to carry her there.

Moments later she stood before the open medicine chest, the small plastic case in her hand. She stared at it. The haze of passion lifted, and she stared harder. Slowly she opened it, then gazed at the rubber disk inside. Closing her eyes, she struggled to calculate the number of days it had been. A glimmer of excitement shot through her, accompanied by a sudden and intense determination that reflected a need as great as any she'd ever known. She

opened her eyes to look once more at the disk, then carefully, quietly, closed the lid and replaced the case on the
shelf.

The medicine chest snapped shut. She stood for a
minute studying her reflection in the mirror. She put her
hand on her stomach, moved it slowly downward over the
silk of her dress. The trembling of her body intensified, but
there was more than passion behind it. Knowing precisely
what she was doing, she turned and left the bathroom.

Jesse stood in the bedroom, staring out at the ocean.
Hearing the soft rustle of her dress, he turned. The look in
his eyes was of a heated anticipation that had built even in
the brief moments he'd spent waiting for her. His tie was
unknotted and hung on either side of the center tab of his
shirt. He'd released the top two buttons.

She was glad he was still clothed. She wanted to undress
him. She wanted to slowly and carefully peel away his
outer layers, to sculpt him and mold him, to forever embed
in him the memory of who she was and what their time
together had meant to her.

Closing the small distance between them, she looped
her arms loosely around his neck. "You look like a god
standing here," she whispered, smiling. "A very handsome
god made of stone, who needs the touch of a mortal to
bring him to life."

"Will you touch me?" he whispered back, too mesmerized by the look of adoration on her face to think seriously
of its cause and rebel. Or perhaps he did know its cause but
didn't care. Tonight he could be greedy. He'd be leaving
tomorrow.

"Oh, yes," she murmured against his jaw. Her lids
lowered and for a long moment she simply savored the
musky scent that was his alone. "Mmm." She inhaled
deeply. "So good."

She brushed her lips back and forth along his skin, its
faint roughness heightening the sensations. Mouthing him
softly, she slipped her hands under the shoulders of his

blazer and pushed the fabric back and off his arms. Trailing her fingers back up those two strong limbs, she next went slowly to work at the buttons of his shirt. Anticipation quickened her breathing, and she reveled in the urgency she felt even as she restrained herself from rushing. Each step was beautiful. Each one she relished.

When his shirt was open, she pressed her face to his warm, hair-spattered flesh. Her hands charted the muscular swells, feeling his shudder, absorbing it with her lips.

"Dear God," he murmured. "I don't think I'm going to be able to take this."

"You'll take it," she whispered with confidence, but she began to ease the shirt from his shoulders. "You'll take it and more. You love it. Confess."

"I love it, I love it," was his hoarse chant as his hands guided her head in its tormentingly slow shift. The feel of her lips on his flesh was like fire. The dab of her tongue did little to quench the flame. He shifted his stance in an effort to steady his legs, but it seemed a losing battle.

Bare from the waist up, he submitted to her sensual manipulation. while her mouth was busy tasting and teasing every inch of his chest, her hands on his back were those of a sculptress. The tactile exploration took her over bunching muscles, into softer hollows. He was sure she'd separately identified each and every one of his vertebrae before she finally granted him a rest from the steady strain of desire that threatened to erupt violently.

"How do you feel?" she asked against his lips once more.

"I'm dying," he grated. "Dying. How can you do this to me, Paige?"

"How can I not?" was her whispered reply, and he understood and agreed and contained the urge to throw her on the floor and take her instantly.

Paige would have nothing to do with "instantly." Setting the pace as she was, she wanted everything to last. If her own body cried out for release—which it did vociferously—she had only to think of tomorrow night and the night after that, and she was in control once again. This night she'd remember, every tiny, tormentingly beautiful moment of it. She'd decided that. So it would be.

Their kisses reflected the duality of their desire, swinging from gentle to fierce and back to gentle, vacillating between the needs of the body and those of the mind. Lips caressed, teeth nipped, tongues repaired the damage only to fuel the hunger. The air was rent with tiny moans, from whose throat Paige neither knew nor cared. The attraction, the fascination, the fire was shared; that seemed all that mattered.

Closing her eyes and pressing her forehead to Jesse's chin, Paige took several long, ragged breaths.

"What's wrong?" he teased. "Trouble breathing?"

"No, no. Just trying to steady the pace."

"Of breathing...or loving?"

"Both," she murmured, knowing the truth of the confession. Her hands seemed glued to his shoulders, as though they wanted to remain forever. Of course, the support was a boon to her quaking knees.

"I could help you out," he offered gruffly. "I'm an expert at taking off my pants."

"I'm sure you are," she drawled, "but I can manage, thank you." Already her hands had moved to the buckle of his belt. She imagined she was wielding a new tool in the sculpting process, still trying to bare the surface of the stone on which she worked.

The belt was unbuckled. Her fingers brushed the firm skin of his belly, and releasing the catch of his trousers was made easier when he sucked in a breath. Catch unfastened. Zipper tab raised. She paused, rubbed her cheek against his breast, swirled her tongue around one dark areola. His nipple was erect; she basked in her success, then furthered it with the tip of her tongue. The ploy backfired when she found herself quivering in contact with the tight nub.

"Hurry...hurry..." Jesse rasped, arching his hips against her hand.

But she wouldn't hurry. She couldn't. If this night was to hold her a long, long time she had to make it last forever. And once a layer had been removed from the stone, it could never be replaced. She wanted to fully appreciate each new facet as it was revealed.

To the tune of the surf beyond the rocks, Jesse's zipper rasped slowly down. She slid her hands inside the plackets, then knelt to ease his trousers over his hips. In this he helped her, stepping out of his loafers so that both trousers and socks could go. When he stood before her wearing nothing but his briefs, she sat back on her heels to look at him. He'd done the same to her that first night. Only now could she appreciate what he'd felt then, an awareness of beauty so intense that her hands trembled at the thought of touching it. She felt awed by his power. In her eyes Jesse was perfection.

She steadied her fingers by curving them around his ankles, then moved them upward over calves that were sinewed and strong. Her hands ruffled hair as they moved, hair that exemplified masculinity in such a small but exciting way. His knees seemed thicker, as if locked in desperation. Corded muscles stood out on his thighs, hard to her touch, growing harder beneath it like living marble, rich and firm.

"You are a work of art," she breathed brokenly. "We sculptors think we have talent, but it's nothing compared to His."

"Religion now," came the low moan above her. "Oh, my God." But it wasn't criticism as much as sheer agony.

"Patience," she whispered as she slid both hands to the backs of his thighs, finding them strong and textured. When she leaned forward to bury her face against his leg, he clutched at her hair.

"I've run out, love! I want you undressed!"

"Me…undressed?" She was so enraptured by what she'd found beneath his clothes that she hadn't yet thought that far.

"That's how it's normally done," Jesse growled, grasping her under her arms and hauling her to her feet. When he began to hurriedly fumble with the back zipper of her dress, she stepped away. This time she was going to do it, she decided. Always before either he'd done it or they'd tugged at their clothes simultaneously. This time would be different. This time Jesse would know exactly how far she'd come from the innocent, near-virgin he'd first made love to so many weeks before.

There was nothing outwardly seductive in her movements as she unzipped the dress, slid it from her shoulders and let it fall in a pool at her feet. Her eyes didn't tease. Her hips didn't sway. Rather, her demeanor was one of conviction and love and, even in spite of the two, the faintest flicker of fear. She needed to please the godlike creature she adored, and no amount of self-possession could hide that need.

Heart thumping, she stepped out of her slip. Hands trembling, she reached back to release the catch of her bra, then eased the lacy confines from her breasts and dropped the wisp of material to the floor. Eyes on his as she closely followed her progress, she rolled down her panty hose and peeled them from her feet. When she stood perfectly naked, she waited for a sign of his approval. For as many times as they'd made love, she'd always needed that. Without it, her determination meant nothing.

He pressed his lips together. His collarbone stood out above wire-taut muscles. His eyes raked her figure with a slowness she'd have thought beyond him at that moment. Only when he met her gaze with eyes that positively smoldered did she feel free once more. Without words he conveyed his own adoration, then he met her hand when she reached out to draw him toward the bed.

With a flick of her wrist the cover was turned back. With a second flick, the blanket and top sheet joined it in a hillock at the foot of the bed. Jesse freed himself of his straining briefs, for just a moment stunning Paige with his ardor. Regaining control then, she urged him down, following with the same innocent sensuality with which she'd undressed.

She stretched out over him, letting her body take part in an exploration of his rugged form. She ran her foot up and down his leg. Her belly familiarized itself with the firmness of his. Her hands worked from his ribs to the concavity beneath his arms, finally propping themselves flat on the sheet as she rose to find his lips with her own.

It was a kiss made all the more heated by the intimate molding of their bodies. Her breasts swayed with every breath she took, nipples brushing against his until every pore, every nerve end had taken flame. Scorched, she drew back. There was work yet to be done—the fine shaping and polishing and finishing that would end in joyous conflagration for them both.

Straddling his legs, she knelt above him for a minute. His eyes were heavy lidded and smoky, his lips slightly parted to aid the labored working of his lungs.

"Paige…" he warned, his fingers sinking into the flesh above her elbows.

He was at the end of his tether, which was just where she wanted him to be. He was going to know what it was like to go nearly mad with want. He was going to know what it was like to be worshiped. He was going to know, once and for all, that there was no other woman, no other woman in the world for him. And he was going to know just how much she loved him, whether he liked it or not!

What took place then was something that Paige could never have consciously choreographed. Driven by the love she had to express, she touched and tasted every inch of his body, finding one part more precious than the next, treating each with fevered reverence. He was writhing, straining toward release when she finally rose and lowered herself onto him. At that moment, without severing their connection in any way, he rolled them over and took the dominant position.

It was only a position, for the dominance was shared. Who drove the other harder, who took the greater pleasure was something neither could determine even when they reached one apex and began a heady climb to the next. Paige only knew—much, much later, when neither could move a limb—that she had indeed found the secret of this stone. Hard though Jesse was on the outside, inside he was filled with love. He spoke it through his body, as Paige did through hers. He murmured it in broken thoughts when the frenzy of passion stripped away that last flimsy layer that shielded his soul. "Yes...oh, love...yes...sweet...I'm yours... dear heart...!"

He'd never have admitted it if she confronted him, so she didn't. But the next morning, when he determinedly packed his things and carried them to the car, the knowledge that for a tiny period of time he'd loved her fully was some comfort.

"Take care of yourself," he said quietly, pausing only to give her a final poignant look before climbing into the car and driving off.

Indeed she would take care of herself, because now she had a secret of her own. With a conviction that was uncanny but very, very real, she knew she was pregnant.

CHAPTER SEVEN

THE FIRST THING PAIGE DID AFTER Jesse left was to take a huge wad of clay from the storage closet, raise it high above her head and ram it mercilessly against the workbench surface. Over and over she did it, pounding the clay from time to time with her fists before lifting it and slamming it down again. Only when her arms were weak from exertion did she stop and sink onto the nearby stool. Her body was tired, but her heart was heavy as stone. When she finally mustered the will to move, she wandered to the beach, where she sat for hours. She stared at the sea, choosing a distant wave, following it in to shore. She looked at the sky and wondered that its blueness could be so vital while her own blue mood was a leaden weight. She searched the sand for Jesse's footprints, but if there had been evidence of his presence once upon a time, the tide had washed it away.

When the heat of the sun began to prickle her skin, she returned to the house to drift aimlessly from room to room. Quiet pierced her ears. Emptiness filled her view. She felt suddenly and strangely alone…and she grew slowly furious. Her life had been fine, just fine before he'd entered it! She'd *loved* silence, *thrived* on solitude. She hadn't needed *anyone*, much less a man, to liven up the day. But that had changed…thanks to Jesse Dallas.

Back in her studio again, she wielded the clay a while longer, lifting it high, slamming it down, relentlessly pommeling it with her hands. If this was a temper tantrum, she was loving every minute of it. Loving it...hating it...suffering inside as though a vital part of her had been cut out and skewered.

When exhaustion took over, she turned her back on the studio and, trailing to the living room, collapsed on the sofa. She dozed; she awoke. Time held little meaning. She lay listlessly out on the deck. She walked the beach again. The sun had begun to lower in the western sky before she realized she hadn't eaten since breakfast. With little enthusiasm she managed to down half a sandwich and a glass of milk, but the sandwich might have been paste, the milk dishwater.

Picking up the book she'd started several days before, she sat on the sofa and tried to read, but her stomach kept knotting and, before long, she sought solace in bed, in the sweet oblivion of sleep. It eluded her for long hours. She tossed and turned, then jumped up, stripped the bed and put on fresh sheets. She'd be damned if she'd have to smell him, too! It was bad enough that she could see him, an ever-present vision wherever she went. Damn him! Damn her own vulnerable heart!

It was long into the night before she finally fell asleep. When she awoke the next morning, she felt vaguely disoriented. Groggily she blinked, then rolled to her side. The other half of the bed was perfectly neat, the pillow as fully fluffed as it had been the night before. Slowly, inevitably, reality set in. She lay board still, fingers clenched into fists by her mouth. Her pulse grew erratic, as though something was squeezing her heart, squeezing and twisting and causing the most excruciating pain.

Then she began to cry.

Tears fell full and fast from her eyes. Soft, soulful sobs slipped through her lips. She curled into a ball, hugging the pillow for comfort, and cried. And cried. Everything she'd done the day before had been for the frustration, the anger, the loneliness she'd felt; this was for the sorrow.

She loved Jesse Dallas with all her heart. Now he was

gone. He hadn't called the night before; she hadn't expected him to. The break had been made and made cleanly. She was simply going to have to adjust.

Wiping the tears from her eyes, she sat up cross-legged on the bed. As minutes passed, her head cleared. Though her limbs still trembled, she knew they'd calm in time.

Determination was an antidote, spreading slowly through her veins, giving her strength. She'd adjust. Oh, yes! She'd resume her life as it had been before *he'd* stepped into it. She'd sculpt. She'd eat, sleep, walk, read, see her friends from time to time. She'd forget that Jesse Dallas had ever been—no, no, she wouldn't do that. She loved him; she'd always love him. And besides, microscopic though it yet was, she had his baby. No, she'd never forget him. She didn't want to forget him. What they'd shared had been too beautiful for words. These memories, plus her own maternal instinct, would guarantee that their child would be born and raised with love.

Placing her hand low on her abdomen, she studied it resting there. A miracle? Love was the miracle. To have a child who embodied that love would be her salvation.

Sitting straighter, she raised her head. Then slowly, her lips curved into the softest, most serene of smiles, and she was ready to face the future once more.

IT WASN'T AN EASY ROAD at the start. Paige went through the motions of normal living, doing all the things she'd done before. But she was repeatedly stunned by how much she missed Jesse. The house didn't seem the same. The outings she took were somehow lacking. The evenings were thunderously quiet. And, of course, there were the cravings. She had only to picture him standing before her and her body began to tingle. The tingle grew to a tremble, then an ache. She ached, damn it, she ached. And there wasn't a thing she could do about it!

Jesse Dallas, whether he'd known it or not, had chipped through the complacency of her existence, finding holes she hadn't known were there, needs she'd prided herself on being above. If they were flaws, she could find no fault with them. Ever the sculptress, she was simply going to have to work around them, to use them to her benefit. It was a challenging project. Jesse had added a new dimension to her life; it would take every bit of her skill and determination to compensate for its loss.

There were times when she was angry or frustrated or hurt, but those times grew fewer, each less intense than the one before. By the end of the first month, she was comfortably back in the routine she'd established before her fateful trip to New York.

Work was her major solace and she poured herself into it heart and soul. The piece she'd started before Jesse had left took shape as a child in the early stages of uterine development. It frightened her at times that she'd begun it even before she'd decided she wanted a baby. She wondered if it reflected a maternal instinct she'd subconsciously harbored for some time, or whether the womanhood that had blossomed under Jesse's caring hand had spawned it. Whatever the case, she took great pleasure in sculpting the small fetally tucked form. There was a liquidity to its shape suggestive of its suspension in amniotic fluid, but there was a realism as well in tiny features— eyelids, ears, mouth. Lifelike fingers and toes emerged from the swirling mass much as had Jesse's fingers from the stone she'd picked up on the beach. Whereas then the fingers she'd sculpted had been masculine, those she did now held the fragility, the innocence of the not-yet-born. When she finished the piece, she found herself thoroughly in love with it. But a mother raised her child to let it go one day, didn't she? It was with reluctance and great, great discipline that she gently crated the stone and sent it off to New York.

She began work on a second piece, this a dancer carved from a piece of yew that she'd let age in her storeroom for just the right amount of time. As she sculpted carefully and with due concentration, the heat of August abated and September came.

Her pregnancy was now fact. She didn't need a doctor's confirmation, so firm had been her conviction from the start. Even had that not been so she couldn't have missed the ripening of her breasts, the shadowy appearance of tiny blue veins, the first subtle changes in her body.

Her joy was tempered only by the awful sickness that set in soon after, a nausea that was far from limited to mornings and prevented her from holding down much of anything she ate. At this point she did see her doctor, who assured her that she was in fine health and that what she was experiencing was perfectly normal for a woman who was six weeks pregnant. When she offered her medicine to control the nausea, Paige refused it, opting instead to follow her doctor's suggestion that she eat small amounts of easily digestible foods at frequent intervals throughout the day. This helped somewhat, though she still had bad moments when she craved nothing more than Jesse's warm, strong hand bracing her in her agony. But he wasn't there. She hadn't heard from him at all. And she had to be strong, if not for her own sake then for that of the child she carried. When she continued to lose weight and called the doctor in alarm, she eased her worries with a chuckle, telling her that soon enough she'd have the reverse complaint. Thus assured, Paige found the sickness easier to accept.

More than once she was grateful to the nature of her profession, which allowed her to take breaks when she needed, to lie down and rest when she felt tired, as she did increasingly. This, too, the doctor assured her would pass, so she didn't fight it and found herself napping regularly each afternoon.

More often than not, the evenings found her curled on the sofa buried in one of the books she'd picked up on pregnancy and childbirth. At these times she'd grow more excited than ever—excited and proud, a little bit frightened, and on occasion sad. She wanted Jesse to be sharing this with her. Miracles in his life had been nonexistent; it grieved her to know that he was missing one now. The knowledge that a baby was growing inside her, that one day it would be a living child to hold and nurture and love, was truly wondrous. As much as he might declare that he didn't want a child, she had a deep conviction that, even against his will, he'd treasure it. It was, after all, a child of his blood. That was the thought that gave her the greatest comfort during the nights that seemed so long.

The end of September found Paige packing her bags and heading for Connecticut. She was looking forward to seeing her family. The grand party that Laura Mattheson had been planning since June had given even her brothers an excuse to come home. When one's father reached a robust and healthy seventy, it was indeed cause for celebration.

Paige's mother knew that Jesse had left. She'd been wonderfully gentle and supportive during those times when Paige had called, feeling down. Paige hadn't yet said a word about her pregnancy. She'd debated long and hard about how to break the news. Not that her parents wouldn't be overjoyed at the prospect of another grandchild, but…Paige wasn't married. For that reason word of her pregnancy might throw them. Wanting nothing to mar the long-planned celebration, she knew she'd have to carefully pick her time. Though her brothers and their families were leaving the day after the party, Paige had planned to stay on a bit longer. That was when she hoped an opportune moment might come.

It didn't quite work that way.

She arrived in Westport on Friday afternoon, with the party planned for Saturday night. Her mother was there to meet her at the door, as beautifully dressed and coiffed as ever, with an added excitement in her eyes.

"Paige!" Grinning broadly, she held out her arms and took her daughter into a fond embrace, which Paige returned with a force that surprised them both. Only at that moment did Paige realize how much she'd missed the warmth of human contact.

Loosening her arms with reluctance, Paige stood back for her mother's inevitable inspection. She'd dressed more carefully than ever, choosing sweater and slacks in coordinating shades of lavender, applying makeup to counteract the slimness of her face and the hollows beneath her eyes, waving her hair as softly as possible around temple and cheek.

Her efforts had been in vain, but then, a mother's eye was by nature keen. "You look tired," Laura said. Her quiet tone echoed the concern in her eyes.

"*You* look marvelous! I like your color."

Laura touched her hair, but Paige's attempt at diversion went no further. "Aren't you feeling well?"

"I'm fine."

"You're still upset by that fellow's leaving."

"His name is Jesse, and I'm, uh, I'm getting used to it."

Wrapping an arm around her daughter's shoulders, Laura led her into the house. Her eyes remained fixed, though, on Paige's face. "This will be a good vacation for you, then. I hope you've brought plenty of things. I thought we could go shopping one day next week. If you want to, that is." Her brows knit. "Are you sure you're not coming down with something?"

Coming *out* with something was more like it. "I'm sure. Is Daddy home?"

"He's gone to the airport to pick up Bill and Angie and the kids. Jason and Annette came in last night. They're at the club with Todd. He couldn't wait to see the pool. Michael and Sheila are driving down with the girls tomorrow morning."

Paige raised her eyes in a sweep around the large front hall of the elegant Tudor home. "This is the calm before the storm, then."

Laura chuckled. "You could say that. But we won't

mind the storm a bit. It's too quiet around here most of the
time. It's the nicest gift for your father—having you
children here with us. It's not often that everyone can make
it at the same time."

"This is a very special occasion. Is he looking forward
to the party?"

"Yes, ma'am. Come. I'll make us some honey tea. That
should put color in your cheeks."

"There is color in my cheeks."

"Artificial. Every speck. You might be able to fool the
world, but you can't fool me, Paige Mattheson." They
were on the kitchen threshold. "Do you want to go on
upstairs while I heat the water?" Her voice took on a
teasing note. She knew how much Paige enjoyed touching
base after being away for a time. "Your room's waiting."

Paige grinned. "Then I'd better hurry. Rooms get very
impatient." Giving her mother a quick peck on the cheek,
she returned to the hall, grabbed her suitcase and started
up the stairs.

Her room was the same as it had been when she'd left
to go to college eleven years before. It wasn't the room of
a child, or a teenager; Mattheson bedrooms had been re-
decorated with regularity as the children had passed from
one stage to the next. Redone the summer before her senior
year in high school, this room was that of a young woman.
Bold florals dominated in shades of yellow and green and
white. It was cheerful, but sophisticated, with French pro-
vincial furniture and just the right touch of softness.

Paige stood at its door feeling strangely melancholy.
Stepping inside, she set down her bag, fingered the back
of the scrolled chair by the dressing table, then approached
the bed and brushed the quilt coverlet with her palm.
Sliding one hip against the bed, she slowly lowered herself
to its yielding surface.

She'd been happy in this room now filled with
memories. These four walls had seen her playing with
toys as an infant, going off to school for the first time, en-

tertaining afternoon chums as pint-size as she in the days before homework had precluded such playtime. They'd overheard hours of inane chatter when, as a birthday gift in her thirteenth year, her parents had installed the Princess phone that lay quiet now on the nightstand.

She smiled, remembering her friends and the fanciful talks they'd had. They'd gossiped and giggled and dreamed, dreamed of husbands and of the children they'd have and the things *they'd* do differently. At the time, there was always pretense of one complaint or another, but Paige knew in her heart that she'd be lucky to give *her* child the very same things she'd had. If she was unable to give it a father, she'd simply have to compensate in other ways.

Taking a long, slightly unsteady breath, she lowered her eyes to her hands, determinedly placed them on the spread on either side of her and pushed herself up. Pausing only to brush her hair and dust an additional bit of color on her cheeks—though her mother might see through the ploy, her father and brothers were sure to be fooled—she headed back downstairs.

Laura was in the breakfast nook off the kitchen, stirring her tea with a spoon, deep in thought. At the sound of Paige's heels on the ceramic tile, she looked up.

"Millie's coming in for dinner," she said, feeling called upon to explain the housekeeper's absence. "She's looking forward to seeing you, but she wanted to spend a little time at home since she won't be taking Sunday off."

"How is she?"

"Remarkable, given the fact that she's sixty-five herself. Actually, it's worked out well. I don't need her full-time, what with all of you off and on your own, so when her arthritis is acting up she stays home. She's promised me, absolutely promised me that the arthritis will behave itself at least through Sunday. I think she's as excited about the party as we are. She'll be in command of quite a fleet in here."

Smiling, Paige slid into the place Laura had set beside

her own. Tea was steeping. A plate of small pastries, with crackers and cheese on the side, awaited her pleasure.

"Is everything set for tomorrow night?" Paige asked, reaching for a cracker nonchalantly. She was acutely aware of her mother's renewed scrutiny.

"I think so. The tent is being set up in the yard in the morning. The tables, chairs and linens should come soon after that. The florist promised me he'd be by at three. The caterers arrive at five. There's really not much that I have to do, other than have my hair and nails done and make sure the children don't play with the silverware once it's set out."

Paige gave a fond smile. "I can't wait to see them. I bet they've all grown."

"Mmm. Todd has. He's the most precocious five-year-old I've ever seen." Her expression of grandmotherly pride would have been complete had it not been for the slight worry crease between her eyes. "Have some cheese with the cracker, dear. It's fresh brie."

Paige's stomach tripped at the thought. She crinkled up her nose and reached for her tea. "Uh…I think I'll pass. Mmm. Sweet. Honey makes it, don't you think?"

Her mother was not thinking of honey, nor did she have any intention of doing so. "What's wrong, Paige? Something is, and you can deny it as much as you want, but you won't convince me. You're pale. You've got shadows under your eyes. And you've lost weight. If there's one thing you don't need, it's that."

Slowly setting down her cup, Paige looked at her mother. It was probably her biggest mistake, for the look of concern on Laura's face chipped at her resolve and she was beset by a wave of emotion. She'd wanted to wait, to have the party over and done with before chancing to say something that might or might not be upsetting. But this was her mother, and they'd always been close. Laura's next words did nothing to ease her dilemma.

"I'll worry until you tell me, darling," she said softly. "You know that. I'll imagine all kinds of horrible things."

"This is blackmail," Paige countered, forcing a smile that didn't quite make it.

"It's the truth. You look as though you've been ill. But there's something else." She paused, holding Paige's gaze. "Something in your eyes. I remember the time you came home from school with a look like that in your eyes. You'd been invited by your art teacher to go to an exhibit at the Guggenheim and, as excited as you were, you were terrified that we'd object."

Paige remembered. She gave her mother a rueful grin. "You did."

"But only until we learned that the teacher's wife was going along. He was young and attractive, that art teacher of yours. You were sixteen years old. It wouldn't have been proper for you to have gone with him alone."

It was all Paige could do to contain the hysterical laugh that threatened to bubble forth. If her mother had thought *that* would have been improper, she could imagine what the reaction would be to the current news. Needing to do something, she nibbled gingerly at her cracker, then wished she hadn't for her stomach was queasy.

"Mr. Antone was a newlywed, mother. He was in love with his wife. He only invited me because he knew how much I'd love the exhibit. Besides, even if his wife hadn't been along, if he'd done anything improper I'd have known how to take care of myself. I knew my way around the city. I'd have caught a cab to the train and come right home."

Laura's watchfulness was as intense as ever. "That's beside the point now, all in the past. Just that look in your eyes brought it back. It's…it's as though you've got something you're dying to tell me, but there's that…that little bit of fear." She put her hand over Paige's and squeezed gently. "You can tell me, darling. I'm strong. I can take it." The tiny hint of teasing took the edge off her concern, though the concern itself remained.

With a soft half laugh, Paige looked down. "You always

did see too much. It wasn't fair, y'know. Every girl has a right to some secrets."

"I know *you*, darling. That's more than some parents can say of their children. And I loved you dearly. I still do." She lifted her hand to tuck a dark wave of hair behind Paige's ear. "Which is why I want you to tell me what's brought you here looking like you can't keep a thing in your stomach, much less get enough sleep."

Her choice of words had been strictly by chance, but something about their juxtaposition brought her to a halt. She glanced down at the half-eaten cracker on the saucer, then back at her daughter's face.

"You got it," Paige murmured.

"You're…pregnant?"

Despite the anxiety Paige felt in anticipation of her mother's reaction, she couldn't contain the soft smile that broke through on her lips. "Yup."

Laura's eyes widened. *"Pregnant?"*

"As in going to have a baby. Looks that way."

Laura straightened. "You can't be serious, Paige. I mean—" she began to sputter "—I mean, you're not married!"

"I know that."

"And you're pregnant." As though to deny it, she shook her head. Not a hair moved. "I thought your generation was expert at making sure this kind of thing didn't happen."

"We are. The techniques are all there and very efficient." She smirked. "It's when you don't use them that funny things like morning sickness occur."

"This is no time to be flip, Paige," her mother scolded. "You're an intelligent girl. I'd have thought you'd have done the wise thing."

"I did." There was not a trace of flippancy in her sober tone. "I chose to have a child."

"You *chose*? How could you *do* that when you're all alone?" She shook her head more slowly this time. "I don't think you've given this proper thought."

"Mother, even if that were true—which it isn't—it's not the issue. The issue is that I'm pregnant. It's a fact." She took a breath, then lowered her voice. "I can't believe you'd suggest I try to reverse it."

"Lord, no!" Laura exclaimed, her pallor growing more marked. "You can't kill that child. It's yours!"

Paige smiled. "Yes, it is mine."

"And you want it, don't you?"

"More than anything. When I think of it getting bigger and bigger by the day, I get giddy."

"Then you throw up," Laura interjected wryly.

"The doctor says morning sickness is a good sign. Besides, it'll pass. You should know that. You had four children of your own."

"And a husband."

Paige sighed. "Things can't always be perfect. I've been pretty lucky so far. I have a career, a home and plenty of love to give a child." Her eyes softened almost beseechingly. "I really do want the baby, Mom. It's mine. Mine—" her voice caught "—and Jesse's."

"Jesse's gone," Laura stated unnecessarily. "Does he know?"

"No."

"But you're going to tell him, aren't you? Surely he'd marry you—"

"No, I'm not going to tell him. I haven't heard from him since the day he left. I was the one who wanted the baby. I never discussed it with him. And I have no intention of calling him with unfair expectations, *least* of all marriage. I don't want anything from him. I don't *need* anything from him…" Her voice dropped with her gaze. "At least not where the baby's concerned."

"But Paige—" Laura's head shot around at the sound of a horn and her expression grew worried. "Oh, dear, that'll be your father." She looked back at Paige even as she stood. "We'll talk more about this later."

Paige caught her hand as she started toward the door.

Her eyes were wide, her voice clipped and urgent. "Don't tell Daddy. Not yet. I don't want him upset before the party."

"He ought to be told," Laura said in the quietly reproving voice she used when she felt her daughter should know better.

"He will be," Paige continued with the same urgency. "I'll tell him as soon as things have quieted down on Sunday. Please, Mom?"

Laura's mouth was pinched as she pondered that for a minute. "I suppose it could wait. I don't want him upset either. Okay, it'll be our secret until after the party. But you'll have to tell him then. The longer you wait, the more hurt he'll be."

Implied in her words was the knowledge that he'd be hurt as it was, and Paige felt the slightest bit guilty at having done something to disappoint him. Then she caught herself. She was an adult and she'd made a conscious decision, knowing what to expect, feeling confident that she could handle the consequences. Guilt was the last thing she should be feeling, particularly when at this moment she felt vaguely ill.

She mustered a weak smile and nodded. Laura stared at her a minute longer, then, squeezing her shoulder, left to welcome the homecoming troop. Paige took several minutes to steady herself before following in her wake.

THE REUNION was a joyous one, growing more so when Jason and family returned from the club and again the following morning when Michael and company arrived. From then on, the house was in a perpetual whirl. Paige threw herself into the festivities and was genuinely happy even in spite of the occasional worried glances sent her way by her mother. If she felt queasy from time to time, the excitement diverted her mind from her discomfort. She was careful of what she ate, determined to pamper her stomach and avoid what she was sure would cause awkward repercussions.

Her father was so thrilled to see her that he overlooked those things that her mother had noticed from the start. With his children and grandchildren gathered around him, he was in his glory. With the addition of a multitude of friends and business associates on Saturday night, he was aglow. Paige shared his excitement with a pride of her own. The enthusiastic gathering was a testament to her father's affability and the high respect in which he was held.

In every respect the party was an overwhelming success. The caterers were gone by midnight, the musicians by one. It was nearly two in the morning before the last of the guests had departed, nearly three before the Matthesons themselves finally went to bed. And it was almost noon on Sunday before Laura crept quietly into Paige's room, sat down on the edge of the bed and gently shook her sleeping daughter's shoulder.

"Paige?" she whispered, then raised her voice a notch. "Darling, it's almost noon." When Paige turned her head on the pillow and sighed, obviously still asleep, Laura shook her shoulder again. "Time to get up, Paige. Paige?"

Opening first one eye then the other, Paige frowned and looked hazily around the room. "Mother," she finally managed through a dry throat. She moaned and turned onto her side, pulling her knees up tight. "What time is it?"

"Almost noon," Laura repeated patiently. "You'd better get up soon or you'll miss brunch completely."

Paige forced her lids wider. "Brunch?" Moaning again, she wrapped her arms around her stomach. Even the word was distasteful to her. "How can anyone think of eating after last night?"

Laura grinned. "The children demanded breakfast at eight. This will be their lunch."

"Breakfast...lunch...how can you do this to me, Mother?"

Laura's grin faded. "Not feeling well?"

"No, no, I'm fine. Just tired. How 'bout I sleep a little longer, then join you all?"

"The boys will be leaving soon. I thought you might want to visit."

Uncoiling her body, Paige pushed herself to a sitting position. With thumb and forefinger she swept the hair back from her brow. Her stomach churned; she swallowed hard against the rising bile. "You're right. I'll just shower and get dressed." Using her mother's shoulder for leverage, she rose, then stumbled into the adjoining bathroom in time to lose what little had remained in her stomach of the evening's fare. She was gasping for breath, bracing herself shakily above the commode when a more steady hand slid around her waist and another smoothed the hair back from her face.

"Better?"

Paige could only nod between increasingly deep breaths. She straightened slowly and covered her mother's hand. "Thanks."

"Don't thank me. I just wish there was something I could do for you."

Leaning over the sink, Paige splashed water on her face and rinsed her mouth, then dried herself with the towel Laura offered.

"You're here, Mom. That's enough."

Laura's expression was unreadable, at least to Paige, who still felt shaky. "Will you be all right now?"

Balancing herself against the sink, Paige nodded and smiled as if to prove it. Her smile must have been lacking, for Laura appeared far from convinced, but when a distant "Grandma!" echoed from the hall, her eyes widened.

"Uh-oh. I'd better catch Melissa before she barges in here. You'll be able to make it into the shower by yourself?"

"Yes, I'll be able to make it into the shower by myself."

"You're sure?"

"Mother…"

"All right, Paige. I'm going." She moved toward the door, shaking her head in renewed dismay. "I'm going."

Alone at last, Paige braced her hands on her hips and hung her head. She'd suspected it wouldn't be easy, but one small part of her had dared hope that her mother would share her excitement. Laura was torn; that much was obvious. Paige had to believe that, in time, she'd come around. Her father might either speed up or retard that process; she could only pray that it would be the former. For, as confident as she was in the course she'd chosen, she desperately wanted, needed, the approval and support of those she loved.

BY EARLY SUNDAY EVENING, Paige was alone with her mother in the house once again. Her father had gone to take the last of her brothers to the airport, leaving a pervasive silence in contrast to the constant noise and motion that had existed such a short time before.

Much as Paige had enjoyed seeing her brothers and their families and had wished they might stay longer, she was exhausted. Within minutes of their departure, she fell asleep on the sofa in the den, rousing only to stumble to bed at her mother's urging, remaining there in the deepest of sleep for the rest of the night.

Morning found her feeling decidedly refreshed. The sun was shining on a magnificent autumn day. Wearing jeans and a sweater, Paige made a slice of dry toast, poured herself a glass of juice and took them out to the deep willow-shaded hollow that had always been her favorite backyard spot. Sliding down against the trunk of a tree, she began to nibble on the toast. Overhead, the breeze whispered through gracefully weeping branches. She looked up at her pale green umbrella, took a deep breath and smiled. The smile froze in place, though, when the sound of footsteps announced the approach of her father. Her eyes collided with his, and she bit her lower lip, let it slowly slide out from between her teeth.

Phillip Mattheson came to a halt several feet from her, his gaze never once leaving her face. He was a handsome man, with his shock of dashing gray hair neatly combed and his skin tanned and weathered from hours on the golf course. The casual slacks and jacket he wore did justice to his still-sturdy build. Only his mouth, set in a straight line, and his dark, somber eyes hinted at his concern.

Paige silently returned his gaze, unaware that her own brimmed with trepidation. But Phillip saw it and softened helplessly. Taking another step forward, he hunkered down by her side.

"How're you feeling?" he asked quietly.

"Okay." She waited cautiously for him to say something. When he didn't, but dropped his gaze to her stomach, then the grass, she knew. "Mother told you, didn't she?" He nodded, eyes still averted, and she went on. "I asked her not to. I wanted to tell you myself."

"When I came home last night I was concerned to find you'd already gone to bed. She was concerned herself. I think she just needed to share her worry." His eyes lifted to the subject of their discussion. Laura was making her way across the yard, carrying two mugs of coffee.

"There's no need to worry," Paige stated as her mother came up and handed one of the mugs to Phillip. Laura did look more relaxed, as though relieved of a great weight. Paige couldn't find it in her heart to be angry. In truth she was envious of a relationship that was so close after all these years.

"Coffee, dear?" Laura extended the second mug. When Paige made a faint grimace in distaste, Laura smiled. "I didn't think so." Lifting the mug to her lips, she spoke against its rim. "I never could drink coffee myself when I was pregnant." She took a sip.

Pregnant. The word echoed loudly. Paige cast a wary glance at her father, only to find him scowling at his coffee. She looked for some diversion, but couldn't bear the thought of either orange juice or toast. Threading her fingers through the grass, she pressed her palm to the ground.

"I'm sorry if I've upset you both," she murmured. "I wish I could have done things the way you might have wanted, but it just didn't work out that way."

"Why didn't it?" her father asked. "From what your mother said, you loved this...Jesse."

"I did—do. But one-sided love can't make a marriage."

"He didn't love you?"

Paige pulled at the glass. "I don't know."

Laura settled herself on the ground. "How can you not know something like that? It's either there...or it isn't."

"I don't think it's as simple as that," Paige replied, voicing the thoughts she'd spent the past two months sorting out. "Jesse may have loved me on one plane, but on another he couldn't cope with the concept of love." She raised beseechful eyes to meet those of her father. "He's a very special man, very sensitive in his way. But he didn't grow up the way we did. His mother resented his existence. His father was nowhere in sight. He was trained in the school of hard knocks and is convinced that that's the only way he can live." She took a breath, then went on with pride. "He's very talented, a successful film editor."

"Your mother told me. How long was it he stayed in Marblehead?"

"Six weeks." She anticipated her father's response and sought to nip it in the bud. "But he wasn't a freeloader. During the time he was there, I didn't open my wallet once. He paid for food, restaurants, movies. He repaired countless things that needed fixing around the house, again at his own expense."

"That was generous of him," Phillip grunted, slipping from his haunches to the ground, stretching out his legs, crossing them at the ankles. Paige knew he was less relaxed than he looked, but her main concern was in defending Jesse.

"It *was* generous. He didn't have to do those things. I was perfectly willing to have him stay as my guest. He needed a vacation, and I thought my house would be the perfect place. But he made it clear at the beginning that he intended to carry his weight."

Phillip seemed unimpressed. "Carry his weight, huh? Looks to me more like he's foisted it on you."

"The baby was my idea, Daddy." She shot a glance at her mother. "I told you that." When she looked back at her father, his expression was guarded. "I decided on my own that I wanted this child. I knew Jesse would be leaving. I also knew that if I'd have suggested it he'd have packed and left right then. So don't blame him for my being pregnant. If anyone's to blame, it's me. If he found out, he'd probably be as furious as you are."

Reaching out, Phillip squeezed her shoulder in a way that gave Paige her first measure of comfort. "I'm not furious, sweetheart. I'm worried. Do you have any idea what you face? Raising a child in this day and age is hard enough under normal circumstances. You're starting with a distinct disadvantage."

"I've thought that all through, Daddy, and I don't think it'll be so bad. I've got a solid career, an ideal one in fact for a single mother. I work at home, so I can gear my schedule around that of a child. I make good money—"

"Money isn't an issue," her father interrupted with a dismissing wave of his hand. "We'll help you out. You know that."

"I do know that, and it's a comfort, but I don't *need* it. I can easily support my child and myself on what I earn. Besides, you've already done so much. Thanks to you I've got blue-chip stocks, interest in any number of real-estate ventures, plus a healthy trust fund that I can tap in case of emergency. I've got a big, beautiful house whose value only increases. I live in a safe area. My neighbors are all well-to-do and reputable—"

"But you'll be alone." This time it was Laura who interrupted. "The material aspect of child rearing is only one part of it. What about the emotional part? How will you explain to your child that he doesn't have a father?"

Paige answered her with the same quiet deliberation. "There are too many single-parent homes nowadays for that to be a problem. With the divorce rate what it is, there'll be plenty of other children in similar circumstances. As for what I'll tell the child when he's old enough to know, I'll tell him the truth—that I loved his father very much, that his father is a special man who would have loved him deeply if he'd been there."

"Do you honestly believe that?" Phillip asked skeptically. "From what you've said, the man didn't want any part of a child."

Paige lowered her eyes. "That was what he said, but I've seen him with children and he's wonderful. I think it's the responsibility he fears, the emotional responsibility. He sees the world as a pretty awful place and he doesn't want to bring a child into it. Maybe he's trying to spare himself some kind of pain."

"How can you be so...so forgiving?" Laura gasped.

"Not forgiving, Mom. There's nothing to forgive. Jesse laid his feelings on the line when we first got together. He was forthright from the start. I'm the one who was slightly devious in letting him believe I was using birth control. No, forgiving isn't the word. Accepting, perhaps. But then, you both taught me that. I can only do my best. That's what you've always said. I can't beat my head against a brick wall if my best isn't perfect. I have to reconcile myself, to accept the facts as they are and be proud of what I did do."

Her voice softened, taking on a pleading note. "That's what I want from you now. Acceptance. The facts are—" she raised one finger "—that I'm pregnant and—" she raised a second "—that I'm very, very happy about it. I want you to be pleased, too." She looked from Phillip to Laura and back. "I want to know that you'll be there to share my excitement when the baby's born, that my child will have grandparents who love him as much as I do." Her hand fell to her stomach in an instinctively possessive grip. "Because I do love this child and I'm going to have it and raise it, and nothing, nothing in the world can change those facts."

Before she could do so much as take a breath, her father had reached out and drawn her into his arms. "We wouldn't want to change them, sweetheart," he crooned huskily, his arms strong about her back. "We're proud of you. Always have been, always will be."

Paige felt her eyes fill with tears and pressed her face into his welcoming shoulder. "Thanks, Daddy," she whispered. "I needed that." When she finally raised her head, it was to seek out her mother. One half wasn't enough; she needed them both.

Laura's eyes were as moist as Paige's, but her lips curved into a tentative smile. "I couldn't agree with your father more, darling." She tipped up her chin. "And if the ladies of my bridge club are shocked, I'll tell them to…to…" As defiant as she suddenly felt, the coarse words on the tip of her tongue couldn't quite make it past her lips. She blushed, then laughed and leaned forward to hug Paige herself. When at last she held her back, it was to look lovingly at her face.

"You've always been a determined one, Paige. I'm proud of that, too. You will, I'm sure, make a wonderful mother." To counter the weepiness she felt, she feigned sudden sternness. "*If* you ever make it. You've got to take care of yourself, dear. Better still—" her eyes lit up "—*I'll* take care of you. Why don't I drive back up with you? I'll only stay a week or so. I can cook and clean and hold your head when you throw up—"

"Mother!" Paige laughed, feeling incredibly lighthearted. "I do believe that's above and beyond the call of duty."

But Laura simply straightened her shoulders. "I did it yesterday and I'll do it again. Nothing is above and beyond the call of duty when it comes to those you love."

IN THE DAYS THAT FOLLOWED, Laura was as good as her word. Though she allowed Paige to sculpt, she permitted her nothing else by way of work. For a woman who had always had a housekeeper, Laura took surprising joy in seeing to all the needs of Paige's home. She cleaned with a vengeance and cooked up a storm, stocking the freezer with so much food that Paige wouldn't have to do much more than operate the microwave oven for the next few months.

Though Paige wasn't used to such pampering, she found that the rest did her good. Whether the improvement had to do with her mother's care or with the fact that the critical first three months of pregnancy were now behind her, she didn't know. But by the time Laura left, Paige was feeling far better than she had in weeks. It was a good thing. For, once more, she was alone.

CHAPTER EIGHT

IN THE WEEKS THAT FOLLOWED, Paige continued to grow physically and emotionally stronger. That she missed Jesse was a given, but she'd come to terms with his absence and was redirecting her energy toward preparation for the birth of their child.

Their child. She did think of it that way. It thrilled her to know that it was Jesse's child in her belly, that she'd always have that little part of him. Oh, yes, she knew that psychologists would say she was loving her child in place of her man, but they were wrong. There was nothing "in place of" about the love she felt for the unborn babe. It was more a matter of "in addition to." The child would have its own love and then some.

By the end of her fourth month, she was filled with energy and sculpting furiously, intent on supplying the galleries with enough work to keep the owners satisfied during that time around the baby's birth when she'd be unable to sculpt. She'd finally told Marjory about her pregnancy, and smiled every time she recalled that conversation.

"You're *what*?"

"I'm pregnant."

"You've got to be kidding."

"Nope."

"*Pregnant?* I don't believe it."

Paige had grinned. "It's true."

"What is this, the second coming? Come on, love. Immaculate conception isn't for mortals."

"It wasn't immaculate conception."

"Then you've been holding out on me. Who is he?"

For reasons she hadn't understood at the time, Paige had never mentioned Jesse's presence when Marjory had called. Now she realized that there had been a part of her that had wanted it to be her secret, another part that had half feared Marjory's inevitable teasing.

Now there was a completely different reason why she wouldn't tell Marjory about Jesse. Though she trusted her, she didn't want to burden her with secrecy. It was a small world. Too easily word could spread. The last thing Paige wanted was for Jesse to learn through the grapevine that he'd fathered a child.

"Who he is is irrelevant," Paige had answered gently. "He was here for a time and I loved him, but now he's gone. I wanted the baby. He doesn't know anything about it."

There had been a long, uncharacteristic silence from Marjory. When she'd finally spoken, it had been on the recovery side of stupefaction. "You are truly remarkable, Paige Mattheson. Cool, dispassionate Paige Mattheson. Ice maiden?" She'd nearly choked in delight. "I still don't believe it!" But she was excited, and Paige was pleased. "If ever I'd expect to hear something astounding from you, it wouldn't have been this! A baby…my God! That's fantastic! You *are* full of surprises!" She'd chuckled. "For your sake, I hope the stars don't converge on the night it's born. No one will ever believe you then!"

Paige had laughed with her, but the conversation had held far deeper import. Indeed, the fact of her pregnancy made lie of the ice-maiden image. There would be those who'd be shocked. But Paige was proud, proud to be pregnant, proud to have done something she wanted to do. Through Marjory's eyes she'd glimpsed a new image of herself. The cool, self-possessed sculptress of stone was going to be a mother.

JESSE DALLAS, of course, knew nothing of this. He only knew, as he held his foot to the gas pedal, that he had to see Paige. For four months he'd worked himself to the limit, praying that one day he'd awaken without her image before his eyes.

It hadn't happened. When he'd pushed himself all the harder, he'd managed only to view that image through a migraine headache. The migraine passed; the image did not. More than once, in desperation, he'd called a number from his little black book. The consequences had been embarrassing. He'd finally given up on that particular potential diversion, fearing for his reputation, if not his sanity.

Exorcism was what was needed, he'd decided. He'd drive up and see Paige, be his arrogant self, provoke what was certain to be anger on her part—after all, he hadn't so much as dropped her a postcard in the months he'd been gone—and then return to New York. He'd be done with her. Free. Oh, Lord, what he'd give for freedom once more!

Leaving the highway, he turned onto the local roads he remembered so well. The trees were bare now, as dictated by the November chill. Though the snows hadn't yet come, there was promise in the air. He'd go skiing, perhaps in the Alps; would even dare, with Paige's image banished once and for all, to pick up a warm and cuddly snowbunny for his evening's delight.

Thoughts of snowbunnies left his mind the instant he turned onto the road that wound along the shore. There was a barren beauty about winter's ocean with its slate-gray hue and prancing whitecaps. The roar of the waves overpowered the hungry purr of his car, and he felt suddenly threatened. He liked this place. Even in winter it beckoned. He wished it had been a rainy day, cold and raw and forbidding. But it wasn't. And he was here. Pulling into Paige's driveway, he stopped the car.

The house looked just the same, blending into the late November winterscape as snugly as it had stood out refreshingly in the summer's heat. Trying to ignore the excitement that flashed through his veins, he tucked his keys in his jacket pocket, pulled up his collar and started up the walk. Thrusting his hands in his pockets for warmth, he approached the door. On impulse, he dragged his keys back out, fingering them, singling out the one that fit Paige's lock. He'd never given it back. Had she had the locks changed?

She hadn't. The key slid in smoothly. He turned it, slowly pushed the door open and looked inside. At once the serenity of the place enveloped him. Even as he tried to deny its grip he was drawn in. Closing the door as soundlessly as he'd opened it, he turned around. The same. It was exactly the same.

Paige was nowhere in sight. He started down the hall toward the bedroom, then turned and headed for the other wing, realizing that she'd more likely be in the studio. He'd surprise her. Perhaps scare the wits out of her. She *should* have had the lock changed. Men were an irresponsible lot.

As always the studio door was open. Jesse found himself slowing as he approached, walking stealthily, with a trace of hesitance. It was almost as if he neared that same invisible barrier he'd encountered when he'd first come here. And as he had then, he now sensed he was intruding. It was callous of him to come back this way, but he'd had to. There'd been no choice.

Taking the last steps with quiet determination, he came to a halt on the threshold and helplessly caught his breath. She was there, head bowed over a piece of stone in her lap. He saw nothing but her. Wearing an oversize sweatshirt that bore streaks of dust, a pair of jeans that hugged her thighs and calves, she was deep in concentration, easing an abrasive strip back and forth over the stone. She wore no mask this time, so her hair fell freely, creating a shimmering shield that hid her features from him.

He took one step into the room, then another. His eyes never left her bent head. Farther he came, slowly, making barely a sound. Barely. But the tile underfoot wasn't as forgiving as the outer carpeting had been. He'd crossed no more than half the distance between them when the heel of his shoe scraped the floor.

Paige's head flew up, her eyes wide in alarm. Her lips parted as if she'd cry out, but no sound came. She stared, blinked, stared again. All color drained from her cheeks. She lowered her head, pressed her eyes shut, rubbed the bridge of her nose. Then she looked up again, this time not so much in fear as in disbelief.

"Jesse?" she whispered.

He could do nothing but nod. His vocal cords seemed stuck.

"You're...here?" Still that incredulous whisper.

Again he nodded.

Her eyes went even wider, and she swallowed once. Then, in a concise burst of movement, she was off the stool and into his arms. The stone she'd been smoothing fell unnoticed to the floor, as did the sandbags on which it had rested and the large burlap mat.

Jesse hadn't been aware that he'd held out his arms until they'd caught her, closed about her slender form and lifted her clear off her feet. For the first time in months and months he felt happy. He closed his eyes, pressed his face to her hair and held her so tightly that his hands crisscrossed her back to grasp opposite sides of her waist. He couldn't believe how wonderful she felt, so warm and soft and tremblingly alive. He couldn't even object to her choke hold on his neck. It made him feel...needed.

"Jesse?" she whispered once more, releasing his neck and pushing herself back so that she could see his face. With great reluctance he loosened his arms, but he didn't let her go.

"It's me." He gave her a crooked smile. "In the flesh."

His attempt at humor sailed over her head. "I can't believe it! Oh, Jesse!" Her arms were about his neck again, squeezing tightly, her breath trembling by his ear. "I can't believe it! I thought I'd never see you again!"

"Now, did I ever say that?"

It was as though she never heard his drawl. "God, it's good to see you!" She pushed back again. "Let me look."

He was enjoying every bit of her excitement. "I thought that was what you did a second ago."

Unfazed, she let her eyes drop his full length. "You look so big," she whispered in near-awe.

"It's the jacket." Suede, with a thick sheepskin lining, the jacket may have indeed magnified his size. But he was a large man even without it.

Exquisitely appreciative, Paige took in the breadth of his shoulders, then looked up at his face again. She brushed back the swathe of sandy hair that had fallen across his brow and frowned. "You look tired. You've been working too hard."

His lips twitched. "You could say that."

"Is the film done?"

"That one, and a second." He paused, watching closely for her reaction. She had to realize that he'd taken at least a few days off between the two. "I'm a louse. I never called or wrote. It's been four months and now I have the nerve to show up on your doorstep. Come on. Tell me what a bastard I am."

To his astonishment, she simply grinned. "In time. God, you look great, baggy eyes and all!" She hugged him again and, for an instant, Jesse thought he'd like to stay forever like that, with her clinging to him as though he really, really mattered. He knew it was an illusion, and wondered why he was suddenly prone to such fancy, but other thoughts were beginning to intrude—like how firm and full her breasts felt against him, how shapely her hips were beneath his now-wandering hands, how perfectly her entire body fit against his. He pushed illusion aside to concentrate on a very real primal drive.

"I need you, Paige," he growled against her ear. "You may not believe this, but I haven't been able to make it with another woman since I left."

"That's quite a confession."

"It's the truth. I tried. Believe me, I tried. But it wasn't any good. You've ruined me."

"I must have. Something's definitely wrong. You haven't even kissed me yet."

He was the one to draw back then, the expression on his face comical in its astonishment. "I haven't?"

"Not…once."

His gaze dropped to her lips, studying them almost hypnotically. Fingers trembling, he slid his hands up to frame her face, caressing her even as they held her still. Then he took a shuddering breath that emerged in a moan and crushed his lips to hers.

His fierceness was just what Paige needed. She didn't care that he'd called other women before he'd come back to her. The only thing that mattered was that he had, indeed, come back.

The kiss she returned was no more gentle than the one he gave. After months of craving, their hunger was mutual and explosive. Greedy lips slanted and grasped. Avid tongues fought for the honeyed moisture beyond. Heated breath mingled, producing urgent moans. And all the while impatient hands clutched shoulders, backs, hips in avaricious reacquaintance.

"Oh, God," Jesse panted, "God, I need you."

"I need you, too," Paige whispered, clinging so tightly to his neck that her arms shook.

"Come on." Unwinding her arms from his neck, he took her hand and began striding across the tile floor. She had to run to keep up as he led her quickly toward the other wing and her bedroom. When he released her to tug off his coat, she dashed into the bathroom, emerging a minute later to find that he'd pulled back the covers and was bare from the waist up.

She thrust her jeans down her legs while he dispensed with his own. Her sweatshirt was just clearing her head when his hands found her breasts. Her entire body quivered with such rampant desire that she thought she'd burst.

"Hurry," she gasped, peeling down her panties, kicking them aside, then reaching for the waistband of his briefs. He released her breasts to assist her. Within seconds they were tumbling back on the bed in each other's arms. Her whisper was hoarse and intense. "I need you! God, Jesse, I need you…inside…!"

He was there then, filling the void that had gnawed at her so long. The groan that came from her throat told of a precious, sweet pain, one he echoed in kind.

They took each other in a frenzy, demanding without mercy or shame. It was as though neither could get enough, as though the physical limitations of their bodies frustrated the emotional bond between them. If Paige was driven wild by the love she felt, Jesse was no less frantic in his need to absorb her whole. Their bodies slammed slickly against each other, hips thrusting in their bid for oneness.

When it came, it was simultaneous and heart-stopping. Paige's breath caught in her throat; Jesse gave a hoarse cry. Their arched bodies were suspended, then shattered in endless spasms that left them quivering.

It was a long time before either spoke, before either could catch his breath to produce so much as a whimper. Paige felt she'd been to heaven and back. She'd never in her life felt so…blessed.

"Ahhhhh," Jesse murmured at last. He pressed his lips to her forehead, left them there while he inhaled shakily, then slid an arm beneath her and brought her curving to his side. "I've missed you, love. Damn it, I've missed you."

She understood his reluctance and it only added to her satisfaction. The fact that he'd come back to her *against* his will said something for the depth of his feeling. True, perhaps the feeling was primarily physical. But it was something.

"I've missed you too, Jesse."

He took one deep breath, and another, then moaned and turned his body toward hers. "You're a witch, I think. You've got me under a wicked spell."

"No spell." She slid her hand across his chest, loving

its damp warmth, loving the way the dark golden hair tickled her palm. "I can't believe it," she whispered, astonished once again. She raised her head to give him an owl-eyed stare. "I keep thinking I've imagined you."

He chuckled. "If you think that was a ghost inside you just now, you've really gone off the deep end."

"No ghost?"

"No ghost."

Smiling, she settled her head back in the crook of his shoulder, rubbing her cheek against the softer flesh beside his armpit. "I'm glad you're here."

"So am I." His eyes trailed down her body then, appreciating it at a more leisurely pace. His free hand soon followed, heating her tired flesh anew. "Your breasts are so full." He traced a faint blue vein, amazed he'd never noticed it before, but before he could ask he was distracted by the responsive erection of her nipple. Dipping his head, he kissed the taut nub. "Mmm. It always was good with us," he murmured. "It still is. I take one look at you and, bam, I'm up. And you're always ready."

His words, uttered in such a husky timbre, were as stirring to Paige as his nearness. She arched against his hip, sliding her leg between his. Her own smoothness against his more textured flesh never failed to excite her. She drew the sole of her foot along his calf to his knee, then reversed direction.

The movement drew Jesse's eyes downward. He slid his hand to her hip, then her belly. His palm caressed it, gliding over and around the faintly curved surface. Strange, his hand remembered a perfectly flat ivory plane. This tiny bulge was new. He frowned for an instant, wondering if she'd gained weight. If she'd been pining over him, surely the opposite would have been the case, particularly since she'd never been a hearty eater.

Skimming her body, he saw that her limbs were as slim and shapely as ever. It was only her belly...and her breasts....

An awful thought jolted him. But...*that* wouldn't have happened. It *couldn't* have. There had been that one episode when she might have been vulnerable, but she'd gotten her period after that. And henceforth she'd been protected. Hadn't she run into the bathroom even today?

His gaze flew to her face. Her eyes were closed, her lips curved in a half kiss against him. When he touched her cheek, she smiled and purred. He trailed his fingers over her throat to her breast, circling its vein-shadowed fullness until she squirmed against him.

He opened his mouth to ask her point-blank, then closed it. If he'd been imagining something that wasn't true, he'd feel like a fool. But…there was one way he could tell. One sure way.

His touch grew more caressive on her breasts, and he eased himself lower until his mouth found hers. His kiss was deliberately seductive, teasing and coaxing while his hand slid lower. She moaned and opened to him, kissing him back, happily stroking his arms and the rippling musculature of his back.

He rubbed her belly, very, very gently, before inching even lower. His fingers were silky, insinuating themselves into her warmth as they'd done so often in the past, evoking the same soft gasps of delight. Deeper they crept, tantalizing her most sensitive spots, finally sliding farther, searching…

Then they were gone.

Dazed and in ecstasy, Paige didn't feel the stiffening of Jesse's limbs. The loss of his touch, though, left her bereft. Opening her eyes to urge him back, she met a scowling countenance that was instant ice to her ardor.

"Jesse?" she asked in alarm, eyes widening. "What is it?"

"Your diaphragm. It's not there."

She swallowed once. "I know."

"Where is it?"

Her heart was pounding but she kept her voice calm. "In its case in the medicine chest."

"Why isn't it in you?"

"I…I don't need it."

As she watched, he flicked his gaze to her breasts, then

her stomach. "And that little dash into the bathroom a few minutes ago?"

She took a tremulous breath. "I had to go." Her voice dropped to a whisper as she confirmed what she knew he'd already guessed. "It's that way with me now."

His jaw flexed once then froze. His blue eyes hardened. His nostrils flared. Then he was pushing himself up on a fist and tipping his head back. "Goddammit!" he bellowed. When he looked back at her, his rage was barely contained. "How did it happen? *How in the hell did it happen?*"

"You know the facts of life," she said quietly.

"Yeah, but that thing was supposed to protect you. Do you mean to say that we're in the small percentage for whom it doesn't work?"

"No. That's not the case."

"Then what is, damn it, *what is*?"

She made no attempt to dodge his gaze. "I didn't use my diaphragm that last night, Jesse. It's as simple as that."

"As simple…you didn't use…" He loomed over her, pinning her shoulders to the sheets. She cringed, but only because she truly believed he was angry enough to hit her. "What in the hell possessed you to do *that*?" he roared, fingers digging into her flesh.

Her lower lip trembled, but her tone remained firm. "I decided I wanted a baby. I knew you were leaving. I believed at the time that I'd never see you again."

"You decided. *You* decided? And I was just the dumb stud in the deal?"

"It wasn't like that. It was *your* baby I wanted."

He released her shoulders abruptly. "Great. You decided you wanted to have *my* baby, so you took things into your own hands. Didn't you have the guts to discuss it with me?"

Feeling as naked in the face of his hostility as she truly was, she struggled up and reached for the sheet. "I knew what your feelings were. You'd made them very clear—"

"Oh-ho, no," he growled, snatching the sheet from her

fingers. "You won't hide from me. If you've got my baby in your belly, I've got a right to see everything!"

In a flare of anger, she faced him. "Right? *Right?* You have no right! You were the one who took off without a second glance, who let four months, *four months* pass without a word." She flung out her hand. "You saw other women, you did God knows what during that time, and never once did you so much as give me a call to see if I was okay." She took a sharp breath. "Don't talk to me of rights, Jesse Dallas! You haven't got *any* in my life!"

In the wake of her outburst, he seemed to gain a measure of control. "That may have been true at one time, Paige," he stated, "but you're carrying my child now. That changes things a bit."

"And just how does it change them? You're free to leave now, to go back to that hard life you feed off. How in the devil does my pregnancy change anything?"

"It's my child—"

She jabbed at her chest. "It's my child, too. And since I'm the only one who wants it, I take sole responsibility."

"I'll bet you do," he snarled.

"And just what is that supposed to mean?"

"It means that I can imagine what little plots you've got in that devious mind of yours. When were you going to tell me, Paige? When it was too late for an abortion?" He took perverse pleasure when she flinched. "When you were on the verge of giving birth and needed someone to hold your hand? Or was I going to get a little court order out of the blue demanding child support?"

Her hand clenched into a fist over her stomach. She tried to still the quaking of her limbs but they refused to obey her silent command. Mustering her pride, she inched up her chin. "I wasn't going to tell you at all. The way I saw it, it was my business, and my business alone. I'd decided I wanted to conceive and I did. I didn't consult you. It wasn't your choice." She kept talking as Jesse stormed up and stalked around the bed to stand at her side, glaring down. "I knew precisely what I was doing *and* what the consequences would be."

"You don't know anything about consequences! You grew up insulated in a suburban cocoon. You haven't the faintest—"

"Don't start in on that!" she interrupted, surging to her knees in frustration. "I'm tired of hearing about the mean world out there. Your view is *warped*. Has anyone ever told you that?"

"Screw that world!" He thrust a pointed finger toward the floor. "I'm talking about the responsibility of day-to-day child rearing. How're you going to sculpt with a squalling kid around? And if you can't sculpt, how are you going to be able to feed it? And even *if* you get beyond the squalling and feeding, how in the hell are you going to be able to give the child what it needs? You're a woman. Just a woman. A kid needs a father, too."

"I may be *just* a woman, but I've got enough love to more than cover what's lacking from a stone-cold father. I've got plenty of money whether I work for the next five years or not, and I refuse to believe that I won't be able to work. Face it, Jesse. Single mothers have been doing it for years now."

"Yeah, I know how well they do it. You forget I grew up in a home like that."

"I'm going to ignore that comment," she stated, deadly quiet.

He made a face and gestured broadly. "I didn't mean that you'd whore. I know you wouldn't do that."

"Well, thank you."

Her sarcasm was ignored as Jesse ranted on. "I'm talking about resentment. When you're in the middle of a tricky piece of work and the baby starts to bawl, you're going to resent it. And it'll only get worse. You take off to go to New York for a show, and you've got this albatross hanging around your neck. You want to date—okay, even an innocent date—and the baby-sitter calls to cancel at the last minute. It'll be hell."

Paige squared her shoulders. "Maybe it was for your mother, but it won't be for me. Because I want this child and I love it already. Don't you see? When it comes to this baby, I don't *care* about my work. I don't care about New York. I don't care about dating. And besides, even if I did need to get away, my parents would be up here to stay with the baby before I could blink an eyelash."

Jesse straightened, hands falling from their imperious perch on his hips. He seemed suddenly unsure. "Your parents? You've told your parents you're pregnant?"

"Of course." She frowned. "Did you think I wouldn't?"

"Were they…angry?"

"Angry? No. Stunned perhaps, at first, and worried, then excited. You see, Jesse, they love me. My happiness is theirs." She sighed. "I wish you could have met them. As parents go, they're so different from anything you've known. They care, truly care about every aspect of my life. They've given me the strength to face things, which is one of the reasons the prospect of single-motherhood doesn't scare me. Furthermore, I know that I can give my child that same kind of strength, so that it will be able to face whatever comes along."

Jesse stared at her. "You're crazy. *All* of you."

"We could say the same about you," she said softly. "You can't begin to imagine the joy of holding a baby in your arms, having its tiny finger curl around yours, having it cling to your neck as if it can't live without you. You can't imagine the pride you feel when it gets its first tooth, when it takes its first steps, when it says 'Mama' for the first time—"

"'It'…'it'…must you make it sound like you've got some kind of neuter being in there?"

There was a petulance in his tone that made Paige smile. "What would you have me say? If I say 'he,' I'd be called sexist. If I say 'she,' I could well be wrong."

Having no answer to that, Jesse's brows lowered. "And

how do you know about the joys, anyway? You've never been a mother and *you* were the baby of your family."

"I didn't say *know*. I said *imagine*. But I do have nieces and nephews and I remember when they were small."

"Somebody else's kid is one thing. You can give it back when it gets to be a pain."

"I won't want to give this one back. I *want* it. I want to be a mother."

Jesse muttered something unintelligible as he turned to retrieve his jeans. "You know, Paige, I never would have expected this of you." His voice jolted with the movement as he angrily pulled the denim over his legs. He tugged up his zipper and straightened. "It's really pretty funny. Remember that day you insisted on going to the doctor? You said you couldn't trust *me*."

She hadn't thought about that day. Now she felt a brief pang of guilt. "I was only kidding."

"Well, it sure as hell worked to your benefit, didn't it?"

"I hadn't planned a thing at the time. You have to believe that, Jesse."

He scooped his shirt from the floor. "When *did* you start planning this little fiasco?" He glared. "A week later? Or two? Or did it come to you when you got your period and realized it hadn't taken that first time?"

She spoke slowly and with deliberation. "I didn't plan a thing until that very last night. It just…came to me when I was in the bathroom."

"Just came to you," he ridiculed. "Like the secret of the stone?"

"No! I—"

"If what you're saying is true," he interrupted, "you couldn't have had much of a chance to think *anything* out!"

"I knew it was right. Call it intuition or whatever, but every sense I possessed told me it was right."

Shirt hanging open, he raked his hand through his hair. "Intuition. Oh, please." The scorn in his voice was mirrored by the disgust on his face. But before Paige could speak to defend herself, he'd turned on his heel and charged out of the room.

She sat in stunned paralysis for what seemed an eternity before reaching for the covers and drawing them up. Then, curling up on the mattress, she struggled to calm herself as reaction set in. She trembled uncontrollably and felt chilled to the bone. Tugging the covers more closely around her neck didn't help. Neither did an attempt to focus her thoughts on the baby whose existence meant so very much to her.

She hurt.

Recollection of how happy she'd been to see Jesse, of how ecstatic their coming together had been on this very same bed, served only to sharpen the pain within. The contrast was stark—from rapture to hell. She wished he'd never come back, if only to have been spared his anger. Surely he'd leave again, this time truly for good. She much preferred to remember him the way he'd been the last time—loving, if she dared say so—than to remember him as the hard, unfeeling man he'd been in his fury just now.

Closing her eyes against the misery she felt, she tried to place what had happened into the overall scheme of things. This was a setback, that was all. She'd go ahead with her plans and do the best she could in pushing Jesse from her mind. A setback, just a setback. Somehow she sensed, though, that she'd be a long time in recovering.

It all boiled down to one thing. Her dream was shattered. Before, when Jesse knew nothing of the baby and she pictured him going about his life in New York, she'd been able to imagine from time to time that, had he known about the child, he might have been pleased. Oh, yes, it was an illusion, but a harmless one. Now, illusion was delusion, thoroughly harmful, totally unacceptable. The sooner Jesse left, the better.

She lay still, listening, wondering where he was. His coat was still on the chair, so he had to be in the house, unless he'd rushed out into the cold with just his anger to keep him warm. She'd heard no door banging, but she hadn't heard him come in, either. Then she'd been engrossed in her work, a plausible enough excuse. Perhaps now she'd been deafened by misery. Spotting one dark loafer across the room, she realized that he couldn't have gone far. Oh, yes, he'd be back, and she sensed there'd be more unpleasantness before he finally left.

With a weary sigh, she pushed herself up. If she had to field his disdain once more, she'd need all the help she could get. Her clothes would be a start; at least then she wouldn't feel so vulnerable.

Sitting on the edge of the bed, she gingerly pulled her sweatshirt on over her head. Her muscles felt stiff and tense and tired, but she knew they simply reflected the ache radiating from her heart. Lifting one leg, then the other, she tugged on her jeans. She stood only for the second it took to ease them up over her hips, then sank weakly back on the bed. Propping herself on shaky arms, she closed her eyes and willed strength to her spent limbs.

That was how Jesse found her when he stalked back into the room. He came to an abrupt halt, taking in her weary pose, her closed eyes, the milky pallor of her skin. She was slower to react, his footsteps having been muted by the rug, but a sixth sense warned her he'd returned, and she opened her eyes and stiffened.

"Are you all right?" he asked evenly.

"Yes." Lowering her gaze, she closed the zipper of her jeans, but when it came to the snap, which was sorely tried at best, her seated position and boneless fingers conspired against her.

Jesse watched her fumblings with a frown. "Leave it undone. You'll only suffocate the kid."

"I will not—"

He cut off her denial. "If you can't even look out for the baby's best interests now, I can just imagine what it'll be like later on."

Paige was incensed. "I've managed just fine up until now, and I'll manage just fine in the future."

"Hmph." He looked around for his socks, then his shoes. "Get something on your feet. We've got things to do."

"What things?" she asked warily.

He sat in the chair and pushed his foot into a sock. "Blood tests. A license."

Paige felt the blood drain from her face. "License?" she whispered.

"That's right. We're getting married."

"What?"

He had the other sock on and was pushing his feet into his shoes. "You heard me." Standing, he eyed her critically. "If you want to change your clothes, fine. You should be wearing looser things, anyway. If you haven't bought any maternity clothes, we'll stop for those, too."

"Wait…just…one…minute." She shook her head, trying to ingest what he'd said. "Back up a little. We're getting *married*?"

"Yes." He was on his feet, clearly annoyed. "Damn it, Paige, you're wasting time—"

"Who's getting married?"

"You and me. Now, get a move—"

"I'm not marrying you!" she cried, bolting to her feet only to sway when myriad bright lights exploded before her eyes. Groping for the bed, she sagged back down, gasping for breath, feeling positively ill. Within seconds her head was being pushed between her knees and a firm hand was rubbing her neck.

"Keep your head down. It'll pass."

"Dizzy…"

"I know. You moved too fast."

She wanted to say that he'd been the one to tell her to move, that he'd been the one to upset her from the start, but she felt too weak to utter a word. With her head down, the blood slowly returned and she revived.

"You're hurting my neck," she murmured.

He raised her shoulders and pushed her hair back from her face. "You're in a cold sweat. Lie down." He was off the bed then and, without his support, she had no choice but to follow his command. When he returned he carried a cool, damp cloth. Sitting beside her on the bed, he pressed it to her forehead.

She put her hand over it and closed her eyes. "I'm not marrying you, Jesse."

"You're carrying my child. You'll marry me."

"You can't force me to."

"You're right. But if you refuse, I'll have to take stronger measures. Once the child's born, I'll go to court for visitation rights. In fact, I may even sue for joint custody. It's the up-and-coming thing. You know, half the year with the mother, half with the father."

Paige's eyes were open now, wide with fear. "You wouldn't," she whispered.

"I most certainly would."

"But...but you don't want the child!"

"Keep your voice down or you'll really make yourself sick."

"Jesse, you can't be serious about all this."

"Why not?"

"You don't want any ties. You don't want a wife. You don't want children."

"I've changed my mind."

"Just like *that*? In ten minutes' time?"

"Seems to me you did much the same, though I don't recall you were in the bathroom that night for more than five."

Closing her eyes again, she turned her face away. "I can't believe this is happening."

"It'll sink in pretty quick. You'll be my wife by the weekend."

Her head flew back. "No!" At his warning glance, she

lowered her voice. "No. You can't marry me, Jesse. You don't love me!"

"Love? What's *love* got to do with anything?"

"It's the basis of most marriages."

"Gimme a break. Most marriages are based on expediency. A man wants a woman to see to his needs, a woman wants a man to give her security. In some cases there may be financial considerations, but most often it's the image of marriage that people fall for. When the image tarnishes, divorce comes into play."

"You are a cynic."

"I think you've said that before."

"Well, it's true. And I suppose the point of expediency in our case is the baby?"

"Good thinking. Your head must be clearing."

Distraught, she rolled onto her side away from him, flinging away the now-tepid cloth as she went. Tucking up her knees, she pressed a protective arm across her middle. "Exactly what do you hope to accomplish, Jesse?"

"By marrying you? I'd have thought it would be obvious." With a sigh, he stood up and walked to the window. It was not quite four, but the sky was darkening already. "Given a choice, I would never have let you conceive. But since the deed's done, I want my kid to have everything I didn't. That means a warm home, plenty of clothes and toys and playmates, the most nourishing of food…and above all, two parents."

Paige turned her head and stared at his back. "*Love*, Jesse. That's what you were missing. If you'd had that, none of the other things would have mattered. You're sadly mistaken if you think that I was happy as a child because of the toys or clothes or food I had. It was my parents' love that made my life." She paused. "So if you don't believe in love, what can you possibly offer our child?"

Without turning, Jesse shrugged. His voice was suddenly more distant, less cool, almost…soft. "I can be there when he's sick, hold him when he's had a nightmare. I can go to his school plays, take him for fries at McDonald's. I can read to him at night and teach him to play chess. I can swing him up on my shoulders and make him laugh."

For the first time since her own nightmare had begun that afternoon, Paige felt heartened. Though he couldn't realize it, Jesse had just given her a glimpse of the man she loved. Not only that, though he'd be appalled if she suggested it, what he'd described just now sounded suspiciously like a demonstration of love. She felt suddenly lighter, as though a great weight was lifting from her heart.

Then Jesse turned and half the weight settled back. His expression was closed once more. If he'd allowed a bit of warmth to seep through when thinking of his child, he obviously had no intention of extending that warmth to her.

"Are you ready to go?" he asked in a tone compatible with his expression.

She pushed herself to a seated position but made no move to rise from the bed. "Jesse, I think you ought to think this out. You may have decided that you want our child, but you certainly don't want me."

"I wouldn't say that," he drawled with unmistakable intent, but a chill remained in his eyes and she was filled with dread.

"Oh, no, Jesse…" she breathed in disbelief.

"Oh, yes, Paige." He began to walk forward. "What greater expedient can a man have than a beautiful woman at his beck and call? It's been damned frustrating these past months. I think you'll meet my needs quite well."

She eyed him defiantly. "I won't marry you. I'll take my chances with the courts."

He continued forward until he reached the bed. "You'll marry me. And you'll marry me soon." He pressed both fists to the sheets and put his face close to hers. Every one of his features was hard. Only with great restraint did she hold still, though her eyes grew wider as he spoke. "That kid is going to have two parents." He enunciated slowly, as though to a dimwit. "And they're going to be husband and wife. Jesse Dallas. Paige Dallas." His eyes flashed with the same iron determination that his clenched jaw conveyed. "If I've got to be responsible for bringing a kid into the world, he's not going to be a bastard like his old man was!"

Finding Paige utterly speechless, he slowly straightened. "Now." He buttoned the cuffs at his wrists. "Are you ready to go?"

"Go?" she whispered hoarsely, then cleared her throat. She was stunned. He'd never said anything about being illegitimate before! Or had he? How many times had he called himself a bastard? Of course, she'd taken it as its less literal meaning. "Uh...I..."

Her arm was grasped and she was helped to her feet. "We'll go to your doctor for the blood tests. That way I can have a good talk with him. When is your next scheduled appointment?"

She frowned and looked down, struggling to think clearly. "I, uh, I saw her last week. I only go once a month."

"Then it's just as well I can meet her now. I don't want to have to wait another three weeks to have my questions answered."

"Jesse, this is really—"

"Shoes, Paige?" He arched his brows, then went to retrieve her sneakers. After staring at them for a minute, he headed for the closet. "These won't keep anything warm out in that cold." He exchanged the sneakers for a pair of low-heeled leather boots, stopped at her dresser for a pair of high wool socks, then set what he'd gathered into her hands. "Put them on. It's getting late. Things will be closing pretty soon for the day. We've got a hell of a lot to do before that happens." His warning stare was designed to keep her protest in check, but he needn't have worried. She was far too overwhelmed by conflicting emotions to utter a sound.

Numb, she pulled on the socks, then the boots. Indeed they'd counter the winter chill. But the chill in her heart? She knew the remedy for that would be far more difficult to find.

CHAPTER NINE

THE WEDDING TOOK PLACE the following Saturday afternoon and was witnessed only by Paige's parents, who'd come in the night before and who insisted on treating the newlyweds to a celebration dinner immediately after the brief civil ceremony. Independent as he was, Jesse's instinct had been to pick up the tab himself. Anticipating this, Paige had been firm. She'd yielded to practically every other demand he'd made—she'd sat by while Jesse had grilled her doctor as though she was unable to take care of herself, she'd dutifully selected the full maternity wardrobe he'd insisted upon, she'd been shunted to bed each night well before she'd been tired—but where her parents were concerned she put her foot down.

"My father will want to take us out afterward, Jesse. Please, don't give him a fight. I'm his only daughter. If he had his way, he'd be walking me down the aisle in a formal ceremony with all of his friends in attendance. Since that's out of the question, give in at least on a dinner."

"Is that what you'd have wanted—to wear a white gown with a long train and go down on his arm with crowds watching?" Jesse had asked coolly.

"Under these circumstances—no. It'll be hard enough keeping up a front for my parents' sake alone."

That, indeed, was her greatest fear. And she tried, she did try, to smile and act pleased. Her mother, as always, saw through the ruse. They'd returned to the house late Saturday afternoon and Paige was sitting on a chair in the guest bedroom while Laura finished packing. Determined to give Paige and Jesse privacy on their wedding night, the Matthesons were driving back to Connecticut that evening.

With her suitcase finally closed, Laura sat on the edge of the bed facing Paige. "I want you to be happy, darling. Are you sure this is what you want?"

Paige gave a dry laugh. "I'd have thought you'd have been thoroughly relieved," she said, but without rancor. "Now I've got a husband. It makes things…perfect." She glanced down at the diamond-studded wedding band Jesse had slipped onto her finger during the ceremony, and twisted it around.

"He has good taste," Laura remarked. "It's a beautiful ring."

"Umm. I think he's determined to let the world know that he's doing it right."

"Your father likes him."

"What's not to like? He's been the perfect gentleman." Indeed, he'd said and done all the right things. Of course, neither Laura nor Phillip had felt the formality of Jesse's hand when it curved around Paige's waist. Neither could they imagine how different his ceremonial kiss had been from the persuasive warmth of the kisses they'd shared at one time. "Do *you* like him, Mom?"

"Yes. Yes, I do. He's intelligent and well-spoken. You make a handsome couple. And, though you may object to my saying this, I think he's done the best thing. You're carrying his child and you have a right to his protection." She held up a hand as Paige opened her mouth. "I know. I know. You're perfectly capable of taking care of yourself. But, as a parent, I have to say I'm relieved that you won't have the pressure of shouldering it all on your own." Her gaze grew more worried. "I only wish you were happier about his return."

"I'm happy enough," Paige murmured, but her voice lacked conviction. She hadn't told her mother the details of her reunion with Jesse, had simply called to say they were getting married.

"Do you want to talk about it?" Laura asked softly.

"Talk about it?"

"Your concerns. Things aren't exactly hunky-dory, are they?"

Strangely, Paige did want to talk. She'd felt so bottled up since Jesse's brusque declaration of intent that she needed desperately to talk. More, she needed her mother's encouragement that she'd been right in agreeing to the marriage.

"No, I wouldn't say hunky-dory is quite the word," she said sadly. "Jesse was furious when he found out I was pregnant. The last thing I expected him to do was to propose marriage." *Demand* was more the case, but it was irrelevant at this point.

"He seems happy enough about the baby now."

"Oh, yes. Funny, he came around very quickly on that issue. He's determined to give the child everything he never had, and I'm sure he'll do it." She remembered the way his voice had grown soft when he'd spoken of those things he'd do with his child. "I do think he'll love our child."

"But?"

The eyes Paige raised to her mother held a world of regret. "Whether he'll ever love *me* is another matter."

"You don't think he does?"

"At one point I might have thought so. There were times when he was here last summer when I might have imagined him to be in love. Then again, when he first saw me the other day, he was as excited as I was. That was before he learned about the baby. I'm not sure he'll ever forgive me for that."

Laura's voice grew exquisitely gentle. "Love doesn't just go away, darling. Even if he's angry at you right now, if the seeds of his love are there and you nurture them properly, they'll blossom."

"That's a pretty image," Paige argued sadly, "but it might just be wishful thinking when it comes to Jesse

Dallas. Don't forget, this is a man who's fed on anger for better than thirty-five years."

"But from what you say, his mother never made the slightest attempt to give. That's where things may be different now. It could be that he just needs coaxing. It could be that he wants very much to love you, but that he's fighting it. All you have to do is persevere. I know you. You succeed when you set your mind to things."

"I know. I'm just not sure it'll work this time." Eyes clouded with pain, she wrapped her arms around her middle. "Jesse is so…remote when he looks at me, when he touches me. I may have gained a loving father for my child, but a loving husband?"

Laura paused then, cautiously studying her daughter's face. "You could have said no, Paige. Why did you agree to the marriage?"

Paige sighed and seemed to sink into the chair in defeat. The look she gave Laura was rife with helplessness. "I love him, Mom. It's as simple as that."

"Then you'll make it work, darling. Just keep at it. You'll make it work!"

HER MOTHER'S WORDS, and the love Paige did in fact feel, kept her going for a while. Jesse sold his New York town house, furniture and all, and moved the rest of his belongings to Marblehead. He set up his Kem machine in one of the spare bedrooms, which he'd allocated as his workroom, and fit back into Paige's daily existence in much the way he'd done the summer before…with several notable exceptions. The warmth was gone. The gentle companionship seemed strained. And, though they shared the same bed, he didn't attempt to make love to her. Not once.

Paige might have blamed the latter on his awareness of her condition, but he'd been right there when her doctor had okayed lovemaking. Right up until the last month, or until she was too uncomfortable, the doctor had said. But Paige was only in her fifth month and not physically uncomfortable at all, and still Jesse avoided her. He was punishing her. She was sure of it. And she let him have his way. All she could do was show him in small and subtle ways—a smile here, a special meal there, acquiescence, understanding—that she loved him. Beyond that, it was up to him.

Christmas came a short three weeks after their marriage and, though Paige had agonized over making the suggestion, Jesse was surprisingly agreeable to spending the holidays in Westport. Sure, he'd like to meet her brothers and their families, and wasn't it good of them all to come in so soon after the September bash? Sure, he'd like to see her parents again. Maybe he'd even try his hand at golf with her father—but no, the course would be closed for the winter. And yes, it'd be nice to see the house where she'd grown up.

Paige dreaded it, again because of the pretense. To have to behave like a loving couple before these people who meant so much to her was going to be difficult. Oh, she was loving enough. But Jesse?

As it happened, her fears were unfounded. For one thing—and she should have anticipated it—there was so much pandemonium in a house filled with ten adults and five children that Paige and Jesse as a couple were hardly noticeable. The youngsters were so high on the Christmas spirit that their enthusiasm took precedence over most else. For another thing—and this Paige hadn't dared anticipate—Jesse quite easily donned the facade of the loving husband. He held her hand, put his arm around her shoulder, smiled and laughed with her in a way that seemed utterly natural.

He got along fine with her brothers, too, and seemed comfortable without being patronizing. Their wives took to him as well, responding quite helplessly to his subtle charm. The children were more shy at first, but after the first snowball fight in the yard the boys were won over. And Paige would never forget his conquest of Sami,

Michael's seven-year-old daughter. On the first day she eyed him from a distance. On the second, she began to position herself by his side whenever possible. On the third, she approached the chair in which he was seated, stood staring at him for endless moments, then whispered, for only his ears and Paige's, who sat on the arm of his chair, "You've got pretty eyes." He'd broken into a smile then and had hoisted her onto his knee, which became her near-constant perch from then on.

Even in the privacy of Paige's bedroom, when she and Jesse were getting ready for bed at night or getting dressed in the morning, Jesse seemed less restrained.

"Uncle Jesse," he repeated, smiling. "I never imagined what I was getting when I married you."

"Are you sorry?" she asked, and was pleased when he confirmed her suspicion.

"Nah. It's fun. They're great kids. And I like their parents."

Still he made no attempt to make love to Paige, and while she sensed that her family had scored points, she felt that she'd scored few. The drive back to Marblehead was made largely in silence. By the time they were inside their oceanfront home once again, Jesse was as aloof as ever.

January came and Paige entered her sixth month of pregnancy. Her stomach was rounding nicely, and she'd gained some weight, though not as much as the doctor wished.

"You're eating properly, aren't you, good healthy things?" she asked at Paige's monthly appointment.

Jesse answered quickly. "She's got all those things on her plate, but she usually leaves half of what's there."

The doctor cast a glance Paige's way. "You shouldn't, you know. You're eating for two."

"I know," she said softly, intimidated with Jesse sitting so imperiously by her side. She wished he'd let her see the doctor alone, but when she suggested it he simply set his jaw and shook his head. He didn't trust her. That much was certain. "I'm just…not that hungry. And I feel worse if I stuff myself."

"By all means don't stuff yourself, but you should try to eat enough. Perhaps you ought to have four or five smaller meals a day."

Paige cringed then, and with good cause. From that time on, Jesse himself presented her with those four or five meals, then stood by while she struggled to swallow. She tried her best, both to eat and to indulge him his protectiveness, but, increasingly, his protectiveness stifled her, particularly as it lacked the warmth she craved.

In the end, when she simply couldn't stomach another bite, they'd argue.

"I can't, Jesse."

"It's for the child. The one you wanted so badly. If you starve it, it'll be no good to either one of us."

"Then *you* eat for it," she snapped, eyes flashing. It took a lot to get her goat, but days on end of Jesse's remoteness had begun to tie her in knots.

"My eating won't do it any good, or believe me I'd do it. As it is, I'm doing everything I can to make sure it's healthy, which is a hell of a lot more than you're doing. You won't nap during the day. You barely sleep at night."

"How would you know that? You sleep like a baby yourself!"

"I know. Believe me, I know. Your tossing and turning wakes me up and I can tell from your breathing that you're not asleep."

"If I'm bothering you," she goaded, "try another bedroom." She'd been pushing to rile him, but she didn't succeed. Jesse simply walked away from her. And he was back in his place in bed that night.

He was playing a game, she decided. It was part of her punishment. His concern for the well-being of the child she carried knew no bounds, but the very contrast between that and his concern for her own emotional well-being was dramatic. At times he'd walk through a room and barely glance at her. Conversation between them was sparse, making meals a horror for Paige even beyond the effort to eat. When he'd appear at nine o'clock and tell her to go to bed, she went, if only to escape the ever-present chasm that stretched between them.

As soon as he could after moving his things, Jesse took on an editing assignment and spent hours holed up with his machine, emerging only to see to those needs of hers that related to the child. Paige, on the other hand, did little sculpting, finding herself more often than not staring at a piece of stone without the slightest idea of what to carve or where to begin. If she'd hoped to find salvation in her work, it failed her, too. She could only pray that once the baby was born, inspiration would return.

During those evenings that they actually spent together in the living room, Jesse was preoccupied studying the baby books she'd bought or one of those he'd subsequently picked up himself. He appeared to be taking a disciplined approach to not only pregnancy and childbirth, but child rearing itself, wanting to know every fact, every possibility, every recommendation.

On occasion, she'd find his gaze wandering to her, his eyes settling on her stomach, or on her ankles, propped on the coffee table. At those times, she'd feel her heart lift in the hope that maybe he'd soften, but no sooner did he catch her hopeful eye than he looked away.

It was like that from time to time in bed, too. She'd awaken in the morning, groggy from a shallow and disturbed sleep, to find his arm around her waist, his hand on her stomach. The latter wasn't unusual; he'd taken his turn at feeling the movement of the baby, but his touch had never strayed to the sexual. These early-morning touches were different, as though it was her flesh he wanted. But she'd no sooner reach to cover his hand than he'd withdraw it. Once she even awoke to a more ardent caress; he was stroking her breasts while he buried his lips against her neck. This time she was careful, holding her breath, afraid to turn or respond lest she anger him. She needed him so badly; her pregnancy had done little to dull that urge. But it was to go unsated. His fingers wandered, grew bolder...then abruptly withdrew and he rolled to the far side of the bed. She was never to know if he'd reached for her in his sleep; if that had been the case, she might have had the hope that a subconscious part of him wanted her, needed her as much as she very consciously wanted and needed him. But his detachment the following morning thwarted her hopes.

He was taunting her, tormenting her. Aching, she'd grit her teeth and try to be grateful for his fleeting caresses, but it became apparent that regardless of what his body felt or did, his mind was set strongly against her. She began, in the long periods of idleness when her hands couldn't seem to find their way around a chisel or file, to imagine what the future would be like. It wasn't a pretty picture. She saw days stretching into weeks, months, then years during which she and Jesse would share a home and a child, go through the motions of marriage with none of the feeling. She wondered if he'd *ever* make love to her again, wondered if he'd seek out other women as he'd done when he'd gone back to New York. She didn't think she could bear that, and found herself agonizing over thoughts of an eventual divorce...but only until she reminded herself of his threat. Joint custody. Her child gone from her for fully half of the year. *That* would destroy her. It was bad enough that Jesse rejected the love she tried to give, but if he were to deny her the only other outlet she'd have, she thought she'd die.

By February, Paige was beginning to feel heavy. Her stomach seemed to stick straight out in front of her—a sure sign of a boy, was the consensus of her mother's bridge group. And there were times—the doctor said they were perfectly normal—when she experienced contractions and her stomach grew rock hard. She'd curve her hand under it for support then and continue with what she was doing. Inevitably, Jesse would be at her in a minute.

"Sit down, Paige. Give it a chance to pass."

"My making dinner won't hurt."

"You don't have to rough it. These aren't the Dark Ages when women worked in the fields, squatted to give birth, then stood right up and went back to work again."

If he'd spoken with concern, she might have listened. But his even tone told another story. In defiance, she'd continue what she was doing until the spasm passed, *then* she'd settle listlessly into a chair. Inevitably, too, he'd berate her for her lack of concern for the baby. One day, when he did, she lashed back with uncharacteristic curtness. Heartsick and exasperated, she felt she'd begun to teeter on the perilous tightrope she walked.

"Get off my case, Jesse. I'd do much better if you'd leave me alone."

"If I left you alone, God only knows what you'd do to my kid!"

"That's not fair. I was doing beautifully until you came along."

"That was before the baby started making demands. It's easy enough to do beautifully when there's nothing to do. Now, though, you've got to eat right and watch that you don't overdo things."

"*Overdo things?* You don't let me do *anything*!" She lowered her voice, feeling dangerously close to tears, and spoke as though to herself. "I think I'm going crazy. I feel cooped up and frustrated. It's been so cold that I can't go anywhere, and now I look forward to each doctor's appointment as if it's a party."

The doctor didn't feel quite that way when she saw Paige several weeks later. Concluding her examination, she remained by Paige's side to talk with her quietly while Jesse went out to the outer office.

"Is something bothering you, Paige?"

"Bothering me?"

"You're dragging. You look exhausted. Your blood pressure's up. And you're still not gaining the weight you should."

Paige's eyes widened in fear. "Is something wrong? With the baby?"

The doctor smiled kindly. "No, no. The baby sounds fine. Its heartbeat is good and strong. *It* seems to be growing well, but I think it's taking its weight pound for pound from you."

"That's all right. I can afford to be slimmer."

"No, you can't. My concern is for both baby and mother. And you don't seem happy. At least, not the way you were at the start of your pregnancy."

Paige wrinkled up her nose and tried to make light of the observations. "Oh, I'm sure it's just impatience. Nine months seems like such a long time sometimes."

"True. But…somehow I didn't think you'd be one to wither under the pressure."

"I'm not withering."

"That's what it looks like to me." She took a breath and spoke with supreme gentleness. "I may be overstepping my bounds here, Paige, but as I said, my concern is as much for you as for your baby. I'm not blind, or deaf. Speaking as one woman to another, I can see the tension between you and your husband. And I do know that the marriage didn't take place until well into the pregnancy. If you want to talk, and I think it might do you good, I'd be glad to lend an ear."

Paige looked away, then closed her eyes and sighed wearily. "I don't think it'll do any good. Jesse wants the baby. It's me he doesn't want."

"That's not what I see. I see a man who's genuinely concerned for you both. Oh, maybe he gets a little carried away, but I think his heart's in the right place."

"Could've fooled me."

"You're not looking as objectively as I am. You have to realize that a man is at his most helpless when his wife is pregnant." When Paige opened her mouth to disagree, the doctor went on quickly. "You're doing all the work. He feels left out. Some men have to compensate by trying their best to take control of the situation."

"He's succeeded."

"Obviously not, since your health leaves something to be desired. And if you don't do something to improve that, the baby may well be endangered at some point. You know, Paige, I'm great at giving advice like this, but I'm not a counselor. I do know of several good ones, if you'd be interested."

Oh, yes, she'd be interested. *Anything* to break though the barrier Jesse had created. But she doubted *he'd* go for that. He wasn't even willing to admit that a problem existed! From all outward signs, he seemed satisfied with the status quo.

"Uh...well, let me discuss it with Jesse," she murmured, doubting she would but needing to appease the doctor somehow. "If we decide to go ahead, I'll give you a call for the referral."

"Will you?"

Paige nodded. From the look in the doctor's eye, though, she knew she hadn't fooled her for a minute.

"And will you try to take better care of yourself? Eat well? Get lots of rest? Keep calm? You're going to have to work things out before that little one is born. It won't be any easier then."

"I know," Paige whispered, feeling more discouraged than ever.

After leaving the office, she thought long and hard about the doctor's suggestion that she and Jesse see a counselor. But she *knew* what was wrong; it was no mystery. Jesse had chosen to put a distance between them. He refused to share himself with her as he'd once done. He resented her. He was angry. That very anger would rule out the possibility of counseling. And the worst of it was that...she didn't even dare ask.

She wondered what had become of the self-confident woman she'd been several months before. For that matter, Paige hardly recognized herself. The zest she'd had for life was gone, as was the optimism, the determination. She'd tried to break through Jesse's shield during the first months of their marriage. She'd tried to be patient and understanding, to show the love she didn't dare express in words, knowing that he'd surely laugh in her face. Finally, she'd given up. She was just too tired, too heartsick to make the exertion.

It was a side of herself she'd never seen before. True, Jesse Dallas had chipped away her cool exterior to reveal the passionate woman beneath, but when he'd chipped further—as he'd been doing these past weeks—he'd hit flaws. One after the other. Weaknesses Paige hadn't known existed. And as disgusted as she was with herself, she didn't know where to turn. For her parents, the doctor, any friends who happened by, she managed to put on a passable facade. After all, she'd made her bed; now she had to sleep in it. But alone once more she was drained. Nothing seemed to matter...nothing except the baby. And though she did her best to eat and sleep well, it was never enough. It appeared that she was letting the baby down, too.

Jesse kept himself busy, finishing one job, starting another with the expressed intention of taking time off after the baby's birth. Paige should have been relieved by his noble stand, but she wasn't. For hours she'd sit alone with a book in her lap, feeling lonesome, wishing desperately for company. When she'd bound up in frustration and begin to pace the room, she'd be stopped either by a sharp pain in her hip—the baby was pressing on a nerve, the doctor said—or a wave of dizziness. This she didn't even *report* to the doctor. So she'd sit down again, limp and discouraged. When she finally heard Jesse emerge from his workroom, she'd begin to tremble not in pleasure but in apprehension.

One afternoon early in March she could take it no

longer. Jesse had gone off to pick up groceries, insisting that she take a nap while he was gone. But she didn't want to nap, and she was sure that if she sat in the house alone for one minute longer she'd truly lose her mind.

Wearing a stylish wool jumper, boots, and her oversize winter coat, she headed for the garage. She couldn't remember the last time she'd driven her car. Jesse was adamant about taking her everywhere she wanted to go. But all along the doctor had told her she could drive, and she had every intention of doing so now.

Sliding behind the wheel became her first major obstacle. When last she'd been in the driver's seat, she'd been much slimmer. Grunting, she leaned forward, tugged at the lever and moved the seat back, then patted her stomach and sighed. She extended the seat belt, then let it slide back, fearing that it would do the baby more potential harm than good. Backing the car carefully from the garage and onto the road, she put it in gear. That was when she faced her second obstacle.

Where to go. If she went into Marblehead, chances were strong she might pass Jesse on the way. He'd try to make her go back, and she wouldn't! She just wouldn't! She needed these few minutes of freedom as badly as she'd ever needed anything. Taking her only other option, she headed away from Marblehead center and drove along the shore route.

After a while she began to feel warm in her coat, and she tried shrugging out of it. But her bulky clothing worked against her so she finally gave up and simply rolled down her window. The air retained its crispness but was milder than it had been in weeks. Her thoughts raced ahead toward the first of May, when her baby was due, and she imagined herself pushing a carriage, breathing in the warm ocean air once more, admiring nature's rebirth even as she displayed her own offspring proudly.

Before she knew it, she was on the road to Boston. Yes, she felt like going there. Perhaps she'd park and walk along

Newbury Street, maybe even stroll through the stores examining the clothes she'd buy when she was her old svelte self once more. She'd be gone for several hours, maybe more, and if Jesse worried, so what! He deserved it, overbearing ape that he'd been! Let him stew, just as she'd been doing since the day he'd so rudely reappeared in her life.

Her third obstacle, though, was her own fatigue. She began to feel it on the outskirts of the city as the traffic picked up, and it grew steadily worse. Stopped at a traffic light, she managed at last to peel off her coat, but she felt little relief when it lay bunched on the seat beside her.

When had she grown so weak? Weren't pregnant women supposed to be endowed with some kind of divine strength? She broke out in a sweat, and when her limbs began to quiver, she thought back on what she'd eaten that day. Breakfast, a midmorning snack, lunch—each meal had been scanty, but she'd eaten no less than normal. That wasn't saying much; possibly it explained her shakiness.

Following the ramp over North Station onto Storrow Drive, she drove until she reached the Arlington Street exit, determined to park and visit the first coffee shop she found.

She never made it. Somewhere alongside the Public Garden, with her foot on the gas and her hands on the wheel, she passed out cold.

RETURNING TO THE HOUSE with several bags of groceries and a book for Paige, Jesse went directly to the kitchen to put the food away. He was grateful that she had taken his suggestion and was sleeping. Damn, but she'd been hard to handle lately. Quite a change from the self-possessed, easygoing woman he'd known the summer before, but then, she was pregnant and having quite a time of it. It was a damn good thing he'd come back when he had; no telling how she'd *ever* have managed on her own!

Storing a carton of milk on the refrigerator shelf, he ran

his hand down its damp surface and, frowning, thought ahead to the future. He wondered what would happen when the baby was born, whether things would thaw between Paige and himself. True, they'd have the child as a diversion, but there still remained the matter of their own relationship.

He'd been hard on her. He knew that. So perhaps he was as much at fault as she. Yes, she'd deceived him by getting pregnant, but she hadn't asked that he marry her, or that he take care of her as he'd done these past months. He'd been angry. He still was. He felt manipulated into something he'd have sworn he hadn't wanted.

And yet…there were times when he imagined it might actually work. He'd seen her family, witnessed the warmth firsthand, and had dared to dream that one day he and Paige might have that, too. Oh, he wanted the baby. He'd never have believed how much. And, yes, he wanted Paige, too. But he wanted that other Paige, the one she'd been before—so independent that every show of affection on her part was a special gift.

She had been affectionate. He remembered each and every gesture. He could have sworn that she loved him…until lately. Lately she hadn't cared much about anything. Lately she'd been without self-assurance, without direction, losing interest even in sculpting. Lately she'd cringed every time he'd walked into the room. Had he done that to her? Had he pushed her too far?

She had no way of knowing that many of the hours in his workroom he spent thinking, wondering, worrying. She had no way of knowing that he felt guilty about things that he wished could be different, that the tension between them was taking a toll on him, too.

For indeed it was. He was confused. And frightened. Frightened to reach out for something that would mean the world to him, frightened of taking that risk and then somehow, sometime, losing. For years it had seemed better to go his own way.

The baby had changed all that. He was committed in one sense. No, he was committed in a far greater sense. Paige was his wife. They were legally married...at *his* insistence. Perhaps that was one of the things that made him uneasy. If she'd come to him of her own free will, perhaps he'd feel more confident where she was concerned.

There were nights when he'd yearned to reach out for her, nights when he had, then pulled back. He was a coward. So what in the hell was he going to do about it? God, he didn't know!

Wearily he stowed the rest of the groceries, folded the empty bags and stored them, then picked up the book and went to check on Paige. At the bedroom door he stopped. The bed was empty, as smooth and neatly made as it had been that morning.

"Paige?" Perhaps she was in the bathroom. He walked to its door. "Paige?" No Paige. Turning, he retraced his steps, calling her name at each door, hearing nothing in return. He searched each room in the wing, then stalked toward the other wing. "Paige! Where are you?"

Her studio was empty, as was his workroom and the guest bedroom. "Damn it, where are you?" he growled to himself as he ran back to the living room and looked out toward the deck. There was no sign of her anywhere. Angrily he slid open the glass door and stepped outside, then crossed the deck and trotted down toward the beach. The snow was gone, but it was cold. Ignoring the chill he felt, he looked first one way then the other, then took off across the sand.

"Paige! Paige!" His voice was caught and swallowed by a wind that seemed as angry as he. Grinding to a halt, he cupped his mouth and yelled, "Paiiiiige!" When no answer came, he ran until the rocks bid him stop, then turned and loped in the other direction. "Goddammit, Paige! Paiiiiige!"

Within minutes, he concluded that she wasn't on the beach. Bounding back up the steps and through the house, he stormed into the garage. *"Goddammit!"* She'd taken her car.

Returning to the kitchen for his keys and coat, he took his own car and headed for town. All the way he simmered. All the way he railed aloud as though Paige were sitting in the passenger's seat. "Of all the crazy stunts! Damn it, you could have told me you wanted to go out! I'd have taken you! So what if you don't get the rest you need! So what if you catch pneumonia! So what if you kill the baby! All right, be selfish if you want! But, God, don't walk out on me this way!"

For the next two hours, he scoured not only Marblehead but also Salem and Beverly, searching all her favorite shops, even those she'd visited less frequently. When the stores had pretty much closed for the day he headed home, keeping such a sharp eye out for her car that he nearly rear-ended one himself.

By the time he arrived back at the house, it was nearly six and dark. He ran from his car to check the garage, then swore vehemently when it was empty. But there was a touch of panic in his tone now, and he dashed into the house and headed for the phone.

By some miracle he managed to keep his voice calm as he called each of her friends in the area. Paige had gone out for a drive and had she, by chance, stopped there? He asked over and over again. But to no avail. No one had seen her. No one had heard from her. For the first time he realized just how much of a recluse she'd become in the past weeks, and he wondered whether to blame it on her condition or on *him*. He hadn't encouraged her to see her friends. What had he said when she'd seemed restless? *Take a nap. It'll do you good.*

It was his fault, damn it! His fault!

But self-reproach would have to wait. Frantic now, he tried to think of where she might have gone. Had she been depressed enough to run home to her parents? A quick forage through her dresser told him that she hadn't packed for an overnight stay, and her suitcase was in the storage closet.

As the minutes crept by, he cursed his helplessness. Fleeting images began to haunt him—images of her having just picked up and taken off with no other goal in mind than escape. He didn't blame her. Damn his stubbornness! If she'd been frozen out, he'd done it single-handedly. She had every right to hate him for the way he'd behaved! He could have showed a little compassion for what she felt. He could have tried to talk with her, to express his feelings, to air his frustration and anger and fear.

Frustration and anger were forgotten now. Only fear remained, and it grew and grew as he struggled to decide what to do. He didn't realize he was sweating until he raked his hand through his hair and found it damp. He tried to think clearly, to keep calm, but it grew harder as the clock ticked on. She'd taken the car, so he couldn't suspect foul play. But what if she'd had a flat, or run out of gas, or…or…

Doing the only thing left to be done, he picked up the phone to call the police. He'd barely punched out the exchange, though, when the doorbell rang. Slamming the phone back down, he raced for the door. Maybe she'd forgotten her key. Maybe she was just too tired to put it in the lock.

But it wasn't Paige whose finger was about to press the bell a second time. It was one of the very same men he'd been about to call.

"Mr. Dallas?"

His heart seemed to stop, his life suspended. "Yes?" he asked in a fleeting breath.

"We've been trying to reach you. First there was no answer. Then the line was busy. So I thought I'd—"

"What is it, man?"

"Your wife. I'm afraid there's been an accident…."

CHAPTER TEN

NEVER IN HIS LIFE HAD JESSE been so terrified. He felt as though his world were about to shatter, as though if he could only put his arms around it, he might hold it together. But his arms were useless; there was nothing to grasp. He had to reach for that world, had to reach for it....

Refusing the policeman's offer of a ride into Boston, he drove his own car at a breakneck pace, running red lights whenever possible in his haste to reach Paige.

The policeman had said she was all right, but what did *he* know? She'd fainted at the wheel and had banged her head when the car had gone into a streetlight. Concussion? Skull fracture? Blood clot in the brain?

Jesse was shaking all over by the time he made it to the emergency room. But Paige had already been admitted, so he had to suffer the wait for an elevator, then the ride to the sixth floor before finally bolting out toward the desk.

The nurse on duty was on the phone, but Jesse was too panicked to wait politely. "Excuse me, but my wife's just been admitted." The nurse continued her conversation, though she did eye him. "Dallas. Paige Dallas. Could you tell me where she is? I've just found out about her accident. I've got to see her."

"Mr. Dallas?"

Jesse's head shot up as a resident approached from behind the desk and extended a hand. "I'm Dr. Brassle. I'll be keeping an eye on your wife."

The hand Jesse placed in the doctor's was boneless and

cold, his voice little more than a fearful gasp. "How is she?"

The doctor smiled. "She'll be fine. Just a mild concussion. But she's very weak. I assume this pregnancy's been hard on her."

"Pregnancy…" Jesse murmured. In his panic about Paige, he hadn't even thought about the baby. When he raised stricken eyes, the doctor was still smiling.

"The baby's fine. Evidently has no intention of making an early appearance. I'd like to keep your wife here for a few days' rest and observation, though."

"A mild concussion?"

"That's all. We took a few stitches, and she's apt to have a good headache for a while, but there's no sign of any deeper problem."

Jesse sagged in relief. "Thank God," he whispered. "Can I see her now?"

"Sure. Room 604. She was very shaky, so we gave her a mild sedative—for the baby's sake more than anything—but we don't want her to sleep long. The nurse will be around every few minutes to make sure she's all right."

"Thank you." Jesse was already starting off. "Room 604?"

The doctor nodded, gesturing broadly down the hall.

It took Jesse a minute to find it, then he stopped to catch his breath and still his hammering pulse before going in.

Her eyes were closed, her face frighteningly pale. A small piece of gauze was taped high on her brow. He approached quietly, flexing his fingers by his sides. He wanted to touch her. God, he *had* to touch her. He had to know that she was all right. He had to tell her he was sorry. He had to tell her that he…that he…

Raising a hand to her cheek, he brushed it lightly. It was cool, so cool. Should it be that cool? He wanted to race out to ask the doctor, but couldn't bear the thought of leaving her side.

Pulling a chair close to the bed, he sat down, took her hand in both of his and raised it to his lips. He'd will her to be all right. He'd will her back into the woman who'd taken his heart. Damn it, she didn't have a right to do this to him! She didn't have a right to tear down every defense he'd built and then just…just take off!

When she took a deep breath, he froze. Slowly she turned her head, even more slowly opened her eyes. It seemed to take her a minute to focus, then her eyes widened. "Jesse?" She barely mouthed the words.

"It's all right, love. I'm here."

She swallowed hard, and her momentary calm seemed to crumble. Her whisper was tremulous. "I'm…I'm sorry, Jesse…oh, God, I didn't mean to do that…"

"Shhhhhhhh." He breathed against her fingers, which clutched his with surprising strength.

"I didn't mean…" Her eyes filled with tears. "I didn't…I'm so sorry…"

The tears were streaming down her cheeks then, and Jesse's insides turned. He'd never seen her cry. Not once through what had to have been a months-long ordeal for her had she cried. But she did now, and he realized the full extent of what he'd done.

Shifting to sit on the bed, he gathered her very gently in his arms. "Shhhh. Don't cry, love. God, don't cry." He tried to be tender holding her, but his arms tightened in need. He buried his face in her hair, aware that his own breath was coming in ragged gasps. "I can't bear to see you cry, Paige. I need your strength. Without it I'm nothing."

Through her sobs she barely heard what he was saying. "Ohhh…Jesse…I should have listened…I'm sorry…I'm sorry…"

"Please, baby, don't cry. Don't cry." He rubbed her back, frightened by the slenderness that contrasted so much with her fullness in front. "I'm the one who's sorry. I drove you out. It's my fault. All my fault."

He continued to caress her, to breathe in the sweet smell

of her hair, to feel her warm and pliant in his arms as he
thought she might never be again. Paige tried to control her
tears, but they flowed on as though from a dam that had
burst. Jesse's nearness, his touch, so wonderfully sweet,
only added to the flow.

"Shhhhh. It's all right. Shhhhh." Closing his eyes, Jesse
knew he'd been given a gift. Paige was all right. She was
here. She was holding him. Burrowing his face more
deeply against her neck, he moaned, "God, I...love you..."

Paige caught her breath on a sob, unsure if she'd only
imagined his hoarse whisper because she'd wanted so
badly to hear those words. Blotting her eyes against his
shoulder, she gripped his arms and pulled back. Her eyes
held uncertainty, disbelief, hope. "Wh-what did you say?"
she breathed unsteadily, then reached up in awe to touch
the damp rivulets on his cheeks.

"I've made a mess of this whole thing, Paige," he
managed. His gaze was blurred and he wanted nothing
more than to bury his face against her until he'd composed
himself. But there was much to be said, and since she'd
already seen his tears... "I know I've put you through hell
these months, but I've been there and back myself today."
He took a shaky breath. "It's been hard for me...accept-
ing all this because...it's contrary to everything I thought
I wanted in life. But when I was racing around in a panic,
not knowing where you were or whether you were hurt or
even alive, I realized that what I thought I wanted just
won't work anymore. I used to think that the real hell in
life would be loving and losing, so I refused to be vulnerable. With you, I couldn't help it. I ran off last summer
because I was scared, but I couldn't stay away. I guess I
compensated by denying what I felt, by striking back, by
trying my best to kill what I thought might hurt me. But
the real hell of it is that I hurt anyway. The thought that I'd
lost you today even before I'd given that love a chance
nearly killed me."

He paused to brush the tears from her cheek, aware of

the astonishment on her face. "I know I haven't got a right to ask this of you. You must hate me for everything I've done. But…" His voice softened, trembling still. "But I'd like another chance, Paige. I'd like another chance to show how much I…I love you. Maybe in time you could…could love me again?"

"I do."

Jesse's heart flipped. It wasn't so much the two small words as the way she'd spoken them that sent him soaring. They were said calmly, factually, with the very same self-confidence that had captivated him from the start.

"You do?"

She nodded, suddenly imbued with a strength that overrode any effects of the sedative. "Love isn't something that starts and stops, Jesse. It's there. It doesn't go away. Even if you'd never come back after leaving in August, I'd have always loved you." Her eyes grew moist again. "For me the hell was in loving you and, day after day, having to face your disdain. I'm sorry I didn't tell you I wanted a baby—"

He stopped her words with one long finger. "Shhhh. Maybe you were right about that. I'd never have consented at the time. But it certainly forced the issue, and I do want that baby so badly."

"What about when it fusses and cries and disturbs your work? What about when we've got plans to go out and the baby-sitter cancels at the last minute? What about when we want to get away for a few days?"

"When it fusses, I'll rock it to sleep. When the sitter cancels, we'll call another. When we want to get away, we'll run it down to Westport. You've had the answers all along. I'm the one who always sees the dark side. And I'm not saying that I can change overnight. The fears of a lifetime aren't easy to erase. But I'll try. Damn it, Paige, I'll try. And if you'd be willing to help…"

The look of joy on her face took willingness one step further. Wrapping her arms around him, she pressed her newly glowing cheek to his chest as his arms made the circle complete.

That was how the nurse found them when she poked her head in a few minutes later. Smiling in satisfaction that her patient was on the mend, she quietly left.

EIGHT WEEKS LATER Paige and Jesse were in much the same position. It was a different bed, a different hospital, a different occasion, but their embrace was no less firm, their hearts no less filled with joy.

"She's beautiful, Paige. Just like you."

"Kinda red and wrinkled, don't you think?"

"Nah. Did you see those tiny fingers?"

"Uh-huh. All ten."

"God, they're cute. I think she's ticklish. When I touch the bottom of her feet, her toes curl."

"That's instinct."

"And her mouth…have you ever seen anything so sweet? All pink and puckering…"

"It is sweet, isn't it?"

"She's a winner, that's for sure. I called your parents. They're out of their minds with excitement!"

"Ahh, I knew they would be."

"They couldn't wait to call your brothers. I also called Sandy and Frank and Tom and Margie and Ben, who, by the way, said he can't win where I'm concerned. He bet on a boy."

"Poor Ben. Did you tell him how hard you worked?"

"You bet. If it hadn't been for me, you'd never have known when to stop breathing deeply and start panting."

"Mmm. Women are pretty helpless in situations like these."

"Okay, okay. So you could've managed. But it was me who would have felt helpless if I'd been stuck outside pacing the floors. I still can't believe it. When the top of her head appeared…"

"I think you saw more than I did. You'll have to tell me about it sometime."

Staring into Paige's adoring eyes, Jesse shook his head in wonder. "Our baby's got so much going for her. She's a lucky little girl."

"*We're* lucky. Does it scare you?"

"A little. I never dreamed I could be so happy. Thank you, Paige."

"Thank *you*, Jesse."

Just then the crib in which their daughter lay was wheeled in by a beaming nurse. The baby was making herself and her needs well-known. Jesse and Paige both looked her way, then looked back at each other and laughed in delight. Popping a warm kiss on Paige's brow, Jesse stood to rescue his daughter and deliver her to her mother.

We hope you enjoyed reading

THE REAL THING

and

SECRET OF THE STONE

by *New York Times* bestselling author

BARBARA DELINSKY

If you liked reading these stories, then you will love
Harlequin® Special Edition.

Harlequin® Special Edition stories show that
every chapter in a relationship has its challenges
and delights and that love can be renewed with
each turn of the page.

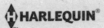

SPECIAL EDITION

Life, Love and Family

Look for six new romances every month
from Harlequin Special Edition!

Available wherever books and ebooks are sold.

SPECIAL EXCERPT FROM

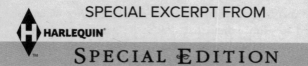

H **HARLEQUIN**®

SPECIAL EDITION

*Lani Vasquez is a nanny to the royal children of
Montedoro...and nothing more, or so she thinks.
But widower Prince Maximilian Bravo-Calabretti
hasn't forgotten their single passionate encounter.
Can the handsome prince and the alluring au pair turn
one night into forever? Or will their love turn Lani into a
pumpkin at the stroke of midnight?*

***

He was fresh out of new tactics and had no clue how to get
her to let down her guard. Plus he had a very strong feeling
that he'd pushed her as far as she would go for now. This was
looking to be an extended campaign. He didn't like that, but
if it was the only way to finally reach her, so be it. "I'll be seeing you in the library—where you will no longer scuttle away
every time I get near you."

A hint of the old humor flashed in her eyes. "I never scuttle."

"Scamper? Dart? Dash?"

"Stop it." Her mouth twitched. A good sign, he told himself.

"Promise me you won't run off the next time we meet."

The spark of humor winked out. "I just don't like this."

"You've already said that. I'm going to show you there's
nothing to be afraid of. Do we have an understanding?"

"Oh, Max..."

"Say yes."

And finally, she gave in and said the words he needed to
hear. "Yes. I'll, um, look forward to seeing you."

He didn't believe her. How could he believe her when she sounded so grim, when that mouth he wanted beneath his own was twisted with resignation? He didn't believe her, and he almost wished he could give her what she said she wanted, let her go, say goodbye. He almost wished he could *not* care.

But he'd had so many years of not caring. Years and years when he'd told himself that not caring was for the best.

And then the small, dark-haired woman in front of him changed everything.

***

Enjoy this sneak peek from Christine Rimmer's
THE PRINCE'S CINDERELLA BRIDE,
the latest installment in her Harlequin® Special Edition
miniseries **THE BRAVO ROYALES,** *on sale May 2014!*

Coming in May 2014 from
Cindy Kirk

THE HUSBAND LIST

Great job? Check. Hunky hubby? Not so much.
Dr. Mitzi Sanchez has her life just where she wants
it—except for the husband she's always dreamed
of. She creates a checklist for her perfect man—but
she insists pilot Keenan McGregor isn't it. With a
bit of luck, Keenan might blow Mitzi's expectations
sky-high....

*Look for the latest in the **Rx for Love** miniseries
from Harlequin® Special Edition®,
wherever books and ebooks are sold!*